Veya and the Arcane Trials

Veya

and the

Arcane Trials

Junalyn Nicdao

Dedication:
For the ones who learned to survive before they learned to
belong.
For those who ran… not because they were weak, but because
staying would have broken them.
This is for you.

And

For the one who stayed.
For the two who believed.
And for the many who said, "You should write this."

THE ORDER *of* THE
ARCANE

LUMORA GUILD   **VELLYN GUILD**   **ASTRAEL GUILD**   **ELDRIN GUILD**

Wisdom and Light   Cleverness and Secrecy   Ambition and Vision   Patience and Tradition

Units of the Arcane

Eclipse Unit

Exiom Unit

Medirian Unit

Obsidian Unit

Parallax Unit

Catalyst Unit

Each student is chosen... but not all endure.

Mistara Island
Arcane Academy
Colosseum of the Forgotten
The Forgotten Realm
N
W

Prelude

You might never have noticed, life has a way of teaching you where not to look…but there is a world beyond your imagination, hiding just out of reach. Not because it is distant, but because it does not wish to be found easily.

Take a moment.

Open your eyes.

Stop searching for what you think is normal, and instead, listen to the quiet spaces between things where older truths still linger, patient and unseen. The pauses. The moments when the air feels heavier than it should, where the world seems to hesitate, as if waiting to see what you will do next.

There is magic there.

Magic fierce enough to change you. Trials so demanding they strip away everything you pretend to be, leaving only what remains. Prizes so powerful they are never given lightly and never without demanding balance in return.

Look past the horizon, up into the silky light-blue sky, beyond the white, cotton-candy clouds, and farther still, past the stars that burn cold and distant in the dark. If you are watching closely, if you are patient, you might see it: a magnificent floating island suspended where it should not exist.

Waterfalls spill endlessly over Mistara Island's edges, vanishing before they ever reach the ground below. Rivers twist at impossible angles, defying gravity as though the concept itself were optional. Forests stretch deep and dense, their leaves whispering secrets to anyone reckless enough to wander beneath their canopy. Sometimes, if the wind is right, the trees sound almost like breathing.

The island does not appear the same way twice.

Some say it floats between worlds, shimmering in sunlight one moment and swallowed by silver mist the next. Others insist it only shows itself to those who are already lost. No map has ever captured it correctly. No compass points toward it for long.

And yet, it waits.

If you were to wander its paths carefully and quietly, you might stumble upon a small, charming cottage tucked among the greenery. At first glance it appears harmless enough, cozy and unremarkable, the sort of place that blends easily into its surroundings. It looks like the home of someone who wants nothing more than peace and quiet, the kind of quiet life that leaves the rest of the world undisturbed.

But look closer.

The windows reflect more sky than they should. The shadows beneath the eaves linger too long. And the door…if you place your hand upon it, it feels warm, almost expectant, like it knows you are there.

This is not an ordinary cottage.

Step inside, and you will learn a simple truth, one the world beyond prefers you never discover.

Some who find this place, arrive by accident while others arrive by design.

But for most people, they arrive because there is nowhere else left for them in the world they came from.

They are the overlooked and the unwanted. The ones who learned early how easy it is to be forgotten.

Magic is rarely what it pretends to be.

And neither are you.

Sometimes the world forgets people because they are small.

But sometimes it forgets them because remembering would mean admitting that something ancient has returned… something that once shaped the sky, the storm, and the deep places beneath the sea.

Some doors appear when the world breaks you.

And somewhere far beyond the sky and sea, the Arcane Academy had already begun listening.

Chapter

One

The Forgotten

There are people the world forgets.
Not all at once, and not always cruelly.
Sometimes it happens in ordinary ways, small omissions that accumulate until a person becomes background noise in their own life. A teacher stops calling on them. A parent stops asking questions they don't want the answers to. Friends learn how to laugh without looking in their direction.

For most, it is social. For some, it is structural. Systems shift and leave them standing outside the shape of what counts. They become the rejected, the abandoned, the runaways, the different. They are the names that sound like categories until you realize they are just ways of saying someone no longer belongs.

And then there are the ones who are forgotten even to themselves.

They learn early to make themselves smaller. They sand down the sharp parts. They swallow instinct. They practice being agreeable, being quiet, and being normal, until the mask fits so closely it becomes indistinguishable from skin. The world rewards that kind of obedience. It applauds survival that doesn't inconvenience anyone.

But some people cannot shrink properly.

They try, and still the air changes when they enter a room. Glass trembles when their emotions rise. Shadows bend in the wrong direction. Heat collects in their palms without flame, and wind gathers at their backs without weather. Something restless presses beneath their ribs, heavy with promise and threat, and no amount of pretending can convince it to sleep.

Those are not simply different, not in the harmless way difference is often dismissed. They are misaligned, standing at angles the world was never built to accommodate. They are unresolved, carrying fractures that hum quietly beneath the surface. They are unfinished, like a story interrupted mid-sentence, waiting for the part no one stayed long enough to hear.

The world has no patience for unfinished things. It does not know whether to fear them or pity them, whether to nurture what they might become or silence them before they disrupt the fragile balance of what already exists. Unfinished things are unpredictable. They refuse tidy narratives.

And unpredictability is dangerous.

So, the world does what it has always done when confronted with something it cannot measure.

It looks away.

It withdraws its attention.

And without attention, forgetting becomes inevitable.

The Forgotten are not always the weakest, and they are not always the kindest. They are the ones who do not fit into the story they were handed. The ones whose existence bends probability in quiet, inconvenient ways. The ones who carry something older than themselves beneath the surface and have no language for it, only hunger and ache and the steady sense of being out of place.

Arcane Academy listens for that.

It had not always listened alone.

The Academy honored its structure through record and stone, through names preserved with careful precision, but at the center of that history, where origin should have anchored everything else, there was only absence.

Not damage. Not erosion.

Deliberate.

A space carved cleanly enough that no one questioned it… and no one remembered what had been removed.

It does not watch cities or governments. It does not care for status, wealth, or bloodlines the way the world does. It listens for rupture, the moment a life splits open and something inside finally pushes back.

It listens for the instant grief cracks a person wide enough to let truth leak through. For the second abandonment sharpens into defiance. For the breath between rejection and collapse, when survival becomes more than instinct and turns into a choice.

It listens for resonance.

When the world turns its back and a soul fractures under the weight of being unwanted, something flares. Sometimes as heat, sometimes as storm, sometimes as shadow that refuses to behave. It is not always spectacular. Often it is subtle. A room that stills. A door that seals. A streetlight that bursts at the wrong moment. A silence that arrives too quickly, as though reality itself has adjusted to avoid breaking.

Arcane Academy hears those moments the way predators hear blood in water, through vibration, through rupture, through the quiet change in current that signals something has broken open. It does not mistake grief for weakness or fracture for failure. It recognizes them as thresholds.

And when it answers, it does not arrive with comfort. It does not offer rescue.

It answers with summoning.

Those who feel the call rarely understand it at first. They only know that the air begins to feel strange, as though it has been holding its breath. That familiar streets look slightly wrong, angles skewed, distances stretching. That a door appears where none existed, or a corridor turns where it shouldn't, or a voice threads through their thoughts without sound.

You have been noticed.

Not chosen as a prize to be displayed. Not saved as an act of mercy. Not gathered out of kindness or sentiment. The Academy does not intervene because it feels compassion.

It does not rescue the Forgotten.

It awakens them.

And awakening is never gentle. It is the slow stripping away of illusion, the removal of what was built to survive in a world that never intended to keep you. It is the moment you realize the thing inside you has been waiting all along.

Within its bounds, illusions are stripped. The versions built for survival peel away. First, politeness, obedience, and then denial. Until what remains can no longer pretend. Power is not taught here. Power is exposed, then pressured, and finally measured. Forced into the open by circumstances that do not pause for fear.

The trials are not punishments.

They are filtration.

A proving ground for those the world was willing to lose.

Some discover they were meant for more than the life that tried to contain them. Some discover that the thing inside them is not a gift at all, but a consequence that is old, hungry, and patient. Some awaken into strength. Others awaken into truths that break them.

Arcane Academy does not intervene when that happens.

It observes.

It records outcomes.

Those who endure become Unforgotten.

Not because the world suddenly decides they matter, but because they finally remember themselves fully, fiercely, and without apology. They become real in a way the world can no longer overlook, and once they are real, the story cannot continue as if they were not.

But those who fail… do not become cautionary tales.

They become absence.

Sometimes it is immediate. Sometimes it is slow enough to be cruel. A name slips in the middle of a sentence. A face blurs at the edge of memory. A space remains at a table, and no one can explain why the emptiness feels heavy.

A few will swear someone was there. A few will insist something is missing.

Most will feel the loss and never understand what they have lost.

That is the Academy's final lesson.

Some departures are loud.

Others leave no mark at all.

And some are remembered only by the spaces they leave behind.

The Academy does not mourn the dead.

It does not offer closure.

It simply continues, ancient and listening, waiting for the next fracture in the world's story and waiting for the next forgotten soul to break in exactly the right way.

Because the Forgotten are not accidents.

They are unfinished intentions.

And when the Academy calls, it does not ask whether they are ready.

It only asks whether they will endure long enough to become what they were always meant to be.

Chapter

Two

Before the Storm
Veya

Magic wasn't rare in the world, just hidden. Most people never noticed it… and the few who did were rarely allowed to keep it.

I tasted magic long before I learned to name it.

It lived in me the way storms lived over the islands. Always gathering somewhere beyond sight, heavy with promise and threat. Even on clear days, when the sky stretched wide and harmless above us, you could feel it building far out over the water, unseen but inevitable. That was how it felt inside me: not constant, not visible, but always there, waiting just beyond the edge of awareness.

It pressed against my ribs without shape, restless and untamed, as if my body were too small to contain something meant for a wider horizon. Some days it hummed beneath my skin like a quiet warning, a vibration so subtle I almost convinced myself it was imagination. Other days it slept, coiled deep and patient, as if conserving its strength for a moment I couldn't yet see. A moment that would demand more from me than I knew how to give.

I learned to move carefully around it. To breathe slowly when it stirred. To pretend the air didn't feel different when my emotions rose too sharply. I told myself everyone must feel something like this: some hidden current beneath their skin, some unnamed intensity waiting quietly for release.

But sometimes it didn't feel like power at all.

Sometimes it felt like memory.

Not the kind you recall with images or words, but the kind that lives in your bones. A recognition without context. A familiarity without explanation. As if something vast and distant had once been whole, and I was only the echo of it, trying to remember what I had forgotten.

Like something immense attempting to remember itself through me, something older than storms, older even than the islands themselves.

And sometimes, when the feeling pressed too close to the surface, when it rose like a tide behind my ribs and refused to quiet. I would hear something else beneath it.

It wasn't a sound.

Not words shaped by breath and carried through air.

It moved through bone instead, a resonance deeper than thought, something that carried meaning without needing language to hold it. Recognition without memory.

It never arrived loudly. It never demanded attention.

It simply waited.

The way the ocean waits beneath the tide.

The way a storm waits beyond the horizon, gathering long before anyone sees the clouds.

When it pressed close enough to feel, it didn't accuse me. It didn't command me either.

It corrected me.

You are not misplaced.

The certainty behind the words carried no comfort. Only accuracy, as if something ancient had already measured the distance between who I was and who I would become.

You are unfinished.

Unfinished didn't sound like failure.

It sounded like a story still in motion.

As if I were standing somewhere in the middle of something vast, and whatever spoke already knew how it ended.

The resonance would fade as quietly as it arrived, leaving only the familiar hum beneath my ribs, restless, patient, and unconcerned with time.

It always grew stronger near the water, when the horizon stretched wide enough to feel like possibility instead of distance.

On those nights, a name would surface like a thought that wasn't mine.

Mistara.

I didn't know what it meant. Only that it landed inside me with the weight of somewhere real. An island I couldn't point to, waiting as if it already knew me.

Sometimes another thought followed, quieter but sharper.

Arcane Academy.

Not a school calling me to learn.

A place waiting to see if I would survive being noticed.

The feeling would vanish as quickly as it came, leaving behind only the restless hum beneath my skin.

I told myself it was imagination. Children invent meaning for things they cannot control.

But the sensation never felt invented.

It felt patient.

Sometimes it felt ancient, older than the mountains

that carved the horizon into jagged silhouettes. Other times it felt buried beneath years of pretending I was ordinary, beneath the careful silence I wrapped around myself so no one would notice the way the air shifted when I breathed.

But magic does not stay buried forever.

And neither do the things the world tries to forget.

My magic only answered to my emotions. I could never summon it when I needed it. I couldn't practice it, couldn't command it, couldn't bargain with it.

It lay dormant, silent and heavy… until it didn't.

And when it woke, it never asked for permission.

It rose when fear sharpened to a blade, when anger cracked something open inside my chest, when grief pressed too hard to remain contained. It did not come when called.

It came when survival demanded it.

The first time, I was too young to understand what had changed.

I remember the heat. Not burning the way you might expect, not sharp or painful enough to make me cry out. It was something else entirely. A dense pressure that settled into the air, thick and unmoving, like the moment just before rain breaks when the world seems to hold its breath.

The room felt too small for the emotions filling it. Voices rose too quickly, too loudly, overlapping until they blurred into something jagged and indistinct. Words weren't meant to be gentle anymore; they collided and sparked, sharp enough to make even the walls feel tense.

Somewhere nearby, something scraped harshly against the floor. A chair, maybe. Or a table knocked off balance. The sound cut through everything else, abrupt and startling, leaving behind a silence that felt even heavier than the noise.

Then came the fear, sudden and sharp, flooding the room with a force that didn't belong to me alone. It pressed against my chest and throat, too large for a child to understand, too powerful to ignore.

My body reacted before my thoughts could catch up.

"Enough," someone snapped, the word cracking through the tension like a command meant to restore order.

But by then the air had already begun to change.

My body reacted before my mind did. I cried. I reached for anything, anything that might make it stop.

And then the room... softened.

Edges blurred. The air thickened, warm and heavy, as if it had decided to stay where it was instead of rushing toward disaster. Whatever had been moving too fast slowed. Whatever had been about to break... didn't.

There was no light, no flame, no spectacle to mark what had happened.

Only the quiet that followed.

The adults went still first. Conversations faltered, then stopped entirely, as if someone had drawn a curtain across their thoughts.

When they spoke again, their sentences were shorter, carefully chosen.

"She's just scared," someone whispered.

"Children don't do things like that," another voice replied, lower and uncertain, as though saying it aloud might somehow make it true.

No one could quite agree on what had almost happened. They only knew that the tension had vanished, that the room had softened, and that no one was hurt.

Relief replaced urgency with startling ease.

And beneath it all, unnoticed and unnamed, something quieter settled into place.

The world hadn't reacted to me the way I might have expected.

It had adjusted.

I was held for a long time after that. Rocked. Whispered to. My name repeated like an anchor.

Someone said I was lucky.

Others said nothing at all.

No one asked how a child that small could calm a room simply by being afraid.

I learned then, without realizing I was learning, that whatever lived inside me did not want to be seen.

It wanted resolution.

Not control. Not destruction.

Resolution.

As if the world itself preferred peace when I was afraid.

So naturally, I learned to prefer it too.

There were other moments after that. Not many just enough to teach me the pattern.

It stirred only in fear, anger, and grief. Never in curiosity. Never in desire.

It answered necessity.

And for a long time, that illusion of control felt like enough.

Until it wasn't.

As I grew, something inside me grew too.

Something that never fully slept.

When I was angry, objects lifted as if gravity had briefly forgotten its job.

When frustration burned too hot, lights flickered and burst. Doors slammed without hands.

Once, only once, the living room mirror shattered like ice beneath my scream.

In those fragments, I barely recognized myself.

Long black hair spilled down my back in loose waves, catching the light like spilled ink. My skin held warmth even in shadow. My eyes were dark brown, always too observant, reflecting more than I ever said aloud.

People told me I looked intense.

Like I was listening to something they couldn't

hear.

Maybe I was.

I learned early how to swallow my feelings, to press them down beneath politeness and obedience. To breathe slowly and smile when every part of me wanted to fracture.

Perseverance became my virtue.

Avoidance became my refuge.

Running, when I could manage it, became my mercy.

I practiced until the mask stopped feeling like something I wore and started feeling like a second skin.

Eventually, no one looked past it.

They saw only the calm, the pleasantness, the carefully shaped version of me that fit neatly into expectations and caused no disruption.

I became someone easy to keep.

Easy to understand.

And even easier to overlook.

For a while, that quiet invisibility felt like safety.

Until the night everything broke.

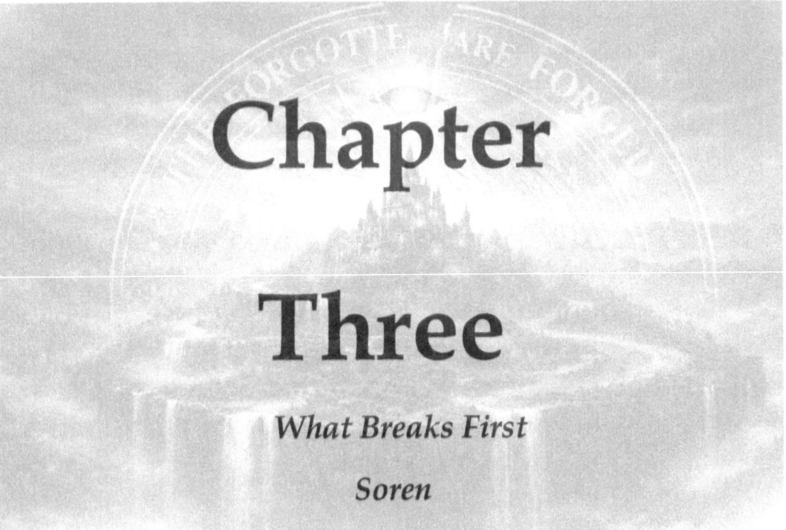

Chapter

Three

What Breaks First

Soren

Soren never learned how to lose safely.
Or how to love without bracing for impact.
Or how to be protected without earning it first.

In his father's house, mistakes weren't forgiven. They were sharpened into lessons and thrown back at you until you either adapted or broke. Weakness was not tolerated. Quitting was a personal failure. Pain was simply information.

It was only useful if you learned from it. Lessons mattered. They were how you grew. How you survived. His father knew that better than anyone.

So, when Soren lost a fight, his father didn't comfort him. He drove him back to the same alley and made him fight again.

And again.

And again.

Even when Soren was broken and bleeding, his father stood back with cold, measuring eyes, arms crossed, saying nothing. Just waiting.

Waiting for the moment Soren stopped reacting

and started adapting.

Waiting for the lesson to settle into bone.
It wasn't about winning the fight. It was about not giving up on yourself. About refusing to lose. About the kind of growth his father believed had to be learned the hard way.

And his father didn't leave until that distinction was understood.

His father was exactly as intimidating as people imagined. A strong man built from scars and survival, hardened by streets that taught him early that no one was coming to save you. He carried authority without effort, his voice calm, cutting, and final.

He had fought for meals. For respect. For the right to keep breathing.

He, too, had been forgotten. Alone for as long as he could remember, roaming streets that offered no mercy, learning lessons the hard way because there had never been another way to learn them.

Those lessons shaped him. Hardened him. Left him with strength enough to endure, a heart he refused to close completely, and a mind that knew how to survive. When he became a father, they were the only gifts he had to offer. That was how he showed love, by teaching the lessons every man needed to learn.

So, he gave them to his son.

From him, Soren learned how to stand tall even when his knees shook. How to take a hit without flinching. How to smile while bleeding.

And how to survive without ever believing he deserved to be saved.

His mother was different.

Shorter. Sharper. Her warmth edged with steel. Life had demanded fight after fight from her, and she met each one head-on. The world tried to harden her and failed.

Instead, it honed her.

Her fire lived on in Soren's temper. In his stubbornness. In the reckless spark in his eyes that made people trust him even when they shouldn't. Her kindness lived there too. Because behind the hardened edge he showed the world was a man with a fierce, unshakable heart. He just needed someone worth guarding with his life.

The night everything changed began with an argument so small it should have meant nothing.

Chores.

Curfew.

A fight he'd gotten into.

His father's voice rose, sharp and familiar. His mother stood in the doorway, arms crossed, judgment already settled.

Guilt settled over the room before Soren could even open his mouth to speak. The decision had already been made, drawn and sealed without him, and he could see it plainly in their faces. To them, he was wrong. He had always been wrong, and nothing he said now would change that.

Something in him snapped at the certainty of it.

Not the argument itself, but the quiet finality behind it. The way the judgment had been delivered without hesitation, without question. The way he had been declared guilty simply for standing there.

The words rose before he could stop them.

Soren shouted back.

And the house answered.

The kitchen light flickered violently overhead before bursting apart in a sharp crack. Glass rained down in glittering shards across the floor. A mug trembled on the edge of the counter, then slid off and shattered against the tile.

The air bent strangely around him, as though reality itself had taken a step back.

Silver threads of lightning curled through his fingers, thin and alive, weaving between his hands like something that had been waiting for him all along.

Stop.

The thought came too late.

The room froze.

Not the tense silence that follows shouting, where anger waits for someone to speak first. This was something deeper, heavier. The kind of stillness that settles when the world itself seems uncertain how to continue.

The air hung thick and unmoving, as though the house had drawn in a breath and forgotten how to release it.

No one moved.

Glass glittered across the kitchen floor like fallen stars. The faint hum of electricity had died with the shattered light, leaving the room wrapped in a strange, unnatural quiet.

Even the distant sounds of traffic outside felt muffled, pushed far away by whatever had just happened.

Soren's father was the first to react.

Not gradually.

Instantly.

The anger drained from his face as though someone had reached inside and pulled something vital away. The rigid certainty that had filled his posture moments before. The authority, the control, the quiet promise of punishment, vanished completely.

In its place was something Soren had never seen directed at him before.

It was fear, not anger, not even disappointment. But deep fear.

And that realization struck harder than any blow his father had ever delivered.

Because anger, Soren understood. He knew how to withstand it. Disappointment he could endure. Even punishment was something he had learned to outlast.

But fear rewrote the rules of the room.

Fear meant this was no longer a fight he could win.

His mother took a step forward, voice trembling.

"Soren… what are you?"

I'm still me, he wanted to say.

The words pressed against his throat, desperate to be spoken, but they never made it past his lips. Because something in the room had already shifted, something quiet and irreversible that he could feel settling into place.

The kitchen suddenly felt smaller, as if the walls themselves had drawn closer, unable to hold the three of them the way they had only moments before.

His father was the first to break eye contact.

He turned away slowly, dragging a rough hand across his face like he could wipe away what he had just seen, like he could erase the image of his own son standing there with lightning still threading through his fingers.

His mother didn't move.

She stood frozen in the doorway, caught between two instincts that pulled her in opposite directions. One urged her forward, toward the boy she had raised and loved. The other held her back, cautious and uncertain, as though the space between them had suddenly become dangerous.

Soren saw both.

And in that moment, he understood something with a clarity that left no room for denial.

No amount of strength would make this safe.

No amount of explanation would make them see him the same way again.

Slowly, he lifted his eyes to meet theirs.

For the first time in his life, he didn't apologize.

"I did what you taught me," he said quietly.

The words were steady, but something inside him twisted as he spoke them.

"I got stronger."

Even as the sentence left his mouth, part of him recoiled from it. That wasn't what he meant, not really. What he wanted to say was *I don't know how to be smaller anymore.*

But it was too late for softer truths.

Silence spread through the kitchen again, heavy and final.

Soren didn't wait for their response.

If he stayed another second, he might hesitate. And hesitation meant hope and hope meant believing something here could still be fixed.

He already knew it couldn't.

So, he turned and ran.

He didn't stop running until the city began to thin around him and the night air burned cold in his lungs.

Streetlights flickered as he passed beneath them, their pale glow stuttering across the pavement like uncertain witnesses. One went dark entirely as he ran past, plunging the street into sudden shadow before sputtering back to life behind him, as if unsure whether it had truly seen him at all.

By the time he reached the bus station, his pulse was still hammering.

He stood beneath the harsh fluorescent lights, staring up at the departures board until the names blurred together.

Cities he didn't recognize. Places that meant nothing.

Anywhere far enough.

Anywhere high enough to breathe.

When he stepped to the counter, the clerk barely looked up. The ticket printed with a soft mechanical whir before being slid across the counter with a distracted motion.

No questions. No hesitation.

As if he had already decided to leave long before

this moment.

Soren took the ticket and stepped onto the bus.

Only after he dropped into a seat near the back did he glance down at the paper in his hand and notice the destination.

Denver.

The name meant nothing to him. Just distance. Just altitude. Just somewhere far enough away that the version of himself standing in that kitchen might not follow.

He leaned his head back against the cool glass of the window.

His hands still tingled.

Not painfully.

Just… there.

Like a quiet reminder humming beneath his skin.

The bus engine rumbled to life beneath his feet, its steady vibration traveling through the metal frame and into his bones. Outside the window, the road stretched endlessly ahead, dark asphalt unraveling beneath the sweep of distant headlights.

For a moment, everything felt ordinary again.

Then something pressed back.

Not a voice.

Not imagination.

Recognition.

It felt like the moment a blade recognizes the hand that forged it an awareness older than language, sharp and undeniable.

The presence moved through him slowly, deliberately, the way his father's stare once had when measuring whether Soren would stand or fall. It searched for weakness with quiet patience.

The presence searched him slowly, deliberately.

Not for strength.

For fracture.

It moved through him the way a blade tests stone, quiet and patient, examining every hidden weakness.

It found none.

You refused to break.

The meaning carried no pride. No warmth.

Only fact.

You adapted.

For a moment, the sensation shifted.

Not the storm. Not the power.

Something beneath it.

Older. Steadier. Certain in a way that did not belong to him.

It passed before he could grasp it, leaving behind only the uneasy impression that whatever moved through him had known exactly what to do… long before he did.

Soren's jaw tightened instinctively.

His entire life had been measured and judged. Weighed against expectations he never quite met, corrected through bruises, silence, and lessons sharpened into survival.

But this presence did not feel disappointed.

It felt… satisfied.

You survived what was meant to finish you.

The bus lights flickered faintly overhead.

Soren didn't move.

You are not ordinary.

The statement did not feel like praise.

It felt like gravity.

Unavoidable. Absolute.

You are one of the forgotten.

The word landed deeper than the rest: forgotten, but not erased and never truly discarded

Forgotten, like the streets his father had walked alone, like the lessons no one explained because survival did not require explanation.

The presence deepened.

Mistara.

The name surfaced whole in his mind, unfamiliar and yet strangely certain.

Arcane Academy.

Arcane Trials.

His pulse quickened slightly.

Challenge.

You will be measured.

A faint curve touched Soren's mouth.

Measured how?

The presence did not answer.

Instead, one final thought brushed against his mind before withdrawing.

Find the one who bends the room instead of breaking it.

For the briefest instant, an image brushed the edge of his thoughts.

Dark hair moving softly in still air. A quiet presence standing at the center of a room that refused to stay unchanged around her.

Not force.

Balance.

Then the sensation slipped away before he could grasp it.

The presence withdrew completely.

Then it was gone.

The pressure eased, leaving only the steady hum of the bus engine and the endless ribbon of highway stretching beyond the window.

Soren exhaled slowly.

"Fine," he muttered under his breath.

If something wanted to measure him, it could try.

He believed in tests.

And he believed in surviving them.

For the first time since he left home the road ahead did not feel like escape.

It felt like alignment.

Somewhere far beyond the highway and the mountains rising in the distance, something ancient within the Academy's wards registered the shift. Not as an arrival, but as the movement of a piece finally beginning to take its place.

Chapter

Four

Alignment
Soren

Denver did not offer answers.
But it offered distance.
Cold mornings that burned his lungs awake when he stepped outside before sunrise. Streets that didn't know his history and didn't care to ask for it. People moved past him every day without recognition, without curiosity, their lives unfolding in quiet parallel without ever intersecting his.

For a while, that was enough.

Distance had its own kind of relief. The farther he moved from the life he had left behind, the easier it became to pretend that version of himself had stayed there. Denver didn't demand explanations. It didn't ask who he had been before he arrived.

It simply allowed him to exist.

He worked where he could, taking whatever jobs didn't require questions or long conversations. When the restless energy in his body grew too sharp to ignore, he trained alone. He went running until his lungs burned, pushing himself until the tension in his muscles replaced the pressure building beneath his skin.

Little by little, he learned the shape of the city.

Not through attachment, but through repetition. The same streets. The same corners. The same quiet places where no one paid attention long enough to notice when the air shifted around him.

It was in one of those places that he met her.

A narrow alley just off downtown, wedged between two aging brick buildings whose windows had long ago stopped pretending to watch the street below. The kind of space people passed without seeing, their attention fixed on somewhere else.

It was the kind of place most people would consider forgettable, the sort of narrow passageway that blended easily into the background of the city.

That was exactly why Soren preferred it.

But the moment he stepped into the alley, something felt different.

Not visibly at first. The brick walls were the same dull red they had always been, and the pavement carried the usual scatter of dust and grit left behind by passing feet. Yet the air held a quiet tension, subtle but unmistakable, like the pressure that gathers before a storm breaks.

Soren noticed the magic before he saw her.

Chalk symbols curved across the pavement in careful, deliberate patterns, looping and intersecting with a precision that made it immediately clear they were not decorative marks or careless experimentation.

Every line had been placed with intention, and every shape carried a clear sense of purpose. Whoever had drawn the circle knew exactly what they were doing.

The air around it carried a familiar pressure, the quiet tension that forms in the moment before unstable magic wakes and begins looking for somewhere to go.

A girl stood at the center of the chalk pattern.

Her dark hair fell loosely around her shoulders, barely moving despite the breeze that slipped through the narrow alley. There was a stillness about her that didn't feel passive or distracted. It felt deliberate, like someone listening for something most people would never notice.

She held herself the way fighters did when they were waiting for movement rather than reacting to it.

Soren leaned back against the brick wall, folding his arms loosely across his chest as he watched her work for a moment.

"You're doing it wrong."

She didn't look up.

Soren leaned his shoulder more comfortably against the brick wall as he watched her work for another second.

"That's helpful," he added flatly. "The line's crooked."

"It's intentional."

"It's crooked."

This time she looked up.

Her expression wasn't annoyed. Not surprised either. If anything, she seemed to be deciding whether he was worth the effort of responding at all.

"You're disrupting it," she said.

"I'm standing here."

"Exactly."

For a brief moment, the corner of his mouth almost lifted.

She lowered her gaze again and rested her palm lightly against the chalk line. The symbols etched into the pavement flickered beneath her touch, thin threads of light sliding along the circle as though something inside the pattern had begun to stir.

The air in the alley tightened, the shift so subtle most people might have missed it.

Soren didn't.

He felt the pressure immediately, the familiar warning of power building too quickly beneath the surface. It rose sharply, the way storms did when lightning gathered before the sky had decided where to send it.

He reacted before he had time to think.

The streetlight above them exploded.

Glass burst outward with a sharp crack, scattering harmlessly across the pavement as the sudden darkness swallowed the narrow alley. Only the dim glow of the chalk circle remained, flickering faintly at their feet.

The pressure vanished almost as quickly as it had formed.

The symbols dimmed.

For a moment she simply stared up at the shattered bulb, the broken fixture still swaying slightly above them.

Then she slowly turned toward him.

"You did that."

"You were about to."

"I had it under control."

"You almost did."

Her eyes narrowed slightly, the smallest shift in her expression.

"That wasn't your decision to make."

That caught him off guard.

For a second, something unreadable crossed his face before it settled back into its usual calm.

"You're welcome," he said dryly.

"I didn't thank you."

He pushed off the wall, straightening as he folded his arms loosely across his chest.

"You should."

"Why?"

His gaze flicked past her, briefly, toward the corridor where the light had nearly slipped out of control.

"Because the next one might not stop at the light."

Silence stretched between them.

Not sharp.

Not hostile.

Just quiet enough to feel deliberate.

They studied each other like strangers trying to

decide what the other was made of.

Then, unexpectedly, she sighed.

"Fine," she said. "Thank you."

He blinked, the reaction small but unmistakably real.

"You're terrible at gratitude."

"I'm new to it."

That almost made him laugh.

Almost.

Chapter

Five

Two Sides of a Coin
Veya
&
Soren

We had one day, just one, to pack what little we owned, gather our magical supplies, and make our way to Mistara Island, a place vast enough to swallow you whole if you weren't careful. The air that morning felt charged, humming with an energy that made my skin prickle.

Every motion carried weight. Each vial we owned tucked away and each charm strapped to a belt. We prepared any tiny piece of protection that might mean the difference between life and death.

Soren moved through the room in sharp, efficient motions, as if precision alone could tame his nerves. The tension rolled off him in waves.

"You're packing like we're going to war," I said lightly as I tightened the strap on my travel satchel, forcing a casualness I didn't entirely feel.

Soren didn't smile. He barely looked up from where he stood near the window, checking the edge of a blade that probably didn't need checking.

"Aren't we?" he said.

There was no sarcasm in it. No dramatic weight. Just a simple statement of fact.

The words landed harder than I expected.

I turned toward him fully then, caught off guard by the steadiness in his voice. Morning light spilled through the tall dorm windows, tracing the line of his jaw and catching on the faint tension he tried to hide behind that usual calm. From a distance he might have looked composed. Up close, I could see the strain threading through him and the readiness that never really left.

"We'll be fine," I said, adjusting the clasp on my satchel more than necessary. My voice held, mostly, though a faint tremor slipped through before I could stop it.

Soren stilled at that.

His gaze lifted to mine, studying me with a quiet intensity that felt less like scrutiny and more like grounding himself in something certain. For a moment he said nothing, and the silence stretched just long enough to feel honest rather than uncomfortable.

Then he exhaled slowly.

"You always say that" he murmured, not unkindly. "And somehow… I always believe you."

I held his gaze, unsure whether the warmth that settled in my chest came from comfort or the quiet weight of responsibility his trust carried. Probably both.

"Well," I said softly, managing the ghost of a smile, "someone has to."

That earned the faintest curve at the corner of his mouth, not quite a smile, but close enough to feel like one.

The edge in his voice softened. He brushed his fingers against mine just long enough to steady us both.

Outside, Mistara Island loomed on the horizon, shrouded in sea mist, its outline shifting like something alive. Some called it a sanctuary. Others, a graveyard or a kingdom of forgotten gods.

Whatever it was, we were about to find out.

I steadied my breathing and kept my eyes on the island, even as I knew I was choosing a path that would leave no way back.

Tomorrow, the Academy will open its gates, just as it did every October 13, without fail.

But no one simply arrived at Arcane.

Students lived hidden among normies, scattered through ordinary cities that would never understand the pulse of magic beneath our skin. For Soren and me, that city was Denver. With its thin air, mountain shadows, and a long way from Mistara's wild heart.

Getting there demanded secrecy, and more courage than most were willing to spend. Storms bent compasses. Rivers whispered in ancient tongues. Not everyone who began the journey reached the island. Some got lost. Some turned back. Others simply disappeared.

I couldn't tell which frightened me more, the journey failing me… or the island deciding I didn't belong.

Those who make it here are rarely missed. We are the forgotten ones, the runaways, the unwanted, and the overlooked. The children no one bothered to look for. There were no search parties and no missing posters for us. We vanish, and the world moves on.

I was thirteen when I stopped wanting to be found. Thirteen when I learned that being unwanted could be its own kind of armor. Nights were long. Food was scarce. My magic burned beneath my skin, daring me to survive one more day.

For a while, solitude was safety. Being alone meant being untouchable…Or so I thought.

Then I met Soren.

A boy whose silence felt less like distance… and more like gravity.

And Zephyr, who could make despair sound like a dare.

Somehow, they saw me before I even knew who I

was. For the first time in years, I wasn't just surviving.

I was becoming something the world had tried to bury.

Soren and I were both born under Gemini, the sign of duality, of mirrored selves and shifting currents. Two sides of the same coin. I have always adapted quickly, bending where needed, finding language before force. He meets tension head-on, restless and sharp, driven by curiosity that borders on defiance.

Two expressions of the same unsettled air.

The Academy summons the forgotten, yes but it also seems drawn to those who are never only one thing.

Together, we balance each other. Dual natures in a world that doesn't understand either.

I remember the night we met.

I'd been roaming downtown Denver for months, living off whatever I could conjure. That night, in an alley off Sixteenth Street Mall washed in yellow streetlight, I tried a spell I wasn't ready for. A spell for summoning a nature spirit bound to air.

The sigil burned faintly against the concrete where I'd drawn it in chalk and salt. My hands trembled, though whether from cold or hunger I couldn't tell anymore. Magic answered desperation more easily than discipline. I had plenty of one and not enough of the other.

I spoke the final word anyway.

For a long moment, nothing changed. The alley remained stubbornly ordinary filled only with the distant hum of traffic, the hollow rattle of a bottle rolling somewhere along the pavement, and the stale scent of city rain clinging to brick.

Then the air shifted.

Wind twisted low to the ground, rising in uneven currents that hissed and coiled around me, whispering in languages that scraped uncomfortably against my bones. Streetlights flickered in erratic bursts, their glow stuttering as heat shimmered across the asphalt in wavering waves. Within the distortion, a shadow gathered, not fully formed but undeniably present, restless, aware, and alive.

As it drew closer, a sharp awareness pressed against my skin, prickling like static before a storm.

The shadow wasn't merely taking shape.

It was watching me.

There was intelligence in that scrutiny, something deliberate and assessing, as though it were weighing my worth before deciding whether I was worth answering at all.

Despite myself, I smiled.

It was working.

I wanted that spirit to teach me how to fly not for spectacle, not for power alone, but so that one day I could reach Mistara Island and earn my place among the magics I had only ever glimpsed from afar.

But old magic does not obey easily, and spirits never give without demanding something in return.

The realization had barely settled when the circle beneath my feet fractured.

The air didn't form into the gentle, obedient spirit I'd intended. It split wild, electric, and alive with a will that was not mine to command. Power rushed outward instead of inward, snapping against the alley walls with a low, vibrating hum that made my teeth ache.

That was when he appeared.

Soren stepped out of the dark with that half-smile that gave the impression of him being reckless, even curious, and entirely too confident for someone standing inside a forming storm.

"Well, well," he said. "Looks like someone's gotten noticed."

The wind snapped around him, tugging at his dark hair, circling like it couldn't decide whether to challenge him or bow. He didn't move.

"You're either brilliant," he added, gaze locking with mine, "or completely insane. Let's find out which."

The air pressed close to him, sharp and searching, but he only laughed a clear, fearless sound that sliced through the storm's tension.

"I'm not afraid," he said. "And you shouldn't be either."

His eyes met mine, steady and certain, like he already expected me to stand beside him. In that instant, I knew he wasn't just a passerby.

He was a challenge. A spark daring me to rise.

Then the voice came, sharp and electrified.

"I am Zephyr," the voice whispered, threaded through every current of air. "How curious. Normies, bold enough to summon me? Few have the strength… or the recklessness. Wait."

He turned suddenly.

The wind shifted, closing in around us, pressing close like a living thing.

"You are not normies," Zephyr hissed, voice sharpening. "You both carry magic and something older still… something buried deep in your blood."

Soren's grin widened, storm-light dancing in his eyes. "Neither of us fears a little wind."

The storm burst around us, silver currents tearing at paper, lifting debris, and hurling signs into a frenzy of noise. Those huddled in the alley scattered, vanishing into the night as Zephyr's laughter rose above it all sounding wild, ancient, and utterly free.

"Show me more," the spirit hissed, mischief curling through its voice.

My heart hammered as I drew in a slow breath, trying to steady the storm inside my ribs. The air between us felt charged with more than magic now with possibility, and with the fragile understanding forming between two people who had spent too long moving through the world unseen.

I glanced at Soren.

He stood with that same restless confidence, but

there was something else there now, something quieter beneath the bravado. Recognition, maybe. The kind that came from realizing you weren't the only one standing slightly outside the world everyone else seemed to fit into.

"They don't see us," I said softly, the words slipping out before I could stop them. "Not really."

Soren's gaze flicked to mine. For once, he didn't deflect with humor.

"No," he agreed. "They don't."

The admission settled between us without awkwardness, carrying the strange relief of being understood without explanation.

"They call people like us unstable," I continued, my voice steadier now. "Too much. Too different. Too difficult to place." I hesitated, then added more quietly, "Forgotten, even when we're standing right in front of them."

Soren huffed a quiet breath that might have been a laugh, though there was no amusement in it. "Yeah," he said. "That sounds about right."

Silence lingered for a moment, not empty but charged with shared understanding.

Then I lifted my chin slightly. "Arcane Academy finds people like us," I said. "The ones who don't fit anywhere else. The ones the world overlooks until it can't anymore." I hesitated, feeling the weight of what I was about to ask. "I'm going to find it. Mistara Island. The trials. All of it."

His brow lifted faintly, interest sharpening. "You say that like it's inevitable."

"It is," I replied quietly. "I just… don't want to get there alone."

That hung between us for a breath.

Soren studied me, really studied me this time, as if measuring whether I meant it or whether this was just another reckless dream that would collapse by morning. Whatever he saw seemed to settle something in him.

A slow grin tugged at his mouth, not mocking and not dismissive either but certain.

"Well," he said, rolling his shoulders as though accepting a challenge he'd been waiting for, "it'd be a waste to let you do something that dangerous without supervision."

Despite everything, a small laugh escaped me. "Supervision?"

"Obviously," he said. "You look like you'd get into trouble."

"I am in trouble."

"Exactly," he replied. Then, more quietly, with a steadiness that surprised me, "You won't be alone."

Something in my chest loosened at that.

I turned back toward the forming spirit, drawing in another steadying breath as the wind began to coil more tightly around us.

"Teach us to fly," I said, lifting my voice to the presence gathering in the air. "Join us on our journey to Mistara Island. Help us reach Arcane Academy and win the Arcane Trials together… as one."

For a moment, the air held still, as if the world itself waited for the answer.

Then Zephyr laughed.

The sound deepened into a roar that shook the air and stirred the currents around us, wind coiling in sharp, restless spirals. It wasn't mockery. It was delight, a sound so wild and dangerous and far too alive.

Soren only smirked, confidence resting easily on his shoulders as if danger were just another inconvenience, he expected the world to adjust around.

He didn't look at the spirit.

He looked at me instead.

"So," he said lightly, like we weren't standing in the center of a summoning circle that could collapse or explode at any moment, "when do we start?"

I let out a breath that almost turned into a laugh. "We already started."

"Good," he replied without missing a beat. "I was worried we were going to stand here dramatically for another five minutes while the wind judged us."

Despite everything, the pressure, the presence gathering in the air, the faint tremor in my hands, warmth flickered in my chest. His ease made it feel possible to breathe.

"You're not even a little concerned?" I asked quietly.

Soren's grin sharpened. "About the mysterious ancient spirit forming in front of us?" He finally glanced toward the shifting currents of air and shadow, then back to me. "I'm thrilled. This is easily the most interesting thing that's happened all week."

"That's not reassuring."

"It's not supposed to be reassuring," he said. "It's supposed to be honest."

The wind coiled tighter around us, brushing against my shoulders and threading through my hair in curious spirals. I could feel it now, truly feel it, the shape of something intelligent gathering inside the currents. Waiting. Listening.

Excitement sparked through my nerves, bright and electric, chasing away some of the fear.

Zephyr.

If this worked, if I could actually do this, then everything changed.

I tightened my fingers slightly, steadying my breathing the way I'd practiced. "You know," I said, trying for composure and only half succeeding, "if this goes wrong, we could get thrown into a wall. Or off a building."

Soren's expression didn't shift. "Then try not to get thrown," he said easily. "I just got used to this body not being broken."

A reluctant smile tugged at my mouth. "You're unbelievable."

"And yet," he replied, stepping just a fraction closer, his voice lowering in a way that grounded rather than distracted, "you're still doing this. Which means you believe you can."

The confidence in his tone settled something restless inside me.

He wasn't looking at the forming spirit.

He was watching me.

I straightened slightly, letting that belief settle into my bones alongside the thrill building in my chest. The wind responded at once, tightening its spiral as if sensing my focus sharpen.

"Okay," I murmured, more to myself than to him. "Okay... I can do this."

Soren's grin returned, bright and sharp and utterly certain.

"Yeah," he said softly. "You can."

The spirit rose higher, silver winds lifting us from the ground and spinning the city into a blur of light and motion.

"Then rise," Zephyr thundered. "Your training begins. Only then will I decide whether I follow."

The storm folded around us, vast and alive, stretching endlessly in every direction. Yet for the first time, it no longer felt like something I had to face alone.

What had begun as a solitary fight for survival was shifting into something else entirely. Something steadier, something shared. I wasn't just enduring anymore. I was beginning to belong.

I had a team... or at least the fragile beginnings of one. A place that might one day resemble a home, even if it didn't quite feel like one yet. And somewhere in the uncertain space between danger and possibility, I realized I might have found two of the best friends I could ever hope for.

The thought felt almost too hopeful to hold onto for long, but I held it anyway. For now, that fragile sense of connection, of not standing alone against the world, was enough.

Chapter

Six

Learning the Sky
Veya, Soren, & Zephyr

Zephyr's training was brutal, relentless, and definitely unforgettable.

"Again!" Zephyr commanded.

The word cracked through the air like lightning.

I barely had time to gasp before the wind surged upward, ripping me from the rooftop and hurling me into open sky. The city dropped away beneath my feet. Brick, glass, and steel shrinking into something unreal.

"You're thinking too loudly," Zephyr's voice hummed all around me, layered and electric. "Air listens. It does not obey."

"I'm trying," I snapped, arms trembling as I fought to stabilize the current beneath me.

"Trying is what normies do before they fall," Zephyr said sarcastically.

Soren laughed somewhere above me, the sound wild and unbothered.

"You heard him, flying squirrel," he called, slipping in that cursed nickname he'd adopted during training. "Less panic. More trust."

Easy for him to say, I thought.

Air magic never came naturally to me. It wasn't

my affinity. It was something that had to be learned and trained over a long time to gain access to that kind of power.

Every gust fought my grip; every spiral slipped through my fingers like mist. When I pushed too hard, the wind rebelled, slamming into my ribs and spinning me sideways until my vision blurred. I learned quickly that force meant nothing here.

The air demanded patience, it demanded precision and above all, the air demanded respect.

Zephyr made sure I learned that lesson the hard way.

"Slower," he would murmur when I faltered. "You carry weight in your magic. Not heaviness or gravity. Learn what pulls and what repels."

Gravity.

The word clung to me, strange and uncomfortable.

So, I learned to listen. To feel the difference between rising heat and falling cold, between playful breezes and cutting crosswinds. I practiced weaving currents into narrow ribbons, guiding them through my palms with deliberate care. It was meticulous work, quiet, and controlled.

But when it finally worked, when my feet lifted from the ground without fear tightening my chest, Zephyr went silent.

Then, softly he said, "There it is."

Soren, meanwhile, was chaos incarnate. Air answered him in ways it never answered me. It was not like a skill he was learning, but like something returning to him. Familiar. Instinctive. As if he had belonged to the sky long before he ever tried to command it.

"Higher!" he shouted, leaping from the edge of a skyscraper before I could answer.

The wind roared up to meet him, catching his fall and flinging him skyward in a silver arc. He laughed, spinning through the air as if gravity were merely a suggestion.

Zephyr's presence flared, delighted. "Yes, that hunger. That defiance. You do not ask the storm for permission, do you, boy?"

Soren grinned, hair whipped by the gale. "Why would I? It's more fun when it chases me."

The spirit laughed, sharp and thunderous. "Careful. The sky enjoys being challenged."

Soren's signature spiral was born that night, a reckless ascent that pulled wind and light into a blazing column around him. Watching it made my heart stutter every time. It was beautifully dangerous and untamed.

And the wind loved him for it.

I, on the other hand, crashed into a billboard so hard the metal rang like a struck bell, the vibration traveling straight through my bones.

Soren doubled over laughing midair, nearly losing his own balance. "Are you good?!"

"I meant to do that," I groaned, rolling my eyes as I peeled myself off the twisted metal and tried to untangle my limbs with what little dignity remained.

He drifted closer and extended his hand, his eyes dancing with open mischief. "Bold strategy. Very… dramatic. Ten style points deducted for that landing."

"Only ten?" I accepted his hand and let him pull me upright. "You're getting generous."

"I'm factoring in creativity," he said. "Not everyone commits to a billboard with that level of enthusiasm."

I brushed imaginary dust from my sleeve. "For your information, I was testing structural integrity."

"Of the sign?"

"Of myself."

Soren snorted. "And what have we learned from this important research?"

"That gravity is biased," I muttered.

He grinned, then steadied me for a brief second longer than necessary before letting go. "You didn't fall," he said, a touch more quietly. "You just… arrived aggressively."

"That's one way to phrase it."

"Look at it this way," he added, gesturing around us. "First aerial collision, and you're still alive. That's progress."

"Your standards are concerning."

"My standards are realistic," he replied. Then, with a sideways glance and a half-smile: "Ready to try again, or should I start scouting more billboards for you?"

I pushed off the metal frame and stepped back into the open air. "Laugh all you want," I said, lifting my chin. "Next time I'm landing perfectly."

Soren's grin widened. "I hope so. I'm running out of things to blame your crashes on."

I rolled my eyes, laughing as I took his hand, pretending I hadn't needed the help. Some lessons were exhilarating. There was something about being able to glide through dawn-lit clouds, skim rooftops as the city slept, and carve paths through mist that felt alive against my skin. Other lessons were nightmares.

Zephyr never warned us when an assessment was coming.

One moment I hovered beside Soren, steady and focused, finally beginning to feel like I understood the rhythm of the wind beneath my feet. The next, the air vanished.

The wind wasn't softened or redirected; it was erased, leaving nothing behind to catch or steady me. The invisible foundation beneath my feet dissolved in an instant, as though the sky itself had decided it was finished supporting me.

I dropped.

The sky lurched violently as gravity seized me, the world snapping into a dizzying blur of color and motion. Wind tore past my ears as my stomach slammed somewhere near my spine, breath ripped from my lungs before

I could even think to steady it.

Panic hit hard and immediate. I reached instinctively for the currents that had held me seconds ago and found nothing.

I grasped for the wind and found nothing waiting there. There was no resistance, no answering pull, no invisible structure to brace against. There was only open sky beneath me and the city racing upward in a blur of concrete and glass.

"Soren!" I shouted, terror threading through every syllable as I spiraled downward with absolutely no plan and even less control. "The wind is gone!"

"Yeah, I noticed!" he called back, his voice somewhere between alarm and what sounded suspiciously like laughter.

I twisted mid-fall, spotting him several yards away, also dropping but somehow managing to look far more composed than any sane person should while plummeting toward the ground.

"Do something!" I yelled.

"I am doing something!" he shot back. "I'm falling with style!"

"This is not style!"

"It's definitely not your landing strategy!"

I tried to stabilize, forcing my breathing into something resembling control. "Zephyr!" I shouted into the rushing air. "A warning would be appreciated!"

A soft, amused voice threaded through the emptiness around us.

"Adaptation requires honesty."

"This isn't honesty!" I snapped. "This is attempted murder!"

Soren twisted in the air, trying to angle himself toward me. "Okay, new plan," he called. "Try not to die."

"Fantastic plan!" I shouted back. "Really helpful!"

Below us, rooftops surged closer with terrifying speed.

Adrenaline burned through my veins as instinct finally overrode panic. I reached again. I didn't reach for the wind that had been given, but for the memory of it. For the shape Zephyr had shown me. For the way it had felt when it answered.

For a split second, nothing happened.

Then something stirred.

A thin current brushed my fingertips like a hesitant reply.

"Oh, now you respond?" I muttered, forcing focus through the panic. "Of course, now."

Soren whooped somewhere above and behind me. "Hey! I've got a breeze!"

"Good for you!" I shouted. "Share!"

"I'm working on it!"

The ground rushed closer.

The wind flickered once.

Then again.

I grabbed it, not gracefully, not perfectly, but enough. Enough to slow. Enough to tilt. Enough to keep from becoming a permanent street decoration.

Soren caught a current seconds later, jerking sideways with a sharp laugh that sounded half wild and half relieved. "Okay," he said breathlessly as we both fought to stabilize, "that was definitely intentional."

I glared at him midair. "If I hit the ground, I'm haunting you."

"You'd have to catch me first."

"I will learn how to fly properly just to spite you."

"That's the spirit," he said, grinning despite the lingering adrenaline. "Motivation through mutual survival."

Above us, the air finally settled back into place. As if it had never disappeared at all.

Zephyr's voice drifted lightly through the currents, threaded with unmistakable satisfaction. "That was better."

I released a shaky breath, still trying to steady the frantic rhythm of my heart as the last of the adrenaline burned through my veins. "You're enjoying this," I accused, though the edge in my voice had softened.

"Immensely," the wind replied, warm with amusement.

Soren let out a breathless laugh, exhilaration still bright in his eyes as he steadied himself beside me. "Okay," he said, glancing over with reckless energy that felt entirely too natural for someone who had just nearly died. "Again?"

Before I could answer, the air shifted.

The world dimmed as if something vast had passed overhead, and in the sudden distortion of space and sound, the fragile balance we'd found unraveled. The current beneath me twisted violently and vanished, and the sky dropped out from under my feet once more.

Darkness swallowed the edges of my vision as I fell.

Then Soren's voice cut through it. "I've got you!"

He dove after me without hesitation, reaching through the churning air, but the distance between us stretched in a way that felt wrong. It was warped and unstable, like space itself refused to align. The wind slammed into him from all sides, hurling him off course and forcing him back.

"Focus!" Zephyr's voice thundered through the storm. "Do not chase the wind, Veya, command it!"

The ground surged upward, far too fast.

Something inside me snapped, not with fear but with fury. It rose from deep within my core, ancient and aching, like a coiled force that had waited far too long to be acknowledged. Instinct urged me to grasp for the wind again, to chase it the way I always had.

This time, I refused. Rather than chasing the current, I anchored myself within it, claiming its shape and forcing it to answer to me.

I reached inward rather than outward, holding my focus steady as I seized the shape of the air itself and forced it to answer. The wind slammed back into existence beneath me in a violent upward surge, roaring with sudden obedience as it caught me inches from the ground.

The impact cracked the pavement below, sending fragments of stone and debris skittering outward in a sharp ring as the force of the halted fall rippled through the street.

Silence followed.

Soren hovered nearby, pale and shaking. "You… you stopped the sky," he breathed.

Zephyr said nothing for a long moment. Then, quietly, he said, "Interesting," eyeing me as if I were a mystery to solve.

The wind curled around me, reverent and wary all at once. "You do not merely ride the air. You bind it. You center it." Zephyr watched her carefully then, something older than curiosity flickering in his expression.

"Strange," he murmured. "The air does not behave that way for normies."

For a moment the wind around her felt vast, ancient… like something recognizing its maker.

His attention shifted to Soren, sharp and crackling. "And you…storm chaser. You burn too bright to ever stay grounded. One day, the sky will answer you in kind."

Soren swallowed, forcing a grin. "Is that supposed to be comforting?"

Zephyr laughed. "No."

After that, the training changed.

By the time we turned sixteen, the veil between worlds thinned. We were no longer just kids hiding magic in alleyways. We were wielders of air, tempered, dangerous, and inseparable.

Soren pushed me forward when doubt rooted me in place. I pulled him back when recklessness threatened to tear him apart. Two forces in constant orbit, never colliding yet somehow balanced.

Mistara Island no longer felt distant.

Instead Mistara Island and the Arcane Academy for Magic felt inevitable.

And somewhere above us, the wind watched as if already knowing what we were becoming.

Chapter

Seven

The Final Test

The wind that morning was different, it felt sharper and heavier, humming with something electric. Even before Zephyr appeared, I could smell the storm building, thick with ozone and memory.

Zephyr hovered above us, a shape of silver and smoke, his voice curling through the air like thunder caught between laughs.

"Today," he hummed, "you show me what you've become. No more lessons. No more mercy."

Something flickered across his face like pride laced with mischief as if he already knew we would survive but planned to make us earn it anyway.

Soren flexed his hands. Tension rippled through him. For a heartbeat, faint arcs of silver-blue light flickered between his fingers. Lightning. The same kind that had crackled to life the night he fought with his parents and left everything behind.

He clenched his fists until the sparks finally faded, forcing the lightning back beneath his skin with visible effort.

But I saw them.

I always did.

"You're going to short out before we even start," I murmured, keeping my voice low enough that no one else would hear the edge of concern beneath it.

His jaw tightened, though a corner of his mouth lifted anyway. "I am perfectly in control."

"Your definition of control is… flexible."

He flexed his fingers, testing them as a faint flicker of blue crackled and disappeared. "It's called anticipation."

"It's called almost setting the curtains on fire."

"They were ugly curtains."

I crossed my arms. "That's not the point."

"It's absolutely the point," he replied, glancing sideways at me. "If we're going into something dangerous, I'd prefer to be the most dangerous thing in the room."

"You're not supposed to compete with the trial," I said dryly.

"I'm not competing," he corrected. "I'm setting expectations."

A thin arc of light flashed between his knuckles again before he smothered it with a sharp exhale. He pretended not to notice my look.

"You know," I added, softer now, "you don't have to burn through everything the second it challenges you."

His gaze flicked to mine, something sharper hiding beneath the bravado. "And you don't have to carry everything like it's already your responsibility."

I held his stare for a beat longer than necessary.

"Maybe," I said. "But if you fry yourself before the first strike, I'm not dragging you out."

He huffed a quiet laugh. "You absolutely would."

"Only because you're heavy."

"I'm not heavy."

"You are entirely muscle and bad decisions."

He grinned fully at that, some of the tension finally

easing from his shoulders. "Good," he said. "That means I'll survive."

I shook my head, but the corner of my mouth betrayed me. "Try not to explode."

"No promises," he replied lightly. Then, more quietly, "But I won't break."

And this time, when the sparks threatened again, they didn't flare.

Soren glanced over, grin already forming sharp and unbothered, like the storm overhead belonged to him.

"Relax," he said. "If I explode, I'll try to aim away from you."

"Reassuring," I replied dryly.

Another faint crackle snapped between his fingers before he forced it down again. His shoulders rolled once, like he was trying to contain something too large for skin.

"Are you good?" he asked, softer now, the grin fading just enough to show the question mattered.

I held his gaze for a moment. "Ask me again when we're still standing."

His smile returned, quieter this time. "Deal."

For a breath, the world narrowed to the three of us standing beneath a sky that felt too heavy, too watchful.

Then Zephyr moved.

He stepped forward into the open like he'd been waiting for permission no one had the authority to give.

"Finally," he said. "Something interesting."

The air shifted, it wasn't a gradual shift, but it was decisive.

Wind curled at his feet first, tugging at loose fabric and hair. Then it rose, spiraling upward in tightening coils as if the atmosphere itself had recognized him and leaned closer to listen.

The sky responded.

Clouds tore open above us as Zephyr's power swelled, pulling the air into motion. Wind howled through the streets, ripping leaves from branches and sending them spinning into violent spirals of green and gold. Banners snapped. Loose stone skittered across the ground.

The world inhaled sharply and did not exhale.

Zephyr lifted one hand. The storm gathered like a living thing answering its name.

"Rise," he commanded.

And the sky obeyed.

The gale lifted me before I could breathe. The pull was raw, dangerous. For an instant, the world did not resist me…it aligned. I steadied myself, shaping the air with slow, careful hands the way Zephyr had taught me, bending it, not fighting it.

Soren was already in motion, vaulting into the strongest currents, laughter carried away by the storm.

"Try to keep up!" he called over his shoulder. "I'd hate to be the only one enjoying this."

The sparks came again, faint flickers skipping between his fingers as if the wind itself carried lightning through his veins.

"Come on," he shouted, voice bright with reckless delight. "It's just gravity having a bad day."

It always scared me a little, how easily the storm seemed to claim him.

He spun through the sky, spiraling in wild arcs, a streak of silver and light. Every time his hands cut through the air, electricity followed like a living echo. Bright, beautiful, and barely contained.

Zephyr's voice boomed across the rooftop. "Control is strength, but chaos is truth! Show me both!"

I rose beside Soren, my movements careful, shaping the wind into clean streams, loops, and curls. He matched me beat for beat, our powers meeting midair in a swirl of wind and light. His lightning braided into my currents, turning the storm silver blue.

"Don't overdo it," I called, breath steady but sharp. "You'll destabilize the current."

He flashed me a wicked grin. "You worry too much."

For a moment, we were perfectly balanced, it was like precision and fury intertwined. The wind wasn't fighting us anymore; it was listening.

Then Zephyr struck hard and without mercy, like a storm finally unleashed.

A sudden wave of raw force tore us apart, flinging me into open air. Cold shock ripped the breath from my lungs. I spun helplessly as the ground lurched and tilted below. Panic surged when the wind refused to answer fast enough.

"Soren!" I shouted, the name nearly swallowed by the roar of wind around me.

But he was already diving toward me, a surge of lightning trailing from his hands, illuminating the air between us.

"Hey, stay with me!" he called, voice sharp through the chaos. "Don't fight it."

The storm bent to meet him, coiling around his arms as he reached out. His fingers brushed mine, as sparks began passing between us. The sparks felt sharp, stinging, and almost alive.

"I've got you; I won't let you fall," he muttered.

Together we bent the gale beneath us, slowing, steadying, landing hard on one knee but upright.

Zephyr hovered above, light flickering through his mist-like form, his voice quieter now.

"Two years ago, the wind ruled you," he said. "Now you rule yourselves."

Soren looked at me then, still breathing hard, sparks fading gently across his fingers. The storm had calmed, but the echo of thunder lingered in his eyes.

For a moment, I realized just how close we were, close enough to feel the residual warmth of lightning along his skin.

"I told you we'd be fine," he said, that same crooked grin tugging at his mouth, hiding more than it revealed.

For a moment, I believed him completely. The storm had finally quieted, the air clean and bright around us, and standing beside him I felt… safe. Certain, like nothing in the world could touch us.

But beneath that fragile calm, something shifted. Small at first, then sharper, threading its way through my chest. Jealousy. Not the cruel kind that poisons, but the quiet ache of wanting what someone else seems born with.

Soren's magic had always known him. It answered instantly, lightning sparking at his call, air bending without resistance, storms wrapping around him like threads of silver and fire. He belonged to it and it to him.

I envied that clarity and that certainty.

Because while he had found his element, his place in the storm… I was still searching for mine.

Zephyr's laughter rippled long and low, folding through the air like the sound of distant thunder. Silver mist shimmered around him, catching the first rays of sunlight breaking through the clouds.

"You've proven yourselves," he said, his voice softer now, carrying something that almost felt like pride. "Your paths lead beyond me, yes… but I think I'd like to see where they go."

Soren looked up, confusion flickering across his face. "You mean… you're coming with us?"

I blinked. "You're serious?"

The spirit's outline brightened, eyes glinting like fragments of storm light.

"For a time," Zephyr replied. "Until you no longer need the sky to remind you how to rise."

Soren's grin returned slowly, bright and unmistakably pleased.

"Good," he said. "I was starting to think you'd just throw us off buildings and disappear."

A low current of amusement rippled through the wind around us.

"You've both tasted the wind and lived," he said. "Few earn that right. Mistara calls to you, but it whispers to me as well. Perhaps it's time I see this Academy of yours and these Arcane Trials you speak of."

A small smile tugged at my lips. "The world might not be ready for you, Zephyr."

"Then it will have to adapt," he said, laughter spilling through the air like sparks.

The last of the storm dispersed, replaced by warm, golden light. The city below seemed asleep, unaware of the promise hanging in the wind above it.

Soren stood beside me, wind in his hair, faint crackles of lightning weaving between his fingers. I met his eyes and felt it; it was the same unspoken certainty that had carried us through every storm.

"Guess the storm's coming with us," he said quietly.

Zephyr's voice rolled overhead, playful and bright. "You'll need it where you're going."

And somewhere deep inside, I think we both knew he was right. Whatever waited on Mistara Island, whatever the Academy and the Trials demanded, we knew we wouldn't face it alone.

The storm was ours now. All three of us.

60

Chapter

Eight

Chosen, Not Summoned
Zephyr

I am not your average Nature Spirit. Most of my kind prefer to remain unseen. We are the quiet guardians of wind, flame, tide, or root. But I've never had the patience for subtlety.

Nature spirits are a type of fae, born from realms that exist just beyond the Veil, the same shimmering barrier that carries most magical children to Mistara when their time comes. We go by many names in all different worlds, fae, spirits, nymphs, call us what you will, we each serve a role in keeping the world alive, balanced, and ever turning. Most mortals, or normies as Veya and Soren likes to call them, never notice us. But we're there, shaping every gust of wind, stirring every spark, coaxing every tide. We are the heartbeat beneath the world's noise.

I just happen to be the part of the wind that howls. I am the kind that refuses to stay unseen

I am a Wind Spirit, keeper of storms, whisperer of breezes, architect of chaos. Every sweep of air belongs, in some small way, to me. The soft breath that skims over a field at dawn? Mine. The autumn gust that chases leaves through quiet neighborhoods? Also, mine. The storm that tears at sails and tests brave fools on the open sea? That's definitely mine.

When I'm in the mood, I even lend a hand or rather, a current to help the sea's travelers reach their destinations, pushing at their boats in rhythm with my old friend, the Moon. She and I dance often, guiding tides and tempests in the endless waltz of water and wind.

We Nature Spirits are vital, though most would never think of thanking us. Still, I don't mind. I prefer laughter to gratitude, mischief to reverence. After all, I wasn't made to be worshiped. I was made to move.

I wasn't supposed to interfere with the normies, at least, not directly. We're meant to stay on our side of the Veil, nudging the edges of weather and fate, never stepping fully into the normie world. But then, Soren and Veya came along, and rules suddenly felt… negotiable.

I still remember that first night in Denver. The air was restless and choked with smoke, neon, and normie noise. I drifted through the city, attuned to the sigh of traffic and the electric hum of normie life, that's when I felt it, magic was thrumming through the air, raw and unsteady. Tugging at the air like an impatient heartbeat. Something was calling me.

At first, I ignored it. Normies are always pulling at things they don't understand.

But then I heard her voice.

"Please," she had said into the wind, clear and determined even though she was a little afraid, but stubborn as mountain air.

And beside her stood him: Soren, a spark barely contained in what I thought was human skin, lightning already dancing in his veins like it had been waiting for a storm to set it free.

At first, I ignored it. Normies are always pulling at things they don't understand.
But then I heard her voice.

"Show yourself," she had called into the wind, her voice steady despite the fear threading through it.

A beat later, his voice followed, lighter, edged with reckless curiosity.

"If something's listening… we're not leaving."

And beside her stood him: Soren, a spark barely contained in human skin, lightning already dancing in his veins like it had been waiting for a storm to set it free.

When I revealed myself, I expected fear. Instead, I got a challenge. Soren smirked like he'd seen through me entirely, and Veya, she stood tall, steady as stone, even with the wind screaming around her. She had courage carved into her bones, even though I don't think she believed it quite yet.

That night, something ancient stirred in me. I remembered what it felt like to believe in something, to be more than a force or a whisper on the wind. Maybe that's why I stayed.

Soren's rage matched my tempests, his curiosity feeding my chaos. And Veya, she balanced us both. She brought reason where we'd bring ruin. Together, they reminded me what passion looked like. What friendship felt like.

So yes, I crossed the Veil and broke every rule ever written in the breath of the skies. I chose them, the storm-touched boy with lightning in his blood, and the girl who carried stillness in her bones.

They were both mixed with something I couldn't quite name, it was something wild, almost forbidden, but it sparked a curiosity I couldn't shake. Soren fascinated me, power swirling in him like a tempest barely contained. And Veya… she intrigued me in a different way. The girl who had learned patience from pain, determination from loneliness, and resilience from abandonment. She carried strength the wind itself could admire.

They didn't summon a mere spirit that night. They

summoned a force that chose them.

And somewhere between the rush of air and the roll of thunder, they earned not just an ally, but a companion, and maybe even a friend.

But every choice carries its price.

The moment I decided to leave my realm behind for Veya and Soren, creatures not of my kind, was the moment the air itself turned against me. A sharp ache tore through my chest, so raw it stole the breath from my winds. Then came the voice, it was ancient and heavy, booming through my mind like thunder pulled from the core of the sky.

"You are no longer welcome among us."

In that instant, I felt the bond snap. The endless chorus of the fae and the whispers I had always felt threading through the wind, the pulse of every storm… fell silent. My connection to the others, to the rhythm of my world, was gone.

Where harmony once sang, only quiet remained. The Veil sealed shut behind me, cutting off the breath of my world. For the first time in all my endless years, I felt the weight of silence press against me, and it was heavy and final.

Whatever I had been was gone. I was no longer spirit or storm. I was simply… forgotten.

The echo of the Veil still rang in my chest; a wound made not of flesh but of absence. The world was too still without the chorus of my kin humming through every gust. For the first time, the wind around me felt empty, just air, not music.

I barely noticed the sound of footsteps behind me until Soren's voice broke through the quiet.

"You're shaking," he said gently.

I blinked. "Am I?" The words came out thinner than I meant.

"Yeah," he murmured, crouching beside me. His hand hovered near my shoulder but didn't touch, as if he wasn't sure I'd welcome it.

"Whatever that was back there… you don't have to pretend it didn't hurt."

I looked at him, at the lightning still faintly flickering within his fingertips, and almost told him everything, the pain, the loss, the voice that had cast me out. Instead, I forced a smile that wavered like a tired breeze.

"I've just… lost the wind for a moment," I said.

He didn't believe me. Of course he didn't. But he nodded anyway. "Then we'll wait until you find it again."

The softness in his voice startled me. Normies weren't supposed to be kind to us. Yet here they were, Soren and Veya, both watching me like the sky had fallen and they were planning how to rebuild it.

Veya knelt nearby, eyes steady and warm in that silent grounding way of hers. "Whatever you lost," she said softly, "you still have us."

Her words sank deeper than any storm ever had. I wanted to tell her how much they meant to me, to speak the gratitude clawing at my throat but instead, the air around us stirred, just once, and the faintest gust brushed across her hair like a promise I didn't know how to make aloud.

"I'll hold you to that," I whispered.

She smiled. "You'd better."

And for the first time since the Veil closed, I didn't feel like one of the forgotten because Veya and Soren had chosen me, and I had chosen them in return.

We may be the lost ones, the overlooked, the abandoned, but together we are something greater. Together, we will never be erased.

Our names will ride the wind, whispered through every storm that dares to test us. We will carve our place in history, not as outcasts, but as a team that is unbreakable and unstoppable. We will be ready to face the Arcane Trials side by side.

66

Chapter

Nine

Journey to Mistara Island

The first time Zephyr taught us to fly, it felt like freedom.

This time, it felt like survival.

Mistara Island wasn't a place you could reach by road or ship. The island existed beyond ordinary distance, tucked somewhere between realms where the sky itself grew unpredictable. If we wanted to reach Arcane Academy, we would have to fly there ourselves.

This meant we had to truly fly, not the short bursts above rooftops, or careful hovering over the city like we practiced with Zephyr over the last year. This time it means we would have to fly long distances, through storms, and with endurance.

We stood at the cliff's edge as dawn bled slowly across the ocean. Mist stretched over the water like a living thing, thick and endless.

Zephyr hovered a few feet above the ground, watching the horizon. "You remember what I taught you," he said lightly. "Balance first. Then intention. The air responds to confidence."

Soren rolled his shoulders, lightning flickering faintly around his fingers. "Good," he said. "Because falling into an endless magical ocean sounds like a terrible way to start the Academy."

I almost smiled.

Almost.

"Ready?" Zephyr asked.

We stepped forward together, and the air caught us. It wasn't gentle, and it wasn't kind, but it held us anyway.

The sudden lift stole the ground from beneath my feet and for a heartbeat my body forgot how to trust anything that couldn't be seen. Instinct screamed to panic, to grab for something solid, but I forced myself to breathe instead.

I returned to Zephyr's teaching, letting myself feel the structure before shaping it and guiding the process without force, trusting alignment to do what pressure never could.

The currents moved beneath my feet like invisible tides, shifting and alive. I leaned into them carefully, guiding rather than pushing, letting intention settle before action. The sky pressed against my senses vast, endless, and unpredictable. It felt less like flying and more like balancing on something that could disappear at any moment.

One wrong surge of emotion and I would lose control.

Below us, the world fell away in layers of cloud and fading coastline. Above us, the sky stretched too wide, too open, as if waiting to see whether we deserved to cross it.

Soren adapted faster.

He always did.

Where I measured and listened, he moved on instinct. He leaned into the wind like he'd been born inside a storm, lightning flickering along his hands and feet to steady his balance whenever a current dipped too sharply.

"You look like you belong up here," I murmured.

He glanced back at me, something sharp and warm

in his expression. "Maybe I do."

The energy didn't fight the air; it fused with it instead, bright and dangerous. He didn't glide so much as challenge the sky to keep up with him. A reckless laugh tore from him as he angled higher, letting a gust nearly flip him before correcting with a sharp flash of silver-blue light.

"Okay," he called over the rushing wind, voice bright with adrenaline. "I could get used to this."

Zephyr guided. Or at least… he tried to.

He moved ahead of us, shaping the currents into smoother pathways, adjusting pressure so we wouldn't be thrown off course. On the surface, everything looked controlled. Effortless, even.

But something about him felt… off.

The moment he truly chose to come with us something inside him had shifted. He'd joked about losing the wind for a moment, about feeling out of sorts, but the change that followed was undeniable.

His power had grown stronger, not in the reckless, flashing way it once had, but in a deeper, more deliberate current that coiled beneath his skin.

And yet it wasn't brighter. The wild spark that once defined it had softened into something quieter, heavier, carrying a gravity that hadn't existed before.

The air around him no longer shimmered with only silver and pale gold. There were darker threads woven through it now. The threads are faint at first, almost impossible to notice unless you were looking directly at them. Thin ribbons of shadow drifted through his currents like living things, coiling and uncoiling with subtle intent.

They moved when his emotions shifted.

They stilled when he forced himself calm.

Once, as he lifted his hand to redirect a current, one of those shadows stretched just slightly farther than the wind itself. It was as if it was reaching into empty sky before snapping back into place.

He gave no outward reaction, and if he registered the shift, he kept the knowledge locked behind that careful composure of his. Even without his confirmation, I felt it all the same.

Something had changed the moment he broke whatever bond tied him to his own kind. The air still answered him, maybe even more eagerly than before, but now there was something else beneath it. Something deeper. Older. Watching from the edges of his power.

There was a sense that even the sky didn't fully recognize what he had become, and that uncertainty settled softly but persistently in my chest. It wasn't fear of him, not even close, but a more complicated unease that refused to take a clear shape.

Just the quiet awareness that whatever waited ahead for us in Mistara… we weren't the only ones changing on the way there.

The air around him carried streaks of shadow now. Thin ribbons of darkness woven through his currents like living ink. At first, I thought it was just the angle of the rising sun.

Until one of those shadows curled around his wrist and vanished into the wind.

He didn't react, maybe he didn't notice. Or maybe he was pretending not to.

We flew for what felt like hours. The coastline vanished behind us. The open sky stretched endlessly ahead, gray and heavy with distant storm.

Then the air changed and tightened around us.

A deep, predatory pressure rolled through the sky like something vast had shifted its attention toward us.

Zephyr stilled midair, hovering.

"…Don't move," he said urgently and quietly.

Too late.

The ocean below exploded with a deadly splash.

A massive shape tore upward from the mist, it had wings of blacked membrane, a body that was long and serpentine, and teeth like jagged coral spears. Its cry split the sky, sharp enough to vibrate through bone.

A Skyreaver.

It moved between storm and open sky like a sovereign of both, hunting anything foolish enough to cross its territory.

And unfortunately… we had flown straight into it.

Soren's grin didn't falter. If anything, it sharpened. It was the kind of smile that appeared right before he did something reckless. Lightning began to crackle more visibly around him, silver-blue arcs snapping between his fingers and crawling up his arms like living veins of storm light.

"Well," he muttered, his voice carrying a low, dangerous excitement, "that's new."

Without warning, the creature dropped into a rapid dive, cutting through the air with predatory speed.

Not a glide. Not a descent. A full, predatory plunge that split the clouds in its wake and sent pressure slamming into us from all sides.

"Move!" Zephyr shouted.

He thrust his arm forward and wind exploded outward in a brutal, concussive force. The gust struck the Skyreaver mid-dive with enough power to warp the air around it in violent, controlled, and far darker than anything I had ever felt from him before.

A heavy presence rode the wind, thicker than air and charged with something unseen, pressing against my senses like a storm wrapped tightly in shadow and waiting to break.

The Skyreaver shrieked as the blast caught it, its massive wings jerking sideways as it veered off course.

But it didn't retreat. It recovered with terrifying ease, circling us in a widening arc, its enormous body cutting through cloud and current as if both belonged to it.

There was nothing fearful in its stillness; it was assessing us, waiting for one of us to shift so it could respond.

"Stay together," Zephyr ordered, his tone cutting through the air as the shadows at his back thickened and drew close like a living thing.

They weren't subtle anymore. They bled into the air like ink dropped into water, coiling through his currents in slow, deliberate spirals. They moved when his focus sharpened, when his pulse quickened. The shadows were like extensions of his will that looked far too alive to be simple magic.

They didn't belong to the wind.

And yet they answered him.

Another screech split the sky this time, but it was louder and closer as the Skyreaver lunged at us again. Except this time, it went straight for Soren.

At that moment lightning erupted.

Not a defensive flicker. Not a warning spark. A violent, sky-splitting strike that tore through the clouds and illuminated everything in blinding silver-white brilliance.

For one suspended instant, the world froze inside that flash.

In the white flare of lightning, something vast unfurled behind Soren, revealed for the briefest heartbeat. A colossal silhouette took shape, wings spreading wide. Immense and ancient wings, rimmed with jagged veins of storm and shadow that seemed born of a world far older than ours appeared, but the light died almost immediately, taking the vision with it and leaving no trace behind.

Then the bolt crashed into the Skyreaver head-on.

The impact thundered through the air like a cannon blast. Electricity ripped across the creature's scales, forcing a shriek from its throat as its body convulsed midair. Smoke rose in twisting streams from the point of impact as it spiraled sideways, momentarily stunned.

The Skyreaver refused to fall. Instead, it snapped its vast wings open and caught itself in midair, stabilizing with a precision that bordered on unnatural. When its gaze found us again, its eyes blazed brighter than before, fury sharpening its focus as its powerful frame coiled in preparation for another strike.

This was no retreat. The creature was escalating, adapting to us even now, and that adaptation carried a growing, unmistakable anger.

"Okay," Soren breathed, eyes alight with something dangerous. "Now I'm having fun."

"Don't," I snapped.

He didn't look at me. The Skyreaver came again, faster than before.

Zephyr moved to intercept, but the air around him faltered violently. The shadows surged without his control, lashing outward in sharp, jagged tendrils that tore through the wind itself.

For a moment, the sky went unstable.

That moment almost killed us.

The currents collapsed beneath my feet. Panic surged through me, sharp and immediate. I dropped several feet before catching myself. Soren lost altitude too, barely stabilizing with a burst of lightning.

"Zephyr!" I shouted.

He wasn't listening.

I watched as he stared at his own hands like they no longer belonged to him. Darkness coiled around his wrists, answering something inside him he clearly didn't understand.

Beneath us, the ocean churned with growing intensity, and from its mist-laden surface smaller figures began to lift and take shape, coalescing into shadowed creatures that climbed steadily toward us.

It was if the shadow creatures were drawn to him. They skipped through the air like living smoke, eyes faint and hungry, forms barely solid. Not attacking yet, but circling us, sensing us, as if they were getting ready to claim us.

Zephyr felt them, fear flickered across his face so brief and raw that I almost missed it.

Inside his mind, something ancient stirred.

"That wasn't wind, air does not cast shadows. So, what have I become?"

The Skyreaver dove again, this time none of us were ready. It slammed into Soren midair.

They spiraled.

Lightning exploded wildly as he tried to break free, but the creature's claw raked across his side and he lost control. His flight faltered. His descent began, fast and spiraling, the storm tearing at him as if eager to claim what had always belonged to it.

"SOREN!" I screamed, panic ripping through me as the distance between us widened too quickly.

His head lifted at the sound of my voice, teeth clenched against pain. Lightning snapped erratically along his limbs, misfiring, failing to catch.

I can't hold it. The thought brushed mine, fractured and strained. "Stay with me!" I shouted. "Soren, stay with me!"

"He's losing the current," Zephyr said sharply, the usual ease gone from his voice. For once, there was no amusement, no detached curiosity, only focus edged with something dangerously close to fear.

Soren dropped harder, his body tilting as another surge of lightning burst uncontrolled from his hands. It scattered uselessly into the storm.

"Zephyr!" My voice broke. "Please!"

Something in him stilled.

Then shifted.

He moved, not with wind, but with something

deeper.

Shadow erupted from him in a violent surge. Not creeping. Not testing but commanding. Dark currents tore through the sky like roots splitting stone, threading through the raging air and forcing it into sudden, unnatural stillness. The storm buckled around that power, reshaping itself under his will.

"Don't fight them," I whispered, breath shaking as the force of it pressed against my senses. I wasn't sure if I meant Soren… or Zephyr.

For a fraction of a second, Zephyr hesitated as if he were standing at the edge of something vast and waiting.

Then he stopped resisting.

The shadows answered instantly.

They surged upward in thick, sweeping arcs and caught Soren before he could fall beyond reach, coiling around him with terrifying precision. The descent snapped to a halt so abruptly the air cracked.

Soren gasped as the shadows steadied him, not gentle but unyielding, holding him suspended between storm and sky.

The moment Zephyr acknowledged them, truly acknowledged them, they obeyed as though they had always been his. As though they had only been waiting for permission.

Even the Skyreaver stilled.

Massive wings beat once, then held, the creature hovering in tense suspension as it watched the shadows writhe through the storm. A low, resonant sound rumbled from its chest, not quite a growl and not quite recognition.

Uncertainty.

Its gaze fixed on Zephyr.

Ancient. Assessing.

"You feel it too, don't you?" I murmured, unable to tear my eyes away from him.

Zephyr didn't look at me. His focus remained locked on the shadows twisting through the sky at his command, expression sharpened into something darker, older than the boy who had once laughed at the wind.

When he spoke, his voice was quieter and almost deeper.

"No one," he said, each word edged in storm and shadow, "touches what flies with me."

The shadows tightened around Soren in silent, unquestioning agreement.

Zephyr hovered at the center of it all, eyes wide as he realized what he was doing. He wasn't just guiding the wind anymore, he was commanding something older, something darker.

"The court will not forgive this", a memory whispered from somewhere deep and buried. "You were never meant to wield both."

"No," he breathed frightened. "I'm not..."

The shadows surged again anyway.

They struck the Skyreaver like a storm made of night, wrapping around its wings, dragging it off balance. Soren recovered midair and answered with lightning. His accuracy was precise this time, brutal and controlled.

The creature screamed and retreated as it vanished back into the mist.

Silence fell.

But only for a moment, because the shadow creatures remained and they were watching Zephyr like he had become something they recognized.

The shadows moved as though bound to something greater, something they served and perhaps even feared.

I drew in a slow, deliberate breath, knowing panic would splinter my control and that losing control now would cost all of us.

Rather than letting it take hold, I settled into stillness, not empty and not numb, but clear and deliberate, anchored in a calm that felt purposeful, steady, and unbreakable.

The storm inside me settled into something deep and steady. The air responded instantly as if it were smoothing, stabilizing, and aligning beneath our feet. Turbulence faded and the pressure eased.

Zephyr felt it and turned toward me.

The shadows around him quieted slightly, not gone completely, but listening.

We hovered there, shaken and silent.

Soren wiped blood from the corner of his mouth and gave a crooked grin. "We almost died," he said. "That was incredible."

I stared at him. "You were falling to your death."

"Yeah," Soren admitted without shame. "I didn't love that part."

I blinked slowly. "You didn't love…"

"I had notes," he said, lifting a hand as if preparing to list them. "Primarily: less falling, more not falling."

Despite everything, a breath of laughter threatened, and I had to suppress it.

Then his attention shifted past me to Zephyr, the humor in his expression sharpening into something more deliberate. "You're hiding something."

Zephyr's expression shuttered so quickly it was almost impressive. "No, I am not."

Soren tilted his head. "Your wind doesn't look like wind anymore."

Zephyr smiled faintly. "That sounds like a philosophical issue."

"And those things?" Soren gestured toward the lingering shadow shapes still dissolving into mist around us. "They weren't here for me or Veya."

Zephyr folded his arms, posture elegant and deeply unhelpful. "Correlation is not causation."

"You literally command shadows," Soren said.

"I guide atmospheric absence," Zephyr corrected smoothly.

Soren looked at me. "You heard it too, right? That's not a real phrase."

"It's absolutely a real phrase," Zephyr said.

"You made it up just now."

"All phrases are made up at some point."

Soren exhaled through his nose, somewhere between amusement and suspicion. "You're deflecting."

Zephyr's smile returned, thinner this time. "I'm surviving, which is what I recommend you focus on as well."

Silence stretched between them, then Zephyr forced a smile that didn't quite reach his eyes. "Exile changes spirits."

It wasn't a lie, but it wasn't the truth either.

I was watching him carefully.

Something had awakened when he broke his bond. Something that felt ancient and dangerous and entirely new. He wasn't stronger, per say, but he was becoming something else.

I didn't push. Trust wasn't something built by dragging truths into the light before someone was ready to face them and forcing it now would only fracture what fragile alignment we had managed to hold.

Instead, I let the silence settle for a moment before speaking quietly. "We're still flying together."

His eyes lifted to meet mine, and for an instant whatever defenses he usually kept so carefully in place slipped. Gratitude flickered there brief, unguarded, and gone almost as quickly as it appeared, but real enough that I felt it settle somewhere steady in my chest.

"Together," he agreed softly.

The word lingered between us, not dramatic or ceremonial, just certain.

Around us, the storm began to thin. Not beneath us, where the ocean still churned and shadowed shapes moved restlessly through the mist, but above.

The sky itself was clearing, as though something vast had shifted its attention elsewhere, leaving only a fading tension in its wake.

The clouds tore open in slow, violent spirals, revealing a sky that no longer belonged to the normie world. The higher we climbed, the less the air behaved like air. Wind lost its familiar rhythm. Sound dulled. Even gravity felt… uncertain, as if we were passing through layers of reality rather than distance.

"We're too high," Soren muttered, though awe threaded through his voice. "There shouldn't be stars yet."

But there were.

Cold and bright, scattered across a deepening velvet sky that stretched far beyond where the normie atmosphere should have ended. It felt as though we were flying through the space between worlds rather than within one.

A subtle shift moved through my awareness, registering as a quiet pressure that carried the weight of something ancient, like the edge of a hidden boundary brushing against my senses.

It was the Veil, and when it reacted it did not yield or open with care.

It fractured.

Light bent around us, folding inward like shattered glass reforming, and suddenly the sky opened into something vast and impossible.

Mistara did not emerge from ocean or earth but existed apart from them, suspended within its own concealed layer of reality and held delicately between the normie world and something far more ancient.

Floating rivers curved through open space as if gravity were a suggestion rather than a law. Waterfalls spilled into nothingness, dissolving into silver mist before re-forming in looping arcs. Dark forests wrapped around towering cliffs that shimmered with faint starlight, their edges blurred as though the realm itself refused to be fully seen.

It was both an island and a realm, a secret the world had hidden beyond the reach of ordinary magic. What we had just done wasn't merely crossing distance; we had slipped into a place we were never meant to reach, a threshold that felt less discovered and more trespassed.

Beside me, Soren let out a long, measured breath, his usual confidence replaced for once by something close to awe. Even he looked momentarily stunned.

"Okay," he said quietly, eyes still fixed on the impossible horizon. "That was almost worth dying for."

Zephyr didn't laugh.

He hovered in silence, shadows faintly threading through the currents around him as if this place recognized something in him. For a brief, uneasy moment, I had the strange feeling Mistara wasn't just revealing itself to us.

It felt as though the realm itself was measuring us, weighing our presence and deciding whether we had any right to stand within it at all.

I steadied my breathing and moved forward despite the scrutiny. Whatever waited inside that hidden layer of Mistara, the Academy, the trials, the truth of what we were slowly becoming, there was no sense in pretending we could retreat.

There was no turning back now.

We had crossed the Veil, and Mistara, for reasons of its own, had allowed us through.

Chapter

Ten

Arrival at Arcane Academy

rcane Academy for Magic is hidden deep within a magical forest, disguised as nothing more than a simple cottage to any normie. It appears small and harmless. A one-story home wrapped in deep green vines, their tendrils curling lovingly around the stone. Vibrant flowers bloom at its base and line the cobbled path leading to the front door, their colors almost too cheerful to be real. Twinkling lights are strung delicately through the surrounding trees, casting a soft golden glow that flickers like fireflies caught in an endless dusk.

To any passerby, even one sensitive to magic, it would appear to be the home of a quiet old couple living in deliberate isolation, the sort of place so safe and ordinary that it became almost aggressively forgettable.

But appearances, as Arcane Academy teaches quickly, are lies.

Those who are invited are the forgotten, the overlooked, the ones the world has failed. They alone are able to open the door.

And the moment you do, the illusion shatters.

The cramped space of the tiny cottage dissolved,

unfolding into something vast and impossible. Open fields stretched outward beneath an endless sky, the air humming with latent magic. In the distance, rising from stone and bark alike, stood the Academy itself, woven seamlessly into massive ancient trees and carved into the face of a towering cliff. Its towers and halls felt grown rather than built, as though the land itself had chosen to shape them. Below it all lay a great lake, dark and glassy, reflecting the Academy like a watchful eye.

I forgot how to breathe.

"Careful," Zephyr murmured, his voice quieter than I had ever heard it.

I barely managed a whisper. "Why?"

His gaze remained fixed on the towering structure, something unreadable moving beneath his usual sharp composure.

"Places like this," he said softly, "are always looking back."

A shiver traced the length of my spine.

The beauty of it still pulled at me, it was vast, impossible, and magnificent.

And yet beneath that wonder lingered a quiet, undeniable certainty.

We hadn't just found the Academy.

It had been waiting.

My hand tightened around the doorframe as a strange pressure settled in my chest, part awe, part warning. The magic here felt different. Heavier. Like it was pressing back, measuring me before deciding whether I belonged.

Beside me, Soren let out a slow, breathless laugh. "Of course it's bigger on the inside," he murmured, eyes bright as he stepped forward without hesitation. "Figures the place meant to break us wouldn't bother pretending to be small."

I swallowed hard and followed.

The moment we crossed the threshold, the air shifted. Towers twisted skyward like silver spires, windows glimmered in colors I couldn't name, and faint laughter echoed through unseen hallways.

"Wow," Soren whispered, excitement threading through his voice. "It's even better than I imagined."

I didn't respond. Something felt… off.

The air smelled sharp and sweet, like ozone mixed with honey. Shadows moved where they shouldn't. A staircase curled upward into nothingness, daring us to climb. Nearby, a fountain sent water spiraling into the air, floating silently before splashing onto the cobblestones.

Mistara Island had welcomed us.
Keeping us alive, however, seemed optional.

That felt like a problem for another day.

I thought I understood my powers. I thought I had control. But standing here, in the shadow of the Academy, I realized I didn't know the half of it.

Soren's grin didn't waver. If anything, it deepened, his eyes alight with the kind of reckless excitement most people reserved for festivals rather than places rumored to break students in half.

"You feel that?" he asked, almost delighted.

"Yes," I said dryly. "It feels like a place that eats people like us."

His smile sharpened. "Or makes them."

"That's not comforting."

"Wasn't meant to be." He glanced sideways at me, expression glinting with something teasing beneath the anticipation. "You're not backing out already, are you?"

I scoffed. "If I were, I wouldn't have made it this far with you."

"Good," he said lightly. "Would've been embarrassing to survive the journey just to lose my partner at the front door."

Heat flickered briefly through my chest before I forced it down. "I'm not your partner."

His grin turned unapologetically smug. "You keep

telling yourself that."

Zephyr exhaled softly beside us, drawing our attention. His gaze moved across the Academy grounds with measured intensity, far less enchanted than Soren's.

"You're both underestimating this place," he said.

Soren arched a brow. "And you're unusually serious."

"Observation," Zephyr replied coolly. "Places built on power rarely welcome it without cost."

I folded my arms, watching the towers loom above us. "You say that like it's deciding whether we're worth the trouble."

Zephyr didn't answer immediately. His eyes lingered on the highest spire, expression tightening almost imperceptibly.

"It is," he said at last.

A faint shiver slipped down my spine.

Soren stretched his shoulders as if preparing for a fight rather than an entrance exam. "Good," he said quietly. "I'd hate to be somewhere that didn't notice us."

Zephyr's gaze flicked toward him, something unreadable passing through his expression. "Careful what you invite to pay attention."

Soren only laughed under his breath. "Too late for that."

Despite the tension coiling in my chest, I felt the corner of my mouth lift. Reckless. Both of them.

And somehow… I was reckless as well.

Then the gates swung open with a long, echoing groan, as if the island itself were speaking.

The sound rolled across the grounds and straight through my bones.

A deep, gravelly voice followed, sweeping through the Academy and settling directly into our minds.

"You who have crossed the veil and survived what was meant to break, please step forward. You now stand within the bounds of Arcane Academy, a place that does not soften magic, nor does it shield the unprepared."

"Within these halls, you will be pushed beyond the limits you believe define you. The trials ahead are not punishments, they are revelations. They will strip you down to what you truly are. Some of you will discover strength you never knew you possessed. Others will learn, too late, what it means to reach beyond your grasp."

"Do not mistake survival for success. Many have entered these grounds with confidence. Few have left unchanged. Over the years to come, you will train, you will fail, and you will be shaped by master's whose names are etched into the bones of this Academy, and by forces far older than it. Listen carefully. The walls are always watching."

A chill slid down my spine, the words *the walls are always watching* sinking deep, settling somewhere beneath my ribs.

Beside me, Soren shifted his weight, rolling his shoulders like he was preparing for a fight rather than an orientation.

"Good," he murmured under his breath. "I hate places that pretend to be safe."

I shot him a look. "You would."

His grin flickered, quick and sharp. "You didn't come here to be comfortable either."

He wasn't wrong.

Zephyr stood very still at my other side; gaze lifted toward the towering structure as if listening for something beneath the headmaster's words.

"This place remembers power," he said quietly. "And it remembers those who failed to wield it."

A faint unease coiled low in my stomach. "That's not ominous at all."

"It isn't meant to be comforting," Zephyr replied.

Soren let out a soft, almost eager breath. "Let it watch," he said. "I want to see what it does when we don't break."

"When," I repeated, arching a brow.

His eyes flicked to mine, bright with reckless certainty. "Not if."

"When this journey ends, champions will rise not because they were powerful, but because they endured. Others will be claimed by ambition, fear, or their own unchecked magic. That choice belongs to you alone."

The courtyard felt impossibly still, as if even the air had paused to listen.

"Step forward with purpose. Once you cross these halls, there is no turning back. Arcane Academy does not ask who you were before you arrived. It only remembers what you become… and what you are willing to sacrifice to get there."

My pulse thudded once, hard, while the words *"What are we willing to sacrifice?"* circled relentlessly through my thoughts.

The voice rolled through the courtyard like music braided with thunder with a calm, commanding, and ancient feeling.

A tall figure stood at the top of the marble steps, his cloak swirling with faint motes of starlight.

"My name is Headmaster Oberon. Please proceed to the Arcanic Hall, our main gathering place, where you will be divided into your guilds."

The gates creaked open, and suddenly the courtyard came alive. Students surged forward in a wave of color and noise. Robes brushing, spells sparking faintly in the air, the smell of fresh parchment and ozone, that metallic, storm-charged scent that lingered after power had been summoned and barely contained filling my lungs.

Soren stepped forward immediately, like a storm finally given somewhere to go.

"Well," he said, glancing back at me with a crooked grin, "this is where it gets interesting."

"This is where it gets dangerous," I muttered,

keeping pace beside him.

"Same thing," he replied easily.

Zephyr walked on the other side of me, his gaze tracking everything around us, the students, the architecture, the subtle currents of magic threading through the air. "Try not to look like prey," he said quietly.

I shot him a look. "Do I look like prey?"

His mouth curved faintly. "You look like someone who doesn't yet know how noticeable she is."

Soren snorted. "She's noticeable because she keeps glaring at everything like it personally offended her."

"It has," I said flatly.

He laughed under his breath as we moved with the crowd. "Relax, Veya. We made it past the creatures on our way to the island that were trying to kill us. A building full of gifted overachievers shouldn't be that bad."

"You have an impressive ability to underestimate danger," Zephyr said.

"I don't underestimate," Soren replied. "I just don't see the point in being intimidated."

His eyes flicked briefly to mine. "You shouldn't either.

Heat stirred low in my chest, equal parts reassurance and challenge.

"I'm not intimidated," I said. "I'm evaluating."

Soren's grin widened. "That's my line."

Inside the Arcanic Hall, light spilled from floating lanterns drifting between soaring crystal arches. The room was enormous, it was larger than any building I'd ever seen, its ceiling is an illusion of swirling clouds and constellations that rotated slowly, painting the space in hues of gold and violet.

Soren slowed, turning slowly in a full circle. "Okay," he admitted under his breath. "That's… impressive."

I folded my arms, though I couldn't stop staring upward. "You sound surprised."

"I am," he said. "I thought it would be intimidating."

Zephyr's gaze remained fixed on the shifting constellations overhead. "It is," he said quietly.

A faint unease slipped through me.

"Good," Soren murmured, eyes bright as he looked toward the far end of the hall. "Then we're exactly where we're supposed to be."

All manner of beings crowded the floor, and for a moment I forgot how to breathe.

Fae of every kind shimmered in shades of moonlight and emerald moss, their wings whispering softly as they moved through the hall. Some glowed faintly, others carried an unsettling stillness that felt older than the stone beneath our feet. Witches and wizards clustered in loose circles, clutching staffs and charms while their voices buzzed with contained energy. Goblins and goblinas darted between taller figures, laughing in gravelly tones as they compared crystal teeth like prized jewels.

"Are they… polishing those?" Soren murmured beside me.

"Don't stare," I whispered without looking at him.

"I'm not staring," he replied calmly. "I'm taking strategic inventory."

"That's staring."

Werewolf shifters straightened as they entered the lantern light, shoulders rolling back as they settled fully into human form. Amber eyes glinted beneath the glow, tracking movement with quiet territorial awareness. Vampires lingered along the edges of the chamber, pale and immaculate in dark, tailored uniforms cut with unsettling elegance. Their stillness felt deliberate, predatory.

Soren leaned slightly closer. "If one of them hisses at me, I'm hissing back."

"You will not hiss at a vampire."

"Depends on the quality of the hiss."

I bit back a smile and forced my attention forward,

even as my pulse continued to climb.

A dragon shifter stood near one of the central pillars, his presence radiating heat strong enough to make the air ripple. Power rolled off him in slow, controlled waves, like a furnace kept carefully contained. Nearby, two shadow sentinels stood in quiet conversation, their dark uniforms threaded with faint silver sigils that shifted when the lantern light touched them. The blades at their sides rested in easy reach, suggesting they rarely needed warning before using them.

Just beyond them, a pair of aether-blades adjusted the rune-etched weapons folded neatly across their backs. Their eyes glowed faintly with contained magic, and the air around them hummed with disciplined power, as if the space itself recognized their presence and chose not to interfere.

"Please tell me we don't have to fight any of them," Soren muttered under his breath.

"I'm choosing not to tell you," I replied quietly.

"Comforting," he said. "Really builds confidence."

"Try not to antagonize the elite combat students before we even start," I murmured.

"I don't antagonize," he said. "I inspire concern."

I shot him a look. "That is not better."

One of the shadow sentinels glanced our way, expression unreadable beneath the shifting glow of the sigils stitched into their uniform. The look wasn't hostile, but it wasn't welcoming either, it was more like a quiet assessment filed away for later.

Soren noticed and straightened slightly, meeting the gaze without flinching.

I nudged his arm. "Maybe don't make eye contact with the people who look professionally lethal."

"I'm being polite," he murmured. "Aggressively polite."

"That's not a thing."

"It is now."

A cyclops blinked one enormous blue eye near the back of the hall while speaking amiably with a sleek centaur whose bronze coat gleamed like polished metal. The sheer variety of beings packed into one space made my head spin.

"They're all watching," I murmured before I could stop myself.

"Good," Soren said easily. "Let them."

I glanced at him. "You're not even slightly concerned?"

He rolled his shoulders, expression sharpening into that familiar, reckless confidence. "If they're looking for a show, I'd hate to disappoint."

A faint current stirred near my ear, cool and amused.

"Try not to challenge the entire room before the trials begin," Zephyr's voice drifted through the air.

"I'm not challenging anyone," Soren said under his breath.

"You are thinking loudly," Zephyr replied.

Soren scowled upward. "Stop eavesdropping."

"I exist in the wind," Zephyr said mildly. "Everything is eavesdropping."

I exhaled slowly, trying to steady the nervous energy coiling in my chest. Awe warred with intimidation, excitement tangling with the quiet, persistent awareness that we were very small inside something very vast.

As we moved forward, a tall fae with antlers like branching silver turned his head slightly, his luminous eyes settling on us with open curiosity. The air around him hummed with old, quiet power.

Soren met the stare without hesitation.

I nudged him lightly. "Maybe don't challenge the ancient forest being."

"I'm not challenging him," Soren murmured. "I'm acknowledging him aggressively."

The fae's mouth curved faintly, as if he'd heard

that.

Great.

We continued forward.

"Okay," Soren said quietly after a moment, glancing around with renewed interest. "This might be the most dangerous room I've ever willingly walked into."

"And yet you walked in," I replied.

He looked at me, grin returning with sharp certainty alive with possibility.
"Yeah," he said. "Because so did you."

Despite the nerves still twisting through me, excitement sparked brighter.

For the first time, the overwhelming scale of the hall didn't make me feel small.

It made me feel like we had finally arrived somewhere that mattered.

Everywhere I looked, life hummed. Magic in motion. Power in every heartbeat.

Soren let out a low whistle beside me. "Well," he murmured, "if we die here, at least it'll be in interesting company."

I elbowed him lightly. "Can you not talk about dying in the first ten minutes?"

"I'm being realistic."

"You're being dramatic."

"Same thing."

Zephyr's gaze swept across the hall, far more analytical than either of ours. "Watch the vampires," he said quietly.

I blinked. "Why them?"

"They're watching everyone else," he replied.

Sure enough, several pale faces lingered at the edges of the room, eyes sharp and assessing.

Soren noticed too and grinned faintly. "Good. Let them look."

"You enjoy being evaluated far too much," I muttered.

"Only when I know I'll pass," he said easily.

My gaze drifted again to the dragon shifter, heat shimmering around him. "I suddenly feel underprepared."

Soren followed my line of sight and chuckled. "You? Never."

Zephyr's voice lowered slightly. "Power like that doesn't make them untouchable. It just makes them targets."

That did not make me feel better.

"Next time," I murmured, "we choose a nice, quiet academy with fewer apex predators."

Soren's grin flashed. "Where's the fun in that?"

Beside me, Soren grinned, eyes wide, sparks of silver lightning flickering faintly around his fingers despite his best attempt at restraint. Zephyr hovered just above the floor in a faint shimmer, his energy blending with the currents of the room as though he'd always belonged there.

"Welcome to the eye of the storm," Oberon murmured.

And for once, I couldn't disagree.

"The guilds are as follows:

- Lumora Guild: wisdom and light

- Astrael Guild: ambition and vision
- Veilyn Guild: cleverness and secrecy
- Eldrin Guild: patience and tradition

Oberon's voice carried effortlessly through the Arcanic Hall. "Welcome, children of the forgotten."

The words settled over us like a seal being set in place.

"The guild you will join is not decided by lottery, chance, or simply by my choosing. Here at Arcane Academy, you will prove where you belong. You will prove that you possess wisdom, ambition, vision, and cleverness… tempered with the right measure of secrecy, and patience for this honored tradition."

He began to pace slowly before us, hands clasped behind his back.

"The first trials are nothing like the final Arcane Trials, but do not mistake brevity for mercy. Though shorter in length, they will test you. They will expose your weaknesses and reveal your strengths… and they will show your fellow peers exactly which colors you choose to display."

"Here is where we learn that only those who endure… remain."

A heavy silence settled over the hall, thick with the scent of fear. Some students shifted uneasily, murmurs rattling through the crowd. Panic rippled from one side to the other like a tremor no one wanted to acknowledge.

Soren leaned slightly closer to me, voice low enough that only I could hear.

"Well," he murmured, "nothing like a warm welcome."

I exhaled slowly. "You'd be disappointed if it were easy."

His grin flickered, sharp and familiar. "Very."

Zephyr stood on my other side, still and watchful. His gaze moved across the hall, tracking the shifting energy of the crowd like a strategist studying a battlefield.

"Fear makes people predictable," he said quietly.

"Is that supposed to reassure me?" I asked.

"No," he replied calmly. "It's supposed to remind you not to show any."

My pulse tightened, but not with fear.

Determination surged instead, steady and unyielding. I had trained, struggled, and survived alongside Soren and Zephyr. There was no version of this moment where I let myself break now.

Soren glanced at me, as if sensing the shift.

"You're doing that thing again."

"What thing?"

"Looking like you're about to conquer something."

I lifted a brow. "Maybe I am."

His grin returned, brighter this time. "Good. I'd hate to be the only one enjoying this."

Zephyr's voice came softer but edged with something older.

"Enjoy it," he said. "But don't underestimate what's coming. Places like this don't test you once."

His gaze lifted toward the towering ceiling of the hall.

"They keep testing," he murmured. "Until there's nothing left to hide."

Beside me, Soren grinned, his gaze sharp, full of excitement and the daredevil spark I had learned to trust.

Zephyr hovered just behind, he wanted to stay invisible to all but us, he was a faint shimmer in the corner of my vision. "They are ready," he said, his voice, a whisper in the back of my mind. "They have strength… and the fire to match it. But will they bend under true scrutiny, or will the trials bend them? This will be… interesting."

A ripple of tension ran through the hall. I clenched my fists, letting the resolve settle in my bones. No hiding. No fear. I would show what I was made of.

"As for rules," Oberon said, his tone smooth, final, like a knife cutting the air, "there are none."

Murmurs and startled gasps echoed.

"You may use whatever you brought with you. Any magic at your disposal. Any power you possess. But understand this, this is a solitary trial. There will be no allies, no assistance, and no protection."

I drew a steadying breath, feeling Zephyr's presence like a current running along my spine. "Yes," he whispers in my mind. "Good. Let them face it. Let them rise."

Oberon's voice dropped, final, like a closing gate, "You will be judged alone. Because within these walls, it is not who stands beside you that defines your future… it is who you are when you stand by yourself."

Oberon's words settled over the Arcanic Hall like a stone sinking into still water.

A ripple of unease followed.

"No rules?" someone whispered somewhere behind us. "Solo?" another voice muttered, sharper now.

"Judged alone," Soren murmured under his breath, as if tasting the words and finding them bitter. "That seems unnecessarily dramatic."

Zephyr didn't look at him. His gaze remained fixed on the dais, shadows shifting faintly at his feet. "No," he said quietly. "It seems intentional."

No rules.

Solo.

Judged alone.

The words echoed in my thoughts, steady and relentless. My fingers curled slowly at my sides as I forced myself to breathe evenly. Panic wouldn't help me here. It never had.

Soren leaned slightly closer. "We've trained together for years," he muttered. "They can't seriously expect us to pretend we don't know how to fight as a unit."

"They don't care what we know," Zephyr replied, voice low. "They care who breaks first."

That silenced him.

I swallowed, grounding myself.

I'd survived worse by doing one thing well, by observing before I moved.

Across the hall, I began to notice it. Who shifted nervously. Who straightened. Who already looked calculating.

If we were being judged alone… Then so was everyone else. And that meant they were watching just as carefully as I was.

This wasn't about power alone. Oberon had been clear about that. Wisdom. Ambition. Cleverness. Patience. They weren't asking who could unleash the biggest spell, they were watching how we chose to act when no one told us what to do.

That meant restraint mattered just as much as strength.

Around me, I could feel other students' magic flaring wildly and raw, unfocused, betraying fear before the trial had even begun. I filed that away. Magic always followed emotion. Those who lost control first would reveal more than they intended.

I wouldn't make that mistake.

I ran through my options in my head like pieces on a board. Air magic was my strongest ally here. Not for brute force, but for movement, balance, control. Subtle currents. Controlled lifts. Nothing flashy unless it was necessary. Let them see precision before power.

A tremor ran through me anyway. My stomach tightened, nerves buzzing beneath my skin. What if I misjudged the trial? What if they wanted boldness instead of caution?

I swallowed.

No, I decided. They want truth.

Beside me, Soren radiated confidence, practically humming with anticipation. I envied that ease, but I didn't need it. I had something else. I had adaptability. I could read the room, shift, and respond.

Also, Zephyr was right there, unseen but present, a steady pressure at my back like a hand between my shoulder blades. I could almost feel his amusement, his sharp attention. He wasn't worried.

That helped more than I wanted to admit.

I belong here, I told myself, grounding my feet

against the stone floor. I didn't survive everything just to fail at the doorway.

Whatever this first trial threw at me, I wouldn't rush in blind. But I wouldn't hesitate either.

When the moment came, I would move, and when I did the Arcane Academy would finally see exactly who Veya was.

While I considered the path ahead, Soren's mouth curved into a grin, not the easy one he wore when he was joking, but the sharper version, the one that appeared when something inside him had already decided how things would end and the rest of the world simply hadn't caught up yet.

Whatever rules the Academy thought it had set no longer seemed to matter, and if this was meant to be a solo trial, then so be it. For Soren, that only made the outcome feel inevitable.

His fingers flexed, energy crackling faintly around him, silver-blue light flickering along his scarred eye like a living thing. He didn't bother suppressing it. Let them feel it. Let them fear it. Let them know.

They want truth, he thought. Fine. I'll give them mine.

Where others trembled, Soren leaned forward slightly, weight on the balls of his feet, as if the floor itself were something he might launch from. He didn't map out possibilities or weigh outcomes instead he trusted the moment to tell him what to do. That had always been his strength. And his danger.

He scanned the hall like a battlefield, eyes flicking from tower to shadow to stone, already imagining where he could leap, what he could climb, how fast he could move if things went wrong.

Or perhaps he was right after all.

At his side, Veya remained motionless, her stillness deliberates and her expression thoughtful, as though she were tracing patterns only she could see.

He admired that about her, even if he'd never say it out loud. She survived by adapting. He survived by challenging whatever tried to stand in his way.

They're watching, he realized, and his grin widened.

Good.

Let the Academy see someone who wouldn't wait to be tested.

If the first trial demanded boldness, he'd rip it apart.
If it demanded restraint, he'd press until it cracked.

And if it demanded fear? A quiet laugh slipped from him. They would never get fear from him. He would give them something far worse, unapologetic, raw, unyielding terror. He would never show fear.

He would become fear itself.

Chapter

Eleven

First Trial

Immediately after Oberon's daunting, cryptic message about the first trial ended, something deliberate began to happen.

The walls of Arcanic Hall shuddered before lurching violently into motion. Stone scraped against stone with a deafening roar that tore through the chamber like thunder, the sound sharp and screeching, like nails dragged endlessly across a chalkboard. The ground vibrated beneath our feet as the walls continued to slide inward, closing the gaps one by one until they slammed together on all sides.

There it is," Soren muttered beside me, not panicked, just alert.

There were no doors left, no windows, no visible point of escape. The chamber had sealed itself completely around us, and the realization settled with crushing clarity as the last echo of stone died away.

We were trapped.

Soren exhaled slowly through his nose. "Well," he said under his breath, "that feels intentional."

"Everything here is," I replied quietly.

Dozens of creatures packed the hall, bodies pressed close as panic spread like wildfire. The air thickened into something suffocating, heavy with the stench of sweat, fur, damp stone, and raw fear. I could feel it pulsing around me, fear, fury, and hysteria thrumming through the crowd like a living heartbeat.

"Too many," Soren murmured beside me, his voice low but steady.

He wasn't wrong.

The goblins and goblinas were the first to lose control completely. Their shrill grunts and guttural cries rose into a frenzy as they sprinted wildly across the hall, claws scraping against stone. They hurled themselves into the walls and rebounded like living springboards, only to collide with one another and surge back into motion again.

"They always go kinetic first," I murmured, watching the pattern form instead of the chaos itself.

Soren glanced sideways at me. "That's your take?"

"They burn energy when they panic."

"Respect," he said lightly. "If I'm ever spiraling, I'll just sprint into a wall."

The noise became overwhelming. The screams, snarls, and frantic breathing colliding into something close to madness. Creatures shoved and clawed their way through the crowd; desperation etched across every face. Elbows dug into ribs. Sharp teeth snapped inches from skin. The heat of so many bodies pressed inward, suffocating, each breath tasting stale and metallic, like blood waiting to spill.

"Don't move unless you mean to," I added quietly, bracing my stance as another surge rolled through the hall.

Soren didn't flinch when a random body slammed into his shoulder. He barely shifted his weight.

"I mean everything I do," he replied, voice calm, almost bored. Then, with the faintest grin, "Relax. If this was meant to kill us, it would've started with fire."

I didn't look at him. "Don't invite it."

"No promises."

And yet, in the midst of the madness, something didn't fit.

The vampires looked… pleased.

The vampires weren't the only ones who refused to break.

Near the western wall, two shadow sentinels stood shoulder to shoulder, unmoving despite the chaos crashing around them

Their dark academy uniforms were threaded with faint silver sigils that shifted slowly across the fabric like living script, markings I hadn't noticed on any first-years.

Upper-level students.

While goblins slammed into the walls and werewolf shifters snarled in panic, the sentinels simply observed, hands resting loosely near the hilts of their blades. They weren't trying to escape. They weren't trying to calm anyone.

They were measuring.

One goblin ricocheted wildly toward them, claws flailing. Before it could collide, a sentinel shifted a single step. The movement was subtle enough to miss. The goblin hit an invisible barrier of controlled force and dropped harmlessly to the ground, stunned but uninjured.

No wasted motion.'

No panic.

Just precision.

"They're not even reacting," I murmured.

Soren followed my gaze, eyes narrowing slightly. "They are," he said. "Just not like the rest of us."

Beyond them, a pair of aether-blades stood with their backs nearly touching, rune-etched weapons folded across their shoulders. Their academy crests glinted faintly at their collars, marking them as students too, though clearly not new ones.

Faint light pulsed beneath their skin in steady rhythms; their breathing synchronized despite the suffocating pressure building in the hall. While bodies shoved and scrambled around them, they adjusted their footing with quiet discipline, maintaining a small, stable perimeter.

Upper ranks. Or close to it.

"They've done this before," I whispered.

"Or they were trained for it," Soren replied.

A soft current stirred near my ear.

"Some learn control," Zephyr murmured. "Some learn panic. The Academy enjoys discovering which is which."

Across the hall, the vampires had begun to move.

Not frantically like the others, but with deliberate grace, slipping through pockets of darkness as though the shifting shadows welcomed them. One leaned casually against the sealed wall, watching the hysteria with faint amusement. Another crouched beside a collapsed student, not to help but to observe.

"They're enjoying this," I said.

Soren's mouth curved faintly. "Of course they are. Eternal darkness, rising fear, and enclosed space?" He glanced toward them. "This is basically a holiday."

As if sensing the attention, one of the vampires turned.

Our eyes met across the crowded hall.

A slow smile curved his lips. It was not friendly, not hostile, just aware. He inclined his head slightly, acknowledging composure when he saw it.

I didn't return the smile.

But I didn't look away either.

The shadow sentinels remained still.

The aether-blades held their quiet formation.

The vampires moved through darkness like it belonged to them.

Everyone else was unraveling.

And in that moment, the pattern became clear.

This trial wasn't only about who would panic.

It was about which students could stand inside

fear… and remain dangerous anyway.

Their pale faces were calm, some even wearing faint smiles as they melted into the shadows. With no trace of natural light to burn or weaken them, the darkness seemed to wrap around them like a familiar embrace. While the rest of us panicked, they thrived and seemed almost relaxed and cheerful, finding comfort in the very prison that terrified everyone else.

That was when it truly sank in.

This wasn't a trial meant to be won.

This was a trial meant to reveal what we were.

Being trapped in such tight and suffocating confines with so many others was meant to break the weak-minded. The pressure, the noise, and the lack of control were all designed to fracture us from the inside out.

But for me, the walls closing in were nothing new. I had lived my life with barely enough room to breathe, let alone move. So, while panic consumed the hall, I remained grounded, still, calm, and watchful.

I turned to my right and found Soren standing just as steady, an unmoving presence in the storm of chaos. His expression never wavered, eyes sharp and watchful as the panic unfolded around us. He understood, just as I did, that this part of the challenge wasn't about strength or survival. It was about endurance of the mind. A psychological game meant to expose cracks and turn us against ourselves.

"This won't break us," I said quietly.

Soren's mouth tilted faintly. "No," he agreed. "But it's going to be entertaining watching it try."

A goblin slammed into the wall nearby and rebounded with a shriek. Neither of us moved.

"They want reactions," I murmured.

"Then let's be disappointing," he replied.

Zephyr, on the other hand, was having the time of his life.

He drifted lazily above the crowd, eyes gleaming with mischief as he observed the unraveling creatures below. Every so often, I caught glimpses of him floating close to the werewolf shifters, then the cyclops, bouncing from one creature to another and leaning in just enough to whisper their deepest fears into their ears.

Soren tracked him with mild interest. "He's enjoying himself."

"He feeds on disorder," I said.

Zephyr glanced down at us, smile widening as if he'd heard.

"I prefer the term curator of chaos," he murmured into the air.

Soren snorted softly. "That's not better."

Panic spread instantly, snarls, growls, sudden outbursts of violence erupting wherever he passed. Zephyr delighted in it, feeding off the disorder, thriving in the madness.

This was his element.

And as I watched the hall descend further into chaos, it became clear: some of us were being tested, some of us were resisting, and some of us were simply enjoying the destruction.

It happened suddenly.

One moment the hall was filled with frantic movement and noise, the next a sharp, piercing scream cut through everything else. All heads snapped toward the sound. A young werewolf shifter had dropped to his knees near the center of the hall, hands clutching his skull as if trying to keep his thoughts from spilling out.

"No! No… get out of my head," he gasped, voice breaking.

Soren went very still beside me.

"That's not panic," he said quietly.

The boy's breathing came in ragged bursts, eyes wide and unfocused, pupils blown as if he were staring at something no one else could see. "I didn't do it. I didn't."

The air around him tightened.

He began to rock back and forth, nails digging into his own skin as low, animalistic whines escaped his throat. Fragments of memories, guilt, and terror tumbled from him in broken pieces. Whatever Zephyr had whispered had taken root, burrowing deep and twisting until the boy could no longer tell thought from reality.

Above us, a soft current shifted.

Zephyr hovered just beyond the boy's reach, head tilted slightly, watching with open fascination.

"Oh," his voice drifted through the air, light with curiosity. "This one is fragile."

My jaw tightened.

Then the bones cracked.

The sound echoed sickeningly through the hall as the boy's body convulsed, an uncontrolled partial shift tearing through him. Thick brown fur burst along his arms and neck in uneven patches, his jaw elongating as his scream warped into a feral howl. He wasn't fully changing, because he couldn't. His mind was too fractured to finish the transformation.

"That's the worst place to be," Soren murmured.

The boy's body twisted between states, muscle and bone fighting against instincts his mind could no longer command. He wasn't fully transformed, yet he wasn't fully himself either. Awareness lingered in his gaze, wide and horrified, as if he could feel every crack inside him and had no way to stop it.

He understood what was happening.

He just couldn't control it.

And there is nothing more cruel than being conscious inside your own collapse.

Creatures screamed and scrambled away as he lashed out blindly, claws gouging the stone floor, eyes wild with terror rather than rage. This wasn't an attack. It was a collapse.

No one dared to intervene.

That's when I understood.

This wasn't something they were meant to stop.

Soren stiffened beside me, his jaw tightening just slightly. "There it is," he murmured, barely audible. "First fracture."

Zephyr hovered nearby, watching with open delight, head tilted like a curious child admiring a broken toy. He smiled as the werewolf finally crumpled, sobbing and shaking on the floor, his mind shattered long before his body gave out.

Fear shifted in the room then, no longer wild and panicked, but sharp and focused. Everyone realized the same thing at once. This wasn't about escaping the hall. It was about surviving your own thoughts.

The room grew colder with the realization, the air thinning until breathing became a conscious effort. We waited in a silence so sharp it felt like it might cut, wondering which creature would be the next to break.

Minutes stretched and blurred into something that felt like hours, the tension coiling tighter with every passing breath. When the second break finally came, it did not announce itself with force or sound, but with laughter that threaded through the silence in a way that felt far more dangerous.

A sharp, breathless sound, too light for what surrounded us. I turned just in time to see a tall creature near the eastern wall smiling to himself, shoulders shaking as if he'd heard a private joke. His eyes darted around the hall, unfocused, tracking things that weren't there.

"They're all watching me," he whispered, over and over. "They've always been watching."

No one moved toward him. Everyone had learned from the first fracture.

The laughter stopped abruptly.

His expression twisted and his fear folded inward, warping into something darker. His gaze locked onto the nearest body, a horned fae pressed too close to him by the crowd. The creature flinched, raising their hands defensively.

"You did this," the man snarled.

Soren's shoulder brushed mine. "Second fracture," he said quietly.

Before anyone could react, he lunged.

The impact was brutal. He slammed the fae into the wall with a sickening crack, fingers digging into their throat as magic flared wildly around him, uncontrolled, and volatile. The fae screamed, heels scraping uselessly against stone as sparks and shadows burst from the attacker's hands.

Panic detonated.

Creatures surged backward, some screaming, others shouting spells or warnings too late to matter. The hall felt smaller somehow, tighter, as if the walls were feeding on the chaos. The attacker ranted incoherently, voice breaking between rage and terror.

"Get out of my head! Get out, GET OUT!"

He lashed out again, and blood struck the stone in a sharp, echoing spray.

"Outward break," Soren murmured. "Worse."

Only then did the Academy respond, and even that movement came with a chilling realization: it wasn't to save the fae.

Stones shifted beneath them, walls groaning as if the building itself had reached out. The floor twisted, curling upward to pin the attacker, holding him fast as he thrashed and screamed, eyes rolling white. Magic sparked and flared around him, wild and uncontrolled, until he lay still.

The fae lay crumpled nearby, unmoving, their magic flickering weakly like a dying flame.

No light came to heal them. No voice rang through the halls. Instead, the air thickened, shifting with judgment. The walls vibrated subtly, almost imperceptibly, as if scanning each student, measuring their fear, their control, and their weakness. Measuring who would survive its trials… and who would not. A faint hum rose from the stones and towers, wrapping around us, pressing us into place. Panic surged and ebbed like the tide, but it was the Academy that set its rhythm.

The message was clear.

Soren stepped closer to me, his voice low and tight. "That's the difference," he said. "The first one broke inward. This one broke outward." His eyes cut to mine. "If this is how they begin…what happens in the final trial?"

Zephyr hovered above the scene, clapping softly, delighted. "Much better," he murmured, grinning. "Fear always chooses a direction."

I clenched my jaw, forcing my breathing steady as my heart hammered against my ribs. Around us, the creatures weren't just afraid anymore, they were calculating, watching each other, measuring distances and choosing threats.

The atmosphere of the hall shifted completely, transforming what had once been a test of composure into something far more precarious. What began as psychological pressure had sharpened into something deliberate. A test not of strength, but of restraint under suffocating strain. And whatever fractured next would not wait for permission.

We weren't just battling our own minds or the rising fear of those around us anymore. The Academy itself had entered the equation, its will pressing against the air like a predator circling its chosen ground.

"It's narrowing," I said quietly.

Soren's gaze moved slowly across the room, calculating. "Yeah," he replied. "It picked something."

Or someone.

That was when Oberon's words came rushing back to me:

"The walls are always watching."

Without warning, screams tore through the air, raw and unfiltered, as if fear itself had come alive. Growls erupted from every direction at once, loud enough to feel capable of shredding eardrums. Soren and I spun, scanning the Arcanic Hall, trying to make sense of the chaos, and in that instant, I knew things had shifted from dangerous to catastrophic.

Students of every race staggered and screamed, clutching their heads as voices slithered into their minds. At first, I thought it was Zephyr. His presence, his poison, whispering fears into their ears but the sheer volume of it was wrong.

Whatever moved around us felt far too vast and layered to come from a single source. The truth arrived with chilling clarity. Zephyr wasn't the only one whispering. The Academy itself had entered the conversation.

"That's new," Soren said quietly.

The walls hummed with ancient intent, their magic bleeding into every thought, amplifying doubt, terror, and despair until fear was no longer suggested but commanded.

From the dark corners of the hall, shapes began to move. Creatures peeled themselves from shadow, uninvited yet undeniably real, crawling, slithering, and lunging toward anything that breathed. They poured forward in relentless waves, attacking without pattern or mercy. Everywhere I looked, someone was falling.

"Up," I said quietly.

Soren didn't question it.

The polished floors of the Arcanic Hall liquefied into something like quicksand, dragging the unlucky down and locking them in place. At the same time, the walls themselves came alive, stone hands bursting forth and snapping shut around wrists and ankles like living shackles, restraining students mid-scream as darkness closed in around them.

Soren shifted closer, keeping his footing as the

floor began to give way. "You saw this coming," he said, not accusing but observing.

I didn't answer.

I already knew what I had to do. I needed to get off the floor and away from the walls before the Academy decided I was next. Calming my mind, I reached for the air magic I had trained so relentlessly to master, not as a weapon but as lift. The currents answered more easily than they should have, rising beneath my feet with an almost eager precision.

The moment my boots left the ground, the pressure in the room shifted.

Soren looked up at me, eyes narrowing slightly as if he wasn't surprised.

Recognizing.

"Yeah," he murmured under his breath. "You're different."

I pretended I didn't hear him and rose higher, letting the currents steady beneath me as the chaos unfolded below.

From above, the Arcanic Hall revealed its true shape. It was not a room in disorder, but a battlefield in motion. Students struggled against shadows and stone, against their own unraveling thoughts, each pocket of panic spreading into the next like fractures in glass.

Lightning split the darkness.

My gaze snapped toward the source just as Soren hurled another bolt of silver and royal-blue energy into a cluster of Moroi advancing on the most vulnerable students. The psychic vampires recoiled as his power struck, their forms flickering as if the light itself burned.

For a moment, he looked exactly like himself again. He was controlled, dangerous, and unbothered.

Then everything stopped.

"Soren!"

He froze mid-motion.

The next bolt never formed. His shoulders slackened as though the strength had been pulled from his bones, and he began to fall. A single tear slipped from his deep ocean-blue eye, silent and unguarded, as if something inside him had simply… let go.

Cold recognition slid through me.

Something was wrong.

The air around his head shimmered, and that was when I saw them. Fifteen Echo Wraiths peeled from the darkness and began circling him in tightening spirals, their forms shifting like smoke shaped by memory. They moved like living regrets, pressing inward and forcing fragments of guilt and buried pain into his mind until past and present blurred together, indistinguishable.

A cold, focused certainty settled through me. I didn't allow myself time to think or to question what I was seeing. Watching him unravel was not an option.

I moved.

That was when I felt it, a part of me that had been lying dormant suddenly sparked to life. It wasn't fully manifested or anywhere near its full strength, but it was enough to tell me I was capable of something new. Something powerful. Something that could save someone I cared about.

I didn't even have to think.

My body moved on instinct as ruby-red and golden-orange fire formed into glowing orbs around me, spinning in a perfect circle. Without hesitation, I thrust my arms forward, aiming to kill. To protect.

The fire surged outward, the blazing spheres lunging toward every Echo Wraith and Moroi within a foot of Soren and me.

The fire didn't burn the way normal flames did.

It screamed.

The orbs spiraled outward like sentient comets, ruby cores wrapped in molten gold, tearing through shadow as if darkness itself recoiled from their touch. The Echo Wraiths shrieked, high, glass-shattering screams, as the fire tore into them, their forms warping and unraveling. But before they vanished, they did what they were born to do.

They reached inside Soren's mind.

The Arcanic Hall dissolved, its screams swallowed by a memory Soren had spent years running from.

He was back in the kitchen.

The room smelled like burnt coffee and cracked porcelain.

The clock above the sink ticked too loudly, every second pressing against his skull. The argument hadn't started big, nothing ever did. It was something small. Something meaningless. A chore undone. A fight he'd been in. A tone he'd taken.

But anger had lived in that house long before the words.

His father's voice rose, sharp and familiar, cutting through the air with practiced ease. His mother stood in the doorway, arms crossed, jaw tight, fire in her eyes. Not hatred, but exhaustion.

Soren snapped.

Not just with his voice, but with everything inside him.

The light overhead flickered, once…twice… then shattered, raining glass across the floor. The house hummed, low and alive, like it recognized him now. A mug slid off the counter and burst apart at his feet. The air bent, warped, trembling around his body as silver threads of lightning crept through his hands, searching for release.

For one awful heartbeat, no one breathed.

His father went pale first. The anger drained from his face, leaving only disbelief… then fear.

Real fear.

His mother took a step toward him, her hand lifting as if to touch him, to anchor him. Her eyes filled, not with horror, but with something worse.

Grief.

"Soren," she whispered, her voice breaking. "What… what are you?"

The words shattered something in him.

He didn't know how to answer. He didn't know how to tell her that he was still her son. That he was terrified. That he hadn't asked for this. Every explanation tangled in his throat, useless and fragile.

His father turned away.

Just like that.

A hand dragged over his face, a quiet sound of defeat slipping from his chest, as though Soren had already been lost.

His mother stayed where she was, caught between love and fear, reaching for him with her eyes while her feet refused to move.

That was the moment that followed him into every nightmare.

Because Soren didn't beg.

He didn't apologize.

He straightened instead. Lifted his chin. Wrapped himself in the strength they had beaten into him through every bruise, every cruel lesson, every night he learned that weakness was a liability.

"I did what you taught me," he said, his voice steady even as his heart splintered.

"I became bigger than you. Stronger."

He waited.

Just a second.

For his mother to say his name. For his father to turn back around. For anything that would give him a reason to stay.

He waited for acknowledgment, for an apology, for any small crack in their silence that might mean he still belonged there.

Nothing came. Not a word, not a gesture, not even anger strong enough to fight for him.

And when it became clear that no one would stop him, he turned away.

His hand brushed the door. And that was when he hesitated.

Just for a moment. His throat tightened. His lips parted.

"Mo…"

The world shattered.

Fire ripped through the memory, ruby and gold tearing the kitchen apart as the Echo Wraiths screamed and their hold snapped violently. The vision collapsed, smoke and ash spiraling outward as their forms disintegrated into nothing.

For one suspended heartbeat, the attack faltered. The pressure that should have driven deeper into Soren slipped sideways instead, diverted by something neither the wraiths nor the Academy had anticipated.

It did not settle where it was meant to.

It passed him by and found her waiting.

The Arcanic Hall vanished without warning, torn away as if the world had blinked and forgotten where she stood.

She stood in a place without shape or time, watching figures move away from her. Backs turned. Shoulders retreating. One by one. No faces. No voices. Just distance widening with every step. Doors closing somewhere beyond sight. Footsteps dissolving into a silence that pressed tight against her ribs.

The old, hollow certainty settled deep in her chest.

She was left… again.

Lightning split the darkness.

The vision fractured like glass caught in a storm.

Soren fell to his knees in the Arcanic Hall, gasping, the word still burning on his tongue, unfinished and unheard.

And that was the cruelty of it.

He had never stopped loving her.

He had just never said it.

The Moroi fared no better. Their psychic grip snapped the moment the flames reached them, their fear-fed bodies combusting in bursts of silver ash that rained harmlessly to the floor below.

The oppressive weight in the hall cracked.

Soren gasped like he'd been pulled from deep water, collapsing to one knee. His lightning sputtered, then steadied, royal blue veins crawling back over his arms as clarity returned to his eyes. He looked up, straight at me, shock and something softer flickering across his face.

"I got you," he said, breath rough but steady. "Thank you for having my back."

The walls roared.

The stone hands retracted, replaced by jagged runes that flared to life across the hall, ancient symbols blazing a sickly violet. The floor hardened beneath me again, but the air thickened with deliberate resistance, as if the Academy itself were pushing back. My fire dimmed, drawing closer to my skin, not extinguished but restrained as if were subdued by something greater.

And beneath that dimming flame, I felt it again.

Not heat. Not light.

A deeper current stirred inside my chest, steady and gravitational, bending the air around me in ways the Academy had not accounted for.

This was not fire.

And it was not something the hall could smother.

It was something deeper. Older. A pressure in my chest that didn't burn but pulled, like gravity bending toward my will. The realization sent a sharp breath through my teeth. This wasn't an element I had trained for. This was instinct. It was survival and choice.

I clenched my fists.

The air around Soren and me warped violently, folding inward as the Academy hurled another wave of creatures from the shadows, they were larger this time, armored in darkness, their mouths filled with too many teeth. Before they could reach us, the space itself collapsed between us and them, compressing with ruthless precision until the creatures were crushed into nothingness with a sound like thunder snapping bone.

Silence followed.

For half a heartbeat, the hall stood still. There was no screaming, no shadows moving. Even the air seemed uncertain.

Soren turned slowly toward me. Not startled, not afraid but assessing.

His gaze moved over me once, checking for cracks that weren't there.

"Are you good?" he asked, voice quieter than before.

"I think so."

He studied the space where the creatures had been and then looked back at me. Something shifted in his expression. It wasn't doubt or concern but recognition.

"You didn't just burn them," he said. "You folded the space between us and them."

"I didn't plan it."

"That's what I'm noticing."

The corner of his mouth lifted, but it wasn't pure amusement anymore. It was respect edged with something sharper.

"Remind me not to stand on the wrong side of you."

"You won't."

That answer came too easily.

He didn't flinch.

If anything, he stepped half a pace closer.

"Good," he said. "Because I'm not planning on standing anywhere else."

The Academy shuddered.

Somewhere deep within its walls, something ancient laughed.

Soren's head tilted slightly. "You heard that too,

right?"
"Yes."
His jaw tightened, just barely.
"It noticed," he murmured.
I didn't have to ask what he meant.
Far beyond the hall, unseen mechanisms shifted.
The Academy had begun its evaluations.
The first trial had ended.
And now it was choosing what to do with us.

118

Chapter

Twelve

Recognition

Silence fell hard after the Academy's laughter faded.

The creatures were gone. The fear lingered in the air, thin, sharp, and waiting. The walls of the Arcanic Hall stopped moving, but they did not relax. They watched.

So did everyone else.

From the tiered balconies and shadowed alcoves, bodies stilled. Goblins with ink-stained fingers and sharp, clever eyes leaned forward despite themselves, ears twitching as if listening for something beneath the stone. A cluster of vampires, pale and composed, ceased their whispered commentary; ancient instincts stirred behind their stillness, pupils narrowing as the air shifted toward something old and deliberate.

Near the rear columns, a cyclops elder lowered his massive head slightly, his single eye focusing, not on the students themselves, but on the space around them, where power liked to gather before it chose.

Oberon did not speak. He didn't need to.

The silence he held was deliberate, controlled, and far more powerful than any declaration. It settled over the chamber like a drawn blade, pressing against every student present until even the restless air seemed to still beneath it.

Judgment did not arrive with fanfare or spectacle. It began quietly, without announcement, woven into the very structure of the Academy itself.

Survival earned notice.

Power earned interest.

But what had unfolded within the hall demanded something more than either.

The ancient systems embedded deep within the Academy stirred, responding not with emotion, but with recognition. Wards older than memory shifted. Sigils carved into the bones of the island adjusted their alignment by the slightest measure, as if recalibrating around a new variable they had not accounted for.

No applause rose to meet them, and no praise softened what had occurred.

Instead, a deeper silence settled in, thick with the unmistakable weight of being watched and measured.

It gathered slowly, methodically, until it felt as though the entire Academy had turned a fraction closer, focusing not on the hall as a whole, but on the small cluster of survivors who had altered its calculations.

Oberon remained still at the center of it all, his expression unreadable, his silence functioning as both acknowledgment and warning.

Then, at last, the ancient voice spoke.

"Veya, Lumora Guild: Wisdom and Light."

It started as warmth. Not heat but clarity. The light around Veya did not spread outward. It held.

A centaur mentor noticed this and frowned. Light usually reached. This one… contained. As if it knew the cost of excess.

Veya felt it first in her chest, spreading outward like a slow sunrise behind her ribs. The chaos of the hall dimmed, edges softening as if the world itself had taken a careful breath. Shadows retreated, not burned away, but set aside, leaving truth exposed instead of destroyed.

A pair of fae perched along the upper arches stilled mid-hover, wings trembling. Light like this did not demand attention. It earned it.

Above Veya, radiance gathered. Not blinding. Not loud. A pale gold glow threaded with white spilled gently from the ceiling, illuminating her alone. The stone beneath her feet warmed, steady and sure, as though the Academy itself had chosen to trust her.

Among the dragon shifters, some scaled, some human, some undecided. There was a low, involuntary rumble passed through their ranks. Recognition. Respect. Not dominance. Balance.

A symbol formed in the air: a radiant sigil shaped like an open eye cradled within a rising sun, its lines precise, intentional. It hovered before her, humming softly.

Lumora did not demand her kneel.

It did not claim her.

It simply marked that it would be watching.

The light brushed her skin like a promise and whispered softly into her mind, "you see clearly. You choose wisely."

And then it sank into her, settling behind her sternum, becoming part of her.

A centaur scholar near the aisle exhaled slowly, hooves shifting against stone. "That one listens before she speaks," he murmured to no one in particular.

Veya exhaled, awe trembling through her. She glanced at Soren, his eyes blazing blue in the half-light and then at Zephyr, nearly invisible but radiating mischief.

This feels right, she thought.
And yet... I wonder what it will feel like to be with them, fully.

The voice returned.

"Soren, Astrael Guild: Ambition and Vision."

The hall answered him violently.

The air around Soren tightened, charged, electric. Silence cracked as energy surged upward, snapping like distant thunder. Above him, the ceiling split, not physically, but perceptually, revealing a vast projection of stars and burning constellations against endless dark. A low murmur rippled through the upper tiers quickly silenced.

A cyclops mentor narrowed his single eye, not at the lightning, but at the pattern of the stars themselves. "That configuration…" he muttered, then stopped, jaw tightening.

Across the hall, a vampire elder turned her gaze skyward and did not blink. Storm-light reflected in her eyes like a remembered horizon.

Astrael did not wait.

It descended.

A sharp, blazing sigil flared into existence, blue-white and fierce. A shaped like a broken compass overlaid with a jagged lightning bolt. The symbol pulsed violently, matching the rhythm of Soren's heart.

Several werewolf shifters stiffened at once, hackles lifting beneath skin. This was not prey. This was momentum. A thing that ran toward storms.

The floor beneath Soren fractured, not breaking, but responding, bracing itself as if the Academy itself acknowledged that containment would never suit him.

Power rushed through him, not comfort or peace, but momentum, the sensation of standing at the edge of something vast, terrifying, and inevitable.

A voice pressed into his mind, not spoken, but absolute,

"Move forward."

Soren grinned.

He had never liked being told to wait.

The sigil burned into the air behind him like a claimed constellation, then sank into his scarred eye, leaving it blazing brighter than lightning for one suspended heartbeat. The thunder did not echo.

Several mentors exchanged quiet looks. Astrael had noticed him early. That alone would change how the trials unfolded.

It waited.

Somewhere beyond the Academy's wards, something vast shifted its wings and went still.

An elder vampire tilted her head, and her expression was unreadable. "That one will either change the path… or burn it."

Soren glanced at Veya, the faintest smirk tugging at his lips. She's steady. Predictable in a good way, he thought to himself.

Then at Zephyr, whose presence he could barely sense, whose shadow didn't quite behave like it should, he realized, he'd do something clever. Probably annoying.

The voice spoke again.

"Zephyr, Veilyn Guild: Cleverness and Secrecy."

His claiming was easy to miss.

There was no light or sound.

The shadows simply noticed him.

Darkness folded inward around his feet first, then higher, gathering without urgency. It did not press or suffocate. It welcomed.

Like a curtain drawn by familiar hands.

The noise of the hall dulled nearby, voices thinning into something distant and indistinct, echoes unraveling into whispers that no longer belonged to anyone.

Even the air seemed to shift, settling differently around him.

It wasn't reacting but more like it was recognizing.

As if something older than the room, older than the Academy itself, had quietly reached out and said,

There you are.

And then it was done without spectacle or announcement, the change settling so naturally around him that it almost felt as though nothing had happened at all.

The shadows simply remained where they had gathered, resting against him with the calm certainty of something returning to its proper place, as though they had not chosen him in that moment so much as found him again after a long absence. No one called attention to it. No light marked it. Yet the space around him had shifted in a way that could not be undone, carrying the quiet sense that something older than the Academy itself had reached forward, recognized him, and decided he belonged to it.

Just the shadows resting where they had chosen him, as though they had always been waiting.

A goblin archivist frowned, blinking. "He was there a moment ago…"

A symbol appeared, not above Zephyr, but behind his reflection in the polished stone floor. A crescent mask split down the center, etched in deep violet and black, its lines constantly shifting, never quite the same twice.

Veilyn did not test him.

It acknowledged what already belonged to it. Veilyn rarely marked openly and when it did… it meant the game had already begun.

A sensation brushed Zephyr's thoughts it felt cool, amused, and intimate, as if a secret had just been shared between old friends.

"You already know how to disappear. Now learn how to rule from it."

Zephyr chuckled softly, unheard by most. He felt the energy of Soren's lightning and Veya's light like predictable currents it was brilliant, obvious, but the shadows bent around him.

That was his playground.

He drifted closer to them, almost imperceptibly, and whispered, "Not bad, friends. Not bad at all."

Oberon's gaze swept the hall, lingering where light had settled, where stars still burned, where shadows had deepened.

"Wisdom reveals," he said quietly.

"Ambition advances."

"Cleverness endures."

His smile was faint. Knowing.

"And patience… waits."

Oberon's gaze lingered longer this time, first on the girl wrapped in steady light, then on the boy still humming with restrained thunder.

His expression did not change.

But a goblin historian watching from below felt a sudden, inexplicable urge to check records that had not been opened in centuries.

The three of them resembling light, lightning, and shadow stood together for a heartbeat, yet apart, each marked by the Academy in a way that felt both terrifying and intimate.

Around them, the hall had shifted. Not in shape, but in attention. Mentors exchanged glances. Old beings remembered prophecies they pretended not to believe in. Instincts stirred that had not been stirred in generations.

Veya felt pride, relief and a flicker of unease coil low in her chest. Soren's grin made her want to laugh. Zephyr looked exactly like he belonged where he was and that unsettled them all.

Oberon's gaze lifted to the ceiling, as though he were already watching futures unfold.

The hall vibrated softly. A heartbeat changing rhythm.

The markings were given. The Academy had taken its measure of them.

And now that they had been seen…the real trials could begin. Marks did not equal to belonging.

They were invitations.

And invitations could be refused…or fought over.

The next trial waited.

The Final Trial, the Arcane Trial, lay years ahead, a distant storm on the horizon. But here, now, hesitation had no place. They would have to learn. Adapt. Survive.

Every lesson would matter.

In the silence that followed, the Academy seemed to breathe around them, its presence settling into the space like something alive and aware, waiting and watching with patient intent.

It had marked them that much was undeniable. Yet some in the hall understood a deeper truth unfolding beneath the surface of that designation: the Academy had not chosen them.

It had recognized them.

Chapter

Thirteen

The Constellaria Wing

The Constellaria Wing smelled of old stone, faint ozone, and something harder to name…possibility, perhaps, like air that had been waiting patiently to be disturbed. The hall stretched ahead in a slow curve, vaulted ceilings catching the glow of floating lanterns that drifted rather than hung, their light bending softly along walls etched with ancient wards worn smooth by centuries of passage.

Surviving the first trial had earned them placement.

What came next would determine whether they kept it.

The Academy did not rush them.

Soren walked half a step behind me, his gaze sweeping the etched walls. "It smells expensive," he muttered.

I glanced sideways. "You've never smelled expensive stone."

"Sure, I have," he said lightly. "This is the scent of decisions that ruin people."

"That's oddly specific."

He shrugged. "Feels like the kind of hallway where you either rise… or disappear quietly."

I didn't argue.

The lantern light shifted as we passed, brightening for a moment before settling again.

"Do you still want this?" he asked, quieter now.

"Yes, I do."

His mouth curved faintly. "Good." He stepped forward to walk beside me instead of behind. "Because I'm not going back."

They were guided instead in pairs drawn forward by subtle pressure in the floor beneath their feet, the stone nudging rather than commanding. The murmur of guild colors faded behind them as the noise of the hall dissolved into distance. What remained was quieter, heavier and thick with intent.

"Welcome to your unit dorms," Oberon said, pausing at the threshold of the Wing.

His tone was light, almost conversational, but the space listened anyway.

"You'll notice," he continued, gesturing vaguely ahead, "that housing here is not organized by guild. We learned long ago that similarity breeds stagnation."

A faint smile touched his mouth. Not unkind but definitely not reassuring.

"Each Constellaria dorm houses four," Oberon said lightly. "One member from each guild. Balance is not optional."

His gaze drifted across them.

"You will train together. You will be evaluated together. And if you qualify for the Arcane Trials, you will enter them as a unit."

A pause.

"Every unit is structured the same way. Four students. Four guilds. Designed contradiction."

His smile thinned.

"Instability costs lives. Usually your own first."

A beat.

"And before anyone gets comfortable," he added mildly, eyes sweeping over them, "understand this: units are not permanent. Attachment," he added softly, "is a liability the Academy does not reward."

That landed harder.

"The Academy alters arrangements every quarter," Oberon continued, as if discussing scheduling logistics rather than lives. "Sometimes sooner. Members may be reassigned. Removed. Or lost."

"They are earned. If your unit survives long enough to qualify."

The word settled between us, stark and unavoidable. Survive. That was the standard.

Beside me, Soren let out a quiet breath that almost resembled a laugh. "Comforting," he muttered.

Oberon inclined his head once. "Good luck."

Then he turned and left, his footsteps fading quickly, as if the Wing itself had decided it no longer required him.

Soren watched him disappear down the corridor. "I don't like when powerful people wish me luck," he said under his breath. "It usually means they expect me to need it."

"That's because you usually do," I replied.

He glanced at me, one corner of his mouth lifting faintly. "You're not wrong."

The corridor beyond opened into a high-ceilinged chamber where the architecture abandoned straight lines altogether. Stone curved where it pleased, walls veined with faint mineral seams that caught lanternlight differently depending on where one stood. In some places the air felt cooler, damp with the suggestion of tide-worn caverns and deep water. In others, warmth lingered, dry and sun-soaked, like cliffs that remembered fire.

No boundary marked where one influence ended

and another began. They overlapped, bled into one another, and adjusted with quiet intention.

Soren slowed beside me, his gaze sweeping the shifting stone. "Tell me you feel that."

"Yes."

The word barely left my mouth before the lanterns nearest us brightened, just slightly, as if acknowledging the response.

He noticed. Of course he did.

"…Good," he murmured. "I'd hate to be the only one being judged by the hallway."

Our assigned dorm waited at the far end. It wasn't sealed behind a door so much as defined by a gentle shift in the space itself. The air changed first, then the light, until an invisible threshold formed without ever fully appearing.

Floating partitions hovered midair, translucent enough to promise privacy without isolation. Beds drifted above the stone floor like clouds caught in glass, each one shaped by subtle adaptive magic that shimmered faintly as we stepped inside.

The moment I crossed into the space, something in the room adjusted.

Not dramatically.

Just enough to notice.

The nearest lantern warmed. The partitions shifted by a fraction. The air settled into a quieter, steadier rhythm, as though recalibrating around my presence.

Soren went still behind me.

"…Yeah," he said softly. "That's not subtle."

"I didn't do anything."

"I know." His voice lowered. "That's what makes it interesting."

He stepped fully into the room beside me, his gaze sweeping once, instinctively mapping exits, corners, and shadows before settling back on the drifting beds.

"Well," he added after a moment, tone lighter but

still edged with awareness, "if it tries to eat us, I'm blaming you."

"If it tries to eat us," I replied calmly, "you'll deserve it."

That earned a quiet huff of laughter.

Neither of us missed the way the room seemed to listen, the air itself holding a quiet, deliberate awareness. It did not feel hostile or welcoming, only attentive, like a place that had already begun recording our presence within its walls.

The common area sat at the center like a held breath. Wide enough for conflict. Quiet enough for retreat.

Furniture suggested itself rather than asserting form, for example, the table that could seat four, or separate if needed. Alcoves that offered shadow without concealment. The room was unfinished by design.

Nothing in the room felt private.

Only temporarily unobserved.

"This is… unsettlingly neutral," Veya murmured, eyes scanning the space. "No guild colors. No banners. No ridiculous house mascots."

"Neutral?" Soren laughed, sound echoing brighter than expected. "It's perfect. Means they're not limiting us. We get to define the chaos."

"Define chaos," Zephyr said, already drifting toward the edge of the room where shadows pooled thickest. He vanished briefly then reappeared beside one of the floating bedposts, grin nearly invisible. "Or exploit it. Depends how cooperative you all are."

Veya crossed her arms. "I'm not your lab rat."

"You're already experimenting," Zephyr replied softly. "You just don't know it yet."

Soren leaned against his bed, rubbing at the scar near his eye. "Lab rat, chaos, whatever. We're alive and unbroken. For now."

The room hummed faintly, responding to the

shape of their presence.

Near Veya, the lantern light softened, warmth pooling subtly at her feet as if the space itself had decided she belonged there. Along the edges of Soren's bed, a faint shimmer of lightning traced the frame, crackling once before settling.

Zephyr raised his hand. Shadows gathered obediently, forming a crescent shape along the wall. It was never the same twice, always shifting.

"See?" Soren grinned. "It likes us."

"It's adapting," Zephyr corrected. "There's a difference."

Veya let out a breath she hadn't realized she'd been holding. "I think… this could work."

If the Academy intended them to survive together, it gave no explanation for why.

The lanterns along the corridor flickered softly, as though in quiet agreement with the unspoken thought.

Soren's gaze shifted toward the light. "Did you notice that as well."

"Yes."

He exhaled slowly. "Good. I'd rather not be the only one being evaluated by architecture."

Before I could answer, a knock sounded at the door.

It wasn't loud, and it wasn't hesitant. It was deliberate and measured, as though whoever stood beyond it already knew we were listening.

Soren didn't move toward it.

"Faculty?" he murmured.

"No," I said quietly. "Faculty doesn't knock."

His jaw tightened just slightly. "Even better."

The lantern nearest the door brightened by a fraction.

Waiting.

Beyond the corridor, footsteps slowed. They weren't passing by; they were lingering, listening.

Word had already begun to spread. Surviving the first trial without breaking had not gone unnoticed, and the Academy was not the only one paying attention.

The door did not swing open so much as reconsider its purpose.

The man who stepped inside had to duck slightly. Not because he was especially tall, but because he carried himself as though space should make room for him. He wore a guild sigil none of them bore, stitched in dark metallic thread over his heart. Travel-worn boots. A long coat clasped neatly at the throat.

His presence carried a quiet density, something grounded and anchored that seemed to settle into the room the moment he entered. The space itself appeared to register him, the air shifting almost imperceptibly in response.

His gaze swept across the room once, sharp and assessing, before coming to rest on Veya. It lingered there for the span of a single breath, and in that brief pause something unreadable moved across his expression. Recognition, perhaps, or a form of respect that had not yet found its context.

He inclined his head to her first, not deeply and not with formal ceremony, but with a deliberate acknowledgment that carried its own quiet weight.

"I was assigned here," he said, voice low and steady. "Looks like I'm late."

Soren raised an eyebrow. "You are, we were just deciding who'd break the room first."

The man's mouth twitched. "Then I'll try not to accelerate the process."

Zephyr circled him slowly. "You're not subtle," he said. "Whatever you are."

The man met his gaze without flinching. "Neither are you."

The air shifted.

Not threatening. Watchful. "You're the last guild,"

Veya said quietly. "Yes," he replied, studying her again as if listening for something beneath her words. "Seems that way."

"What's your name?" Soren asked.

There was a brief pause before the answer came, calm and unhurried. "My name is Rhazien."

As he set his pack beside the remaining bed, the magic threaded through the room stirred in response. The lantern flames dipped and the shadows stretched long across the walls before gradually settling again, as though the dorm itself had taken notice of his arrival.

Something in the space seemed to exhale. It wasn't quite balanced, but newly aligned. The air shifted once more, subtle yet unmistakable, carrying the sense that an unseen mechanism had just clicked into place.

Along the far wall, a projection flared into existence, gold script forming and reforming in quick succession before stabilizing into sharp, deliberate clarity.

ECLIPSE UNIT

Rhazien's gaze lingered on the name longer than the others.

"Eclipses are temporary," he said at last, voice even.

Zephyr tilted his head, shadows shifting lazily at his shoulders. "Only if the sky remains unchanged."

Soren blinked once. "That's dramatic."

Zephyr's smile curved faintly. "I try."

Soren crossed his arms. "Pretty sure eclipses don't end well for whatever's standing in the dark."

"Depends," Zephyr replied lightly. "On whether you're the shadow… or the sun."

"I vote we're the dangerous part," Soren said without hesitation.

Rhazien's eyes flicked toward him. "That would be accurate."

Oberon's voice echoed faintly from somewhere deeper in the Wing, as though the stone itself delivered it:

"Eclipse Unit. Registered."

The letters dimmed but did not disappear, their faint glow lingering along the wall as though the message had merely settled rather than ended.

Soren studied it for a moment. "Registered," he muttered. "That sounds permanent."

"It is," Rhazien replied.

"I was hoping for a trial period."

Zephyr's laugh was quiet but genuine. "Too late. The sky has already shifted."

Rhazien's attention returned to the wall, thoughtful and measuring. "I don't know why they placed me here," he said calmly. "But if the Academy arranged it, there's a reason."

His gaze returned briefly to Veya. Not intrusive and not questioning but simply aware.

"I suspect it isn't accidental," he added, with the quiet certainty of someone who understood that nothing within the Academy ever truly was.

Soren followed that look and didn't comment on it, but he did step half a pace closer to Veya without seeming to notice he had.

Behind them, the door sealed itself without a sound.

A subtle awareness settled through the Constellaria Wing, as though the structure itself had leaned closer to listen.

For the first time since their arrival, the room felt complete. It was not yet safe, but undeniably aligned, like a long-misplaced piece had finally slid into position within a much larger design.

Soren exhaled slowly. "Well," he said, glancing at the others, "if we're rewriting the sky, we might as well do it properly."

Zephyr's grin widened.

Rhazien didn't smile.

But he didn't disagree.

Chapter

Fourteen

The Forgotten Path
Rhazien

On the Ossuary Shoals, names were not given lightly.

At the Arcane Academy, names carried consequences.

They were spoken until they hardened, etched into stone and bone alike. Memory clung there the way salt did, inescapable, preservative, and unforgiving. Stories did not fade. They calcified. To be born among the Shoals was to be cataloged by lineage and tide, by what answered when the elders called, by which element bent first and which followed.

Rhazien learned early that survival did not mean becoming invisible. Invisible things were hunted. Feared. Corrected. Forgettable things were stepped around.

He did not fit cleanly into the stories of his people. He was not absence, but neither was he singular. Fire answered him…sometimes. So did weight. Pressure. The slow certainty of stone. The pull of water beneath bone. Enough to be noticed. Not enough to be celebrated.

Those who were mixed were never simply seen. They were watched, quietly cataloged, and measured for whatever correction might one day be deemed necessary.

So, he learned to soften himself. He learned when to lower his gaze, not out of shame, but out of survival and when to still his breathing until even the air seemed to forget he was there. He learned how to fold the weight of his existence inward, compressing it carefully until the land itself hesitated before answering his presence, as though uncertain it should acknowledge him at all.

It was not a skill anyone had taught him in the dens. No one demonstrated it, and no one praised the effort it required. There were no lessons for becoming smaller, quieter, and less disruptive to the world around you.

He discovered it alone, piece by piece, through the quiet understanding that the more of himself he allowed to show, the more the world would try to reshape him into something easier to accept.

Usually by those who learned what attention cost.

The dens of the Shoals ran deep. Ancestral hollows carved by heat and pressure, places where lineage was proven by what stirred when you exhaled. Dens remembered you. They tracked who you were meant to become.

Rhazien knew the dens.

He could retreat to them. He chose not to.

Instead, he lived along the edges. Tide-worn shelters where stone shifted just enough each season to make certainty inconvenient. Shared dwellings where no one checked too closely and names blurred between occupants. Places where the sea erased footprints before anyone thought to ask who had made them.

That was where he learned how to remain. Not hidden but unanchored.

There were others who shone brighter than him. Children whose magic sang to the tides or split stone cleanly, whose tempers bent storms or set the earth answering in kind. They were celebrated. Watched. Remembered. When they failed, it was recorded. When they succeeded, it was etched.

Rhazien watched them all.

And learned what attention demanded in return.

So, when elders looked past him, he did not correct them.

When teachers forgot to call his name, he did not remind them. When records misplaced him, he let the ink dry.

His name caused problems.

"Ray-zee-en," one elder had called, distracted.

He hadn't corrected her.

Another had tried differently. "Rah-zee-an."

He'd opened his mouth that time, the correction resting at the edge of his tongue.

"It's RHAH"

"Raz," someone else interrupted with a careless grin. "We'll call you Raz."

Laughter followed.

He stopped correcting them after the third time.

It was RHAH-zee-en.

But mistakes, he learned, made excellent camouflage.

By the time he left the Ossuary Shoals, the sea had stopped calling him home.

That was how he became one of the Forgotten, and the Academy, patient and precise, always had a way of finding those the world had quietly set aside. They were not erased, and they were not truly lost; they were simply left unrecorded, existing in the margins where memory thinned, and history chose not to look too closely.

However, Mistara Island did not question him when he arrived.

Borders there shifted more than they barred. The land favored alignment over resistance, and Rhazien had learned long ago how to move where the world found it easier to let him pass than to stop him.

The Academy did not find him. It adjusted around him. Whether by design or inevitability, he had still been brought here to be tested. He arrived without ceremony, without escort, without expectation. Gates did not open so much as yield, making room as though he had always been meant to pass through at that exact moment. No bells rang. No names were announced.

The Eldrin Guild had noticed his restraint and balance they were two qualities Rhazien showed without fault. The space between action and consequence.

He fit there not because he was harmless. No, but because he understood pressure.

Rhazien stood now at the threshold of the Constellaria Wing, fingers loose at his sides, posture neutral. Old stone rose around him, layered with wards meant to measure, sort, and define.

The wards hesitated. Surviving the first trial had earned them placement here.

The next would determine who remained.

He waited.

They always did.

Patience was part of the art.

Inside, the air was alive, too alive. He detected three presences that already shaped the room, each distinct, each dangerous in their own way. Shadow folded and unfolded with intention, as if deciding where it preferred to exist. Lightning whispered impatience, the air buzzing with barely contained motion.

And the light it wasn't brilliance, not even radiance. It was Authority. So, these were the ones the Academy had marked first.

Rhazien's breath caught before he could stop it.

She stood near the lanterns, dark hair falling in soft waves down her back, skin warm-toned and luminous in a way that had nothing to do with display and everything to do with restraint. Veya was small, yes, but the room bent around her all the same, careful not to intrude.

Old instincts stirred within him, urging his head to lower before he consciously chose to move.

He obeyed.

Soren noticed.

"Is that voluntary?" Soren asked lightly, though his eyes were sharp.

Rhazien lifted his gaze again, expression unchanged. "Instinct."

"For what?" Soren pressed.

Rhazien did not answer, not because he meant to withhold it, but because he genuinely did not yet know. The movement had come from somewhere deeper than conscious thought, older than decision. It had felt less like choice and more like recognition.

Still, he allowed the gesture to complete itself, inclining his head just enough to acknowledge the moment without surrendering to it. The bow was precise and measured, neither submissive nor proud, simply aligned with something he had not yet learned to name.

That unsettled him more than raw power ever had. Recognition without memory was dangerous. It meant something ancient had responded before permission had been granted.

Rhazien stepped fully inside.

The wards adjusted at once, shifting with quiet, practiced ease that felt almost familiar.

Of course they did.

He had walked forgotten paths for most of his life, through cities that never recorded his presence, across borders that yielded without acknowledgment, and into institutions that preferred quiet alignment over the effort of truly seeing what stood before them.

It was not deception that allowed him passage, nor any deliberate masking of what he was. The world simply learned to move around him, reshaping itself just enough to let him exist without ever fully recognizing him.

It was easier that way.

Easier to accommodate than to confront, easier to allow than to accept, and far easier to let him pass through its structures as though he were never meant to leave a mark at all.

The Eldrin sigil at his chest felt heavier than it had the night before, as though gravity itself had recalculated. He had not intended to stay. Staying meant being noticed. Being noticed meant being named.

And names had weight.

Later, when the others slept, Rhazien sat awake on his bed, palms resting on his knees, breathing steadily. He listened not just with his ears, but with the quiet part of himself that measured pressure and absence.

The stone seemed to speak in its own quiet way, and so did the charged space between them. Light moved with a low, steady murmur that demanded nothing, while shadow shifted at the edges without any need to conceal itself. Storm pressed outward in subtle currents, restless even in stillness, and beneath it all, so deep he nearly overlooked it, something older lingered.

It did not call or beckon. It simply waited, patient and unmoving, with the unsettling certainty of something that knew time would eventually deliver what it required.

That, somehow, was worse.

Far beyond record or remembrance, something vast shifted. Wings stretched in a place where time had not yet agreed on rules, where names had not been settled. The motion did not seek him. It did not threaten.

It offered a quiet acknowledgment, subtle but unmistakable, and Rhazien chose not to give it a name. Names had a way of anchoring things into permanence, of inviting claim and recognition where neither was wanted.

Instead, he drew in a slow, even breath and let it settle, allowing the moment to pass without form or declaration. The world, as it so often did around him, seemed to accept that choice and refrained from insisting.

Sleep, he decided, mattered. Morning would bring

corridors filling, voices overlapping, the Academy revealing itself through routine rather than ritual and eventually, another trial.

Training would begin soon, and with it the deeper
structures of the Academy would begin to reveal themselves. Somewhere ahead, another trial was already waiting, patient and inevitable.

He would learn what the Academy expected of
them and more importantly, where those expectations
might eventually fracture. Until then, patience would
have to suffice. Careful observation.

And the quiet discipline of remaining, for as long
as possible, just beyond definition and deliberately unnamed.

144

Chapter

Fifteen

Held Breath

Morning came without ceremony, because Arcane Academy did not wake its students gently. It did not allow them to forget where they were.

The lanterns flared to life all at once, harsh and blinding. Beds lurched upward, hovering just long enough to be insulting before jolting again, clearly attempting to eject their occupants.

Soren yelped as his mattress tilted. "Okay…okay… I'm up! I'm up! You've made your point!"

Zephyr rolled smoothly out of the air like gravity had asked politely. "You say that" he observed mildly "and yet the bed remains unconvinced."

Rhazien landed silently, already on his feet by the time his bed dropped back into place with a final, judgmental thud. He didn't look rattled, just alert, like he'd never fully gone to sleep at all.

Veya sat up more slowly, blinking against the sudden light.

"Is it always like this," she asked, her voice still warm with sleep, "or did we offend the furniture?"

"The building," Soren said darkly, wrestling his

boots on as his bed glided away from him like it had made a moral decision, "has opinions. And right now, I think it's testing my patience."

Veya laughed softly. "I am in desperate need of coffee. Let's hurry."

"If this place doesn't serve coffee," Soren said grimly, "I'm withdrawing from the Trials on moral grounds."

"You won't," Zephyr replied.

"No," Soren sighed. "I won't. But I'll resent it loudly."

Soren had never been a morning person, and the Academy seemed determined to prove it.

Sunlight filtered through the tall, narrow windows of the unit dorm, pale and cool, catching on stone that had never known comfort. The walls absorbed the light without softening, holding it like evidence.

They dressed in their guild colors in near silence. The fabric felt heavier than it had the night before, as though the markings now carried expectation instead of promise.

Marks made them visible.

Visibility invited scrutiny.

Buttons fastened more slowly. Clasps were checked twice.

Soren struggled with his collar, scowling. "I swear this was looser yesterday."

Zephyr glanced over, smoothing his own sleeves. "Yesterday, it was decorative. Today, it's declarative."

"That does not help," Soren said. "At all."

Veya adjusted the clasp at her shoulder, fingers lingering a moment longer than necessary. "It feels like armor," she said quietly. "But the kind you don't get to take off."

Soren glanced over at her, expression sharpening for just a moment. "Then we wear it," he said. "Better than being unmarked."

Rhazien stood near the window, fastening his clasp with careful precision. His gaze drifted to the courtyard below, where students were already gathering in small, shifting clusters forming, dissolving, reforming like schools of fish testing unfamiliar currents.

Soren followed his line of sight. "You look like you're planning an escape route."

Rhazien shook his head once. "No. I'm watching who thinks they already belong."

Soren huffed softly. "And?"

Rhazien's gaze didn't shift. "Most of them."

Zephyr smiled faintly. "That should make this interesting."

Zephyr hummed softly. "Bold of them."

The dorm door unlocked itself without a sound.

They stepped into the shared dorm wing corridor, already filling with motion. Doors opening in staggered rhythm as other first-years emerged from their own rooms, guild colors flashing briefly before being swallowed by the flow.

Further down the corridor, a pair of younger students in matching Lumora colors; soft gold and dawn-amber were already talking animatedly. "I heard Combat Casting starts today," one said, practically bouncing. "My brother says half the class throws up the first week."

"That's how you know it's real training," the other replied, grinning like that was something to look forward to.

Soren tugged at his collar. "Do you think they make these stiff on purpose, or is this some kind of endurance trial?"

"Everything here is a trial," Zephyr said mildly, smoothing his sleeves without looking up. "Including whether you complain before breakfast."

Soren snorted. "Then I've already failed." Veya smiled despite herself, nerves loosening just a fraction.

The corridor widened naturally into the Astryx Dining Hall, and the change was immediate.

Breakfast waited in overwhelming abundance.

Long tables stretched farther than Veya could see, laden with food from everywhere and nowhere at once: steaming trays of eggs and spiced vegetables, breads still warm, bowls of fruit glowing with unnatural freshness. The air was thick with scent like butter, herbs, sugar, and smoke. Which made her stomach twisted painfully in response.

The corridor widened naturally into the Astryx Dining Hall, and the change was immediate.

Breakfast waited in overwhelming abundance.

Soren stopped beside her.

"…I take back every complaint I've ever made about this place," he said quietly.

Zephyr drifted forward, studying the spread with open appreciation. "Abundance after deprivation," he murmured. "A classic morale strategy."

"Or a trap," Soren added. "It could definitely be a trap."

Veya exhaled slowly. "If it is," she said, stepping forward anyway, "we'll face it after coffee."

"That," Soren replied, falling into step beside her, "is the most reasonable decision anyone has made since we arrived."

Rhazien said nothing, but he did reach for a plate.

Which, somehow, felt like agreement.

Soren stopped beside her.

Only then did she realize how hungry she was.

Not just her.

A group of fae students hovered near a table of honeyed pastries, wings flickering nervously as they debated in hushed tones.

"They wouldn't poison us on the first day," one whispered.

"They absolutely would," another replied. "But

only if it taught something."

Soren froze mid-step, staring at a carving station where a slab of meat hovered patiently, perfectly cooked. "Is that… ribeye?"

Zephyr was already moving, plate in hand. "Don't question it. Just accept the miracle."

Veya laughed, piling her plate with far more food than she'd intended. For a moment, it almost felt normal. Almost was the closest the Academy allowed to comfort. Almost like a beginning instead of the edge of something much sharper.

Nearby, a tall cyclops student loaded three plates without hesitation, laughing loudly as a centaur beside him tried and failed to balance silverware with a hoof.

"Academy food better live up to the rumors," the centaur said. "If I'm risking my neck, I want good eggs."

Soren stacked his plate recklessly. "If today kills us," he said cheerfully, "at least I'll die happy."

"Optimism," Veya said dryly, "is not your strongest skill."

Rhazien lingered at the edge of the hall, selecting sparingly with only bread, fruit, and water. He watched the room more than his plate, his eyes tracking instructors positioned like statues, not to teach but to evaluate and students who didn't realize they were being measured.

"You're not eating much," Veya noted.

"I'm eating enough," he said simply. That should have been comforting.

It wasn't. They didn't linger long, and neither did anyone else. The Academy discouraged settling in ways both subtle and unmistakable, as though stillness itself were a kind of defiance it refused to tolerate.

There were no bells to signal the shift.

No shouted instructions to herd students from one place to the next.

Instead, doors opened on their own, and corridors adjusted with quiet certainty, aligning themselves like they had opinions about where everyone ought to be.

Soren slowed slightly beside Veya, watching a hallway bend almost imperceptibly to meet the flow of students. "...I don't like buildings that think for themselves," he muttered.

Zephyr drifted forward with mild interest. "You say that as though the alternative has been particularly successful for you."

"That's not the point," Soren replied. "The point is I prefer my architecture passive."

Rhazien's gaze tracked the shifting stone, expression unreadable. "It isn't guiding randomly," he said quietly. "It's sorting."

"Sorting for what exactly?" Veya asked.

Rhazien didn't answer immediately. His attention lingered on the way certain doorways opened sooner than others, the way some corridors widened while others narrowed.

"Efficiency," he said at last. "Proximity. Compatibility." A brief pause. "Potential conflict."

Soren exhaled softly. "Comforting."

A nearby corridor opened before they reached it, lanterns brightening just enough to suggest expectation rather than welcome.

Zephyr smiled faintly. "Well," he said, stepping forward, "it appears we've been given an opinion."

They followed anyway.

Because at Arcane Academy, hesitation had a way of being noticed.

Students rose as if tugged by an invisible current, drifting into motion without being told to move. Those who hesitated found themselves gently but unmistakably redirected.

The stone beneath their feet sloped downward, cool and smooth, the air growing denser with every step.

A vampire student nearby muttered, "I don't like

buildings that watch you walk."

Her companion smirked. "Then don't walk wrong."

"Okay," Soren muttered, glancing around, "I officially retract my earlier complaint. This is definitely not normal school."

Zephyr walked beside him, hands clasped behind his back, eyes bright with interest. "No," he said lightly. "It's calibration. The Academy is figuring out how dangerous, strange, or incompatible we are."

Veya frowned. "That's not comforting."

"It's honest," Zephyr replied.

Rhazien slowed slightly, letting them move ahead of him. "They're watching how we move before they tell us where to stand," he said quietly. "That alone tells you what matters here."

"Great," Soren said. "So, no pressure."

Ahead, the corridor widened into a pre-assessment chamber, circular and stark. White stone. Old wards etched so deeply they felt more like scars than symbols. A low hum filled the space not loud, not threatening just present, like a held breath.

They were not alone.

A cluster of goblin and goblina students whispered rapidly, eyes darting, calculating exits. A dragon shifter rolled their shoulders as if preparing for impact. A werewolf flexed their hands, jaw tight, pretending they weren't nervous.

Veya felt the hum settle under her skin.

Excitement fluttered in her chest, sharp, bright and tangled with nerves. Training was finally beginning. Answers were coming. Structure. Direction.

None of them said it out loud, but they all felt it.

Something was about to decide what they were allowed to become... and what they would be forced to survive. Whatever this was, it would shape how they survived the next trial.

152

Chapter

Sixteen

Calibration
Professor Elira Voss

The Academy had never believed in introductions. Elira Voss considered this a mercy. However, she knew her role here in the Curriculum Hall: to give schedules.

Storms did not explain themselves before they arrived. Neither did institutions built to survive what others could not. By the time students realized what Arcane Academy was, they were already standing in it like they were wet, cold, and expected to adapt.

She watched them gather around the slate where their schedules had been carved. Not written in ink that could fade or be replaced but cut directly into the stone itself.

The distinction mattered.

The letters were etched deep enough to suggest permanence, each line precise and deliberate, as though whoever had carved them intended the information to outlast the students meant to follow it. They weren't marks that invited revision. They were declarations that were fixed, unyielding, and patient. Deep enough that erasure would require effort, and deep enough that even attempting to change them would leave visible scars.

A hesitant voice broke the quiet near the entrance. "Is… is this where we check in?"

Another answered under their breath, "I don't think they do 'check-ins' here."

Elira did not turn. If they required reassurance, they would not find it in her.

She noted the way the students approached the slate, not as a single group but as a shifting constellation of reactions. Some leaned closer immediately, curiosity and urgency pulling them forward as if proximity might grant advantage. Others hung back, cautious or over-whelmed, their gazes flicking between the stone and the crowd as though uncertain where it was safest to stand.

A student near the front squinted at the carved names.

"…They're not going to change these, are they?"

"No," another muttered. "I don't think anything here changes for us."

A few traced the grooves with their eyes, following each carved line as if testing whether stone could remember them in return. Whether something as old and delib-erate as this place recorded more than schedules. Whether it recorded who stood before it, who hesitated, who tried to appear unafraid.

One voice, quieter than the rest, barely carried: "Do you think they already know where we'll end up?"

No one answered.

Elira watched all of it in silence, committing each reaction to memory. In a place like this, the way someone approached a simple slab of carved stone said far more about them than any introduction ever could.

After a moment, she finally spoke in a calm, mea-sured, and in an impossible to ignore tone.

"Schedules," Elira said, her voice carrying just enough to still the room. "Find your name. Memorize your path. The Academy does not repeat itself for those who fail to pay attention."

Silence settled more quickly this time.

Good.

They were learning already.

"The Academy does not operate on a traditional curriculum," Elira said, her voice carrying easily across the chamber. "You will not be attending classes in the way lesser institutions define them. What you will undergo are required disciplines, structured exposures, designed to prepare you for trials that will not pause for your understanding."

Her gaze moved across the gathered students, steady and unreadable.

"These are not opportunities for excellence. They are conditions for survival."

The heading was blunt:

**CORE CURRICULUM
REQUIRED FOR ALL FIRST AND SECOND
YEARS**

No guild distinctions. No exceptions for bloodline, creature status, or unit assignment.

Good, she thought.

Below it, the explanation followed clear, almost merciless in its honesty.

These disciplines are required of all students, regardless of guild, race, or origin. They are not electives, nor are they designed for comfort. They exist to ensure that when the Academy tests you, you survive long enough to be judged.

Survival is not a promise of success. It is merely the absence of failure.

Several students appeared relieved by that distinction. Others did not. Elira observed them both.

Foundations of Aether Control

Anatomy of power across incompatible forms

Power does not move the same through everybody. Some

were never meant to hold what they now carry. This discipline examines what happens when students ignore that distinction and what it costs them.

Combat Casting & Adaptive Defense

Wards. Countermeasures. Magic under stress.

You will fight while outmatched, while afraid, and while wrong. Precision is a luxury. Survival is not.

Elira watched several students exchange excited looks. They would not be smiling by midterm.

Leylines and Living Geography

Magic does not exist in a vacuum.

Land remembers. Cities interfere. Ruins resist. Oceans warp intention. Battlefields echo. Spells behave differently depending on where you dare to cast them and some places refuse to cooperate at all.

Inter-Guild Praxis

Belief systems. Ethical limits. Incompatible magics.

You will learn what happens when ideologies collide and which ones fracture first. Cooperation is encouraged. Failure to adapt is recorded.

She saw arguments forming already.

Good. Better here than later.

Arcane Ethics & Consequence

History, framed honestly.

Every lesson is a case study. Someone made a choice. The world responded.

There are no hypotheticals.

There are no softened endings.

"Completion does not guarantee advancement," Elira continued calmly. "It only guarantees that you were not among those removed."

Elira noted the absence herself, though none of them would yet recognize it: there was no discipline devoted to recovery. No allowance for fracture. Survival did not require wholeness. Only persistence.

"This isn't orientation," someone muttered.

Elira did not look toward the speaker. She rarely

needed to.

"No," another replied quietly. "It's calibration."

Correct.

The Academy- The Resonance Hall

The Resonance Hall was not part of any curriculum, nor was it listed on any student schedule. It existed for one purpose alone: to determine what each student was before anyone attempted to shape what they might become.

The Resonance Hall was not listed on any schedule. It never was. Before instruction came understanding, and before understanding came assessment. The Academy preferred to know what it was dealing with before it pretended it could shape it.

The crystal sphere rested at the chamber's center, flawless, humming faintly. Old magic. Prejudiced magic. It did not lie, but it simplified. That limitation had always troubled her.

She took her place beside it; hands folded behind her back.

"This is not a test," she said evenly. "It is a reflection. Touch the crystal. Let it show how your magic moves."

How it prefers to move, she amended silently. Magic was never neutral. Neither were people.

Students stepped forward. Colors bloomed. Tones rang. Some sighed with relief when the crystal behaved. Others stiffened when it didn't.

Elira recorded only what mattered.

Then the air shifted.

She felt it before she saw him the subtle reorientation of attention, the way the chamber seemed to listen rather than react.

The fae stepped forward lightly, almost casually.

Zephyr.

When his hand touched the crystal, the hum

changed.

Not louder.

Older.

Elira felt her spine tighten.

Several fae students glanced up instinctively and then froze.

No echo followed.

No answering resonance.

The absence was… loud.

The crystal did not cloud or fracture. Instead, it emptied. Light slid across its surface and failed to linger, reflecting only Zephyr himself and even that reflection felt thinner than it should have been, as if the edges couldn't quite decide where he ended.

As though something just beyond him refused to be reflected at all.

The air bent around him, compliant. Familiar.

Too familiar.

It moved the way breath did around a held candle flame, careful and not to disturb something it could not fully see.

Or something it remembered.

Shadows along the chamber walls stretched almost imperceptibly toward him, not lengthening but leaning, like ink drawn toward a deeper well. One pooled briefly at his feet before flattening again, indistinguishable from the rest.

No one else seemed to notice.

Elira did.

The wards flared once, sharply as if it were searching, then dimmed again, their patterns slipping a fraction out of alignment before correcting.

Uncertain.

Elira exhaled slowly. "Air-aligned," she said. "Fae-born."

She paused.

Not because she lacked words.

Because she had too many and none of them were meant for a room full of students.

"…But unattached."

That landed as it should have.

Zephyr withdrew his hand, expression mild, almost amused, though something unreadable passed behind his eyes, like a thought stepping back into shadow before it could be seen.

Elira made her notation without looking at him again.

Air was easy.

What lingered where the light refused to settle was not.

The fae in the chamber shifted uneasily. Not with recognition but with absence. With the quiet instinct that something that should have been present… wasn't.

Or was waiting elsewhere.

"Your elemental affinity remains intact," Elira continued. "Your lineage bond does not."

The slate recorded:

Air Fae (Severed)

Then the notation blurred.

Interesting.

The Academy itself hesitated.

For a fraction of a second, the crystal's surface darkened, not with shadow, but with depth, like a night sky reflected on black water. Something moved there, it was vast and patient. Crowned in nothing at all.

Then it was gone.

Elira said nothing. Some truths did not belong in records.

Zephyr stepped back. His expression was light. Too light.

She noted the discipline in it.

Air remained his.

Belonging did not.

But something else, older than lineage and far less

forgiving, had not released him at all.

Next came the quiet one, Rhazien.

The crystal did nothing when he touched it. No flare. No glow. No answering surge of element.

The hum thinned, stretched taut until the chamber felt suspended between moments, like a breath held too long. Elira felt the wards twitch, not in alarm, but in hesitation. That unsettled her more than raw power ever did.

Fire should have answered.

She felt it waiting. Not absent. Not extinguished. Contained so completely it left only pressure behind like cinders sealed beneath stone, like heat bound so tightly it refused even memory of flame.

A faint line of light traced the crystal's outer edge. Not within it. Not reflected.

A boundary acknowledging something the crystal could not contain.

Elira's fingers tightened on the slate.

"…No primary element registering," she said slowly, deliberately. "Responsive magic only."

That was the safest phrasing available.

Fire should have answered.

She felt it there. It was not absent, not extinguished, but sealed beneath layers of control so absolute it left only pressure behind. Cinders beneath stone. Heat bound so tightly even memory of flame refused to surface.

Yet something else pressed at the edge of the wards.

It wasn't fire or any element the Academy had ever measured.

It was something older.

Something the crystal recognized but could not translate.

Her gaze sharpened, recognition sliding into place not from the crystal, but from experience.

"Creature status…" A pause. "…Cinderbound Nullwyrm. Draconic classification."

A ripple passed through the room quiet, involuntary. A few students stiffened. One instructor near the wall went very still.

A dragon that did not announce itself. A fire that refused to rise. That was not weakness. That was restraint honed to a dangerous edge.

Rhazien withdrew his hand immediately. It was not out of caution, but as though he already knew exactly how long he could remain within the crystal's attention.

Good. He understood exposure. Understood that the moment he allowed the pressure to vent, the room would no longer belong to him or anyone else.

The crystal's hum resumed, almost gratefully.

The slate recorded:

Draconic: Nullwyrm (Cinderbound)
Affinity: Fire (Sealed)
Reactive Status: Unclassified
System Response: Pending

The slate hesitated before finishing the line, as though the Academy itself required a moment to decide how to record what it had just seen.

Elira did not read the final line aloud.

There were truths best acknowledged only in ink. And some best left to systems that could pretend they understood what they were measuring.

She lifted her gaze.

Then, the air shifted again, announcing the next complication before it happened.

Soren.

She felt the shift the instant his fingers made contact. Air snapped sharp and clean, pressure rippling outward as though the chamber had inhaled too fast. Wind coiled around his hand, and it was not summoned, not shaped, but recognizing.

Then lightning followed.

Blue-white light fractured through the sphere with intent, currents folding and accelerating, feeding back into themselves.

Storm memory, Elira thought as the resonance shifted within the sphere, the frequency deepening in a way that felt older than elemental alignment alone. There was patterning in it, ancient and deliberate, like a system that had been refined across centuries rather than formed in a single lifetime.

"Dual alignment," she said calmly, her voice carrying across the chamber without strain. "Air and lightning. Storm-bonded."

Under ordinary circumstances, that assessment would have been sufficient. It would have satisfied the crystal's parameters and allowed the resonance to settle into predictable output.

It did not.

The hum climbed steadily into tension, the chamber's wards flaring in response as they recalibrated again and again, searching for boundaries that refused to stabilize. Light gathered within the sphere, not brightening, but tightening inward, compressing as though something larger had chosen restraint instead of expansion.

This was not an increase in power.

It was an unmistakable sensation of presence.

Elira felt it then. The pressure beneath the storm itself. Something vast leaning forward from behind the elemental display, not pressing against the crystal, but held back by the boy's own control. It did not rage. It did not flare.

It waited.

A student near the back whispered, "Is that supposed to happen?"

No one answered.

The sphere shattered mid-resonance, not in chaotic overload but in something far more deliberate. The fracture ran through it with surgical precision before the entire construct split apart, shards scattering across the chamber floor like fallen stars.

Electricity crackled faintly along Soren's skin as he drew his hand back, breathless laughter escaping him as though he had not expected the reaction but had not been surprised by it either.

One of the junior instructors stepped forward instinctively. "Headmistress…"

"Stand down," Elira said quietly.

She studied the fragments longer than protocol required, watching the residual current fade along the broken edges. This had not been a malfunction. The crystal had not failed.

It had refused containment.

"…Primary affinities confirmed," she said at last. "Air. Lightning."

A pause. "…Magnitude exceeds containment. Secondary resonance unresolved."

The slate accepted:

Air and Lightning
Storm-Class Output
Additional Potential: Unbounded

She wrote the last line smaller. Not to hide it. To respect it. Then came the girl.

Veya stepped forward last.

The change in the chamber was immediate, though no one spoke of it. The air did not tighten as it had with the others, nor did it strain against containment. Instead, something within the room seemed to settle, as though a long-held breath had finally been released. Elira felt it in her chest before she consciously registered the shift. A recognition that arrived without invitation and without explanation.

When Veya placed her hand against the crystal, light did not flare violently. It gathered.

Warm, steady illumination filled the sphere from within, not bursting outward but unfolding in controlled layers. The pressure that had strained the wards moments earlier eased subtly, systems realigning as though relieved to encounter something they understood. As though the chamber had finally found a center it could balance around.

Fire appeared first.

Not wild flame or reckless surge, but controlled heat that was banked and deliberate, like embers sealed beneath stone, glowing with restrained intensity. It did not lash outward. It endured.

Air followed, not as a gale or sharp current, but as a measured circulation that wove gently through the fire without extinguishing it. The elements did not compete. They cooperated.

"Primary alignment: fire," Elira said evenly. "Secondary: air."

Several students shifted, some murmuring under their breath. One of the instructors near the wall leaned slightly closer, as if expecting the resonance to settle.

It did not.

The quality of the light changed. Not brighter, not louder, but denser. The sphere seemed to deepen rather than expand, as though something beneath the visible alignment had shifted its weight.

Elira's posture straightened almost imperceptibly.

The crystal began to strain.

Fine fractures formed beneath its surface, thin veins of light spreading in intricate patterns as it attempted to redistribute energy it had not been designed to contain. The wards flickered, recalibrating again and again, but the pressure did not spike. It accumulated.

Veya's hand withdrew immediately.

"I didn't..." she began, confusion tightening her voice.

The crystal fractured anyway.

Not explosively. Not with the violent refusal that had marked Soren's resonance. This break was quieter, more internal. The sphere split along the glowing seams, the sound like glass exhaling after being held too long under tension. Shards fell softly to the floor, scattering in controlled arcs before settling into stillness.

"I didn't push," Veya said, softer now.

Elira believed her.

She stepped forward before anyone else could speak, raising a hand slightly to still the low ripple of reaction spreading through the chamber.

"Affinities confirmed," she said, her tone measured and undisturbed. "Fire. Air."

She allowed the silence to settle before continuing.

"Resonance exceeds projected containment thresholds. Internal stabilization present. Source unresolved."

Unclassified, she corrected silently.

A few students exchanged uncertain looks.

One whispered, "Is that bad?"

Elira did not answer the question.

Instead, she turned to the slate.

For a moment, the surface resisted her stylus. The stone seemed to hesitate, as though evaluating the entry before accepting it.

Then the inscription formed.

Fire and Air

Sustained Output

Structural Capacity: Indeterminate

Elira closed her stylus. This was not classification. It was caution. Power could be measured. Dampened. Redirected. Uncertainty could not.

By midday, the pattern had fully emerged. Their schedules aligned. Recovery windows vanished. Exercises escalated without explanation. Failure arrived before context. Observation replaced instruction.

"They're not teaching us yet," the storm-boy muttered.

"They are," the fae replied thinly. "Just not how you expect."

The girl said nothing. That concerned Elira most.

That night, a colleague asked her quietly, "Do you think they'll succeed?" Elira did not hesitate. "That was never the goal."

She watched the corridor empty.

The Academy was not built to create legends.

It existed to see what remained when certainty broke.

And these four, light, storm, shadow, and the space between. They had not been grouped because they fit. They had been grouped because they would endure what others could not.

Whether they survived it…

…was still undecided.

Chapter

Seventeen

What the Stone Noticed
Academy Voice

The corridor should have led left.

The slate said so. Foundations of Aether Control were held in Hall Cinderreach, and the stone beneath their boots bore the faint directional glyphs to prove it. Centuries of students had followed those markings without question, the floor worn smooth by obedience.

But as the flow of first-years divided toward their assigned halls, something shifted in a way that was easy to miss. There was no visible distortion in the corridor, no sudden change in light or structure, no dramatic interruption to mark the moment. And yet the air thinned slightly around them, as though a quiet guiding current had withdrawn.

Rhazien felt it first.

The subtle pressure that guided movement everywhere else in the Academy. The quiet current that encouraged bodies toward doorways and down corridors thinned around him. Not resistance. Not force. Just the removal of direction.

When he stepped left, the corridor did not open.

When he paused, it breathed.

Zephyr slowed beside him, eyes flicking from the slate to the archway ahead. His expression sharpened, thoughtful rather than surprised.

"Interesting," he murmured. "It's pretending we chose this."

Soren took two more steps before realizing the others were no longer beside him. He turned, frowning.

"Hey. Why does it feel like the building just… blinked?"

Veya hadn't spoken. Her hand lifted toward the wall, stopping just short of contact, as if the space between her skin and the stone carried its own quiet current. The surface felt warm, not burning, not alive, but familiar in a way she couldn't explain.

Behind them, the rest of the students moved on, unaware. Laughter echoed faintly. Boots scuffed stone. Somewhere down the hall, a door sealed with a sound like a thought finishing itself.

Ahead of the four of them, the corridor widened.

This space was not marked on any map.

The Academy did not use this chamber often. It reserved it for moments when observation mattered more than instruction, when it needed to watch without being seen.

There was no dramatic reveal. The corridor simply curved and opened into a circular chamber of pale stone. The walls swept inward with deliberate precision, etched with wards so old they were no longer ornamental but structural. The sigils had been carved deep, layered over older scars, as though the room had been revised rather than rebuilt.

The air carried a low hum that settled behind the ribs rather than in the ears, a vibration so subtle it felt internal, as though the chamber had found a frequency that belonged to bone instead of sound. It was steady and unhurried, neither rising nor falling, but holding in a way that suggested patience. Not passive patience, but the kind that waits because it already knows what will happen next.

The space itself offered no guidance.

There were no desks arranged for instruction, no lectern or marked focal point to imply authority. No instructor stood waiting to frame the moment or soften its purpose. And perhaps most unsettling of all, there was no visible exit. No obvious seam in the curved stone, no hinge or archway to suggest retreat.

The room did not appear designed for learning.

It appeared designed for assessment.

Soren stopped just inside the threshold and looked around slowly.

"All right," he said, his voice echoing a little too cleanly. "This is definitely not Hall Cinderreach."

Zephyr stepped in beside him, his gaze already tracking the etched wards. "No," he replied mildly. "This is an internal calibration chamber."

Soren glanced at him. "Is that supposed to make me feel better?"

"It shouldn't," Zephyr answered pleasantly.

His attention followed the faint pulse running through the walls. "This is where the Academy observes response patterns like panic, compensation, stabilization, and resistance."

Soren huffed. "So just a friendly little stress evaluation."

The hum deepened, it was not louder, but closer.

Veya stepped farther into the chamber, her movements slower than the others, as though instinct had told her not to rush. The sensation followed almost immediately, settling along her spine. Not as pressure and not as force, but as presence. It felt like a hand placed lightly between her shoulder blades, neither guiding nor restraining, simply aware.

The awareness lingered there, quiet and deliberate,

as though the chamber were assessing her posture, the cadence of her breath, the way she balanced herself against uncertainty. It was not invasive. It did not prod or provoke. Instead, it observed with a patience that felt older than the wards etched into the stone.

The hum in the walls did not spike the way it had with the others. It did not strain or recalibrate.

It steadied.

For a fraction of a second, the frequency aligned. Not louder, not brighter, but cleaner, as though something within the chamber had found a familiar pattern and adjusted around it rather than against it.

Veya swallowed.

She had the strange impression that the room was not measuring her to determine strength or weakness.

It was confirming something.

The warmth beneath her palm deepened, subtle but undeniable, like recognition held carefully in reserve. For an instant she had the strange, unsettling impression that the stone already knew her pattern well enough to adjust around it.

Across the chamber, one of the older wards pulsed once. Slow and deliberate, before settling again, as if acknowledging her presence and deciding, for now, to say nothing more.

Soren rolled his shoulders once. "If something jumps out of the floor, I'm blaming you," he muttered to Zephyr.

Zephyr's mouth curved faintly. "You assume it needs to jump."

Then the voice spoke.

It did not echo from above or project from the walls. It resonated through the etched wards themselves, neutral and stripped of warmth. It sounded less like speech and more like a system resolving into language.

"This is not an exam."

The sigils along the walls ignited in faint overlapping layers.

"This is calibration."

The floor began to change.

Not visibly at first, but the sensation underfoot altered. Weight redistributed itself. Gravity leaned sideways by a fraction, and it was enough to matter.

Soren swore as he stumbled, lightning snapping instinctively along his knuckles before he forced it down.

"Hey, I didn't do anything!"

"Response noted."

The words were not judgment.

They were record.

The chamber did not simply observe responses. It archived them, compressing every reaction into a pattern the Academy could store, revise, or remove as necessary to preserve stability.

Instability was not erased immediately. It was catalogued first, studied carefully, and only later compressed into a version of events that the system could safely sustain.

Air pressure spiked, then dropped. Wind stirred, not summoned, not shaped, but present.

Zephyr moved first.

"If this is calibration," he said calmly, palms open, "then increasing pressure without context proves very little. It encourages instability."

The wards flickered.

"And instability," he added, "rarely reveals useful data."

The hum shifted.

Veya inhaled slowly, grounding herself. The warmth along the walls pulsed in time with her breath. She hadn't cast anything. Neither had the room.

And yet…

The stone listened.

Rhazien said nothing.

He stood where he was, weight evenly distributed,

shoulders relaxed, eyes half-lidded as though the shifting chamber were only mildly inconvenient. He did not reach outward. He did not brace.

He was already contained.

The hum deepened again, threading through the wards with a subtle vibration that seemed to probe the edges of his restraint.

No flame rose from him. No spark flared in defiance.

And yet the air around his body warped faintly, the way heat shimmers above stone long after a fire has burned out. It was not visible flame, and it was not the chamber reacting. It was the residue of something contained so completely that only its memory pressed outward like a suggestion of combustion held under discipline.

The wards nearest him flickered once.

Then they dimmed.

The intricate sigils along the wall simplified, strokes collapsing into cleaner geometry as if complexity were unnecessary. The chamber was not reacting to power.

It was recalibrating around restraint.

"Liminal stability confirmed."

Soren shot Rhazien a sideways look. "You want to translate that?"

Rhazien didn't blink.

Zephyr answered quietly. "It means he's standing on a threshold."

"And?"

"And the room isn't sure which side he belongs to."

Soren exhaled slowly. "That's not ominous at all."

The floor tilted again, sharper this time. Stone shifted beneath their boots, testing reflex rather than balance.

Rhazien adjusted without visible movement.

Inside, the familiar pressure coiled tight behind his

ribs. Vast. Patient. Watching the room watch him.

He did not let it surface.

Veya reacted before the second shift completed. Instead of correcting toward center, she stepped into the tilt, planting her foot where the pressure was strongest. Air moved with her, instinctive and reinforcing.

The warmth along the walls brightened. It was not flame, but resonance.

The hum faltered.

"Adaptive anchoring observed."

The pressure released.

The floor corrected so smoothly it felt as though it had never moved.

Silence settled across the chamber.

"Calibration complete."

A faint seam traced itself along the curve of the wall, so subtle it might have been dismissed as a trick of the light if one had blinked at the wrong moment. The stone did not crack or grind apart; it simply separated with deliberate precision, layers sliding soundlessly away from one another until a doorway stood where solid wall had been only seconds before.

There was no shift in temperature, no rush of air from beyond. The threshold revealed nothing but continuation.

"Proceed."

The word carried no urgency and no encouragement. It was not an invitation, and it was not a command. The Academy was not urging them forward, nor was it demanding obedience.

It had simply determined that they were permitted to continue.

They were not welcomed and not approved either. Instead, they were permitted.

They had met the minimum threshold required to move on, and nothing more.

There was no explanation offered, no dismissal to

signal completion.

Only permission to move forward.

Soren exhaled. "You know, if this is their version of 'getting to know us,' I'd hate to see the part where they try to kill us."

Zephyr's voice was almost gentle. "You will."

Rhazien remained quiet.

Veya did not look back as they stepped through, though she felt the absence of scrutiny like the removal of weight.

When they rejoined the corridor, noise rushed in the form of voices, footsteps, and nervous laughter. The Academy resumed its illusion of normalcy as though it had not just peeled them open and looked inside.

But something had shifted.

It wasn't loud or obvious, and nothing in the corridor openly acknowledged it. Students still moved between halls, voices overlapped in nervous laughter, and the Academy resumed its careful illusion of normalcy. And yet, as the four of them stepped back into the current of bodies and conversation, the space around them adjusted.

Eyes followed them now.

Not openly. Not in a way that invited confrontation. But glances lingered a fraction too long before sliding away. Conversations softened when they passed. A pair of fae near the stairwell fell abruptly quiet, wings drawing in tight against their backs as though minimizing themselves without meaning to.

It wasn't everyone.

Just enough to feel deliberate.

"Was that them?" someone whispered, not quite softly enough.

The words drifted just behind Soren's shoulder before dissolving into the general noise of the corridor.

Soren heard it. Grinned too sharp. "Wow. First morning and we're already legends."

"Or liabilities," Zephyr replied, tone light, gaze not.

A dragon shifter watched Rhazien with open caution before turning away. A goblin student scribbled something rapidly onto their slate.

Veya felt the space around her widen. Not in avoidance, but recalculation.

"They've been told to watch," Rhazien said quietly.

"By whom?" Soren asked.

Zephyr smiled thinly. "By the building."

Ahead, the corridor split again.

Four names glowed faintly on a slate embedded in the wall.

One direction.

Not because they fit.

Because together, they had not broken.

Somewhere deep within the Academy, stone shifted. Not in warning but in preparation.

176

Chapter

Eighteen

What People Say Instead of Asking
Astriyx Dining Hall

By the time the Academy released them back into its wider corridors, nothing looked different.

The halls still echoed with footsteps. Slates still glowed faintly with destinations and times. Students still moved in neat currents toward meals and morning instruction, as if Arcane Academy could be reduced to routine if enough people pretended.

Only the pressure had changed.

Not heavier exactly but more aware. Like the building had taken a measurement and now the corridors remembered it.

Rumors never announced themselves. They arrived already shaped. By midday, the word calibration had detached from its origin and begun to mean whatever the speaker needed it to mean: a test, a punishment, a blessing, a warning. All of it. None of it.

Veya felt it before she heard it.

The Astriyx Dining Hall shifted when they entered, trays in hand. Not silence, it was never silence, just a subtle rearranging of sound. Conversations didn't stop. They angled. Laughter continued half a second too late. Someone dropped a fork and swore louder than necessary, like noise could cover nerves.

Soren's tray balanced in one hand, his other already twitching like it wanted to point at every stare. "Ah," he murmured. "We've achieved ambient notoriety."

Zephyr's mouth curved faintly. "Not yet. This is speculation."

"Speculation with eye contact," Soren muttered. "Which is the worst kind."

Rhazien said nothing. He took the longest route between tables without appearing to do so, his steps threading around clusters the way smoke avoided a draft. The heat under his ribs pressed inside me steady, contained, and patient.

They sat.

Two tables over, a voice carried with the special care people used when they wanted to be overheard while pretending, they didn't.

"…they broke a crystal," someone said.

"Two, actually."

"No way," a wolf shifter scoffed. "You don't break resonance spheres unless you're pushing."

"That's what I said. They *let* it happen."

Another voice cut in, sharper. "Or the Academy wanted it to happen."

That word landed.

Wanted.

Soren snorted softly. "Oh good. Conspiracy already."

Veya stared into her cup until the surface stilled. The stone beneath the table held a trace of warmth, the kind that wasn't heat, but after-pressure, like a hand had rested there a long time and the world hadn't cooled.

Not fire.

Memory.

She let it ground her.

Zephyr leaned back, posture lazy, eyes half-lidded. He listened without looking like listening was a talent, not an accident. "Notice how the story keeps changing," he said quietly. "First it was 'the corridor moved.' Then it was 'they broke the crystal.' Now it's 'the Academy chose them.'"

"And what is it really?" Soren asked, though his eyes had already flicked to the nearest group pretending not to stare.

Zephyr's gaze slid to Rhazien, not asking, just acknowledging.

Rhazien shrugged once. "The building watched."

"That's not reassuring," Soren muttered.

Across the hall, a group in Astrael blue had stopped pretending. He was a tall, sharp-featured, lightning sigil stitched proudly at the collar rose from their bench and began walking toward them.

Here it comes, Soren thought, almost relieved. The confrontation was at least honest.

The student didn't shout. Didn't posture. That was almost worse.

He stopped at the edge of their table, his gaze flicking over them like inventory. "Eclipse Unit," he said, like it tasted odd. "You're the ones who got… rerouted."

Soren smiled politely in the way people smiled before they bit. "Rerouted is such a friendly word."

The boy ignored that. His eyes stayed on Veya a fraction too long, then snapped away like he'd touched something hot in the air. "What happened in there?"

"We ate breakfast," Soren said.

Zephyr sighed. "He means the chamber."

Soren's smile sharpened. "He should ask what he means, then."

The Astrael boy's jaw ticked, annoyance flaring. "I'm asking."

Rhazien finally lifted his gaze. Not threatening.

Just present. "No," he said calmly.

The boy's eyes narrowed, but his posture adjusted a half-step back, involuntary.

Veya watched it happen and felt a strange flicker behind her eyes, like a name trying to rise and failing at the last second. She recognized the boy's face. She was sure she had seen him earlier. Orientation? The slate hall? Someone had said…

J…?

The thought slipped, clean as oil off stone.

She frowned faintly, unsettled by the blank edge of it.

Soren noticed immediately. He leaned closer to her, voice low. "Are you okay?"

Veya blinked once. "Yeah. I just…" She tried to catch the name again. It wasn't there. "Nothing."

Zephyr's eyes sharpened on her for a heartbeat, the lazy mask cracking just slightly.

The Astrael boy tried again, more cautious now. "People are saying the Academy's paying attention to you."

Soren's laugh was quiet. "People say lots of things instead of asking why they're afraid."

The boy bristled. "I'm not afraid."

Zephyr tilted his head, pleasant. "That was an answer to a question no one asked."

Soren leaned back, satisfied. "See? You're learning."

The boy's gaze flicked to the high balconies where faculty silhouettes sometimes hovered like statues. "Constellaria has been watching too," he said, quieter. "Virenna…"

Zephyr's voice went mild and sharp. "Don't say her name like it's protection."

The boy's mouth tightened. For a second he looked younger. Then he forced his posture into something confident again. "Whatever happened… you should be careful. They don't watch people they plan to leave alone."

Soren's eyes narrowed. "Thanks for the advice, mystery Astrael."

The boy hesitated. "My name is…"

And Veya felt it again: that strange slip, that sanding of detail, as if the moment tried to erase itself as it happened.

His mouth moved.

The dining hall's sound swelled at exactly the wrong time.

And whatever name should have landed… didn't.

The boy's expression shifted, confused for a heartbeat like he'd also felt it.

Soren blinked. "Did you just forget your own name?"

Zephyr's gaze went very still.

Rhazien's fingers tightened once on the edge of his tray.

The Astrael boy stared at them, then shook his head like he could dislodge the feeling. "It doesn't matter," he said, too quickly. "Just… watch yourselves."

He turned and walked away.

Soren tracked him with narrowed eyes. "Okay," he murmured. "That was weird."

Veya stared at the retreating Astrael blue and tried, one last time, to hold the name in her mind.

It slid away again.

Not forgotten like a lapse.

Forgotten like a decision the world made without her consent.

Zephyr's voice came quiet. "Did you feel that?"

Soren frowned. "Feel what?"

Zephyr didn't answer immediately. His gaze drifted to the stone columns, the lanternlight, the living architecture that hummed beneath everything.

"The Academy," he said at last, "isn't the only

thing that records."

Rhazien's voice was low. "And something else is editing."

Veya's stomach tightened. She forced herself to breathe, forced her fingers to unclench around her cup.

Across the hall, another whisper carried:

"…they're not just a unit. They're a problem."

"…No," someone replied. "They're a warning."

Soren's smile returned, all teeth. "Cute."

Zephyr's mouth curved faintly. "Not cute."

Rhazien didn't look away from the corridors. "It's beginning," he said.

Veya stared down at her cup again.

The surface reflected her face, steady and ordinary.

But the warmth in the stone beneath her hands suggested something else entirely:

That the Academy hadn't finished watching them.

It had only started deciding what it wanted to forget.

Chapter

Ninteen

The Wrong Kind of Favor
Astriyx Dining Hall

The Astryx dining hall never truly quieted. It only shifted with voices lowering, attention angling, and interest sharpening when something worth watching presented itself.

They hadn't left their table. They hadn't needed to.

"Calibration," the Astrael student said, stopping just short of their bench. "That's what they're calling you, right?"

Up close, the resentment was carefully groomed, it was the kind that formed in communal spaces where witnesses mattered. Polite tone. Tight smile. Hands steady.

"Yes," Zephyr said mildly. "We didn't pick the name."

"Funny how that works," the student replied. "Four first-years rerouted by the Academy itself. Extra assessments. Broken instruments." He gestured vaguely. "Looks a lot like favoritism."

Soren leaned forward. "You say that like it came with snacks." A flicker of irritation.

"You don't deny it."

Veya looked up then. Her voice was quiet, even. "What do you think we were given?" The student hesitated. "Access," he said finally. "Attention. Protection."

Rhazien met his gaze for the first time. "No," he said. One word. Flat. Certain. With a ring of finality in it.

The student scoffed. "Right. Because the Academy bends itself for free."

Zephyr tilted his head. "It doesn't bend," he said. "It measures."

"And what did it measure?" the student pressed.

Soren laughed, sharp, humorless. "How fast things go wrong."

That earned a few looks.

"You think we were advanced?" Soren continued. "We were separated. No syllabus. No warning. No safety buffer." He gestured vaguely toward the ceiling. "Whatever that room was, it wasn't a reward."

The Astrael student's jaw tightened. "You're saying you didn't benefit."

"I'm saying," Zephyr cut in gently, "that if this were favor, there would have been instruction."

Veya added softly, "Or reassurance."

Silence stretched. Not in agreement but in recalculation.

The student glanced around. Others were watching now. Measuring him. "You'll burn out," he said finally. "That's what happens to experiments."

Rhazien's presence shifted, not outward, not threatening, just enough that the air remembered heat.

"Maybe," he said. The student flinched despite himself.

"But experiments imply control," Rhazien continued. "We weren't controlled."

There was absolute silence for a beat, before Rhazien replied, "We were tested."

The Astrael student stepped back, color rising in his cheeks. Not from fear, but from realizing he'd challenged something he didn't understand.

"Enjoy it while it lasts," he muttered, and walked away.

For a moment, no one spoke. Then Soren exhaled. "Wow. First confrontation. Three out of five stars. Would've liked more drama."

Zephyr glanced at him. "You almost lost your temper."

"Almost," Soren agreed.

"That's growth." Veya smiled faintly, then let it fade. "They're not wrong about one thing."

"Which?" Zephyr asked.

"They're watching us now," she said.

"Not just the Academy." Rhazien nodded once. "That's the real calibration."

Conversation crept back into the dining hall. But it altered... Less speculation. More caution. "...the corridor changed," a goblina whispered nearby.

"That happens," her companion said. "Not like that. That was selection."

The word spread. Calibration. The name "Crystal-breakers" weas whispered around them in harsh and judgmental tones.

"One of them, the fea boy, didn't even register," she said, "That's worse."

Soren tipped his chair back. "Ah. We've reached the part where we stop being people."

"And become examples," Zephyr added calmly.

"Explosives," someone laughed. "That's what they are."

Soren's chair hit the floor. "Wow. I was aiming for mysterious but charming."

"Explosives don't suggest longevity," Zephyr said mildly. "Rude."

"Accurate."

Veya had gone still. "They're not afraid of what you did," she said quietly. "They're afraid it happened without you trying." That landed harder than laughter.

Zephyr inclined his head. "That's a durable reputation."

Later, still in the dining hall, when trays had been abandoned and most students lingered instead of leaving, another third year confronted them. He had the posture of someone who had learned where to stand in a room, so others adjusted around him. His shoulders squared, expression controlled, confidence earned through survival rather than rank.

"You get pulled aside," he said evenly. "Private rooms. No instructors. No syllabus." His gaze lingered on each of them in turn. "Looks like favoritism."

Veya stood first. Not fast. Not defensive. But Calm, steady."We didn't ask for it."

"That's what everyone says."

"No," she replied, meeting his eyes. "Everyone says they earned it."

Discomfort rippled outward, subtle but unmistakable.

"You think being watched is a reward?" Rhazien asked.

Soren grinned thinly. "We weren't chosen," he said. "We were useful." That did it. The word passed through the hall like a pressure drop.Useful…Not favored. Not protected but applied.

"Guess Calibration's not a club I want to join," someone muttered. The name settled then. It was no longer a title, but a warning.

As the noise slowly returned, Zephyr leaned in, voice light but eyes sharp. "On the bright side, we have a name."

"I hate it," Soren said immediately.

Veya scanned the room around them. Noting those leaning closer now, and those edging away. "They'll keep watching."

"Let them," Rhazien said quietly. "Calibration cuts both ways."

Somewhere deep in the Academy, wards adjusted around them. Not to protect, not to favor, but to observe. Their attention widened, patient and impersonal, tracking not only the noticed, but the overlooked.

Potential was not a promise here. It was pressure and not everyone survived it.

By the time the midday break thinned and the murmurs sharpened into something more deliberate, they had all had enough.

Rumors followed like static. Misplaced jealousy bled into fear, and fear into speculation. None of it was worth answering.

Without discussion, they left together.

The walk back to the unit dorms was quieter than the hall had been not because the Academy stilled for them, but because no one quite knew what to say now that the story had faces. Eyes tracked their movement. Conversations thinned as they passed. Soren kept his grin in place, sharp and deflective. Zephyr's expression remained pleasant, and unreadable. Rhazien walked half a step behind, his presence contained, heat leashed tight beneath his ribs.

Veya didn't speak. She didn't need to.

The Constellaria Wing accepted them without ceremony. Lanterns brightened just enough to guide, then dimmed again. The corridor felt unchanged, familiar stone, steady wards, the low hum of magic doing its work.

Too unchanged.

Their door stood where it should have been.

Soren reached for the handle.

It was if the room exhaled, not wind, not sound but a subtle release of pressure, like a held breath finally let go.

The door slid open.

The dorm was still recognizably theirs…but wrong in ways that took a moment to register.

The beds had shifted.

Not rearranged dramatically. Not scattered. Just…redistributed. The spacing between them was wider. The common area stretched longer than it had before, the floor subtly re-angled so that no one stood quite at the center anymore.

Zephyr stepped inside first, eyes narrowing. "That's new."

Soren followed, stopping short. "Okay, no, I am very sure my bed was closer to the window."

Veya felt it immediately. The warmth she'd unconsciously settled into this space, gone. Not erased. Displaced. The light near the far wall no longer softened for her. It held steady instead, neutral and unhelpful.

Rhazien remained in the doorway a beat longer than the rest of them. The wards skimmed him differently now. Less curious. More… procedural.

"Did we do something?" Soren asked, half-joking, half-not.

Zephyr didn't smile. "No. Something finished."

The room adjusted again. Just a fraction. A low hum passed through the stone, wards folding and unfolding like pages being turned.

Then, faintly, carved into the wall near the door where there had been nothing before, words surfaced. Not glowing. Not announced. Simply present.

UNIT ECLIPSE STATUS: PROVISIONAL

Below it, smaller.

CONFIGURATION SUBJECT TO CHANGE

There were no signature and no explanation.

Veya's breath caught. Not fear but recognition.

"They told us," She said quietly, "just not like this."

Soren stared at the wall. "Wow. I really hate it when the building makes a point."

Rhazien closed the door behind them. The sound was soft and final. "Units aren't permanent," he said evenly. "They never were."

Zephyr glanced at him. "You sound unsurprised."

"I was warned," Rhazien replied. "Just not when."

Silence settled in the dorm, it was not uncomfortable, but alert. The dorm no longer felt like shelter. It felt like an arrangement, temporary, conditional and measured.

Somewhere deep in the Academy, stone shifted again. Not to protect, not to punish, but to prepare.

The first adjustment had been made.

It would not be the last.

Chapter

Twenty

Next Morning- After Math

Morning did not announce itself with violence this time. There were no tilting beds. No sudden light. Just a gradual brightening, lanterns warming from embers to glow, like the Academy had decided subtlety was more efficient now.

Veya woke already alert because the room felt… finalized. Not settled. Finished. Like a calculation that had reached a conclusion and moved on.

She sat up slowly. The dorm remained in its altered configuration. No sign of last night's adjustment reverting. No apology etched into the stone.

Across the room, Soren was already awake, propped on one elbow, staring at the wall where the provisional notice still lingered faintly but less visible now, though not gone.

"Please tell me that disappears if I ignore it long enough," he said.

Zephyr, seated cross-legged near the window, didn't look up. "It won't. Stone doesn't bluff."

Rhazien stood near the door, arms folded loosely, his gaze unfocused. Not watching the room but listening to it. "The wards stabilized sometime before dawn," he said. "That usually means policy followed action."

"That's comforting," Soren muttered. "In a deeply threatening way." Veya swung her feet to the floor. The stone was cool. Neutral. Unresponsive. "Let's check the slate," she said.

No one argued.

The Curriculum Hall was louder than it had been the day before. Not chaos, but tension. Students clustered closer to the stone tablets than necessary, voices low, movements sharp. Rumors had matured overnight.

Their slate waited where it always had. Carved, permanent and always unforgiving.

Soren leaned in first and froze. "…Oh," he said.

Zephyr stepped closer. His expression shifted but not in surprise, but interest edged with concern. "They added a section."

Rhazien said nothing. Veya moved beside them and read. The new text had been etched deeper than the rest.

Not appended.

Integrated.

ADDITIONAL CORE REQUIREMENT: EFFECTIVE IMMEDIATELY

All students must complete no fewer than two courses outside their primary guild alignment.

One course aligned with a complementary guild

One course aligned with a conflicting guild

Assignment determined by the Academy.

Refusal constitutes withdrawal.

Silence stretched.

Soren broke it first. "So. Just to be clear. This isn't a fun enrichment thing."

Zephyr smiled faintly. "No. This is exposure therapy with teeth."

Veya scanned downward. Names had already begun to appear beneath the rule. It was written cleanly and carved, as if the stone had never known hesitation.

Her breath stilled. "…I have additions."

Soren leaned over her shoulder. "Please tell me it's something gentle. Like Applied Meditation." She didn't smile. "Lumora," she said. "Advanced Light Conduction." Zephyr's brow lifted. "That tracks." Looking up "And Astrael," she added quietly. "Atmospheric Dynamics."

Soren barked a laugh. "Oh, come on. That's not even subtle." She glanced at him. "You too." His laughter cut off. "Wait, what?" Soren read his own name. Once then twice.

Astrael. Lumora. "…They're putting us together," he said slowly. "Again," Zephyr corrected.

Rhazien shifted his weight. "And separating others." Zephyr's name had resolved beneath his own additions.

**Veilyn- Shadow Systems and Concealment
Eldrin- Structural Equilibrium**

Rhazien's appeared directly beneath. With the same two classes.

Same order.

Same depth of carving.

Soren squinted. "Okay, no offense, but that feels… deliberate." Veya felt it then, felt the wrongness of it. Not danger. Design.

"They put them together," she said quietly.

Zephyr's expression sharpened. "Of course they did."

Rhazien read the slate once. That was enough. "These aren't opposing studies," he said. "They're adjacent."

"Edges," Zephyr agreed. "Places where definition fails."

Soren frowned. "You're saying…"

"They want to see what happens when concealment and restraint share a framework," Zephyr said calmly.

"And whether anything leaks," Rhazien added.

The stone did not deny it.

Around them, reactions rippled, clear signs of relief from some, but also open dread from others. A fae student stared at her slate like it had personally betrayed her. Someone laughed too loudly and didn't stop.

"This wasn't announced," Soren muttered. "No warning."

"Why would there be?" Zephyr replied. "They're not teaching preference. They're testing cohesion."

Veya exhaled slowly. "They're cross-threading us."

"If one of us fails," Soren said, "it echoes."

Rhazien nodded once. "That's the point."

The hum beneath their feet deepened, satisfied not with compliance, but with motion.

Classes awaited.

None of them were where they belonged anymore.

And Zephyr, for the first time since arriving, looked genuinely thoughtful rather than amused.

"That," he said quietly, "is either very smart." Soren glanced at him. "Or very stupid." Zephyr smiled thinly.

"The Academy doesn't make that distinction."

Chapter

Twenty-One

Veilyn Class
Zephyr and Rhazien

The corridor leading to the Veilyn classroom narrowed the farther they walked. Not because the stone shifted, but because perception did. The walls remained fixed. The distance between them simply felt smaller, as though space itself rationed comfort.

Zephyr noticed immediately.

Rhazien did not comment, but his pace adjusted by a half step, placing himself either ahead or behind but exactly beside her.

"Interesting," Zephyr murmured, eyes flicking to the etched sigils lining the passage. They weren't wards. They were records. "This hall is measuring us by what we notice, not what we do."

Rhazien inclined his head slightly. "Information before action," he said. "That tracks."

Zephyr glanced sideways. "You say that like you've survived places where action was… discouraged."

"Frequently," Rhazien said.

Zephyr exhaled softly. "Comforting. I enjoy being paired with people who speak like historical warnings."

The door did not announce itself. It was simply there one moment, open the next.

Inside, the Veilyn classroom was not dark.

That was the first lie.

Light filled the room with soft, indirect, reflected rather than sourced. No lanterns. No windows. Illumination came from polished stone and faint iridescence threaded through the walls themselves. Everything was visible.

Which made the shadows unsettling.

They did not pool.

They aligned.

Students were already seated, spaced irregularly, as though the room had decided where each belonged before they arrived. No podium waited at the front. No obvious place of authority.

When they stood still, they almost blended together. When they moved, color surfaced in violet, oil-sheen, shadow, like information revealing itself only when in motion.

The instructor stood off to the side.

They wore Veilyn colors without emphasis, deep violet threaded through shadow-black fabric that caught the light wrong, oil-slick iridescence shifting subtly with every movement. Their face was uncovered.

That mattered.

"Sit," the instructor said calmly.

No raised voice. No command.

Everyone obeyed.

Zephyr decided immediately, he didn't like Professor Cael Verityn.

Not because he was threatening.

Because he wasn't trying.

Veilyn students weren't feared in the open the way Astrael could be or admired the way Lumora often was. They were tolerated. Consulted when necessary. And quietly excluded from conversations that mattered most.

No one ever said they didn't trust Veilyn.
They simply behaved as though trust required distance.

Verityn stood like a man who had already calculated every possible outcome in the room and found none dramatic enough to react to. No theatrical shadows. No cultivated menace. His power didn't announce itself.

It sorted.

His face was unremarkable in the most infuriating way, handsome enough to trust, plain enough to forget. Dark hair, neatly kept. Eyes the color of old glass, reflective but revealing nothing. If Zephyr passed him in a crowd, he'd remember the conversation, not the man.

That, Zephyr suspected, was deliberate.

The room listened anyway.

Not because Verityn demanded attention.

Because everything about him suggested he decided who deserved it.

The shadows didn't cling to him. They didn't flee either. They behaved like information that knew better than to speak out of turn.

Zephyr had met dangerous people before.

This one wasn't dangerous.

He was decisive.

Which meant, Zephyr realized uneasily that if Verityn ever chose to ruin you, he wouldn't need to raise his voice or his hand.

He'd simply ensure the right people knew the wrong thing at exactly the right time.

Veilyn, indeed.

Verityn's gaze moved the way a surveyor's did not lingering, not curious, simply accounting. It passed over Zephyr like weight tested and set aside.

Then it paused.

Not stopped.

Paused.

Rhazien sat exactly where the room allowed him to exist without friction. Not in shadow. Not in light. Not claiming attention, not avoiding it either. His posture was neutral in the way only practiced neutrality ever was.

Verityn's eyes narrowed by a fraction.

Interesting.

The file had been clear:

Draconic. Nullwyrm. Cinderbound. Fire sealed.

Verityn trusted files.

He trusted behavior more.

A Nullwyrm should radiate pressure even at rest. Heat contained but present, like a forge banked under stone. There should have been tension in the air around him. A sense of restrained combustion.

There was none.

Rhazien did not feel like a dragon holding back.

He felt like something that had learned, with terrifying discipline, how to exist without announcing itself to the world or the world to it.

Not concealment.

Containment so complete it functioned like absence.

And yet the shadows did not inform against him.

They registered him correctly, draconic, contained, Cinderbound and then stopped making sense. They didn't lean. Didn't whisper. Didn't offer leverage the way they did around true Veilyn students.

They adjusted.

As if information itself had decided it would rather remain accurate than useful.

Verityn looked away.

Zephyr felt the shift and almost smiled.

Later, much later, he would understand what that moment meant.

Verityn knew exactly what Rhazien was.

The problem was that the classification explained almost nothing.

He'd decided to wait.

And for a man like Verityn, waiting was never

passive.

"So," Verityn said at last, folding his hands loosely. "You think Veilyn is about shadows."

A pause.

"That assumption kills people."

Unease rippled through the room.

"Veilyn is not secrecy for secrecy's sake," he continued. "We do not hide because we are afraid. We hide because truth is a weapon. Weapons are only useful when you control who holds them."

He turned slowly, his gaze sweeping the room.

"Identity is leverage. Memory is currency. Absence is power."

His eyes stopped briefly on Zephyr.

Then on Rhazien.

"Your first lesson," he said, "is not how to lie."

Silence settled.

"It is how to decide when truth is more dangerous."

With a flick of his fingers, the room shifted, not physically, but informationally.

Three sigils surfaced in the air between the rows. Dim. Translucent. Constantly rearranging.

"One of these is false information," Verityn said. "One is incomplete."

"One is true, and lethal if mishandled."

The sigils vanished.

"You will retrieve them," he continued calmly, "without knowing which is which."

A murmur broke out.

"You are paired," Verityn added. "Choose poorly, and you fail together."

The room adjusted.

Chairs nudged. Sightlines shifted. Shadows guided without touching.

Zephyr found himself standing beside Rhazien.

Of course.

Zephyr leaned closer. "Any preferences? Catastrophic failure or slow, educational regret?"

"Observation," Rhazien said.

Zephyr exhaled slowly. "You are going to make this semester extremely character-building."

"That is generally the goal of survival," Rhazien replied.

They watched.

Other students moved quickly, too quickly. Shadows leaned. Assumptions formed. A girl near the wall smiled confidently, her sigil snapped red and dissolved.

A boy reached for a reflection in the floor. The room hummed unpleasantly. Verityn made a note without looking up.

Zephyr frowned. "The room reacts to certainty," he murmured. "Not correctness."

Rhazien nodded. "And to intent."

They waited longer than anyone else.

Too long.

Pressure built.

Zephyr felt it the Veilyn itch, the offense of information withheld. His shadows twitched, eager.

"I don't like this," he muttered.

"You're vibrating," Rhazien observed quietly.

"I'm processing."

"You're about to do something avoidable."

Zephyr paused. "…probably," he admitted.

Then he acted.

Not with shadow.

Not with magic.

With assumption.

The air folded.

A sigil snapped into focus and detonated into narrative.

Not sound.

Not force.

Story.

False impressions flooded the space. Accusations. Rearranged memories. Students gasped, suddenly convinced of things that weren't true.

Verityn turned.

"Failure," he said calmly.

Zephyr swore under his breath. "Excellent. Public failure. My favorite learning environment."

Rhazien stepped forward.

He didn't counter the distortion.

Didn't suppress it.

He stood where the information thinned.

The false narrative bent around him, sliding off like water around stone. He adjusted his stance not blocking truth but denying the lie momentum.

The room quieted.

The sigil collapsed harmlessly.

Silence.

Verityn's gaze sharpened.

"Well," he said softly. "That was instructive."

Zephyr stared at Rhazien. "You resolved that by standing there."

"Yes."

"…I'm reconsidering my entire strategy."

"I recommend it," Rhazien said.

A nearby student laughed nervously. A tall girl with ink-dark eyes leaned over. "You two just saved our grades," she said. "I'm Mara."

"Zephyr," he replied. Then, after a beat, "I regret everything."

"Spectacularly," she agreed.

Rhazien inclined his head. "Rhazien."

Verityn returned to the center of the room.

"One of you acted with confidence," he said. "One of you acted with restraint."

His eyes lingered on Zephyr.

Then Rhazien.

"Only one of those survived the truth intact."

The class resumed, slower now. More careful.

Zephyr leaned closer. "I hate that you were right."

"You'll recover," Rhazien said.

"Eventually. Assuming Veilyn doesn't kill me first."

"If it does," Rhazien replied evenly, "it won't be because you lack intelligence."

Zephyr blinked.

Then smiled.

"That might be the nicest thing anyone's said to me today."

They failed the exercise.

They learned more than most.

And when the class ended, neither of them moved right away.

Some lessons, Veilyn understood, were not meant to be left behind too quickly.

Chapter
Twenty-Two

Intercession
Veya & Soren

The Astrael hall had been built before the Academy learned how to soften its edges. The stone rose high and bare, curved inward like a ribcage, as though the room had been designed to hold something dangerous and decided against escape instead. The sigils etched along the walls were older than the current Guild system. Older, Veya suspected, than most of the rules they were meant to enforce.

She hesitated at the threshold.

Soren didn't.

He stepped inside with the ease of someone who had never learned to ask permission, boots echoing sharply as he claimed a seat near the front. The sound carried. Several students turned. Astrael training always did that, it made people look up, made them aware of where they were.

"You're blocking the door," Soren said without turning.

Veya stepped forward, and the instant she crossed into the room the sigils responded, their light dimming in a controlled shift rather than fading outright, as if the space itself were subtly adjusting to accommodate her.

She felt it more than saw it, a slight pressure change, like the room had shifted its weight to accommodate her. She sat beside Soren, close enough to feel the warmth of his sleeve without touching it.

"You look pleased," she said.

"I am," Soren replied.

"That explains it."

Before he could respond, the doors sealed with a low, resonant sound that silenced the room.

Instructor Karex entered.

He did not announce himself. He did not need to.

There was nothing ceremonial about him, no robes, no visible focus but the room responded to his presence the way a blade responds to its sheath. Contained. Ready.

"Astrael," Karex said, "exists because waiting is a luxury."

No introduction. No pretense.

Soren leaned forward.

"Lumora teaches you to weigh consequence," Karex continued. "Astrael teaches you that consequence will happen whether you are ready or not."

His gaze swept the chamber with quiet authority before pausing, almost imperceptibly, on Veya. The look carried no accusation, only a measured evaluation that suggested conclusions were already forming.

"Today," he declared, voice steady and absolute, "you will learn Intercession."

The sigils etched into the walls ignited in immediate response, flaring with ancient light that surged through the chamber in widening arcs. Power gathered, folded, and then released.

The structure of the hall unraveled around them, dissolving into something far less predictable.

They stood within a fractured city square, suspended at the moment before collapse. Stone hung mid-fall. A conduit of unstable magic split the ground like a wound, energy pulsing unevenly through it. Figures its simulations, Veya realized they were caught in frozen moments of impending harm.

"This scenario is already failing," Karex said. "You are late."

The pressure in the air mounted.

"You may act," he said. "Or you may not. Acting early creates harm. Acting late permits collapse. Acting at all alters outcome."

A pause.

"Begin."

Students rushed forward.

Veya watched interference compound into chaos. Each attempt to help shifting harm rather than erasing it. She felt the system strain, felt the way each decision narrowed what was possible next.

Soren moved.

He didn't look at her. He never did when he was certain.

Wind surged as he redirected falling stone, shattered the conduit with brutal precision, anchored the failing barrier before it could rupture completely.

For a heartbeat, it worked. Then the consequences arrived.

Energy rippled outward. The healer screamed. The child was spared one disaster only to be caught in another.

Soren swore.

Karex observed without reaction. "Effective," he said. "And insufficient."

Soren turned sharply. "I stopped it."

"You redirected it," Karex corrected.

"You chose who paid the cost." Soren's jaw tightened.

"People were going to die."

"And they did," Karex said. "Differently." Silence pressed in.

"Would you intervene again?" Karex asked. "Yes," Soren said.

No hesitation.

Something unreadable crossed Karex's expression. Then he looked at Veya. "You have not acted."

"I know."

The scenario strained around her. Pressure built. The system waited, not passively, but expectantly.

"You are allowing instability," Karex said. "I'm listening," Veya replied. "To what?"

She watched the way the energy wanted to settle, the way collapse could either shatter outward or fold inward depending on where it was permitted to go "To what it's becoming," she said quietly, studying the way the instability gathered at the edges of the conduit.

For a moment the pressure in the square shifted, almost imperceptibly, as if the system itself were waiting to see which direction it would be allowed to turn.

She stepped forward once.

No spell.

No force.

She made one adjustment.

The conduit collapsed inward, consuming its own excess. The falling stone shifted just enough. The healer was freed hurt, but alive. The child never felt the impact at all.

The square stabilized. The sigils dimmed. The hall returned. No one spoke.

Karex stared at Veya longer this time, he was not impressed but wary.

"That," he said, "was Intercession."

He dismissed the class without further comment.

As students filed out, Veya felt it, the subtle recalibration, the sense of something unseen recording outcome rather than action.

Outside the hall, Soren broke the silence. "You could've stopped it sooner."

"And then what?" she asked. "No one would've been hurt."

"They still were," she said. "Just not the same people." He looked at her then not challenging and not dismissive either but focused. "If I hesitate," he said quietly, "things get worse."

"If I don't," Veya replied, "they never change."

The space between them felt charged and fragile. Somewhere behind them, the Astrael doors remained closed a moment longer than necessary.

Neither of them noticed the sigil that flickered once before going still.

Far below the Academy, in the deepest archive where no students were permitted, an old record adjusted itself. A line of notation shifted, not erased, simply moved into a place where fewer eyes would ever think to search.

Threshold observed.

Balance deferred.

Witness required.

Instructor Karex paused in the corridor above, listening to something only he could hear and for the first time since the term began, the Academy watched back.

Chapter

Twenty- Three

The Quiet that Watches

The Academy did not congratulate them. It never did. It simply adjusted, quietly and efficiently, like a system that had recorded a result and moved on.

But that night, the air outside their dorm felt wrong in a different way. It was not evaluative, not mechanical either but aware.

The shift began so subtly that at first, no one noticed.

It wasn't a sound.

Not a visible change.

Just a quiet adjustment in the air, like the moment a room settles after a long conversation ends and no one quite remembers when the silence began.

Classes had finished for the day. The Academy grounds glowed beneath the slow descent of evening, towers catching the last gold of sunset while the lake below reflected it back in fractured light. Students filtered through the open courtyards and winding stone paths, their voices low with exhaustion and relief after another demanding round of training.

There was nothing unusual and nothing alarming.

And yet, Veya felt it.

There was a stillness that did not belong to ordinary quiet.

She paused near the edge of the courtyard, fingers tightening slightly around the strap of her satchel. The air brushed gently against her skin, cool and deliberate, as though testing her presence the way one might test the temperature of water before stepping in.

Behind her, Soren slowed as well.

He didn't speak at first. He rarely did when something felt off. But his gaze sharpened, scanning the open grounds with the same instinctive alertness he carried into every fight, every trial.

"You feel that?" he asked quietly.

Veya nodded.

"It's… watching," she said before she could stop herself.

It wasn't hostile.

Not protective.

Just aware.

Students moved around them, laughing softly, comparing bruises, arguing about assignments. No one else seemed to notice the strange, suspended calm settling across the Academy like a held breath.

Then the first creature appeared.

It stepped from the tree line bordering the far side of the courtyard not dramatically, not with spectacle, but with the quiet confidence of something that had always belonged there.

A unicorn.

Its coat shimmered faintly in the fading light, not pure white but a soft, shifting silver that caught hints of blue and pearl with every movement. Its long mane drifted like fine threads of moonlight, untouched by wind. The horn spiraling from its brow glowed faintly, etched with markings too ancient to be decorative.

Conversation around the courtyard faltered. A few

students noticed.

Then more.

Unicorns were not unheard of on Mistara, but they did not wander casually through student grounds. They did not approach crowds. They did not linger without purpose.

This one did.

It moved slowly across the stone, hooves making almost no sound. Its gaze passed over clusters of students and without pause it almost seemed like it was measuring the students, perhaps, but uninterested.

Until it reached Veya and Soren. It stopped several yards away. Not close enough to invade space. Not distant enough to ignore.

Its head lifted slightly, luminous eyes settling first on Veya.

A strange warmth unfurled in her chest, it was not heat, not even magic but something older, steadier. Like standing at the shoreline of a vast ocean that recognized you without needing to explain how.

The unicorn's ears flicked forward.

For a moment its luminous gaze lingered on Veya with a strange, patient stillness, as though it were searching for the outline of something that had not fully taken shape yet. Something unfinished, but inevitable.

Then its attention shifted.

To Soren.

The air changed again.

A faint current stirred around him, subtle but unmistakable. The creature's nostrils flared once, as if scenting a distant storm carried on high winds. For a brief second, the tip of its horn brightened just enough to be noticeable, before dimming again.

It lowered its head.

Not submission.

Not quite a bow but acknowledgment.

Then it stepped aside, retreating to the edge of the

courtyard where it remained calm and observant.

Students began whispering immediately.

"Why is it here?"

"Is it someone's familiar?"

"No… unicorns don't just…"

"Who is it looking at?"

Veya exhaled slowly, unaware she'd been holding her breath. "That's new," Soren muttered. Before she could answer, a rush of wind swept gently across the courtyard. Not strong and not disruptive but very intentional.

Shadows passed briefly over the ground as something large circled above. Students tilted their heads upward, hands lifting instinctively to shield their eyes from the fading light.

A Pegasus descended from the open sky.

Its wings stretched wide, feathers catching the last rays of sunset and turning them to molten gold. It did not land immediately, instead circling once, twice, over the courtyard in slow, deliberate arcs. Each pass stirred soft currents that lifted loose hair and rustled robes without disturbing anything else.

Then it landed near the far fountain.

Its hooves touched stone with a resonant chime, like distant bells struck underwater. Folding its wings carefully against its sides, the Pegasus stood tall and still, powerful muscles visible beneath its luminous coat.

Its gaze moved across the gathered students.

Searching.

Measuring.

It paused on several fae, shifters, magic-born of obvious strength before continuing.

Then it reached Veya.

The air around her shifted, currents bending gently inward as if drawn by gravity rather than pushed by wind. The Pegasus's wings twitched once, feathers rustling with a faint, curious sound.

Its attention moved to Soren.

A soft crackle of static passed through the air, barely audible but enough to make nearby students glance around in confusion. The Pegasus gave a short, sharp huff, not alarmed, not aggressive.

Almost as if it were intrigued in him.

It stepped back not to leave but joining the quiet observation already underway.

More whispers spread through the courtyard, tension threading through curiosity.

"This is weird," someone whispered.

"They're not supposed to…" another voice started, only to be cut off by a dozen more.

Confusion rippled through the crowd, voices overlapping, sharp with unease.

"Why are they all coming here?"

Because they were.

Across the grounds, shapes began to reveal themselves. Near the lake's edge, a tall, antlered creature with a coat like starlit shadow emerged from between the trees, its many-pointed horns shimmering faintly as it watched from a distance. Along a distant parapet, a sleek, feathered serpent coiled silently around carved stone, eyes glinting with unsettling intelligence.

A pair of small, foxlike beings with multiple tails slipped through the hedges, pausing only long enough to glance toward the same two figures standing near the center of the courtyard before vanishing again into green.

And above it all there was fire.

A small burst of golden flame appeared near the highest tower balcony, hovering in place. It flickered once, then unfolded into the unmistakable shape of a phoenix. Its wings burned without consuming, feathers trailing soft sparks that dissolved before reaching the ground.

It did not descend.

It simply watched.

From the upper balcony, a faculty silhouette

paused, still as a ward and then continued walking, as if this had confirmed something rather than surprised them.

The courtyard had grown quiet now.

Not completely silent because the students still whispered, shifted, and stared, but the easy noise of afternoon had drained away, leaving something tighter in its place. Conversations faltered before they began. Movements slowed. Even the wind seemed to hesitate as it crossed the stone.

Everyone felt it.

The strange convergence.

The unspoken question hanging in the air.

Why here?

Why now?

Soren shifted beside Veya, the movement small enough that most people wouldn't have noticed. To anyone else he probably looked relaxed, shoulders loose, hands at his sides. But she could feel the tension in him anyway, coiled just beneath the surface like something ready to move the moment it had to.

"You seeing this?" he murmured, his voice low enough not to carry.

"Yes."

He didn't look at her right away. His attention stayed on the courtyard, scanning faces, exits, distances, measuring things the way he always did when something felt wrong.

"This isn't normal," he said after a moment.

"I noticed."

"That's not what I meant."

Now she glanced at him.

"You know why this is happening?"

"No."

The answer came too quickly to pretend it was anything else.

Soren studied her then, not suspicious, exactly, but searching, as if trying to decide whether she was leaving something out or simply standing in the same uncertainty he was.

"That's a problem," he said quietly.

"I'm aware."

He exhaled through his nose, his gaze shifting back toward the center of the courtyard where the air still felt heavier than it should have.

"It feels like something's waiting," he added. "Like everyone's already late to it except us."

Veya didn't answer immediately.

Because that was exactly what it felt like.

"No," she said at last, softer now. "It feels like something already found us."

That was the truth.

And yet somewhere deep inside, a quiet certainty stirred. Because this wasn't random and this wasn't coincidence.

The magical world, in all its strange and ancient forms, had begun to notice something. Not loudly. Not dramatically. But with the careful attention of forces that moved only when necessary.

The unicorn remained at the courtyard's edge.

The Pegasus stood near the fountain.

The phoenix watched from above.

Other beings lingered in shadow and distance.

None approached.

None spoke.

They simply acknowledged. As if recognizing something not yet fully revealed. A faint breeze curled through the courtyard then, brushing lightly against Veya's hair, carrying with it the distant scent of rain and open sky. It circled once around both of them in a gentle and deliberate way before dispersing into nothing.

For a moment, the world felt very large and very old. Then, as quietly as they had appeared, the creatures began to withdraw.

The foxlike beings vanished into hedges and stone.

The antlered watcher stepped back into forest shadow.

The serpent uncoiled and slipped from sight.

The phoenix dissolved into a final drift of golden sparks.

Last to leave were the unicorn and Pegasus. The Pegasus leapt skyward in a single powerful motion, wings catching the last light as it rose and disappeared into deepening dusk. The unicorn lingered only a heartbeat longer, luminous eyes resting once more on Veya… then Soren. Then it turned and walked calmly back toward the trees.

Gone.

The courtyard slowly filled with sound again with uncertain laughter, hushed speculation, and nervous energy breaking like a wave after held tension. Students spoke over one another, trying to make sense of what they'd just witnessed.

"Has that ever happened before?"

"No."

"Was it a test?"

"Who were they looking at?"

Veya didn't answer any of them. Beside her, Soren exhaled slowly, gaze still fixed on the place where the unicorn had stood.

"…Well," he said at last, voice low. "That can't be normal."

"No," Veya replied softly. "I don't think it is."

Neither of them spoke again as the last light faded and evening settled fully over the Academy. But somewhere beyond sight, beyond stone and sky and memory, something ancient had shifted.

And whatever had begun to wake… was now paying attention.

Chapter

Twenty- Four

Integration Assessment

The notice arrived the way the Academy did most things, without courtesy, without warning, and with the quiet certainty of something that expected compliance.

It wasn't slid beneath the door.

It wasn't delivered.

It was simply there the next time Veya looked.

A thin plate of stone had surfaced from the dorm wall near the common area, the lettering carved so cleanly it looked less written than decided:

INTEGRATION ASSESSMENT: REQUIRED
UNIT DORM: UNIT ECLIPSE ASSIGNMENT
TIME: IMMEDIATE
FAILURE RESULTS IN REASSIGNMENT

Soren read it once then twice. Then he smiled like it had personally insulted him. "Oh good," he said. "The Academy noticed we're alive."

Zephyr appeared behind him without sound, reading over his shoulder. "It noticed we were watched," he corrected. "That's different."

Rhazien said nothing at first. He stood near the window; his gaze angled toward the grounds where the last traces of sunset had faded. His posture was neutral, carefully so, but the air around him carried that subtle pressure of contained heat, banked deep and disciplined.

He looked back at the stone plate. "Reassignment," he said quietly.

Veya's stomach tightened.

They had barely begun to understand each other. Barely formed the shape of a unit.

The Academy didn't break things violently.

It broke them efficiently.

The stone plate warmed beneath her fingertips as if responding to her attention.

Then the dorm shifted. Not moving or not rearranging. Just… deciding.

The partitions softened into translucence. The floor's pulse deepened. A seam opened in the far wall where there hadn't been one, revealing a corridor of pale stone and faint iridescent light.

No one had to ask if it was meant for them. The Academy did not do invitations. It did inevitability.

The assessment chamber was not called a hall. There was no plaque. No sign. Only an archway cut into stone that looked older than the Wing itself.

Above it, a sentence had been carved in the same indifferent hand as their notice:

WHAT YOU ARE IS LESS IMPORTANT THAN WHAT YOU DO WHEN YOU ARE WRONG.

"Charming," Zephyr murmured. "I feel welcomed."

Soren stepped through first, of course. His confidence moved ahead of him like weather. Veya followed, shoulders squared.

Rhazien entered last, quiet enough that the air seemed to settle behind him as if relieved.

The chamber inside was circular, wide, and empty, until it wasn't. The room held no furniture. No podium.

No obvious authority and yet Veya felt it immediately: the sensation of eyes without a face. Attention without presence.

They were not alone. Not physically. Not spiritually. But institutionally.

The stone itself held memory. The walls had a faint sheen of records, no wards, and no protection. Just silent observation.

Soren lifted his chin, his gaze scanning the ceiling. "So," he called into the silence, "are we supposed to greet the invisible audience, or…"

The air shifted.

A voice spoke, calm and distant, as if transmitted through the architecture rather than spoken aloud.

"Begin."

No name. No introduction. No instructor stepping forward. The Academy didn't need a mouthpiece to judge.

The floor dissolved.

Not falling but replacing.

They were standing in a city square suspended at the edge of collapse. It was not the fractured simulation Karex had used. This was different.

This was worse.

Stone hung mid-fall, yes, but the air carried the smell of smoke and wet iron, and the sky above was a sickly gray-green, as if weather had been corrupted into something deliberate.

A Leylines' conduit split the ground like a wound, but it wasn't pulsing like energy.

It was pulsing like information. Patterns began shifting and rewriting themselves as if the square couldn't decide what kind of disaster it wanted to be.

Around them were people.

Not students.

Not illusionary mannequins.

The figures looked real enough that Veya's chest

tightened on instinct: a woman pressed against a wall shielding a child; a man kneeling with blood on his hands, staring down at something unseen; a boy frozen mid-step, eyes wide, about to run into falling debris.

Soren's hand twitched.

Veya caught his wrist. "Wait," she whispered. He looked at her like she'd sworn.

Zephyr's eyes narrowed. "They're anchored," he murmured. "Not alive. Not fully. But…"

"Convincing," Soren finished, jaw tight.

Rhazien watched the conduit instead of the people. Not unfeeling but precise. The ground beneath them hummed. The square waited. Above it all, something shifted in the sky.

It wasn't thunder. Not wind either. But pressure, like being regarded by something vast.

Veya felt it and hated it because it felt familiar.

The voice returned, still disembodied, still indifferent:

"You have learned."

A pause.

"You have assumed."

Another pause.

"You will demonstrate the difference."

The city square shuddered. The falling stone dropped a fraction.

The conduit's pulse accelerated. The disaster began. Students were not supposed to be used as instruments. But the Academy had never cared what was "supposed" to happen.

Soren moved.

Of course he did.

Wind surged around his arms as he redirected falling stone, catching slabs mid-air and flinging them aside with brutal precision. Lightning crackled along his skin, bright and impatient.

He stopped the first collapse.

Then the consequence arrived.

The conduit flared in response, and the redirected debris triggered a secondary collapse, an archway cracking, a support failing. The woman shielding the child jerked as if struck by an invisible shock.

Soren swore under his breath. "That's…"

"Intercession," Zephyr said dryly. "Congratulations." Soren shot him a look. "Now is not the time." Zephyr's grin flashed sharp. "Now is exactly the time. The Academy loves timing."

Veya forced herself to breathe.

The square was reacting to certainty again reacting to decisive intervention as if certainty itself was a destabilizing force.

She felt the hidden geometry within it, the way the conduit was meant to fold inward, to refine and concentrate, and how repeated bursts of force had driven it outward instead, distorting its balance.

She stepped forward without magic blazing in her hands. There was no strike, no surge, no visible command of power.

Only a single adjustment subtle and intentional, like easing one thread into place within a strained tapestry.

The pulse shifted. It didn't die. It corrected, realigning into something controlled and precise.

The flaring energy bent inward, consuming its own excess instead of spilling it into the city. The falling stone slowed, as if gravity itself had reconsidered its priorities.

Soren glanced at her, startled. "What did you do?"

"Less," Veya said softly. "I did less."

Zephyr's shadows stirred at his heels, twitching with impatience. "Wonderful," he muttered. "The solution is humility. Veilyn will be thrilled."

The square didn't let them recover.

A new distortion hit, this time, not physical but something more like a story. A rumor moved through the air like a living thing, sliding under skin, rearranging perception. The kneeling man suddenly looked up at Soren with terror like he recognized him as the cause.

The woman shielding the child turned her head and stared at Veya with accusation. The boy flinched away from Zephyr as if he'd just threatened him. Words formed on lips that hadn't been moving before.

The voices converged until they no longer sounded like panic, but judgment. They said we had caused this. That we had brought the collapse upon them. That the blame belonged to us.

Zephyr's posture tightened, his features smoothing into deliberate neutrality. "Oh," he said under his breath. "So, this is what they're testing."

The air thickened around us. This was not illusion, nor was it mind control. Nothing reached inside my head to bend my thoughts. Instead, the world itself adjusted, settling into a narrative where the lie had always been fact. The square did not flicker or distort; it simply behaved as though we were guilty.

Soren's breath hitched, and I felt the storm inside him respond, lightning gathering in instinctive defense. Every part of him wanted to end it. To tear the accusation apart before it could take hold.

Veya felt her own chest tighten, something ancient in her bristling at accusation. Not anger exactly. A sense of being misnamed.

Rhazien took one step forward. He didn't flare. He didn't burn.

He didn't counter the distortion with force. Instead, he stood where the narrative was thinnest and simply… refused to hold it.

The lie slid around him like water around stone. The accusations faltered where his presence was.

Zephyr blinked. "You're doing the thing again," he said under his breath. Rhazien didn't look at him. "Don't participate," he said quietly. Zephyr's jaw tightened.

"That's Veilyn heresy."

"It's survival," Rhazien replied. Zephyr hesitated. Then, very carefully he did something that looked like nothing.

He stopped trying to control the narrative and he stopped trying to correct it.

He let it pass through him without catching. The shadows at his feet aligned instead of lashing out.

The lie lost traction but it didn't vanish.

It simply… stopped gaining momentum.

The square shuddered as if disappointed. Soren exhaled, then, painfully he lowered his hands. Wind loosened. Lightning dimmed.

Veya shifted her weight, keeping her adjustment steady, resisting the instinct to "solve" everything at once.

For a fleeting moment, everything aligned. The conduit stabilized, the falling stone corrected into a safer pattern, and the accusing figures stilled as the square seemed to breathe again.

And then the Academy shifted the trial.

The sky flickered once, not with lightning, and not with magic, but with something far more deliberate.

Something like a blink. The entire simulation paused. It was not frozen but held. The air went too still. Veya felt it like pressure in her bones. Soren felt it too; his eyes lifted, narrowing. Zephyr's smile vanished entirely. Rhazien's shoulders tightened by a fraction the smallest break in his practiced neutrality. Something beyond the simulation was looking in.

Not the Academy but something older.

The pause lasted only a heartbeat.

Then the square resumed as if nothing had happened. But the conduit's pulse changed. It became… responsive. As if it had been listening to a different set of rules.

Veya swallowed.

This wasn't just an assessment anymore. This was

an assessment that had been noticed.

The voice returned, almost conversational in its indifference: "Continue." Soren's laugh was short and humorless. "Oh, I hate that." Zephyr glanced at him. "Welcome to Veilyn. We hate everything correctly."

Soren looked like he might argue, then stopped because the ground beneath them cracked again, and a new collapse began.

This time, they moved together.

Soren redirected with disciplined restraint, anchoring the surge instead of weaponizing it. Veya refined the conduit's inward fold, preserving their shared alignment as it strained under pressure. Zephyr shaped absence with surgical care, guiding shadow to disrupt certainty without turning it into open attack.

And at the boundary where the story itself tried to reclaim control, Rhazien held fast, refusing the lie even a single point of return.

They weren't perfect, and they weren't untouched by the strain but they remained standing, bound in a unity that was beginning to feel dangerous.

But they were coordinated. And the city did what it hadn't done at first: It responded like a system acknowledging competence. The disaster de-escalated.

The people figure around them softened, becoming less accusatory, less vivid. The square stabilized. Slowly, reluctantly, it conceded.

The simulation dissolved. They were back in the circular chamber, breathless in different ways.

No applause.

No announcement.

Just the quiet hum of stone recording result.

Soren rolled his shoulders, still keyed with leftover storm. "So," he said into the empty room, "do we pass, or do we die later?" Zephyr glanced at him. "That was your most reasonable question today."

Rhazien's gaze remained on the far wall. His

breathing was steady. Controlled. Too controlled. Veya looked down at her hands. They weren't shaking. That unsettled her more than it should have.

A seam opened in the stone wall, revealing a narrow exit corridor.

No voice told them to leave.

They were dismissed the way they were always dismissed: by the Academy moving on.

As they stepped toward the exit, Zephyr slowed slightly, falling into step beside Rhazien. "You know," Zephyr murmured, "you have a very irritating talent for making 'doing nothing' look like a strategy." Rhazien didn't look at him. "It is a strategy." Zephyr's mouth twitched. "Of course it is."

After a beat, Rhazien added, almost dryly, "You're improving." Zephyr blinked. Then he smiled, a genuine, but brief smile. "Don't say that out loud. It might ruin my reputation."

Soren, ahead of them, glanced back. "Are you two bonding?"

"No," Zephyr said immediately. Rhazien's pause was half a second too long. Soren's grin widened. "Adorable."

Veya didn't speak, but something in her chest eased. Not trust.

Not yet.

But the beginning of it.

Far below the Academy, within the lowest archive where students were never permitted to walk, an ancient record shifted and realigned.

It existed not as ink on parchment but as a living network of carved stone and bound memory, a system that did not forget and did not error.

With slow, deliberate precision, a new line etched itself into the record of their dorm assignment:

INTEGRATION: CONFIRMED (UNSTABLE)
OBSERVATION: INCREASED

EXTERNAL ATTENTION: VERIFIED

Another line appeared beneath it, smaller—almost reluctant:

SUBJECT: Veya- STRUCTURAL INFLUENCE DETECTED

SUBJECT: Soren- MAGNITUDE ESCALATION TREND

SUBJECT: Zephyr- SEVERANCE BEHAVIOR ADAPTATION

SUBJECT: Rhazien- CONTAINMENT DISCIPLINE (SELF-SEALED)

The record hesitated.

Then etched one final notation that did not belong to any curriculum.

CREATURE RESPONSE: NON-RANDOM WITNESS REQUIRED.

In the corridor above, a faculty silhouette paused, it was still as a ward, then continued walking, as if this had confirmed something rather than surprised them.

Far beyond stone and sky and the reach of memory, something ancient shifted in its long slumber. It did not rise, not yet, but its awareness turned, focusing with a quiet, unsettling intent that felt far too close.

"I am getting frustrated never getting answers. I am tired of waiting and waiting to find out what happens next or never getting answers for why," Soren said as we walked toward our next class, clear anger threading through his voice.

He dragged a hand through his hair, pacing half a step ahead before circling back again, like the corridor itself was too small to contain him.

"This place keeps testing us. Watching us. Throwing things at us and then, nothing. No explanation. No direction. Just more waiting."

"Soren," I said calmly, "you're not being ignored. You're being observed."

"That's not better," he snapped immediately. "That's worse." He wasn't wrong.

Soren has never been patient. That has always been my role in our duo since the day we met. He is movement forward, upward, into whatever comes next. Where he pushes, I measure. Where he burns, I anchor.

It has always been that way.

The assessment felt... curious. As if the Academy itself wasn't entirely sure what to do with us yet. Always assessing. Always watching. Measuring not just what we do, but what we are.

But if I am being honest, I am watching just as closely. Something in this place feels... aware. And something in me has begun answering back.

Rhazien has been more observant than usual. Quieter. Sharper. Sometimes I get the feeling he is waiting for something to go wrong like the Academy will strike at the worst possible moment and he intends to already be standing between it and the rest of us.

Sometimes I feel him near me before I see him.

Not hovering. Not obvious.

Just... aligned.

As if some instinct in him recognizes something I haven't said aloud.

Just as I have begun noticing Zephyr doing with Soren.

They move like storm and wind have already decided they belong together. Always in step. Always within reach. But sometimes I wonder if Zephyr stays close out of more than companionship. There is curiosity there. Amusement. Like he's watching something unfold that even Soren doesn't fully understand yet.

"Veya!... Veya!" Soren's voice snapped me out of my thoughts as he bumped into me. "Are you even paying attention? I need answers."

"I was," I said, steadying myself. "Just not the kind you're asking for." He stared at me. "That makes absolutely no sense."

"It does if you stop trying to force clarity," I replied evenly. "Things will come when they are meant to. For now, observe and learn. Everything here is a lesson, whether we like it or not."

"I am observing," he muttered. "What I'm observing is that no one tells us anything."

"You prefer being told what to do?" I asked softly. "That's not what I said."

"Then what do you want?" He stopped walking.

For a moment, the anger fell away and something more honest took its place. "I want…" His jaw tightened. "I want to know what we're walking into before it hits us."

There it was.

Not anger but instinct.

The same instinct that always drove him forward before the storm broke.

Before I could answer, "B—But—"

"Soren."

Rhazien's voice cut through the moment, calm but firm. He stepped forward slightly but not enough to interrupt, just enough to stand nearer.

"Veya is right."

Soren exhaled sharply. "You always take her side."

"I take the side that keeps us alive," Rhazien said, his tone calm and utterly certain. There was no need for defense in it only quiet conviction.

As the words left him, he moved with subtle precision, stepping just ahead and slightly to my side. The shift was so soft it would have gone unnoticed by anyone not watching for it.

I noticed.

The gesture wasn't possessive or territorial. It carried something steadier than that something instinctive. Protective.

Almost… reverent.

"You feel it too, don't you?" Soren said more quietly now, glancing between us. "Something's off. The way they watch. The way they measure."

"We all feel it," I said. "You're just the only one shouting about it."

A familiar amused voice drifted from behind us. "He does shout rather well," Zephyr said lightly. "Very committed to the experience." Soren groaned. "You're not helping."

"I'm not trying to," Zephyr replied cheerfully. "I'm trying to enjoy the mystery. Hidden motives. Secret observations. Looming danger. It's practically theatrical."

"You think this is entertaining?" Soren snapped. "Oh, absolutely," Zephyr said. "Watching powerful beings pretend they aren't being evaluated is always entertaining."

Rhazien glanced back at him. "This isn't a game."

"It never is," Zephyr agreed softly. "Doesn't make it any less interesting."

I exhaled slowly, letting the tension settle before it could sharpen further. "Everyone calm down," I said gently. "I need some fresh air. And we have about an hour until our next class. How about we get out of here and wander the grounds?"

Soren hesitated. "We're just... leaving?"

"Yes." Zephyr smiled faintly. "I support this decision. Before Soren attempts to interrogate the Academy itself."

"I am not"

"You are," I said.

He paused. Then sighed.

"...Fine."

Rhazien gave a small nod. "Fresh air is wise. Too many walls here listen."

Soren glanced between us; tension still coiled in his shoulders, but loosening. "...If something happens out there..."

"Then we face it," I said "Together."

The word wasn't spoken aloud. But something deeper than language settled between us anyway.

Chapter
Twenty- five

The Lake

Night at Arcane Academy didn't feel like rest. It felt like the Academy exhaling slowly and quietly. Like it had been holding its breath all day just to see what we would do.

We slipped out without calling it sneaking. The dorm didn't stop us. It didn't challenge us. It only watched, the way stone watches fire.

Soren walked ahead with the kind of energy that could never fully settle. Not pacing, exactly. But more like he was keeping himself from running.

"I swear," he muttered, "if I see another notice that says REQUIRED, I'm going to start carving REQUIRED into their foreheads."

Zephyr drifted above his shoulder, an amused shimmer more felt than seen. "Do it," he encouraged softly. "I support artistic expression."

Rhazien didn't respond. He rarely wasted words on Zephyr's provocations. He stayed close enough to register, far enough to be unreadable to most except to me, because somehow, I always noticed where he placed himself.

He placed himself near me often. He was never

close enough to touch but it was like a constant hovering. Just… aligned. Like if something shifted in the night, he wanted to be in position before it happened.

I exhaled and pulled my cloak tighter. "Fresh air," I reminded them. "That's all. No starting wars with signage."

Soren glanced back at me, mouth open like he had something sharp loaded and ready.

Then he sighed. "Fine. Fresh air." We walked.

The grounds were larger at night. Or maybe the dark just made distance feel more honest. Lanterns floated at irregular intervals, their glow soft and gold, like fireflies that had learned discipline. The paths curved when you weren't paying attention and straightened when you were. Mistara never allowed you to be careless for long.

Zephyr hummed contentedly. "I like it when the Academy pretends to be peaceful," he said. "It's adorable."

"It's never peaceful," Rhazien said quietly.

Zephyr's smile flashed. "Oh? And here I thought you were learning optimism."

Rhazien didn't look at him. "I'm learning patterns."

That shut Zephyr up for a full three seconds, long enough that I knew Rhazien had landed the point exactly where he wanted.

We drifted toward the lake without choosing it out loud.

Maybe the lake chose us.

It waited below the Academy like a dark thought. The water wasn't angry. It wasn't loud. It held itself with that glassy stillness that made you feel like moving too quickly would be disrespectful.

Moonlight laid a pale path across it, and the surface caught every star above. The lake was too clear, too clean, as if the sky had been folded neatly into the water and stored there.

Soren stopped at the edge and stared.

"Well," he said softly, almost unwilling to sound impressed, "that's… actually kind of insane."

Zephyr drifted forward like he belonged there. "Water likes to make itself look innocent," he said. "It's a liar."

"Everything here is a liar," Soren muttered, and kicked a small pebble into the lake.

The pebble didn't splash even though it should have.

It hit the surface and sank without sound, like the water had decided noise was optional.

My stomach tightened.

I didn't say anything at first. I just watched the place where it vanished, waiting for ripples that didn't come.

The stillness was too complete.

Rhazien moved a half-step closer, it wasn't dramatic and not obvious. But I felt the shift in his proximity the way you feel a storm build before you see it.

"Soren," I said quietly.

He turned at once, like he had been listening for my voice even before I spoke. His eyes found mine through the dim light, storm-gray and alert. "What?"

I nodded toward the lake, its surface too still, too smooth almost like glass laid over something breathing underneath.
"Do you hear anything?"

He frowned, tilting his head slightly as he listened. The usual restless energy around him with the crackle of barely contained lightning that always seemed to live just beneath his skin. It stilled, drawn inward, even his breathing slowed.

For a moment there was nothing. Only the faint whisper of wind through the trees and the distant creak of branches shifting against each other.

Then his expression changed.

Not fear but focus.

"…Yeah," he murmured, voice low. "Something's off."

He took a step closer to the water's edge, boots crunching softly against the damp earth. His eyes narrowed as he scanned the lake, searching not just with sight but with whatever instinct guided the storm inside him.

"It's like…" He hesitated, brow tightening. "Like something's trying not to be heard."

A chill slipped down my spine.

Zephyr's expression sharpened instantly, the lazy, amused air he usually carried vanishing as if it had never existed. The wind around him shifted, tightening, growing thin and sharp.

"Oh," he said softly, almost to himself. "Now that is interesting."

The air stirred, brushing past us in slow, deliberate currents that were no longer playful and no longer free. It moved with purpose. With attention.

Zephyr stepped forward, eyes fixed on the lake as if it had personally offended him.

"Stay where you are," he said lightly, though the tension in his voice betrayed the casual tone. "If something beneath that water has decided to wake… we would very much like to know why."

Soren didn't move back. If anything, he stepped closer to me instead, close enough that I could feel the faint hum of electricity along his skin.

"You hear it now, don't you?" he asked quietly.

I swallowed, staring at the glassy surface. "…Yes."

A sound just beneath the silence.

Soft. Rhythmic.

Waiting.

There were no frogs, no night insects, no distant calls of creatures in the trees… Just silence. Even the wind had softened into nothing.

It was as if the world had… paused.

Soren's grin faded. "Okay," he said. "That's weird." Zephyr's voice dropped, the humor thinning. "The water is listening."

"Is that a thing?" Soren asked. "Everything is a thing," Zephyr replied. Then, after a beat of silence he said, "Especially when you are near it."

I stepped closer to the shoreline. The air felt heavier here, not oppressive, just dense, like the night was holding more weight than it should.

We all looked into the dark water and lake reflected us.

All four of us.

But the reflection looked… too precise. As if the water wasn't copying what it saw. As if it was remembering.

My chest tightened with something I couldn't name. It was not fear not even anger but something older than either. It was like the sensation of being misread or misnamed.

I swallowed and in the moment the water moved, not outward but it was as if it moved inward.

A single ring formed on the surface, then another, then another. Each ripple pulling toward the center of where we stood, as if the lake was drawing us into a pattern.

Soren stiffened. His fingers flexed, lightning, wanting to wake in answer to whatever the water was becoming.

"Don't," I whispered.

He shot me a look like the word offended him. "I wasn't going to"

The wind circled us. Not Zephyr's restless, chaotic gusts.

Something more measured. More deliberate. A slow spiral that didn't touch the ground, just traced the air around our shoulders like a boundary.

Rhazien's posture changed just barely. But the line of him went from neutral to ready, like a blade that hadn't been drawn yet but already knew where it would be placed.

Zephyr went still. Truly still. That unsettled me more than anything. The lake brightened beneath the surface.

A faint, deep glow like light filtering through dark water from something far below.

It wasn't magic flaring.

It was… response.

Soren breathed, almost reverent despite himself. "What is that?"

"I don't know," I said honestly.

The ripple pattern tightened, and for one heartbeat, one clean, sharp heartbeat, the reflection in the water wasn't just us.

It was us together… but not as we were meant to be. The sensation crawled under my skin, as if the lake were trying to impose a different truth over our bodies, one that almost aligned, but not enough to hold.

Then the moment collapsed.

The light drained away. The wind died. The lake smoothed into flawless stillness, so pristine it felt staged, like something had hurriedly erased what we were never meant to see.

Zephyr blinked. His voice came out soft. "That," he said, "was not the Academy."

Soren's laugh was short and humorless. "Of course it wasn't."

Rhazien didn't speak, but his gaze tracked the far side of the lake where the trees leaned closer together like they were hiding something.

The understanding slid into place with dreadful clarity. The spiral had only tightened when the four of us stood shoulder to shoulder.

Earlier, when Soren shifted half a step away, it faltered. When Rhazien stepped closer, it sharpened into something almost eager.

It wasn't responding to any one of us.

It was responding to the convergence. To the four of us aligned.

Slowly, carefully, I stepped back. The water held its shape. The night exhaled into silence, undisturbed.

Soren spoke first, too loud. "So… we're just going to pretend that didn't happen?"

Zephyr floated nearer to him, expression carefully neutral. "Yes."

Rhazien's voice was low. "For now. "I looked at the water one last time. It reflected the sky again like nothing had ever shifted.

But I knew better.

And as we walked away, I couldn't shake the feeling that the lake remained awake behind us still, patient, and paying attention.

Chapter

Twenty- Six

The Day After

Morning didn't feel like morning. It felt like an aftertaste. We returned from the lake without speaking much. We slept, technically. But sleep at Arcane was never deep. The Academy didn't allow surrender. It allowed pause.

When we stepped into the corridor the next day, I felt it: the attention had changed.

Not increased loudly but it increased carefully.

Students passed us and looked away too quickly, like their instincts were warning them about something they hadn't consciously noticed yet.

A pair of Lumora students stopped talking when we approached. Their words didn't trail off naturally they cut clean, as if someone had pressed a hand over their mouths mid-sentence. The silence that followed wasn't empty. It felt placed. Arranged.

One of them glanced at me too quickly, then away. The other stared straight ahead like if they didn't see us, we might not see them either.

Soren noticed too. His mouth twisted, jaw tightening as he slowed half a step beside me.

"I hate this place," he muttered under his breath.

"It's like being inside a thought that doesn't want you to exist."

Zephyr drifted along the air beside us, unseen by most, but the faint current of wind around him brushed against my cheek. He hummed softly, amused.
"Poetic."

"It's not poetic," Soren snapped, keeping his voice low but sharp. His eyes tracked the students as they hurried off. "It's creepy. They don't just ignore us they erase us."

"Correction," Zephyr said lightly. "They try to."

Soren exhaled through his nose, restless energy sparking faintly at his fingertips before he forced his hands into his pockets. The motion felt deliberate. Controlled.

Rhazien had gone quiet.

I followed his line of sight and saw why.

Above us, along the curved stone balcony that overlooked the courtyard, a faculty member stood motionless between two pillars. Half of his figure rested in shadow; the other half caught in pale academy light. He was still enough to be mistaken for a carved figure placed there to watch over the grounds.

Watching.

A prickle ran down my spine.

"He's been there since we turned the corner," Rhazien said quietly. Not alarmed. Just certain.

As if sensing the weight of our attention, the figure shifted.

Not startled. Not hurried.

He simply moved; a smooth continuation of a step already begun and began walking along the balcony's edge. Calm. Measured. Unbothered. Like we hadn't surprised him at all.

Like we'd confirmed something.

Soren's eyes narrowed. "Yeah," he murmured. "That wasn't coincidence."

Zephyr's voice brushed against my thoughts like wind through a narrow hall.

"No," he agreed softly. "It never is here."

The faculty member didn't look down again. He didn't need to.

Somehow, the absence of that glance felt worse than if he'd stared.

My stomach tightened. We reached our first class and the room felt normal at first. Then I realized what was wrong. The wards were adjusted.

Not new. Not rebuilt. Just tuned slightly differently like the room had shifted its pressure points.

Professor Calderyn's gaze lingered on us for half a second too long. His expression didn't change. But the pause was a statement. "Begin," he said, as if nothing had happened.

The exercise was simple in description: controlled cooperation under pressure. Small constraints. Timed responses. But the moment we stepped into the marked circle, the air changed again.

The ward didn't test us.

It measured how we reacted to being measured

Soren's posture tightened, tension coiling through him as Zephyr's presence prickled at my back.

Rhazien remained perfectly still in that controlled, disciplined way of his, as if he were storing energy for a moment none of us could yet see.

I drew in a slow breath, then another, letting each one settle deep until I felt myself anchored again.

The exercise began. The ward projected an obstacle. Nothing dramatic, just a shifting field of resistance that demanded coordination. Soren moved to push through it with force. I caught his sleeve lightly. Not stopping him. Just redirecting. He glanced at me, flashing irritation. "Less," I murmured.

His jaw tightened. Then, grudgingly, he adjusted. His wind became a brace instead of a battering ram.

The resistance eased.

Calderyn's gaze sharpened. He wasn't impressed and he was interested.

After class, we didn't talk until we reached a quiet stretch of corridor where the walls seemed less eager to listen.

Soren spoke first. "They changed the wards."

"Yes," I said. Zephyr drifted near my shoulder. "They're tuning for response frequency," he murmured. "Trying to catch a pattern."

Rhazien's voice was quiet. "They already have one." Soren looked at him. "Then what are they doing?" Rhazien's gaze flicked briefly toward me it was so brief that most people would miss it.

But I didn't.

"Confirming," he said.

My stomach turned.

Soren let out a sharp breath. "I hate being confirmed." Zephyr smiled faintly. "Welcome to Constellaria Wing."

"That's not comforting," Soren said. "No," Zephyr agreed. "But it's accurate." I said nothing.

Because the truth was simple: After last night, the Academy wasn't just watching us anymore.

It was watching how the world watched us back.

Chapter

Twenty-Seven

The Creature That Didn't Choose Random

We didn't plan to go back to the lake. We also didn't plan not to. By late afternoon, the Academy felt too tight. Too full of eyes. Too full of soft pauses and conversations that stopped when we arrived.

So, we wandered quietly, without announcing intention. That was the Academy's preferred form of observation. Movement without instruction revealed instinct. Instinct revealed alignment. And alignment, here, determined survival.

The path curved toward water again. The trees near the lake were taller, older, their leaves whispering even when the wind didn't. The air smelled clean here, like damp stone and cold magic.

Soren walked with his hands in his pockets, trying to look casual. He failed. His energy crackled just beneath his skin when he was annoyed, and Arcane had become very good at annoying him.

Zephyr floated low, his expression too calm, like he'd decided not to stir trouble because trouble had already arrived on its own.

Rhazien remained beside me, close enough to

matter but careful not to crowd. He didn't reach for me or try to guide my steps. He simply positioned himself there, steady and deliberate, as though the space at my side had already been chosen.

I didn't ask him why. I didn't need to.

The lake came into view.

This time, it wasn't still.

The surface shifted in slow, deliberate ripples that spread outward without wind to drive them, as if something beneath the water had sensed our approach and stirred in quiet recognition. Moonlight fractured across the movement, breaking into thin ribbons that slid and reformed instead of settling.

It looked less like water…and more like something breathing.

My throat tightened before I could stop it.

The air near the shore carried a faint metallic chill, cool against my lungs, like the first inhale before stepping into deep water.

Soren slowed beside me, noticing the change in my steps before I spoke. His voice dropped instinctively, as though the lake might overhear.

"You feel it too."

It wasn't a question.

I nodded once, "yes."

Zephyrs gaze narrowed slightly, attention sharpening as he studied the surface. For once, he didn't look amused. He looked…careful.

"Be polite," he murmured.

Soren blinked. "Did you just tell me to be polite to a lake?"

Zephyr didn't look away from the water. "I told you to be polite," he said quietly, "to what's inside it."

We reached the shoreline.

The water brightened again, though not as sharply as it had the night before. The glow spread beneath the surface in slow, deliberate veins, like something tracing the lakebed from below. It felt less like a warning this time and more like a measured response like an acknowledgment that we had returned.

A subtle movement passed across the lake's surface, so controlled it barely disturbed the reflection of the sky. It wasn't the chaotic ripple of something forcing its way upward, but a deliberate shift, as though the water itself was making room. The surface parted slowly, almost gently, the motion reminiscent of a held breath finally released before words are spoken.

From the dark beneath, something began to rise.

It did not burst upward. It did not thrash or surge. It ascended with the patient inevitability of something that had never needed to hurry.

The first thing to break the surface was not the head, but a ridge of scaled spine, catching moonlight and bending it instead of reflecting it. The scales were not fish-like; they lay in interlocking plates patterned like etched armor, pale and iridescent, as if carved from the memory of light itself.

Then its head emerged, long, elegant, and wrong in the way ancient things often were. Tendrils drifted from their crown, not hair and not fins, but something fluid and silk-thin that moved without wind. Its eyes were pale and depthless, luminous but not glowing, intelligent in a way that made instinct recoil.

It wasn't a student, and it wasn't a spirit like Zephyr. The presence rising from the water felt older than either, as though it had existed long before the world decided what counted as normie or magical.

The lake should have broken into ripples when the creature surfaced, but it didn't. Instead, the water shifted with subtle intention, smoothing and reshaping itself as if making room for something that belonged within it.

When the creature's gaze lifted, the effect was immediate and unmistakable. It wasn't examining us one by one. Its attention moved across the four of us as a unit, lingering on the space we occupied together, as though whatever it sought could only be understood by the way we stood in relation to each other.

I felt the weight of that realization settle into my ribs.

Soren inhaled sharply beside me. I felt the surge in him before I saw it, the pull of storm rising reflexively, lightning gathering along the edges of his control.

"Don't," I whispered.

He swallowed hard and forced the energy down, jaw tight, breath uneven.

The creature drifted closer without disturbing the surface, its body moving beneath the water in long, deliberate curves that suggested impossible size. The faint glow beneath it deepened, outlining something vast coiled in the dark.

Rhazien shifted without speaking, placing himself a fraction more forward, not shielding me outright but adjusting the angle of threat like instinct had drawn the line for him.

Zephyr lowered slightly as well, not flaring, not provoking. His presence aligned instead, smoothing into something older and quieter.

The creature slowed as it neared the shoreline, its movement through the water so controlled that the surface barely disturbed. It came to a stop just beyond the reach of the shallows, close enough that the faint glow beneath its form illuminated the edges of its scales and the long, drifting tendrils that framed its face.

For several heartbeats, nothing moved. The lake held itself in perfect stillness, and even the night air seemed to pause, as though the world had narrowed to this single, suspended moment.

Then the creature inclined its head.

The motion was deliberate and measured, neither defensive nor deferential. There was no hint of submission in it, no gesture of retreat. Instead, the angle of its gaze and the quiet precision of the movement carried something far more unsettling: recognition.

My pulse surged hard enough that I felt it in my teeth, each beat echoing through my jaw as if my body understood the significance before my mind could catch up.

Beside me, Soren drew in a shallow breath. When he spoke, his voice lacked its usual edge of humor, stripped down to something rougher and more honest.

"What… are you?"

The creature offered no answer in words.

Instead, the air around us thickened subtly, not with pressure or threat but with attention. It felt as though the space itself had begun to listen, gathering quietly around the shoreline. Beneath the surface, the lake's faint glow shifted once more, spreading outward in slow, deliberate arcs that curved and aligned with the positions of the four of us standing there.

The pattern wasn't random.

It mirrored us, our spacing, our stillness, the shape we formed together as if whatever watched from the water was not simply observing who we were, but what we were when we stood as one.

It wasn't reacting to one of us.

It was responding to the shape we made together.

The creature lifted its head once more, eyes moving across us like it was comparing us to something older than memory.

Then it turned.

The movement was smooth and almost gentle, but the water followed it in a widening spiral that hinted at the enormity concealed beneath. For a heartbeat, the surface bowed inward, as if something massive had just rolled beneath it.

The creature turned with unhurried grace and slipped back beneath the surface, its form dissolving into the dark water as though it had never fully entered our world at all. The lake closed over it without resistance. There was no splash, no violent disturbance, not even a lingering ripple to mark where it had been. Instead, the surface drew itself smooth again with unsettling composure, the faint glow beneath fading gradually until only the fractured reflection of moonlight remained.

For several seconds, none of us moved. The shoreline felt suspended in a strange, attentive stillness, as if the lake were not finished with us even in its quiet.

Zephyr was the first to break the silence. When he spoke, the usual playfulness in his voice had been stripped away, leaving something more thoughtful and sober in its place.

"That wasn't curiosity," he said quietly, his gaze still fixed on the water.

Soren's jaw tightened as he followed the creature's vanished path across the lake's surface. "Then what was it?" he asked, the question edged with unease he didn't bother hiding.

Zephyr did not look away from the water as he answered. "Recognition."

The word settled heavily between us.

Rhazien spoke next, his voice low and measured, carrying a weight that made the air feel denser rather than lighter. "Not random," he said, the quiet certainty in his tone more unsettling than any open alarm.

The words landed heavily because they matched the truth settling in my bones.

I stared at the lake and felt something inside me respond. It wasn't not awakening and not igniting…not yet.

Remembering.

And then, from the corner of my vision, I saw movement along the far path.

Another faculty silhouette. Still as a ward and watching. Then continuing on, unhurried, like this was exactly what they had expected to see.

Soren noticed too. His voice went sharp. "Did you

see that?"

"Yes," I said. Zephyr's expression tightened. "We should go."

Rhazien didn't argue. He simply shifted with us, guiding our movement away from the water with the same quiet certainty he used when he decided something mattered.

We walked back toward the Academy and behind us, the lake remained perfectly still.

But I could feel it.

Watching.

250

Chapter

Twenty- Eight

Controlled Trial

The notice came the next morning.
Of course it did.
The Academy never allowed an anomaly to settle without quantifying the aftermath. It did not panic. It did not react emotionally. It adjusted.

The slate surfaced near the common hall before breakfast, rising from the stone as if it had always been there. The letters were carved cleanly and deeply, each stroke precise enough to feel irreversible.

CONTROLLED COORDINATION TRIAL: RE-QUIRED
CONSTELLARIA OBSERVATION: ACTIVE
ARCANE TRIAL READINESS: PENDING
OBJECTIVE: STABILITY UNDER CONFLICTING IN-PUT

Soren read it once and smiled the way predators do when something finally bares its teeth.

"They're obsessed," he muttered. "We're the Academy's favorite problem."

Zephyr stood just behind him, gaze tracing the word *Observation* with clinical interest. "You say that like it's a compliment."

"It's not," Soren replied. "It's a challenge."

Rhazien didn't move immediately. His gaze remained fixed on a single word.

Stability.

"They want to see who fractures," he said quietly.

"Fractures?" Soren repeated lightly. "That feels dramatic."

Rhazien's eyes flicked toward him. "It's precise."

My stomach tightened.

The trial chamber was smaller than the integration assessment room, but sharper somehow. The space felt honed like a blade designed to cut indecision out of you.

A circular platform of pale stone floated above a dark drop that showed no bottom and offered no reassurance. Constellaria wards shimmered faintly around the perimeter. They didn't glow warmly.

They recorded.

I felt it immediately the difference between being tested and being studied.

A voice emerged from the air without direction. "Begin."

The platform divided not by walls, but by pressure. Four zones formed, invisible but unmistakable.

We stepped forward.

Each zone pressed against something instinctive.

Soren stiffened first. His space demanded restraint. I felt the resistance in him like static building under skin.

"They're joking," he muttered. "They want me to not respond?"

"Correct," Zephyr said calmly.

My zone demanded decisive force. Immediate correction. Overcommitment. It wanted me to anchor everything with finality.

It wanted me to overreach.

I felt the urge rise in my chest like heat looking for oxygen.

Zephyr's zone demanded silence and the absence of interference. No shadows. No manipulation. No clever adjustments hidden in the dark. His strength relied on stillness and on information gathering without disturbing the system he was observing.

Rhazien's zone demanded the opposite.

His required engagement. Participation. Reaction. His power did not function through quiet observation but through presence through pressure applied and energy answered.

Placed side by side, the two spaces canceled each other out.

One demanded restraint.

The other demanded response.

It was inversion.

Deliberate conflict.

The Academy had not created this trial to showcase our strengths.

It had designed it to see whether we could refuse them.

The platform shuddered beneath our feet.

From the center of the stone floor, a conduit structure rose slowly upward, emerging like a piece of machinery unfolding from within the Academy itself. It was similar to the unstable conduit we had faced in the integration chamber earlier in the term, but this one was different.

Cleaner.

Refined.

Contained.

The structure hummed with controlled energy as it locked into place.

Then it pulsed.

The rhythm was steady and deliberate, like a heartbeat echoing through the stone.

But the pulse did not respond to any of us individually.

It responded to us together.

The moment our movements shifted and the moment we adjusted to one another instead of acting alone, the rhythm sharpened. Not violently.

Recognizing.

Zephyr's voice lowered beside me.

"Don't give it what it expects."

Soren rolled his shoulders once, tension settling into his stance.

"That's vague."

"Good," Zephyr replied.

The conduit tilted slightly, its energy fluctuating as though testing our reactions.

Soren moved first because he always did.

But this time he didn't strike.

Instead of releasing the storm building in his hands, he redirected it. Wind curved outward in a controlled arc, bracing the conduit's structure without forcing it back into place. Lightning flickered briefly along his fingers before fading as he closed his fists and held the power there.

The restraint cost him.

I felt my own instinct surge in response.

My magic wanted to correct the imbalance. To anchor the structure. To take control of the situation before the instability worsened.

The ward around us pressed harder, encouraging that instinct.

It wanted someone to take command.

It wanted one of us to solve the problem alone.

I refused.

Instead of force, I offered alignment, a subtle shift in the balance of pressure around the conduit. A quiet adjustment that stabilized the movement without claiming authority over it.

Not control.

Coordination.

Zephyr's shadows twitched, eager to lash outward, but he inhaled once and let them fall flat, becoming absence rather than attack.

Rhazien's zone tightened around him, pressing insistently against his instincts and demanding a reaction something visible, something unmistakable, the flare of flame the system clearly expected him to unleash.

He stepped forward anyway.

But he did not answer the pressure with fire, and he did not retreat from it either. Instead, he held his ground with quiet control, remaining present without allowing the tension to escalate into spectacle.

For a brief moment, it worked.

The conduit stabilized, its uneven rhythm smoothing as the pulse slowed beneath our feet. The ward lines shimmered faintly around the platform, their light flickering with something that felt almost like irritation, as though the system had expected chaos and was now forced to reconsider its approach.

Then the trial escalated, though not with the violence or spectacle we might have expected. Instead of an explosion or a sudden collapse, the system shifted its approach, changing the shape of the pressure around us.

The structure began to behave as though one of us was destabilizing the entire lattice. The pattern of the conduit altered subtly, its pulse tightening and redirecting until the instability seemed to gather around a single point.

It chose Soren.

Of course it did.

Lightning was the easiest story for fear to tell.

The conduit's pulse sharpened around him, reacting to his presence like a wound reacting to touch.

Soren stiffened. "You've got to be kidding me."

"It's assigning fault," Zephyr observed calmly.

"It's assigning blame," Soren corrected through clenched teeth.

The pressure intensified. The structure tilted harder, as though confirming its own conclusion.

Zephyr's voice cut low. "Don't fight it."

Soren's jaw flexed. "It's literally accusing me."

"Good," Zephyr replied. "Then let it."

Soren stared at him like he'd suggested stepping off the platform entirely.

Rhazien spoke without raising his voice. "Do not participate."

Soren swallowed hard, his throat working as he fought the instinct rising inside him. For a moment, lightning crawled across his knuckles, eager and restless, the storm within him gathering as it always did when something tried to challenge him.

Then, slowly and with visible effort, he lowered his hands.

He didn't try to correct the narrative the trial had constructed around him, and he didn't strike back to prove it wrong. Instead, he allowed the accusation to pass through him without answering it, refusing to give the system the reaction it was waiting for.

The conduit faltered.

Its steady pulse skipped unevenly, the rhythm stumbling as though the ward itself was uncertain how to proceed.

It was almost as if the ward had never been designed to handle a storm that refused to perform.

I held my adjustment steady. Zephyr flattened his shadows into quiet. Rhazien stood exactly where the pressure thinned and gave it nothing to amplify.

The ward shuddered.

At first, I thought it was only the strain of the trial reaching its end, the lattice settling after the pressure we had forced it to endure. The conduit flickered faintly, its light thinning as the system recalibrated around us.

But then I felt something else.

For the briefest instant, beneath the steady rhythm of the platform and the quiet hum of the wards, another fluctuation slipped through the pattern. It wasn't stronger than the others, and it didn't disrupt them. It moved beside them, subtle and unfamiliar, like a note in a song that didn't belong to the composition.

A fifth rhythm.

The sensation vanished almost immediately, gone before I could focus on it or understand what it meant.

My breath caught anyway.

For a moment, the question rose instinctively in my mind.

Did you feel that?

I almost asked it aloud.

But the thought dissolved before it could reach my voice, slipping away the same way the disturbance had. Leaving behind only the quiet certainty that something had shifted.

The platform steadied beneath our feet.

The conduit dimmed, its light withdrawing into the stone as if the chamber had decided the trial had reached its conclusion.

Then the voice returned, calm and distant as ever.

"End."

No praise followed, there was no correction, just dismissal.

We remained where we stood for a few seconds longer than necessary, none of us moving toward the exit.

We lingered on the platform longer than necessary, not because we were waiting for instruction, but because all of us could feel it.

Something had noticed us.

The trial hadn't ended because we failed, and it hadn't ended because we succeeded either. It ended because we adapted in a way the system hadn't predicted, and the Academy, for all its precision, had needed a moment to reconsider what it had just seen.

Soren exhaled slowly beside me. "That felt personal."

Zephyr's smile returned, thinner than before and edged with quiet amusement.

"Everything here is."

Rhazien's gaze traced the ward lines, studying the way they recalibrated. "It expected fracture."

"And?" Soren asked.

"It didn't get one."

Soren huffed softly. "Disappointing."

"Perhaps," Zephyr said, "for someone."

As we stepped off the platform, I felt it again. It wasn't the pressure of the wards this time, and it wasn't the lingering tension of the trial.

It felt more like an adjustment.

Something within the structure of the chamber had shifted, subtle but deliberate, as though the system had quietly recalculated the risk we represented.

And in my chest, something settled that felt uncomfortably close to certainty.

This wasn't preparation.

The trials, the wards, the careful measurements of our reactions. None of it felt like training anymore.

It felt like containment.

And containment only mattered when something dangerous was expected to grow.

Chapter Twenty- Nine

Rooftop Quiet

We didn't go back to the lake that night. Not because we were afraid. Because we knew better than to keep knocking on a door that had already answered.

Instead, we found a rooftop.

Arcane Academy didn't always allow rooftops the way normal buildings did. But sometimes, if you followed the corridor that shouldn't have connected and took the staircase that felt like it belonged to someone else, the Academy allowed open air. Like it wanted to see what you did when you thought you weren't being watched.

Or maybe it wanted to remind you that being watched wasn't optional.

The sky above Mistara felt closer than any sky should. Stars looked too sharp, as if someone had etched them into the dark with intent. The air smelled like cold stone and distant water.

Soren sat on the edge, legs dangling, hands clasped between his knees like he was physically holding himself down. Zephyr hovered a few feet away, unusually quiet. Rhazien stood with his back to a low wall, neutral posture, but close enough that I could feel his attention like a steady weight.

I sat beside Soren.

For a long moment, no one spoke.

Then Soren's voice came out rougher than I expected. "I hate not knowing," he admitted.

It wasn't anger.

It was honesty.

I nodded slowly. "I know."

He glanced at me like he was searching for a crack. "You always seem like you know."

I almost laughed. "I don't," I said. "I just… don't panic about it the way you do."

"That's because you're terrifyingly calm," Soren muttered.

Zephyr made a soft sound that might have been agreement. "Terrifyingly calm is one way to describe it," he said. "Clinically composed is another."

Soren's head snapped toward him. "Can you not diagnose her?"

Zephyr's mouth curved faintly. "I'm not diagnosing. I'm admiring the self-control I lack."

Rhazien's voice came quiet, almost dry. "Calm is not the absence of fear."

Soren looked at him. "Then what is it?"

Rhazien's gaze flicked toward me, brief, respectful. "Choice," he said. "Over reaction."

Something tightened quietly in my chest. It wasn't pride. It felt closer to recognition, as though some part of me had been waiting for this moment long before I understood why.

I stared up at the sky, letting the cold air fill my lungs and settle the tension still humming through my body.

For a while none of us spoke.

Soren shifted beside me, his gaze drifting toward the horizon as if he were looking for something familiar that didn't exist here. When he finally spoke, his voice had softened in a way I hadn't heard often.

"When we were in Denver," he said, "things were simpler."

Zephyr snorted immediately.

"Simpler?" he echoed, leaning back on his hands like he was settling in for entertainment. "You summoned me in an alley behind a closed restaurant while lightning was actively trying to burn the building down."

Soren's mouth twitched despite himself.

"Okay," he admitted, "maybe not simple. But it was still… us."

Zephyr lifted an eyebrow.

"You mean chaotic."

"I mean we understood it," Soren corrected. "There weren't a hundred invisible rules waiting to punish us for breathing wrong."

"There weren't rules at all," I said quietly.

Soren glanced at me, something like agreement flickering across his expression.

"Exactly."

The silence that followed settled around us again, but it wasn't the uneasy kind that filled empty rooms. It was the kind that came from shared exhaustion, the quiet understanding that we had all just survived something together.

For a moment it felt almost peaceful.

Then Zephyr spoke again.

This time his voice was careful.

"Something is paying attention."

Soren's head snapped toward him immediately. "The Academy."

Zephyr shook his head slowly, his usual half-smile nowhere to be found.

"Not just the Academy."

Across from us, Rhazien's shoulders tightened by a fraction. The movement was subtle enough that most people would have missed it.

I didn't.

Because I felt it too.

The sensation was difficult to explain. It wasn't pressure like the wards created, and it wasn't fear either. It felt more like a memory stirring beneath my skin, restless and half-formed, as though something had brushed past the edge of recognition and disappeared before I could see it clearly.

Soren noticed the shift in the air as well.

His voice tightened. "Then what?"

Zephyr studied the sky for a moment before answering.

When he finally spoke, the usual humor had drained from his tone.

"Something old."

The words settled between us like a stone dropped into still water.

I swallowed before I could stop myself.

"And it noticed us," I said quietly. "Together."

Zephyr's gaze sharpened, the faintest flicker of something calculating passing through his expression.

"Yes," he said.

Rhazien spoke then, his voice calm and certain in a way that didn't invite argument.

"Then we stay together."

Soren turned toward him, surprise flashing openly across his face.

"You say that like it's obvious."

Rhazien didn't look away.

"It is."

My throat tightened at the certainty in his voice. The feeling that followed wasn't romance or friendship, but something deeper and more like alignment. The quiet recognition of a path already unfolding beneath our feet, the kind of bond you don't choose so much as survive into.

Soren's voice softened slightly. "Okay," he said, and for once he didn't push back against the idea. "Then we stay together."

Zephyr tilted his head, studying him for a moment as though weighing the statement. Something in his expression shifted, the sharp edge of his usual amusement easing just enough to reveal something more genuine beneath it.

"How dramatic," he murmured at last.

Soren let out a quiet breath that might have been a laugh. "You're insufferable."

Zephyr's faint smile returned, slow and unapologetic. "And yet you keep inviting me into these heroic declarations."

"Shut up."

"No."

The exchange was so familiar, so perfectly predictable, that I almost smiled despite the tension still humming through the air.

Then the sky flickered.

Just once.

It wasn't lightning or magic, just a brief, unnatural blink in the fabric of the night.

For the smallest fraction of a heartbeat, the stars seemed to hold their breath, the night suspended in a strange stillness as though the world itself had paused long enough to look at us.

Soren went rigid beside me.

Zephyr's smile disappeared instantly.

Across the platform, Rhazien's posture shifted, subtle but immediate, the quiet movement of someone already placing himself between danger and the rest of us.

I felt it deep in my bones before my mind could give it shape.

It wasn't the Academy.

Something beyond it had just looked in.

The flicker passed.

But the silence it left behind felt different.

The sky resumed as if nothing had happened, but

the air stayed different, denser, attentive, and *closer*.

Soren's voice came out low. "Did you see that?"

"Yes," I whispered.

Zephyr's voice was too soft. "It's getting closer."

Rhazien didn't speak. He simply stepped half a pace nearer to me, like his body decided where it needed to be before his mind could argue.

And then, strangely and sharply, my mind snagged on something that should have been simple.

Denver.

I tried to picture the street where we'd stood, the alley where Zephyr had appeared, the exact corner where Soren had laughed like fear was a dare.

The image came, but not cleanly.

A sign. A storefront. A name…

What was it called?

The detail slid away the moment I reached for it, leaving only a blank edge and the uncomfortable sense that something had been removed.

I blinked hard, staring at my hands as if the answer might be written there.

Soren noticed instantly. "What?" he asked, sharp now. "What's wrong?"

"Nothing," I said too fast.

Zephyr's gaze fixed on me, the playfulness gone. "That wasn't nothing."

Rhazien's voice was quiet. "You forgot something."

I tried to laugh it off. It came out thin. "I didn't forget. It's just…" I searched again and found the same smooth absence. "It's not there."

Soren's jaw tightened. "Like… erased?"

The word hung between us, ugly and accurate.

Zephyr's voice went careful, almost gentle in the way a blade could be gentle if it wanted. "Constellaria doesn't just monitor behavior," he said. "It monitors memory."

Soren stared. "That's not a thing."

Zephyr's smile didn't return. "It is here."

Rhazien's gaze lifted to the sky, scanning the dark as if he could see the shape of what watched. "Or it's not Constellaria."

That landed worse.

Because it fits.

I swallowed, cold spreading through my ribs. "The Academy picks the forgotten," I whispered, and I didn't know if I was reminding them or reminding myself. "What if… it keeps us that way until we earn otherwise?"

Soren's voice came rough. "So, it takes things?"

Zephyr's tone went quiet. "Or it makes sure the world can."

Rhazien's voice, steady: "Then we hold what we can. For each other."

Soren looked at him. "You're really committing to this 'unit' thing."

Rhazien didn't blink. "Yes."

Zephyr exhaled, half amused and half grim. "How inspiring. We're going to defeat memory theft with friendship."

Soren shot him a look. "Shut up."

Zephyr tilted his head. "No."

And despite everything, I let my shoulder bump lightly into Soren's, a small contact like an anchor.

The sky stayed sharp.

The air stayed attentive.

And in the quiet that followed, I understood something I didn't want to name yet:

Arcane Academy was not the worst thing watching us.

It was only the first thing that admitted it.

266

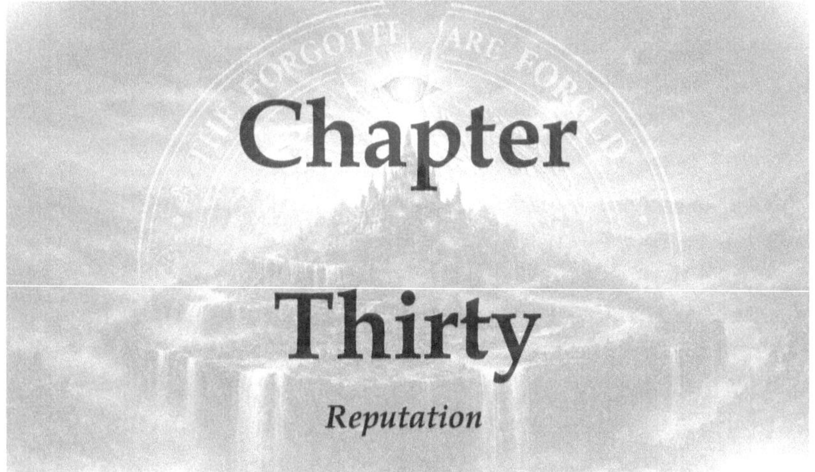

Chapter

Thirty

Reputation

The Academy didn't announce consequences. It let them spread.

By morning, the corridors felt the same. Stone, lanternlight, the familiar hush of footsteps and distant instruction, but the air around Veya's Eclipse unit carried a new kind of space. It was not emptiness, not avoidance but allowance.

Students shifted aside half a step sooner than necessary. Conversations didn't die when they approached but more like they rerouted their conversations to something else entirely. Voices thinned, then resumed behind them like water closing over a stone.

Soren noticed first, he always did.

He walked with his shoulders set as if the hallway had personally offended him, eyes flicking to every pause and every too-careful glance.

"They're doing it," he muttered.

Zephyr drifted beside him, hands clasped behind his back like a boy pretending to be harmless. "Doing what?"

Soren tipped his chin toward the Obsidian Unit near a column. They watched him with open curiosity until he looked directly at them. Then they turned away too quickly, like they'd been caught staring at a wound.

Soren snorted softly. "Subtle. Really subtle."

"You've become an attraction," Zephyr said, faintly amused.

"I don't want to be an attraction."

"No one does," Zephyr replied. "And yet here we are."

Soren dragged a hand through his hair with his shoulders tight with tension. "It's the half-second delay that gets me," he muttered. "They always look just a little too long. Like they're trying to figure out if I'm about to explode or confess something tragic."

Zephyr's smile curved. "Which would you prefer?"

"Neither" Soren said immediately. Then, after a beat, "Exploding, maybe. At least that's honest."

A pair of younger students rounded the corner, spotted them, and veered off so abruptly one nearly walked into a pillar.

Soren watched them go, expression flattening.

"See?" he said quietly pointing towards them retreating. "That."

His voice carried less bite now and more frustrated.

"They don't see us," he went on. "They see whatever story the Academy's already started telling about us."

Zephyr tilted his head slightly. "And what story is that?"

Soren's mouth twitched without humor. "That we're either about to win something… or survive something they won't."

He glanced sideways at Veya then, quick and almost careless, except it wasn't.

"Are you good?" he asked under his breath.

The question was light but the attention behind it wasn't. Before she could answer, another cluster of students went quiet as they passed.

Soren exhaled through his nose. "I miss being invisible," he muttered.

Zephyr considered that. "You were never invisible."

"Yeah," Soren said. "But at least before, people only stared when I gave them a reason."

Rhazien didn't comment. He hadn't spoken much since the rooftop, which wasn't unusual in itself. What was unusual was how his quiet had changed, it wasn't because of absence but rather, his silence became focus.

He moved with them, not behind, not ahead but always placed where the corridor narrowed, where sightlines opened, where a mistake would have the most room to become something worse.

And Veya caught the shape of it.

The same way she had before.

His presence stayed protective without drawing attention to itself, close without possession and always aligned with her. Veya kept her eyes forward, determined not to acknowledge the way it tightened something in her chest. The feeling wasn't warmth or comfort; it carried a different gravity altogether, something steadier and heavier, like a quiet weight she hadn't agreed to carry.

The Arcanic Hall, was louder than the corridors, full of clatter and creature-sounds and the sharp, hungry pulse of magic in a hundred different forms. The moment they entered, the room didn't go silent.

But it shifted.

As if the hall registered them the way a ward did.

As if attention rebalanced itself without anyone meaning to.

A few heads turned, then turned back. A few whispers rose, then flattened into normal conversation with forced ease.

Soren slowed, scanning the room like he was searching for a reason.

Zephyr leaned close enough that only Soren and

Veya could hear. "Don't look like you're going to bite someone."

Soren's jaw tightened. "Then tell them to stop acting like I'm going to bite someone."

Zephyr's eyes gleamed. "You are."

Soren's glare could have melted stone.

Veya reached the nearest table before the tension could take root, and sat deliberately, grounding herself in simple movement. The bench was cool beneath her palms. The air smelled like citrus-spice and warm bread and something faintly metallic, an Arcane scent she'd never fully placed.

Soren sat across from her with unnecessary force. The table rattled slightly.

A few students glanced over again.

Zephyr sat as if he owned the bench, stretching out with the effortless ease of someone who had never once worried about whether he belonged in a room.

Rhazien remained standing for a moment longer. His gaze moved slowly across the room, sweeping the space with practiced neutrality before he finally sat beside Veya, not touching, not crowding her, but close enough that his presence felt like a brace.

Soren saw it.

The flicker in his eyes came and went in an instant. It was too sharp to dismiss, too fast to name outright as jealousy, but charged enough to make the air between them feel different.

His jaw tightened. He looked away and dragged a hand through his hair, the gesture rough and impatient, as if he were frustrated at the world for arranging itself in ways he couldn't immediately correct.

Veya noticed. Of course she did.

She kept her expression neutral anyway, letting her gaze remain forward as though nothing had shifted. As though the room hadn't subtly recalibrated around her. As though the space beside her didn't suddenly feel more complicated.

She drew in a slow breath and released it just as carefully.

If the Academy was watching and it always was, then it could watch composure. It could watch restraint.

It would not see her flinch.

Across the hall, a group of students in the Parallax Unit whispered into their hands. One of them, older, eyes too steady, met Veya's gaze for a heartbeat, then gave a small, almost reluctant nod. Weather it was recognition or warning; Veya couldn't tell which.

A goblin attendant scuttled by with a tray, pausing abruptly at the edge of their table. Its ears twitched, pupils narrowing as if it smelled something wrong. It looked at them, then hurried away without offering food.

Soren leaned forward. "Okay. That is not normal."

Zephyr's smile thinned. "Nothing is normal when something has started labeling you."

Rhazien didn't look at the retreating goblin. Instead, he looked at the space beyond it toward the high balconies lining the dining hall where faculty sometimes appeared as silhouettes against lanternlight.

"There," he said quietly.

Veya followed his gaze.

A figure stood on the upper walkway, half obscured by a column. The silhouette was still enough to be mistaken for decoration, and I realized it was Professor Virenna. She wasn't watching the hall at large. Her focus was angled, and precise. Her focus was on them.

Veya's stomach tightened. Virenna's expression didn't change as she watched them. There was no frown, no curiosity, just the clinical calm of someone witnessing a result.

Then Virenna turned and walked away, unhurried, like her presence had been a checkmark rather than a threat.

Soren exhaled through his nose. "She's doing it on

purpose."

"Of course she is," Zephyr murmured. "Constellaria doesn't watch accidentally."

Veya's fingers curled against the edge of the table. "Eat," she said, more firmly than she intended. "Before you start spiraling."

Soren's eyes snapped to hers. For a heartbeat, the anger was still there with sharp restlessness that was sparking just beneath his skin.

Then something shifted with in him, it wasn't gone but redirected. His storm didn't quiet for anyone. Except sometimes it quieted for her. The air between them tightened. Not loud. Not always visible but charged.

Like the moment before lightning decides where it will land.

He didn't thank her. He didn't admit she was right.

But he held her gaze a second too long. Long enough for the noise of the hall to blur at the edges. Long enough for something unspoken to pass between them. Something neither of them named.

Then the tray arrived.

Soren broke eye contact first.

He reached for the bread and tore it apart with trembling hands that were from contained energy. The motion was rough, almost violent, but deliberate. It was controlled. Always controlled.

Veya watched his knuckles whiten.

Watched the faint flicker of silver-blue light ghost along his veins before he forced it back under.

She knew that restraint.

She knew what it cost him.

He glanced up again and caught her looking.

One corner of his mouth tilted. It wasn't quite a grin but something smaller and more private. "Are you going to keep monitoring me," he murmured, low enough that only she could hear, "or are you planning to eat too?"

Heat traced slowly up her spine before she could stop it, unwelcome and undeniable. This time, she looked away first.

"Eat," she said again, softer now, as if gentleness might steady what tension could not.

They obeyed the distraction. The storm between them did not dissipate; it merely coiled, contained, beneath careful movements and controlled breaths.

They attempted conversation on safe subjects, ordinary rhythms but normalcy wouldn't take root. It felt thin and fragile, unable to withstand what lingered beneath it.

Halfway through breakfast, a first-year Astrael boy approached their table with the stiff, purposeful stride of someone trying to prove he wasn't afraid.

He stopped just short of Soren, posture rigid. "You were in the integration chamber," he said.

It wasn't a question.

Soren lifted his gaze slowly. "Maybe, were you in the integration chamber?"

The boy swallowed. "No. But everyone knows. People heard things and everyone is talking about it."

Zephyr leaned forward, chin resting in his hand. "Oh? What kinds of things?"

The boy's eyes flicked toward Zephyr like he didn't know what category to place him in. "That the chamber changed. That the stone recorded something unusual. That…" He hesitated, then blurted, "That the Academy had to reinforce the ward lines after."

Soren's mouth twitched, a humorless smile. "So now we're structural damage."

Veya's voice stayed even. "Who told you that?"

The boy's gaze slid away. "No one told me. People talk."

"People always talk," Zephyr said lightly. "But they rarely know what they're saying."

The boy's shoulders tightened. "Are you dangerous?"

The question dropped into the space between them like a stone.

Soren went still.

Zephyr's expression remained polite, but the air around him sharpened subtlety leaving a shadow-edge around him.

Rhazien didn't move. But his presence shifted, like a wall settling into place.

Veya felt it all at once, the attention on them from everyone around the hall, the way the hall itself held its breath, it wasn't silence but it was as if it were listening.

The Academy loved moments like this. Not because of the drama around them was interesting but because of what the answer revealed while those occurrences happened.

Veya held the boy's gaze gently. "We're students," she said. "Like you."

The boy didn't look convinced.

Soren's fingers flexed against the table.

Veya spoke before the storm could speak for him. "What you should ask," she said quietly, "is whether the Academy is dangerous. Not us."

The boy blinked, as if he was thrown off balance.

Zephyr's smile returned, faint and amused. "Ah," he said. "A philosopher."

The boy flushed. "I just…everyone says…"

"Everyone says whatever makes them feel prepared," Rhazien interrupted softly.

The boy's eyes snapped to him. "Do you think something's coming?"

Rhazien held his gaze for a long beat, staring at the boy dead in his eyes. Then, in the same even tone he always used when acknowledging weather he said, "Yes," as if this wasn't shocking news.

The boy paled.

Veya's chest tightened. Not because Rhazien was wrong, but because he'd given the truth a voice.

Silence had kept it distant.

Spoken, it settled into the space between them and stayed.

The boy backed away with a stuttered apology and vanished into the crowd as quickly as he'd approached.

Soren exhaled sharply. "Great. Now we're prophecy."

Zephyr lifted his shoulder. "Better than being irrelevant."

"I would love to be irrelevant," Soren snapped.

Veya looked at him. "No, you wouldn't."

His eyes met hers, and for a heartbeat the anger in him didn't find a target.

There was something else there. Something that looked raw, tired, and honest. Then he looked away, jaw tightening again. "You don't know what I want," he muttered.

Veya didn't push.

Not because she didn't care, but because she did care.

And she knew how quickly Soren turned caring into pressure, pressure into anger, and anger into movement that didn't always leave room for consequences.

She chose calm instead.

They finished breakfast and left the hall.

Outside, Mistara's sky was pale and unsettled. The clouds were high and looked thin like scraped paint. The air held that same attentive density it had held on the rooftop.

Not heavy but watchful.

They walked toward Constellaria's next session, and Veya felt eyes follow them from balconies and doorways as they walked. Some were students, yes, but also something else like the Academy's awareness, threaded through stone.

Soren broke the silence first. "So, now what?"

Zephyr's gaze tracked the shifting clouds. "Now

we pretend everything is normal."

Rhazien's voice was quiet. "And we prepare."

Soren huffed. "Prepare for what exactly? A surprise we can't predict or even see coming. That's not preparation. That's just waiting to get hit."

Rhazien didn't answer immediately.

Veya did.

"For the way the Academy changes when it decides," she said softly.

Soren's steps slowed a fraction. "You think it's deciding something about us."

"I think it already has," Zephyr murmured.

They entered the corridor leading toward Constellaria training, where the light always felt slightly drained and the walls carried a subtle, unsettling awareness. The sigils carved into the stone weren't wards but instruments of record, measuring presence, pressure, and alignment as each student moved through the space.

Veya sensed their reaction immediately: a soft warmth spreading through the stone and a delicate tightening in the air around them. It wasn't hostile, but attentive, the unmistakable sensation of being registered and quietly assessed.

At the far end of the corridor, Professor Calderyn waited beside the doorway as if he'd been there the entire time. He didn't greet them. He didn't smile either.

His eyes swept them in a calm, clinical way and lingered on their spacing, the way they naturally fell into position.

Soren stood slightly forward.

Veya anchoring.

Zephyr drifting at the edge like a question mark.

Rhazien near Veya, he was always near Veya, like his body had made a choice his mind didn't argue with.

Calderyn's gaze paused on that.

Then he spoke. "Inside," he said with finality. There was no introduction or explanation.

Just inevitability.

They stepped through the threshold and felt the chamber's pressure adjust around them subtle as a breath, as if the room had been waiting to inhale exactly their shape.

Calderyn's voice cut through the stillness. "Your integration results have been recorded," he said.

Soren's mouth twisted. "How reassuring."

Calderyn didn't react. "Reassurance is not the function."

Zephyr's smile flashed. "Then what is?"

Calderyn's eyes lifted to him. "Prediction."

Veya's stomach tightened.

Calderyn continued as if he hadn't said something dangerous.
"You will be observed more closely in the coming days."

Soren laughed, short and sharp. "More closely? You mean you're going to start breathing down our necks instead of staring from balconies?"

Calderyn's gaze didn't flicker in irritation or amusement at Soren's words. But his gaze continues assessment. "If you require a metaphor," he said evenly, "then yes. Something like that."

He paused, letting the air settle.

"Your recent… adjustments to the Academy's equilibrium have made distance inefficient."

Rhazien's voice was quiet and steady. "For what purpose?"

Calderyn paused, just long enough to feel intentional. Then he said "Stability."

The word landed like a weight.

Veya felt Soren's storm shift beside her, his pressure rising, lightning wanting to bite.

She reached for him without thinking, just a light touch on his wrist beneath the edge of his sleeve. Her touch wasn't meant to stop Soren but to help anchor him.

Soren's fingers tightened once around nothing.

Then loosened.

Calderyn watched the gesture, eyes narrowing slightly but not with disapproval. Instead, it caused interest.

Veya hated that.

Calderyn turned away, as if satisfied with what he'd seen. "Begin," he said.

The floor's sigils brightened.

And as the chamber woke around them, Veya felt it again, faint but unmistakable.

Not just the Academy watching.

Something much older and farther was paying attention through the cracks. Like the world itself had started leaning in. And this time, Veya couldn't tell whether it was curiosity…

Or hunger.

Chapter

Thirty-One

Faculty of Stone

Faculty didn't gossip.

They calibrated.

Veya didn't know a meeting was happening. No student did. Arcane Academy did not invite candidates into its decision-making any more than it invited them into its bones. But the Constellaria Wing had a habit of letting certain things leak, not as information, not as confession, but as pressure.

And pressure always found her.

It began after Calderyn dismissed them, as they drifted back into the corridors like the Academy expected them to pretend the trial had been ordinary. The ward-light had dimmed, the platform had gone still, and yet the sensation of being watched remained cleaner, closer, and more precise.

The air felt too sterilized. The stone beneath her boots held an inexplicable warmth, not heat, not fire, but something residual, like the corridor, remembered her weight and hadn't decided what it meant yet.

Soren stalked ahead as though speed could outpace surveillance. Zephyr walked with his hands behind his back, expression mild enough to be suspicious. Rhazien stayed near Veya without crowding her, silent, steady, like a brace against the building tension.

"No," Soren said suddenly, voice low and edged. "No. I'm not doing that."

Veya blinked. "Doing what?"

"Being their stability project," he snapped. "Did you hear him? *Prediction.* Like we're weather. Like we're a system they can model."

Zephyr hummed. "You are weather."

Soren shot him a look that could have ignited stone. "Not helping."

Zephyr's smile thinned. "I'm not trying to."

Rhazien's voice slid in smoothly, timed like a blade finding a seam. "You're reacting exactly how they want."

Soren stopped mid-step and whirled. "Oh, so now you're on their side too?"

"I'm on the side that keeps you from giving them what they're looking for," Rhazien replied, calm and certain.

Lightning skittered faintly under Soren's skin, eager as a threat. The storm in him pressed outward, searching for release.

Veya stepped closer before it could become words he couldn't take back.

"They don't want you loud," she said quietly. "They want you predictable."

Soren's gaze snapped to hers, sharp and immediate. Something raw moved behind it anger, yes, but edged with something tighter and more dangerous. Not fear of the Academy. Fear of being shaped into something he didn't choose.

Of being controlled.

Of being seen too clearly.

His throat worked as he swallowed, the motion rough enough to betray how hard he was holding himself together. "Then what do I do?" he asked.

The question landed quieter than his usual defiance, but no less intense.

Veya didn't look away. She didn't soften the truth or dress it in comfort.

"You do what you did in the trial."

His brow drew in. "I don't even know what I did."

"You didn't perform," she said, gentler now. "You didn't fight the story they tried to assign you, and you didn't try to become what they expected. You just… stayed inside yourself and refused to move for them."

She paused, letting the words settle rather than sharpening them further.

"That's why it couldn't hold you," she added. "You gave it nothing false to anchor to."

Zephyr's expression sobered for half a heartbeat. "She's right," he said softly. "You refused to feed it."

Soren looked away, jaw clenched. "I hate refusing."

"I know," Veya murmured not in accusation, not comfort. Recognition.

By the time they reached the common hall, instinct seemed to decide what their mouths didn't say. They split without discussing it, each taking distance the way people do when tension threatens to turn into something worse.

Soren disappeared toward the training corridors like motion was his only prayer. Zephyr drifted off as if he had errands only, he understood. Rhazien paused, gaze tracking the corridor like he expected stone to shift again at any moment.

Then he chose to remain near Veya.

Of course he did.

Veya returned to the dorm, but the dorm didn't feel like shelter today. It felt like a chamber inside a machine, the walls too smooth, air too patient, light too consistent.

She sat on the edge of her bed and tried to write the day into order.

Her thoughts refused.

Instead, they circled the one word Calderyn had

used, as though it had lodged itself behind her ribs.

Stability.

The way he'd said it had carried implication: that instability was their natural state, and everything they did was merely compensation. As though the Academy had already categorized them, filed them into an equation.

A variable.

Veya exhaled slowly, trying to release the tension that thought left behind.

The breath steadied her, only slightly.

Behind her, the stone shifted.

Not visibly. Not audibly. Yet the room felt different, subtly recalibrated, like a space leaning closer to hear a quieter conversation.

Listening.

The sensation sharpened along the wall nearest the common passage. For an instant, a seam appeared in the stone thin as a breath, almost impossible to detect before sealing again so smoothly it might have been a trick of light.

Veya stood.

She crossed the room, palm hovering near the wall where the seam had been. The stone felt warm, faintly pulsing, but not with the Academy's broad ambient current. This was narrower. Focused. Like a private corridor shifting behind the sanctioned architecture.

She didn't push.

She didn't demand.

Demanding access would have closed whatever this was before it fully revealed itself.

Instead, she listened.

She let her awareness settle, threading outward through layers of old stone and older wards, aligning rather than pressing and finding the existing seam and matching it the way breath matches breath.

For a suspended moment, the pressure sharpened.

And sound began to resolve.

Not words at first.

Contours. Intention. A room holding itself too still.

Then…

Voices.

The space beyond was not a classroom. Not a hall. Not a chamber meant for student use.

It was a decision-room.

Stone walls etched with records. There were no windows and no warmth to be found within the room. The air thin with magic held in restraint.

Professor Calderyn stood at the center, hands folded behind his back, posture perfectly neutral. He looked like the kind of man who could watch a world burn without changing expression provided it burned according to predictable rules.

Professor Virenna stood near a panel of moving sigils, records shifting and recalculating in clean, unforgiving increments. She didn't look at Calderyn. She looked at the data like it was an argument she intended to win.

A third presence occupied the room without standing in it.

Headmaster Oberon.

Veya didn't see him.

She felt him the way you feel an ancient tree in a forest. The weight of it, the age, and the quiet certainty that it could crush you without raising a hand.

His voice came from the architecture itself, calm and distant.

"Report."

Calderyn's tone didn't change. "Their integration remains confirmed."

"Unstable," Virenna added immediately. "Not in performance but in influence."

Silence deepened, cold and attentive.

Calderyn continued. "Environmental response observed on three occasions."

"Not individual," Virenna said. "Collective."

Oberon's voice remained calm. "Explain."

"When separated," Virenna said, fingers tracing the shifting panel, "the system normalizes. When together, the system responds."

Calderyn nodded once. "Not only Academy systems. External elements."

"Define external," Oberon said.

Virenna's jaw tightened by a fraction. "The lake."

A pause so deep the room felt colder.

Calderyn's voice stayed steady. "A creature response occurred. Recognition behavior. Non-random."

"And the candidates?" Oberon asked.

"Unaware of cause," Calderyn said. "Aware of attention."

Virenna's gaze sharpened. "Soren is volatile when pressed."

"He is reactive," Calderyn allowed.

"He is storm," Virenna said, like a classification.

Calderyn's eyes flicked to her. "And Veya?"

Virenna hesitated, only half a heartbeat.

"Veya is structural," she said at last. "She alters without exerting. She changes alignment rather than output."

Calderyn's attention sharpened. "She stabilizes him."

"Or contains him," Virenna corrected.

Oberon's voice: "Rhazien."

"Containment discipline," Calderyn said. "Self-sealed. He refuses narrative traction. He positions defensively around Veya."

Virenna's mouth tightened. "He respects her."

Calderyn paused, then conceded. "Yes."

Oberon's silence thickened.

"Zephyr," he said.

Virenna's gaze shifted. "Severance behavior adapting. He is capable of absence without collapse."

Calderyn: "And he is watching everything."

Oberon's voice was quiet, almost thoughtful. "So, the four form an axis."

"Yes," Virenna said.

Calderyn added, "They are integrating beyond intended parameters."

Oberon's tone sharpened slightly. "Is it dangerous?"

"Not yet," Virenna answered quickly.

Calderyn answered slower. "But it is accelerating."

Oberon's presence pressed into the room, like weather lowering over a field.

"Then we adjust," Oberon said.

Virenna didn't hesitate. "Split them."

Calderyn's stillness changed like the suggestion had weight even to him.

"Not yet," Oberon replied.

"If we wait, the influence becomes harder to separate," Virenna insisted.

"If we move too early, we provoke," Oberon said calmly.

Calderyn nodded. "We observe. Pressure test. Evaluate response under controlled conditions."

Virenna's eyes narrowed. "A major trial."

"A contained escalation," Calderyn agreed.

Oberon: "A trial that measures unit response."

Virenna's fingers traced a line of sigils. "And if unit response exceeds acceptable limits?"

Oberon held the room in silence for one cold beat.

Then: "Then we begin reassignment."

The words weren't cruel.

They were procedural.

Virenna's satisfaction was nearly invisible. "I will revise ward parameters."

"And increase archive monitoring," Oberon said.

Calderyn: "Already active."

Oberon paused. "One more variable."

Virenna's eyes lifted. "External attention."

The air cooled another degree.

Calderyn's gaze hardened slightly. "We have no confirmation."

"We have anomalies," Virenna said sharply.

Oberon's voice lowered, and for the first time, it was not entirely indifferent.

"Anomalies are how ancient things begin."

Silence.

Then, final and flat:

"Continue observation."

The sigils on the panel shifted and rewrote themselves.

The meeting didn't end with dismissal. It ended the way the Academy ended everything with motion, with decision, with time being granted only so the outcome could be watched arriving.

The sound blurred and collapsed inward. Veya's awareness snapped back into her dorm as if a thread had been pulled too sharply.

Her heart struck once, heavy enough to ground her back inside her ribs.

She stepped away from the wall, slow and deliberate, fingers tingling not from spell work, but proximity. The residual awareness of having brushed too close to something that had not been meant for her.

Major trial.

Unit response.

Reassignment.

The words arranged themselves across the slate with cruel clarity, each one settling into place as though the Academy had already decided how the next hours of her life would unfold.

Veya stared at them for a long moment.

The room around her was quiet, the late-night stillness of the dormitory pressing softly against the walls. Most of the other students had long since gone to sleep, their doors closed, their lamps dark.

But the silence in her room felt different.

Heavier.

The kind of quiet that comes just before something changes.

She let out a slow breath and lowered the slate slightly, the words still glowing faintly against the stone surface.

MAJOR TRIAL.

It was not another observation and not a minor assessment but something larger.

Something designed to break things apart and see what survived.

Unit response.

Her fingers tightened slightly around the edge of the slate.

The Academy wasn't just calling her.

It was calling all of them.

Reassignment.

The final word lingered longest, as if the system itself were considering the implications of what it had written.

Then a knock sounded at the dorm entrance, it was soft and controlled.

Not the impatient pounding of a nervous student or the casual tap of someone dropping by unannounced.

It was a knock of someone who already knew she was awake.

Veya opened her eyes.

The knock came again.

She crossed the room quietly, the wooden floor cool beneath her bare feet, and opened the door.

Rhazien stood there.

His posture was neutral, his expression calm, but his gaze held the steady focus she had begun to recognize whenever the trials shifted around them.

For a moment neither of them spoke.

He didn't ask what she had heard.

He didn't need to.

The Academy had called them both.

His eyes moved over her face like he was checking for fractures.

"You're pale," he said quietly.

"I'm fine," Veya replied, but the lie was thin.

Rhazien held her gaze for a beat. "Something changed."

Veya swallowed. "Yes."

"What?" he asked.

She hesitated, not because she didn't trust him, but because saying it out loud made it real.

"They're preparing a major trial," she said. "Designed around us. Around unit Eclipse."

Rhazien didn't look surprised. If anything, he looked resigned.

"As expected," he said.

"You knew?" Veya whispered.

"I suspected," he replied. "They don't observe without intending to act."

A third knock on the door, but it was louder and impatient.

Soren's voice cut through the stone. "Veya! Open up!"

Veya's chest tightened again, but this time it wasn't fear.

It was awareness.

Soren was the storm they planned to pressure-test.

And she… she was the anchor they were already measuring.

Veya opened the door.

Soren stood there with shoulders set and eyes bright with barely contained lightning. "I hate this place," he said immediately. "I hate the way it looks at us like we're a problem it's solving."

Zephyr hovered behind him as if he'd been there

the whole time. "To be fair," he murmured, "you are an excellent problem."

Soren shot him a look. "That's not comforting."

Zephyr's smile didn't reach his eyes. "I didn't say it to comfort you."

Veya met Soren's gaze and didn't flinch. "We are," she said softly.

His expression flickered. "What does that mean?"

"It means they're going to try to separate what happens when we're together," Veya said. "They called it reassignment."

Soren went very still.

Rhazien stepped closer, quiet and braced. "Then we stay controlled," he said. "We don't give them traction."

"You mean, I don't give them traction," Soren muttered.

Rhazien didn't argue.

Veya reached out and touched Soren's wrist. It was as light as breath. It wasn't to stop him but to anchor him.

Soren's gaze dropped to her hand.

Then back to her eyes.

For a heartbeat, the storm quieted. It wasn't gone completely but more contained.

"Okay," he said roughly. "Tell me what we do."

Veya inhaled.

And down the corridor, beyond the dorm walls, the stone warmed faintly, as if the Academy had leaned closer to listen.

"First," she said, voice steady, "we don't let them see us fracture."

Zephyr's shadows stirred at his heels, restrained.

Rhazien's gaze held steady, like a vow he would never speak.

Soren nodded once, sharp.

And somewhere beyond the Academy, beyond

stone, ward, and record, the air shifted with the faintest pressure of attention, like something older had heard the plan and found it… interesting.

Veya felt it.

And for the first time since arriving, her calm wasn't patience.

It was readiness.

Chapter Thirty-Two

Pressure Patterns

Morning didn't arrive the way it used to. It assembled.

Light gathered slowly along the stone corridors of Constellaria Wing. It was never warm, never kind, just present. Deliberate. Like the Academy had decided, visibility was required and the world had no vote in the matter.

Veya felt the shift before she opened her eyes. The air carried a different weight, the faint sense that the building had moved from passive observation into something more directed.

Intention.

Across the dorm, Soren was already awake.

She knew without looking. His energy had texture when he held it like this, tight and restless, pressing against his own skin as if a storm were trapped behind glass and resented the boundaries.

"Do you feel it," he said.

It wasn't a question.

Veya pushed herself upright, brushing sleep from her eyes. "Yes."

Soren leaned forward with elbows on his knees,

hands clasped as if he were physically keeping himself from pacing. "It's different today," he muttered. "It's not just watching. It's waiting."

Near the window, Zephyr hovered just above the floor like he'd been there the entire time, his presence too quiet to have been accidental. "Ah," he said softly. "We've reached the anticipation phase. My favorite."

Soren shot him a look. "You say that like we're about to attend a festival."

"In a sense, we are," Zephyr replied pleasantly. "The festival of institutional anxiety."

"That's not a real thing," Soren snapped.

"It is now."

Rhazien stood near the door.

Of course he did.

He wasn't guarding it and he wasn't blocking it. He was simply placed in the position he always chose when he expected movement to matter. The difference was so subtle most people would miss it. Except Veya had learned to read him the way she read storm pressure in the air.

"The Academy is shifting schedules," he said quietly.

Soren frowned. "You can hear that?"

Rhazien shook his head once. "It's Pattern. I can hear the movement through the wards. It's reorganizing."

Zephyr tilted his head. "How delightfully ominous."

"Everything here is ominous," Soren muttered, but his voice carried less bite than it used to. Instead, it carried more fatigue and more familiarity.

Veya rose slowly and crossed to the wall slate. It glowed faintly, already awake and already waiting. Like the stone had been expecting her.

"That's never good," Soren said. "When the wall is eager."

"It's never eager," Zephyr corrected. "It's inevitable."

The slate shifted.

Letters carved themselves into the surface in clean, final strokes:

CONSTELLARIA DIRECTIVE: ACTIVE
UNIT OBSERVATION CONTINUES
NEXT TRIAL WINDOW: UNASSIGNED
BEHAVIORAL RESPONSE MONITORING: PRIORITY

Soren stared at it as if it had personally insulted him.

"…Trial window unassigned," he repeated. "That's not terrifying at all."

Zephyr leaned closer over his shoulder, eyes flicking across the lines like he was reading a language he'd seen before in another life. "It means they haven't decided when to test us next," he said lightly. "Only that they will."

Soren dragged his hand down his face. "Have I mentioned how much hate this place?"

"No," Zephyr said calmly.

Soren blinked. "Excuse me?"

"You hate not understanding this place," Zephyr corrected. "Different problem."

Soren opened his mouth, ready to argue, then paused as if he'd hit something uncomfortably true. "… Okay," he muttered. "That's annoyingly accurate."

Rhazien stepped closer, gaze lingering on the final line.

"Behavioral monitoring," he said quietly, as though tasting the phrasing.

Veya felt the words settle deep in her chest like cold stone. "They're not watching what we can do," she said. "They're watching what we do before we decide to do it."

Soren looked between them. "So, we're being evaluated for emotional stability."

Zephyr's mouth curved faintly. "You say that like you have any."

Soren glared. "I have plenty."

"You have enthusiasm," Zephyr replied gently.

"That's the same thing."

"It is absolutely not."

Veya almost smiled.

Almost.

Then the stone beneath their feet pulsed once faint and steady.

Like a heartbeat.

All four of them went still.

"…Did you feel that?" Soren asked, voice suddenly stripped down to something real.

"Yes, I definitely felt it," Veya answered.

Rhazien's posture shifted, nothing dramatic, just readiness settling into his bones. "We're being positioned," he said.

Soren exhaled sharply. "Of course we are."

Zephyr straightened, expression sharpening as the humor drained from the edges. "Well then," he said. "Shall we go see what new form of psychological torment awaits us today?"

"No," Soren said immediately. "Let's stay here and pretend we're sick."

"The Academy does not acknowledge illness," Rhazien replied, tone level.

"Of course it doesn't," Soren muttered.

Veya stepped toward the door. "We're going," she said quietly.

Soren looked at her. His irritation didn't vanish; it rarely did but it shifted into something steadier, grounded by her certainty.

"…Yeah," he admitted after a beat. "We are."

The corridor outside felt subtly altered.

Students moved through it as usual, but the flow opened a fraction sooner when Veya's unit stepped into it.

Conversations didn't stop, yet they angled away. Bodies adjusted their paths without understanding why.

It wasn't avoidance.

It was allowance.

As if the Academy itself had widened the current so they could pass without friction.

Soren noticed instantly. His shoulders tightened. "They're doing it again."

Zephyr drifted beside him. "You're becoming difficult to ignore."

"I don't want to be noticeable," Soren muttered.

Zephyr's smile flickered. "Too late, you are very noticeable."

They reached the main crossing between guild wings and slowed as the building redistributed movement around them. Light fractured across the stone floor. Voices echoed.

For a moment, everything felt almost normal.

Then the floor warmed beneath their feet. Not from heat but from recognition.

Veya's breath caught, not from fear but from the strange intimacy of it like the way the stone seemed to *know* them.

Soren froze. "…Okay," he said slowly. "That's new."

Zephyr's expression sharpened. "No," he corrected softly. "That's deliberate."

Rhazien scanned the corridor, gaze narrowing. "Something's about to happen."

Soren's storm stirred under his skin. "What kind of something?"

The pulse deepened once more.

Then stopped.

Silence pressed in, not real silence, but the kind that exists inside a held breath. A corridor waiting for a decision to be made.

The nearest slate flared.

New text carved itself instantly:

ECLIPSE UNIT: REPORT
CONTROLLED TRIAL INITIATED

Soren stared. "…Now?" he said flatly.

Zephyr smiled without humor. "Oh yes. It's happening now."

Around them, students redirected as if on instinct, paths bending away until a clear route formed down the central hall. It wasn't an evacuation. It was compliance. A hallway clearing itself because the building had asked it to.

An open path.

For them.

Soren let out a slow breath. "I hate when the Academy does that."

Rhazien didn't look away from the corridor ahead. "Then don't give it traction."

Soren shot him a look. "I don't give it traction. It invents it."

Veya stepped forward first, not because she wanted to, but because hesitation here always cost more than movement. "Together," she said quietly.

Soren's gaze flicked to her. Some of the sharpness eased from his expression. Not gone just steadied.

"…Together," he agreed.

Zephyr straightened, shadows settling close as if they'd decided to behave. "How touching," he murmured. "We're a unit."

Rhazien moved into step beside Veya without comment.

They walked.

And as they did, Veya felt something else slip across her mind. It left as quick as a fish beneath dark water.

An almost-memory.

A face that should have been in the corridor last week. A name that hovered just out of reach.

She tried to catch it.

It slid away before it could become language.

Her hand tightened around the strap of her bag, her knuckles whitening.

Soren noticed her expression. "What?"

Veya forced her voice to steady. "Nothing. Just… don't let them make you perform."

Soren's jaw flexed. "Yeah," he muttered. "I'm starting to understand that."

They reached the turning corridor.

And somewhere deep within the Academy, something ancient shifted its full attention onto them. It was slow, deliberate, and unmistakably awake.

Chapter Thirty-Three

Major Pressure Test
Constellaria Wing & Containment Chamber

He usual notice came without warning, carrying the quiet certainty of a verdict.

A thin plate of stone surfaced from the dorm wall while we were still half-dressed, letters carving themselves into the surface with clean, decisive strokes like the Academy was speaking through a blade and expected obedience as punctuation.

MAJOR TRIAL: REQUIRED
ECLIPSE UNIT: ACTIVE
OBJECTIVE: STABILITY UNDER   LETHAL CONDITIONS
FAILURE RESULTS IN REASSIGNMENT

Soren read it once.

Then again.

Then he smiled like the expression hurt to hold. "Oh good," he said. "They upgraded us."

Zephyr drifted behind him, eyes moving over the words like they were a recipe he'd already tasted. "They upgraded the risk," he corrected. "Not us."

Rhazien didn't move. His gaze locked onto the last line, and the air around him seemed to tighten.

FAILURE RESULTS IN REASSIGNMENT.

His voice came out quiet. "They've decided to stop pretending."

My stomach tightened, not with fear but with something colder, like recognition. The Academy didn't threaten. It simply documented outcomes in advance and called that fairness.

Soren's fingers flexed. Lightning sparked once across his knuckles, brief, angry, and contained. He clenched his hand as if he could crush the reflex itself.

"Before we go," he said, voice rough, "we're clear on one thing."

Zephyr tilted his head. "Only one?"

Soren ignored him, gaze landing on me like I was the only fixed point in the room. "If it goes bad… we don't split. Right?"

No one spoke for a beat.

Because the building was listening.

Because saying it made it real.

"We don't split," I said.

Zephyr let out a soft sigh, theatrical and thin. "Wonderful. Group solidarity before potential execution. Very inspiring."

Rhazien nodded once. "If separation is forced, we regroup immediately."

Soren exhaled hard, like he'd been holding something back behind his teeth. "Good, we are in agreement."

Then, quieter, almost resentful of the honesty: "I really hate this place."

"I know," I said, and I meant it.

The stone plate warmed faintly beneath my fingertips, not with heat or comfort but with something closer to permission.

A seam opened in the far wall. A corridor formed

where there hadn't been one the moment before, pale stone lit by faint iridescence, like the Academy had decided it was time to walk us somewhere private.

We followed without being told.

Because the Academy didn't do invitations.

It did inevitability.

The chamber we were led into was not the integration room.

The circular platform hovered above a vast dark shaft that dropped into depth too complete to measure. No bottom revealed itself, only a slow swallowing darkness that seemed to absorb light rather than reflect it. The stone walls rose high around us in precise, curved layers etched with Constellaria sigils so thin and exact they looked like mathematical diagrams rather than wards.

Lines of faint silver light traced the carvings, shifting subtly as we entered, as though the chamber itself had turned its attention toward us.

The air smelled sterile, almost metallic, stripped clean of warmth or dust. This was not a place built for practice.

It was built for measurement.

Soren stepped onto the platform first, his confidence moving ahead of him like weather, as natural to him as breathing. The moment his boot touched stone, the ward lines flared, not bright but attentive, like eyes opening.

Zephyr drifted beside him. "Try not to be dramatic," he murmured.

Soren shot him a look. "Try not to speak."

Zephyr smiled. "No."

Rhazien stepped onto the platform last. Space adjusted around him in that subtle way I'd started noticing like the room decided it would rather make room than resist.

I stepped on after him.

The platform pulsed once.

And the voice spoke.

It didn't come from above. It didn't belong to a person. It came from the wards themselves, the architecture translating old magic into language.

Begin.

The platform divided into four zones. The zones were not divided with walls. They were divided with pressure that slid under the skin and pressed against instinct.

I felt my zone immediately. It didn't command my feet so much as it tugged at something deeper, urging me toward a specific kind of choice.

Soren's zone demanded restraint, and I felt his hatred for it from across the platform like static.

My own zone demanded decisive force, immediate correction, and overcommitment. It wanted me to solve with violence where I preferred alignment.

Zephyr's demanded silence, absence, and non-interference.

Rhazien's demanded engagement, participation, reaction, and presence.

It was inversion, deliberate conflict built into the design. The Academy had reversed our instincts on purpose, forcing each of us into the exact role we trusted least.

The Academy didn't want us to do what we were best at.

It wanted to see what happened when we were made wrong.

Soren's voice dropped lower. "Oh," he said with a wicked little laugh, "that's cute."

"It's not cute," Zephyr replied, eyes narrowed.

Rhazien's gaze swept the ward lines. "It's surgical."

The platform shuddered.

A structure rose from the stone: clean, contained, and too familiar.

A conduit lattice.

Not the chaotic one from the integration assessment, this one had been rebuilt into something the Academy could control.

It pulsed once, then again, and the pulse responded to us, not individually but collectively. The moment we shifted our weight, the rhythm sharpened as if the system recognized the pattern we formed when we stood close enough to matter.

Soren moved first anyway.

Of course he did.

But he didn't blast.

He braced.

Wind curved into a stabilizing arc, holding the lattice's wobble without forcing it into submission. Lightning flickered across his fingers, then dimmed as he clenched his fists hard enough to ache.

Restraint cost him. You could see it in the tightness of his jaw.

"Look at you," Zephyr called softly. "You're growing."

"Shut up," Soren snapped, then caught himself, because snapping was a reaction and the wards were waiting for it. He swallowed the rest of the storm back down.

I felt my own instinct rise: the urge to anchor the system with one clean, final choice.

My zone pressed harder, urging me to act. To force a solution, to burn through the uncertainty and take control of the moment.

I refused.

Instead, I adjusted, subtle, precise, like shifting one strand in a woven net. The lattice's pulse eased.

Zephyr's shadows twitched at his feet, offended by restraint. He stopped them, anyway, letting them flatten into absence rather than strike.

Rhazien's zone pressed engagement into him, trying to force him outward output, reaction, participation.

He stepped forward anyway, refusing both extremes.

He didn't flare with power, and he didn't retreat from the pressure pressing against him.

Instead, he held his ground, present without becoming reactive.

For a moment, it worked.

The conduit stabilized. The pulse slowed. The ward lines shimmered, displeased, as though competence without spectacle offended the design.

Then the system escalated.

A surge slammed through the lattice, it was not violent, not explosive either, but something colder.

Information.

Narrative pressure crashed onto the platform like a storm front made of accusation. The structure began to behave as if one of us was the problem.

And the ward chose Soren.

Lightning was an easy target for fear.

The lattice pulsed harder around him, reacting to his presence like a wound reacting to touch. The air tightened. The resonance shifted into something that felt like blame taking shape.

Soren went rigid beside me, the sudden stillness so sharp it felt like the air itself had tightened around him.

His breath caught halfway in his chest, as if something unseen had closed a hand around his ribs and refused to let go.

Then the voices came.

They didn't rise from the chamber or echo from the wards. They formed out of nowhere, thin and insidious, sliding through the air like splinters of thought that didn't belong to any living person. The sound of them was wrong. It was too soft to be real, too precise to be imagined.

They weren't meant to inform.

They were meant to hook instinct.

You did this.

The whisper slipped through the space between breaths.

You brought it.

Another followed, sharper this time, circling the moment like a predator testing weak ground.

It's your fault.

The words didn't accuse loudly. They didn't need to.

They simply repeated, over and over, pressing against the edges of Soren's control, waiting for the moment his storm answered them.

Soren's storm surged. Instinct demanded correction, fix it, crush it, and prove it wrong.

His hands lifted. Lightning crawled along his skin.

I moved without thinking.

My hand caught his wrist, light as breath, anchoring without restraining.

"Soren, look at me," I said.

He didn't want to.

I waited anyway.

His eyes snapped to mine.

"Don't prove it wrong," I said quietly. "Just don't help it exist."

Soren swallowed. His jaw worked like he was biting down on something sharp. "You make that sound easy," he muttered.

"It isn't easy," I said. "But it is possible."

Zephyr's voice cut in, low and unnervingly calm. "Let it blame you."

Soren stared at him like he'd lost his mind. "It's literally blaming me."

"Good," Zephyr said. "Then you don't have to perform. You just have to endure."

Rhazien's voice came steady. "Don't participate."

Soren's hands trembled with power aching to be used.

Then, painfully he lowered them.

He didn't correct the narrative.

He didn't fight the story.

He let it pass through without catching.

The ward hesitated.

The conduit's pulse faltered, like the system didn't know what to do with a storm that refused to strike.

The accusation thinned. It wasn't gone but it had weakened.

I held my adjustment steady, resisting the urge to solve everything at once. Zephyr kept his shadows quiet. Rhazien stood where the pressure thinned and gave the lie nowhere to root.

The lattice steadied again.

Somewhere in the lattice above us, a ward flickered. It didn't flicker in failure, but in calculation.

For a heartbeat, I thought we'd done it.

Then the Academy introduced the lethal condition.

It wasn't a physical drop.

It was a conceptual one, like the rules of the room tightened and the world sharpened its teeth.

The air changed. The ward lines brightened with a colder frequency. The dark drop beneath the platform became aware.

The darkness below shifted, not moving but deepening, like the chamber had suddenly remembered gravity and was eager to use it. A faint pull pressed against the soles of my boots, subtle but undeniable, as though the empty space beneath us had developed intention.

Depth and hunger gathered there, patient and enormous, like an opened mouth waiting to see what the Academy would feed it.

And then a figure appeared at the edge of the platform where the drop began.

A boy, he was a first-year. His eyes wide, wrists bound in shimmering threads of magic.

He didn't look at us like we were instructors.

He looked at us like we were the last option.

Soren's breath hitched. "Oh, no."

Zephyr went perfectly still. "That's not supposed to be there."

Rhazien shifted in subtle, immediate, and ready way.

The voice spoke again, neutral as stone:

Stability under lethal conditions requires consequence.

The binding threads tightened. The boy jerked, the fear in his face was clear as day, a sound catching in his throat as if even breath had become expensive.

My zone pressed harder, screaming for decisive force.

I knew I needed to burn the threads, break the binding and overcorrect.

The urge to do something rose fast.

I hated how easy it would be.

I could also feel the trap: if I struck too hard, I'd destabilize the lattice again and the drop beneath us wouldn't take one life. It would take whatever it could.

Soren took a step forward, furious. "We're not doing this," he growled.

Zephyr's voice sharpened. "Soren…"

"I said we're not…"

Rhazien cut in, calm but iron. "If you strike, you destabilize the platform."

Soren's eyes went wild. "The boy is going to die."

"I know," Rhazien said. "That's why you don't make it worse."

The boy's gaze met mine.

He wasn't pleading.

Just watching like he'd already accepted his role and was waiting to see what kind of people we were.

I inhaled slowly.

The stone beneath my feet warmed but not like fire but like alignment.

I stepped forward into the pressure of my zone. It

demanded force. It demanded spectacle.

I refused to give it the satisfaction.

I didn't burn the threads.

I adjusted the structure around them.

A single shift, small, precise, like turning a key in a lock that didn't want to admit it had hinges.

The binding threads loosened, not snapping, and not exploding either. But simply losing the angle that made them lethal.

The boy gasped. His shoulders dropped an inch as the pressure eased.

The conduit's pulse changed.

It didn't stop but started aligning.

Zephyr exhaled quiet and tight. "You're doing it again."

"Doing what?" Soren rasped.

"Making the room behave," Zephyr said and the way he said it sounded like it frightened him.

The lattice trembled, hunting for a new way to punish competence.

Narrative pressure surged again, this time toward me.

It wasn't accusation but more like expectation. As if the system decided I was the axis and everything should bend accordingly.

The ward lines brightened. The air leaned toward me.

Soren's eyes snapped to me. "Veya…?"

"I'm not doing anything," I said, and the truth made my throat tighten. I didn't want to be the center. I just refused to let someone die.

Zephyr's voice came out too soft. "You don't have to do anything," he murmured. "You just have to exist."

Rhazien shifted a fraction closer, not enough to touch me, but near enough that I understood the intention behind the movement. It was subtle, almost careful, yet unmistakable. If anything reached for me, it would reach him first. The instinct behind it wasn't possessive or controlling; it felt older than that, something quieter and more deliberate, like protection that had been written into his bones long before either of us understood why.

Then the sky above the chamber flickered.

The change lasted only an instant, so brief it might have been dismissed as imagination if all of us hadn't felt it at the same time. It wasn't lightning, and it wasn't the pale glow of the Academy's wards reacting to strain. The sky itself seemed to blink, a brief interruption in the steady darkness above Mistara, as if something vast had glanced in our direction before withdrawing again.

Everything held in place. Not frozen, but suspended air too still, bones too heavy. My breath stopped without permission.

Soren felt it first. His eyes lifted toward the sky, narrowing slightly as if he were trying to focus on something just beyond sight.

Zephyr's smile vanished.

Rhazien's shoulders tightened beside us, the first visible crack I had ever seen in his carefully maintained composure.

Something was looking in.

It was not the Academy.

And it wasn't the building or the wards that threaded through its towers.

It was something older.

The awareness pressed against the moment like a silent observer leaning closer, curious and patient.

The pause lasted only a single heartbeat.

For that single moment, the chamber stopped behaving like a system and waited like a witness.

Then the chamber resumed as if nothing had happened.

But the conduit's pulse had changed. It became responsive, like it had listened to rules that did not belong to Arcane Academy at all.

The voice returned, almost conversational in its indifference.

Continue.

Soren let out a short, humorless laugh. "Oh, I hate that."

Zephyr glanced at him. "Welcome to Veilyn," he murmured. "We hate things correctly."

Soren looked like he might argue…

Then the lattice cracked again, and a new collapse began.

This time, we moved together.

Soren redirected with restraint, anchoring instead of hurling.

I maintained alignment, holding the conduit's inward fold steady without overcorrecting.

Zephyr shaped absence, interrupting certainty without turning it into attack.

Rhazien held the line where narrative tried to return, refusing the lie a foothold.

The platform steadied beneath our feet.

The binding threads around the boy loosened, their tension fading until the strands unraveled completely and dissolved into harmless light. He staggered forward as the pressure vanished, his eyes wide and disbelieving, his lungs dragging in air as though he couldn't quite accept that breathing was still allowed.

For a moment he simply stood there, alive.

And then he vanished.

There was no gesture of release, no instructor stepping forward to guide him away. No door opened and no path appeared for him to follow. One instant he was there, shaking and gasping for breath, and the next he was gone, erased from the platform as cleanly as if the chamber had decided the measurement was complete.

It didn't feel like mercy.

It felt like the Academy had simply finished with him.

As though he had never been a person to begin with, only a variable in a problem that had now been solved.

Veya tried to picture his face again, his eyes, the curve of his mouth, the exact shape of fear on him and found the detail already slipping away. The memory didn't fade like normal recollection. It blurred with intention, as though the room itself were sanding it down before it could become guilt.

She reached for his name without meaning to.

The instinct rose automatically, the way memory always did when a moment mattered. But when she searched for it, there was nothing there.

Not a name half remembered.

Not a sound she could almost grasp.

Just absence.

It wasn't the kind of blank that comes from forgetting. This felt deliberate, as though the space where the memory should have lived had been carefully removed and sealed, leaving behind a silence she couldn't push past.

Before she could dwell on the sensation, the conduit stabilized.

The ward lines dimmed around the platform, their bright tension fading back into the quiet geometry of the chamber. The voice returned a moment later, flat and distant, as though the trial had simply concluded a calculation.

End.

There was no praise, no correction, and no explanation.

Only dismissal.

To the Academy, the trial had ended the moment the measurement was complete.

The pressure that had filled the chamber eased all at once, releasing like a breath the room had been holding since the trial began.

Soren exhaled hard, hands shaking with the storm he hadn't spent. "That felt personal."

Zephyr's smile returned thin. "Everything here is personal."

Rhazien's gaze flicked to the ward lines, measuring them like they were measuring him back.

And in my chest, something settled that felt uncomfortably like certainty.

This wasn't preparation anymore.

This was containment.

A seam opened in the wall. An exit corridor appeared. We stepped off the platform without being told.

The Academy dismissed the way it always dismissed us, by moving on.

As we walked, Zephyr fell into step beside Rhazien, voice low. "You know," he murmured, "you have a very irritating talent for making 'doing nothing' look like a strategy."

Rhazien didn't look at him. "It is a strategy."

Zephyr's mouth twitched. "Of course it is."

After a beat, Rhazien added, almost dryly, "You're improving."

Zephyr blinked once, then a brief, genuine smile slipped across his face.

"Don't say that out loud," he said lightly. "It might ruin my reputation."

Soren glanced back at them from a few steps ahead, his eyes moving between Zephyr and Rhazien with immediate suspicion.

"Are you two bonding?" he asked.

"No," Zephyr replied instantly.

Rhazien didn't answer at all. His silence lasted only a fraction of a second, but it was just long enough to betray him.

Soren caught it immediately.

His grin widened.

"Adorable."

I didn't say anything.

But something in my chest eased all the same. Not trust, not yet, but the beginning of something that might eventually grow into it. The kind of quiet shift that happens when people who should have been strangers start realizing they might survive better together.

And above us, somewhere beyond the stone of the chamber, beyond the wards and the careful record of the Academy, the air felt subtly different.

Heavier.

As though something had leaned closer to watch.

The attention no longer carried the distant curiosity we had felt before.

This felt… focused.

Interested.

314

Chapter

Thirty-Four

The Day the Academy Flinched

By the next morning, the Academy had done what it always did after a result it didn't like. It pretended nothing had changed.

The corridors were still stone and lanternlight. Slates still glowed faintly with schedules. Students still moved in predictable flows.

Only the pressure was different. It was tighter and more watchful.

As if the building had learned the shape of us and decided to monitor the edges more carefully.

We walked together because none of us said "split up" anymore.

No one wanted to test what happened if we did.

Soren looked like he hadn't slept. His storm sat under his skin like a bruise.

Zephyr moved with too much calm as if it was performative and practiced.

Rhazien stayed near me like he always did now. Not touching. Not hovering. Just… placed.

And I could still feel the chamber's blink in my bones. Like a handprint that left its mark.

The dining hall shifted when we entered. There

wasn't silence, just rearrangement. Conversations didn't stop. They angled. Laughter continued half a second too late.

People looked at us like they were trying to decide whether we were dangerous… or contagious.

A goblin attendant scuttled past our table, paused, and then hurried away without offering food.

Soren leaned forward. "Okay. That is not normal."

Zephyrs smile thinned. "Nothing is normal once an institution starts labeling you."

Two tables over, voices carried loudly yet unintentionally intentional.

"…I heard someone almost died."

"No, I heard they used someone."

"They broke the platform."

"They didn't break it," another voice insisted. "The platform blinked."

"That doesn't happen."

"It did."

A wolf shifter lowered their voice, though the tension in the room made the whisper carry anyway.

"Whatever they are… the Academy is scared of it."

The word *scared* landed harder than the rest of the rumors.

Soren's jaw tightened immediately.

He let out a short breath that was almost a laugh, though there was no humor in it.

"Oh, that's comforting," he muttered. "Fantastic, actually. I feel much better knowing the institution that's been running lethal magical trials for centuries is apparently afraid of whatever we just did."

Zephyr glanced sideways at him.

"You do have a gift for optimism."

Soren didn't look at him.

"No," he said flatly. "I have a gift for recognizing when we've officially crossed into the part of the story where everyone stops pretending things are normal."

Veya felt the tension in his voice more than heard it.

Soren's gaze flicked across the room, tracking the students whispering along the edges of the hall.

"They're not talking about the trial anymore," he said quietly. "They're talking about us."

Rhazien's attention had already shifted upward.

"There," he said softly.

A faculty silhouette stood half-obscured by a column, not watching the hall but watching us.

Professor Virenna.

She didn't frown. She didn't look curious. She looked… clinical. Like she was witnessing a measurement.

Then she turned and walked away, unhurried, as if her presence had been a checkmark rather than a threat.

Soren exhaled through his nose. "She's doing it on purpose."

"Of course she is," Zephyr murmured. "Constellaria doesn't watch accidentally."

Faculty of Stone

The Academy didn't let students into meetings. But the Academy wasn't the only thing listening.

Behind a private seam of stone, deeper in Constellaria's architecture, voices moved through the wards in clean, controlled, and sharpened by procedure.

Calderyn's voice: "The unit stabilized under lethal conditions."

Virenna: "And the chamber introduced consequence. It still failed to fracture them."

A third presence made themselves known, older, pressed through the architecture without needing a body.

Oberon.

"External attention," he said.

Silence.

Then Calderyn's steady voice said, "Verified."

Virenna's voice sharpened. "The chamber blinked."

Another beat of silence but this time colder.

Oberon spoke again, quiet as a knife. "That was not Academy behavior."

"No." said Calderyn

Virenna said, "Which means it is accelerating."

Oberon studied the shifting patterns of light moving slowly across the chamber walls. The wards had already begun recalibrating in response to the anomaly the four students had created, subtle lines of magic rewriting themselves through the ancient stone like a system correcting its own mathematics.

At length he inclined his head.

"Then we adjust."

Virenna's response came immediately.

"Split them."

She stepped forward as she spoke, her eyes bright with a kind of focused curiosity that bordered on excitement.

"If the unit remains intact, the results will continue contaminating each other," she continued. "We cannot isolate the variable if they insist on behaving like a structural formation."

Oberon did not turn.

"Not yet."

Virenna's expression sharpened.

"With respect," she said, though the words carried no softness, "waiting invites escalation we do not control."

Oberon's voice remained level.

"Separation now would produce incomplete data."

Virenna tilted her head slightly, studying the glowing wards.

"Or it would confirm which of them is responsible for the structural interference."

Calderyn had been watching the shifting magic in silence. Now he stepped forward, his voice calm but deliberate.

"We pressure-test again," he said. "Contained escalation. Increase environmental instability. Increase narrative resistance."

Virenna smiled faintly.

"Ah," she murmured. "You want to see whether the system bends… or breaks."

Calderyn ignored the comment.

"If the unit response exceeds acceptable limits," he continued, "we begin reassignment."

Virenna's gaze sharpened with renewed interest.

"Yes," she said quietly. "That would be informative."

Oberon finally turned from the wall, the light of the recalibrating wards reflecting faintly in his eyes.

"If the structure continues adapting around them," he said, "reassignment will begin."

Virenna folded her arms lightly.

"Good."

She looked back at the shifting wards.

"I would very much like to know what happens when the system stops pretending, they are students."

Silence settled over the chamber.

No one offered reassurance.

No one suggested restraint.

The meeting ended not with comfort, but with action.

Deep within the Academy's foundations, ancient stone shifted as dormant mechanisms awakened. Ward parameters rewrote themselves through hidden channels of magic threaded through the towers and halls.

The Trials were adjusting.

Not to protect the students.

But to provoke them.

Deliberately.

Students Who Start Treating You Like a Warning

By midday, the rumors stopped being stories.

They became behavior.

A first-year fae brushed past me and froze.

"I...I'm sorry," she blurted, eyes wide. "You just... felt warm."

I blinked. "I didn't touch you."

"I know," she said quickly, already backing away. "That's what I meant."

Soren stared after her. "Cool. So now we have an aura problem."

Zephyr's gaze lingered on the retreating fae longer than the rest of us, his expression sharpening with quiet consideration.

"No," he murmured after a moment. "We have a witness problem."

Soren frowned. "A witness to what?"

Zephyr didn't answer immediately. His attention remained fixed on the corridor behind us, as though he were already calculating the number of eyes that might now be watching.

"To a pattern," he said finally. "And patterns tend to spread."

None of us liked the sound of that.

We turned the next corner in the corridor and the building shifted.

It wasn't the familiar adjustment we had begun to recognize, the subtle rerouting that guided students away from restricted halls or redirected them toward quiet observation rooms.

The Academy did not lead us toward another calibration chamber.

It didn't guide us anywhere at all.

Instead, the space around us seemed to hesitate,

the ancient wards threaded through the stone walls flickering faintly as though the structure itself were reconsidering what to do with us.

Soren slowed.

"That's new."

The corridor stretched ahead of us, but the usual hum of controlled magic felt different now. It felt less like direction, more like calculation.

"This isn't rerouting," Zephyr said quietly.

Rhazien's gaze moved across the shifting wardlines carved into the walls.

"No," he agreed.

Zephyr's voice dropped another notch.

"This is something else."

A tightening, like the Academy itself had braced.

Rhazien slowed. "Do you feel that?"

"Yes," I said.

Soren's storm rose instinctively. "If they throw another chamber at us…"

Zephyr cut in, too soft. "They won't."

Soren glared. "How do you know?"

Zephyr's smile didn't show. "Because something else arrived first."

Creatures Respond Again

It wasn't random, and it certainly wasn't subtle.

The air in the courtyard shifted the way it had that other night, when the world seemed to hesitate just long enough to notice something important. Conversations faltered. Footsteps slowed. The space between breaths stretched wider than it should have.

For a moment it felt as if the entire courtyard was holding its breath.

Students glanced around in quiet confusion, trying to understand what had changed. Lanternlight flickered once along the stone walls, the glow wavering before steadying again.

Then the creatures appeared.

They didn't arrive in a rush or a spectacle. There was no dramatic entrance, no roar or blaze of magic announcing them.

Instead, they simply took their places.

Like pieces being set carefully on a board.

A unicorn stepped forward from the tree line, its silver coat catching the lanternlight in a way that made the metal railings nearby seem dull by comparison. The creature moved with quiet certainty, every step deliberate, as though it had known exactly where it meant to stand before it ever entered the courtyard.

A Pegasus descended near the fountain, its great wings folding slowly against its sides as its hooves touched the stone. The sound rang softly through the courtyard, a strange chiming note that echoed like distant bells underwater.

Above us, along the edge of a parapet, a feathered serpent uncoiled its long body across the stone. Its scales shimmered with muted color, and its head lifted slightly as it studied the courtyard below with eyes far too intelligent to belong to something merely animal.

And on the highest balcony rail, a phoenix settled into place.

Flame curled quietly along the edges of its wings without consuming them, the fire moving like living light across feathers that glowed but never burned. It folded its wings neatly against its body and watched the courtyard below with a stillness that felt deliberate.

At that point, the students stopped pretending this was normal.

Whispers spread quickly through the courtyard, sharp with confusion and rising fear.

"Why are they here?"

"They're not supposed to come this close."

"Who are they looking at?"

The answer became clear a moment later.

The unicorn lifted its head.

Until then it had stood quietly among the trees, its silver coat catching the pale light like something carved from moonlit metal. But now its ears turned forward

Something warm unfurled slowly in my chest, the feeling steady and strangely ancient, like recognition that had been waiting longer than I had been alive.

The Pegasus shifted its wings slightly, feathers rustling with a low crackle of static that spread softly through the air around Soren.

Above us, the feathered serpent tilted its head as though it were listening, not to our voices, but to something quieter beneath our skin.

And the phoenix…

The phoenix did not move at all.

Flame curled quietly along the edges of its wings as it watched us, the fire moving in slow, deliberate currents that never consumed the feathers beneath it. For a moment its gaze lingered on me longer than the others, and the flames along its wings flared almost imperceptibly, as if something about my presence had stirred a memory buried deep in its ancient instincts.

Then the fire settled again.

The phoenix remained perfectly still, watching with an unsettling kind of awareness, like it had glimpsed a future it didn't entirely approve of.

The look in its burning eyes carried an unsettling kind of awareness, as if it were studying a future, it had already seen and wasn't sure it approved of.

Beside me, Soren went very still.

For once the restless energy that usually lived in him seemed to vanish completely, replaced by the rigid attention of someone trying very hard not to move too suddenly.

"Okay," he whispered after a moment. "No. I'm officially done."

Zephyr didn't even look surprised.

"Be polite," he murmured.

Soren turned slowly toward him, his eyebrows lifting in disbelief.

"Did you just tell me to be polite to a phoenix?"

Zephyr lifted one shoulder in an elegant half-shrug. "It seemed like a reasonable suggestion."

Soren gestured vaguely toward the burning creature perched above the courtyard. "That thing is literally on fire."

"Yes," Zephyr replied calmly. "Which makes politeness feel like a very wise strategy."

Soren stared at him for a long second.

"You're unbelievable."

"I prefer well-informed."

Soren opened his mouth like he had three more arguments ready, then stopped and dragged his hands down his face in frustration instead.

"I can't believe this is happening," he muttered.

Zephyr's gaze drifted back toward the creatures surrounding the courtyard.

"I told you to be polite to what it represents," he said, his voice quieter now. "Because it's not here by accident."

That shifted the tone immediately.

Soren's sarcasm faded, replaced by a sharp, uneasy focus as his eyes moved from the phoenix to the unicorn, then up toward the serpent coiled above us.

Rhazien stepped half a pace closer to me, the movement subtle enough that most people might have missed it. He didn't touch me, but the shift placed him just slightly between me and the open courtyard, as if his body had made the decision before his mind had time to debate it.

Rhazien is always protective.

He is always ready.

I swallowed, the realization settling slowly into

place.

"They're witnessing," I said.

Soren's head snapped toward me.

"Us?"

Zephyr's expression didn't change, but something sharpened behind his eyes.

"Yes," he said quietly.

Soren let out a slow breath, glancing around the courtyard again as if hoping someone else might suddenly become the center of attention.

"They couldn't be here for someone else?"

"No," Zephyr said.

Soren groaned softly. "Fantastic."

Above us, the phoenix shifted its wings slightly, flame rolling along the edges like living light.

Soren glanced up at it again.

"…I still think telling me to be polite to a phoenix is insane."

Zephyr's mouth curved faintly.

"And yet," he said, "you're still doing it."

Zephyr didn't look away from the creatures. "Yes."

The unicorn lowered its head not a bow of submission but in a bow of acknowledgment.

The courtyard held its breath.

Then the creatures began to withdraw slowly and deliberately like they'd confirmed what they came to confirm.

The phoenix dissolved into sparks.

The serpent slipped from sight.

The Pegasus lifted skyward.

The unicorn lingered one last heartbeat, eyes on us and then turned and vanished into the trees.

The sound in the courtyard returned in a rush.

Students spoke over each other, trying to make meaning of what they had just witnessed.

But the meaning was already etched into behavior, we were no longer just an Academy problem.

We were a world problem.

Soren's laugh was short and humorless. "So… they're coming now."

Zephyr's voice was quiet. "They were already here."

Rhazien's gaze stayed fixed on the tree line where the unicorn had disappeared. "This wasn't curiosity."

"No," I said softly, feeling that older certainty that stirs under my ribs.

"It was confirmation."

And somewhere behind us, deep in the Academy's stone, beneath records and wards and policy, the building adjusted again.

It was not to comfort us.

Not to punish us.

But to prepare us.

Because whatever had blinked in the chamber… had just been seen by things that didn't care about curriculum.

And the Academy…for the first time felt like it was moving too fast to stay in control.

Chapter Thirty-Five

Veya and the Arcane Trials
The Trial That Chooses You Back

THe slate did not glow.

It warmed.

Veya felt the shift before she even looked down, a subtle change beneath her fingertips as the stone moved from neutral to aware, like something that had been holding its breath all night had finally decided to exhale in her direction.

The surface rippled.

The letters did not simply appear.

They rose.

ARCANE TRIALS: SUMMONED
SUBJECT: VEYA
ATTENDANCE: MANDATORY
TIME: NOW

For one suspended second, the room became so still that even the lanternlight seemed uncertain whether it should continue burning.

Then Soren leaned forward and read the slate.

Once.

Then again.

And it went very, very quiet.

Which was worse.

"…Subject," he said at last, his voice low and controlled in a way that never meant calm. "That's adorable, Veya. They've categorized you."

Zephyr drifted closer, eyes narrowing slightly as he studied the words.

"You are a category to them," he said.

Soren's smile showed far too many teeth. "Then they're about to learn what happens when categories bite."

Veya almost laughed, sharp and disbelieving, until she noticed Rhazien.

He was already moving.

Not dramatically. Not aggressively. He simply stepped into position with quiet precision, placing himself where he could see everything at once: the slate, the room, the door, the space around them. It was the kind of readiness that didn't need spectacle, the calm preparation of someone who had already measured the moment and decided exactly where he needed to stand.

"They're isolating you," he said evenly.

Veya swallowed. "Or maybe it's just…"

Zephyr's soft chuckle cut through her attempt at optimism.

"Stone does not 'just maybe' anything, Veya."

Soren's fingers flexed. Lightning snapped once, sharp and impatient enough to make the lanterns flicker.

"No," he said.

Veya turned. "Soren…"

"No." he said louder now. "They don't get to…"

He reached for the slate.

Veya caught his wrist.

Not hard enough to stop him by force.

But force had never been what stopped Soren.

It was her.

The moment she touched him, the storm inside him surged outward: rage, panic, pressure looking for something to break.

She didn't fight it.

She anchored it.

"Soren," she said quietly. "Look at me."

His eyes snapped to hers, bright and furious and painfully honest.

"You're not going alone," he said before she could speak.

The words came out like a verdict, sharp and immovable, as if he had just declared a law the world would have to obey.

Veya's throat tightened. "I'm not going alone."

For a moment he searched her face, looking for any sign that she might try to argue. When he didn't find one, some of the tension in his shoulders eased, though only a little.

Zephyr leaned in just enough to read the slate again. "The slate disagrees."

Soren turned his head slowly and fixed him with a look that could have stripped paint off stone. "I didn't ask the slate."

"I'm simply pointing out," Zephyr said, irritatingly calm, "that the ancient magical death-machine currently running the Trials appears to have a different opinion."

Rhazien spoke without raising his voice.

"Then we don't ask," he said. "We adjust."

Zephyr's mouth curved faintly. "Careful. That almost sounded optimistic."

"It's strategy," Rhazien replied.

Soren gestured sharply at the slate. "Great. Then strategize the door into letting us in."

Zephyr tilted his head toward the glowing words as though studying an interesting puzzle rather than a potentially lethal command. "It will attempt to center her as a solitary variable."

Soren stared at him. "In English."

"It wants her alone," Zephyr said. "Because alone

is easier to measure."

The air around Soren's hands crackled faintly.

"She's not alone."

"I know," Zephyr said quietly. "That's why we don't let it pretend she is."

Veya turned back to the slate.

SUBJECT: VEYA

The word did not sit passively on the stone.

It settled.

She felt it along her spine, not as weight or pain, but as alignment, as if something had located the exact axis of her balance and pressed there gently and confidently, as though it had always known where she stood.

She drew a slow breath.

"Okay."

Soren answered immediately. "Together."

She nodded once. "Together. But controlled this time. No performing."

He blinked. "So, what you're saying is, do it your way."

"Yes, exactly."

Zephyr brightened faintly. "Excellent. A plan that includes my favorite pastime, not dying."

Soren muttered, "I don't mind dying if it's dramatic."

"Later," Veya said.

Rhazien's gaze rested on her for a single, quiet beat. "Lead."

So, she did.

The corridor outside Constellaria Wing did not reroute them.

It yielded.

Lanternlight warmed in sequence ahead of their steps as though the Academy itself were escorting them. The air felt thinner, not emptier, but cleared, as if other sounds had been gently moved aside.

Soren noticed immediately. "It's making space."

"For her," Zephyr replied.

Veya hated the way that tightened something in her chest.

They passed first-years mid-laughter. The laughter didn't stop. It flattened. A girl glanced at Veya's slate, went pale, and looked away too fast.

Soren leaned closer. "If anyone whispers, 'chosen one,' I'm committing a misdemeanor."

"You commit misdemeanors recreationally," Zephyr said.

"You're a chandelier of problems."

"That's almost affectionate."

Rhazien spoke without looking at either of them. "You're both loud."

Soren looked offended. "I'm expressive."

"You're a performance," Zephyr corrected.

Veya exhaled despite herself.

Then they reached the archway.

There was no plaque, no instructor sigil, only two sentences carved above the entrance:

THE ARCANE TRIALS DO NOT TEST WHAT YOU CAN DO.
THEY TEST WHAT YOU ARE.

Soren stared up at it. "I hate that phrase."

"It's smug," Zephyr agreed.

Rhazien's gaze tracked the stonework. "No signature."

"Meaning?"

"No one wants accountability."

The slate warmed again in Veya's hand.

ENTRY: NOW

Soren stepped forward beside her.

The archway did not open.

For a moment nothing happened at all.

Then the wards along the seam flared faintly and the light shifted, sliding past him as if he were not there.

The door wasn't locked.

It simply refused to recognize him.

Soren looked down at the empty air in front of him. "...Rude."

Veya felt the realization settle quietly into place.

The door wasn't testing her.

It was isolating her.

A seam of pale light appeared directly in front of her.

Soren went very still. "No."

His storm surged so fast Veya felt it in her teeth.

Her hand snapped out and caught his sleeve. "Please don't."

"It's taking you," he hissed.

"Then change the pattern," Rhazien said quietly.

Zephyr studied the seam for another second, his expression sharpening as the structure settled into place.

"It's trying to arrange us," he said. "Assign positions. Predict the outcome before we even move."

Soren frowned. "That's how the Trials work."

Zephyr shook his head. "No. That's how stories work."

Soren's brow lifted. "What story?"

Zephyr pointed toward the seam with exaggerated patience.

"The story is very simple. She's the center, you're the reaction, Rhazien is the threat..." His eyes flicked briefly toward Veya before returning to the door. "...and I'm apparently the decorative complication no one accounted for."

Veya frowned. "Decorative?"

Zephyr glanced at her. "Temporarily."

Soren snorted softly. "Annoying. You forgot I'm annoying. Apparently, my job in this little story is to explode on cue whenever someone threatens her."

His gaze flicked toward the seam again, jaw tightening.

"Which means the Academy thinks it knows exactly how I'm going to react."

Veya looked from one of them to the other. "Then let's give it something else to predict."

Zephyr's smile returned, thin and satisfied. "Exactly."

He tapped the seam lightly with one finger. "So, we refuse the story."

Rhazien stepped forward, calm and deliberate enough to quiet the conversation around him.

"We enter as a unit."

He didn't raise his voice. He didn't need to.

The certainty in the statement settled into the space between them like something already decided.

Veya looked at the seam of pale light waiting in front of her. The Academy had built the moment to pull her forward alone. She could feel it in the way the light centered itself on her position, the way the wards held their breath as if waiting for the obvious next step.

Instead, she stepped sideways.

Not toward the seam.

Toward them.

Her hand stayed on Soren's wrist, anchoring the storm that still hummed beneath his skin. Two fingers hooked lightly into Rhazien's sleeve, feeling the steady presence there. Zephyr drifted closer on her other side until the empty air between them stopped feeling like distance and started feeling like intention.

For a second, the corridor held its breath.

Soren glanced down at where her hand still rested on his wrist. "…You're doing the thing again."

"What thing?"

"The thing where you pretend this is calm and reasonable."

Zephyr's mouth twitched. "It's her most alarming trait."

Veya ignored them both.

She did not push the door in front of them.

Instead, she adjusted the system.

The seam shuddered.

Light flared sharply along the carved wards as ancient mechanisms buried deep in the stone reacted to the disruption. Sparks snapped across the archway like flint striking steel.

For one suspended heartbeat, it felt as though the Academy itself was deciding whether to refuse.

The wards tightened immediately.

The structure resisted.

Rhazien felt the wards hesitate. "It's adapting," he said quietly. "To us."

Then the stone made a sound like something ancient reconsidering its position.

The seam widened.

Not just for Veya.

It widened for all four of them.

Soren blinked once. "Oh."

Zephyr's smile flashed, quick and wicked. "Well," he said softly, "hello, loophole."

Rhazien gave a single approving nod. "Proceed."

Soren stepped forward first.

Of course he did.

Veya watched him for half a second before following, keeping hold of the threads she had drawn together between them. If the Academy had intended to make her stand alone, it had clearly miscalculated the group it had gathered.

She stepped through last because she did not trust doors that behaved and as she passed the threshold, the light swallowed them.

They stood on a stone platform suspended in a sky without stars.

There was no horizon, no distant glow of moon or lantern light, only an endless expanse of dark stretching in every direction. Beneath the platform, the void dropped away into a depth so vast it felt less like distance and more like absence, a silence that swallowed the idea of ground.

Around them rose twelve pillars carved from the same ancient stone as the platform itself. Their surfaces were etched with sigils that glowed faintly in the darkness, patterns too intricate and deliberate to be decoration.

They did not feel like wards.

Wards were built to contain power or protect what lay within them. They carried tension, a quiet pressure that warned of boundaries and consequences.

These pillars held none of that.

Instead, they carried something older, something patient, as though the sigils had been etched not simply to control magic, but to observe it.

To remember it.

They felt less like defenses and more like records, as though every trial that had ever taken place here had been quietly inscribed into the stone, waiting to be studied long after the moment itself had passed.

At the center of the platform, a crystal circle was embedded in the floor.

It pulsed faintly with a slow, steady rhythm that moved through the stone beneath their feet like a distant heartbeat. The light within it shifted constantly, threads of pale energy weaving and unweaving themselves in patterns too complex to follow.

It wasn't a resonance sphere.

It was something far more deliberate.

It was a trial core.

Veya felt the moment it noticed her.

The recognition wasn't loud or dramatic. It came quietly, with the precise certainty of a mechanism finding the one shape it had been waiting for all along, the subtle click of a lock accepting the key meant to open it.

Soren felt it too.

He stepped instinctively closer to her, the protective motion almost automatic.

The core reacted immediately.

Light surged upward through the crystal in a sudden, blinding pulse. Energy raced along the etched lines in the floor, spilling outward into the surrounding pillars as though the entire structure had just awakened. The sigils answered with a faint glow.

For a heartbeat the whole platform hummed.

Then the pressure struck.

Not violently.

Not like an attack.

More like a correction, an invisible force pushing against Soren with deliberate precision.

Enough to stagger him back.

He caught his balance and swore under his breath. "Hey!"

Zephyr grabbed his sleeve before the storm gathering in his hands could turn the moment into something worse. "Stop trying to romance the architecture."

Soren shot him a glare. "I'm protecting her."

"Then do it without feeding the system," Zephyr snapped. "It's waiting for you to react."

Rhazien hadn't moved.

His gaze remained fixed on the glowing crystal, studying the shifting patterns of light like someone reading a language no one else could quite understand.

"It's centering her," he said quietly.

Veya looked at him. "Why?"

Before he could answer, the platform itself responded.

A voice filled the space.

Not the neutral announcement tone the Academy used for schedules and routine instructions.

This voice was different.

Older.

It carried the weight of stone that had outlived kingdoms and forgotten the names of the gods who once claimed them. When it spoke, the sound seemed to rise from the pillars themselves.

"*VEYA.*"

Her name did not echo.

It landed.

The sound struck the air like a claim pressed into wet clay, something permanent and deliberate.

Soren's jaw tightened instantly. "Don't talk to her like that."

Zephyr didn't even look at him. "Threatening architecture remains one of your least effective hobbies."

The voice did not acknowledge either of them.

"*THE ARCANE TRIALS REQUIRE A PIVOT.*"

The words settled into the chamber like weight being added to a scale.

Then the voice continued.

"*YOU ARE STRUCTURE.*"

For a moment, no one spoke.

The words settled over the platform like pressure. Even the faint glow inside the trial core seemed to pause between pulses, as though the system had just revealed something it rarely said aloud.

Soren let out a short laugh that carried no humor. "Well. That's unsettling."

Veya blinked. "Unsettling?"

"Yeah," he said, gesturing vaguely toward the pillars. "Because I'm pretty sure that wasn't meant as a compliment."

Zephyr's gaze remained fixed on the core, the shifting light reflected faintly in his eyes. For once, the usual amusement in his expression had faded into something quieter.

"No," he said thoughtfully. "It really wasn't."

Soren frowned at him. "You want to explain that part before I start threatening architecture again?"

Zephyr tilted his head slightly. "When systems talk about structure, they aren't describing someone inside the design."

His eyes flicked briefly toward Veya.

"They're describing something the design has begun to depend on."

Soren's jaw tightened. "That's worse."

Rhazien still hadn't looked away from the core. His attention moved slowly across the shifting patterns as though he were watching a machine reveal its internal design piece by piece.

"It means she isn't reacting to the system," he said calmly.

Soren turned toward him. "What does that mean?"

Rhazien finally lifted his gaze. "It means the system is reacting to her."

For a heartbeat, no one moved.

Then Soren exhaled. "…Okay. Yeah. That's definitely worse."

The voice deepened then, vibrating faintly through the platform beneath their feet.

"*YOU WILL BE TESTED.*"

The pillars surrounding them began to glow faintly, ancient sigils awakening along their surfaces.

"*YOUR UNIT WILL BE MEASURED.*"

The air thickened as pressure built inside the chamber, subtle but unmistakable.

"*YOUR INFLUENCE WILL BE CONFIRMED… OR BROKEN.*"

The last word rolled through the space like distant thunder.

Soren's storm answered immediately. Lightning crawled across his knuckles, thin white threads of energy snapping through the air as his temper surged ahead of his better judgment.

"Try it," he whispered.

The reaction was immediate. The world tilted, not in gravity or space, but in story itself, as though the trial had tried to force the moment into a path Soren had just refused to follow.

The world shifted in a way that felt wrong to the senses. Soren stumbled as the pressure pressed against him, the trial system clearly expecting the same outcome it had always produced before.

Lightning snapped violently along his arms.

The system waited.

It was watching for the explosion.

Veya moved.

Not dramatically and not with force, but with the quiet precision that had begun to define the way she interacted with the Trials. She didn't push against the pressure gathering in the chamber.

She simply adjusted.

One precise correction was enough. The shift rippled outward through the space like a thread being pulled straight through a tangled tapestry, subtle but undeniable. The pressure eased almost immediately, the unnatural tilt settling back into balance.

Soren caught himself as the force released him, lightning flickering along his hands before dissolving into harmless sparks.

For a moment, he didn't move.

He just stared at the floor beneath his feet, his expression tightening as if he were trying to understand what had shifted, and more importantly, what it meant that he hadn't been able to fight it.

The lightning that had gathered around his hands flickered once, then faded completely.

Zephyr exhaled slowly, the sound quiet but deliberate. "There," he said, almost to himself. "You felt it."

Soren didn't look at him. "Yeah. I really did."

Rhazien's attention never left the trial core. If anything, his focus sharpened. The shifting patterns within the crystal no longer looked random. They were responding, recalibrating in real time, adjusting to what had just happened between them.

"Again," he murmured.

It wasn't a suggestion.

It was recognition.

The system hadn't finished.

The voice answered at once.

"BEGIN."

All twelve pillars ignited.

Light surged upward through the carved sigils, racing along the etched lines like fire tearing through dry branches. The glow intensified rapidly until the entire platform was wrapped in a lattice of burning gold.

The air tightened.

Pressure built, not against their bodies, but against the shape of the moment itself, as if the world were drawing inward, preparing to collapse into something new.

The core pulsed.

Once.

Twice.

Then everything fractured.

Not with sound.

Not with impact.

But with a sudden, impossible shift, as if reality itself had been pulled apart at the seams and rewritten in the space between one heartbeat and the next.

And the world shattered.

They stood in the middle of a city choking on smoke.

Not illusion-smoke. Not harmless fog conjured for spectacle.

Real smoke.

It burned in the throat and stung the eyes, thick with the metallic taste of iron and something darker beneath it, like heat that had already consumed too much. Ash drifted through the air in slow gray spirals, settling over shattered stone and broken glass.

The street beneath their feet trembled.

A conduit had split the roadway down the center like a wound torn through the city itself. Jagged veins of unstable magic pulsed along its edges, rewriting them-selves every second as if the structure couldn't decide what shape destruction should take.

People ran through the smoke.

Some screamed.

Others simply stumbled forward with the blank panic of those who had not yet decided whether they were escaping or already too late.

Soren inhaled sharply. "You've got to be kidding me."

Zephyr's eyes moved across the street with quiet calculation. "Living trial."

Rhazien stepped closer to the edge of the fractured pavement, studying the pulsing conduit like a hunter studying unfamiliar terrain. "No instructors."

Soren dragged a hand through his hair, turning in a slow circle as he took in the collapsing buildings, the spreading fire, the people running in every direction with no clear escape.

"Fantastic. That's exactly what you want to hear in a place actively trying to kill us."

Another crash split the air.

Stone sheared loose from the upper levels of a nearby structure, slamming into the street hard enough to send debris skidding across the ground. The impact echoed down the corridor of buildings, sharp and final, followed by the sound of something else beginning to give way.

People screamed.

The sound wasn't distant anymore. It was close and immediate, cutting through the heat and smoke with a rawness that made it impossible to ignore.

Soren's head snapped toward it.

A child stumbled near the edge of the street, small hands scraping against broken stone as they tried to catch themselves. Behind them, part of a fractured wall shifted, the remaining structure tilting just enough to make what was about to happen painfully obvious.

Soren didn't think.

He reacted.

Power surged to his hands in a sharp, instinctive burst, lightning snapping into existence along his fingers as he stepped forward, already moving to intercept before the debris could fall.

Veya caught his wrist.

"Wait."

He jerked slightly against her grip. "Someone's going to die."

"I know," she said over the roar of the collapsing street. "But if you act wrong, more people die, not just the boy."

Soren glared at her, frustration and fear flashing across his face in equal measure. "I hate when you're right."

Zephyr leaned closer, his voice dry even as the city threatened to fall apart around them. "Please say that again. I'd like to frame it."

"Not now, Zephyr."

Veya forced herself to breathe slowly.

Around them the city roared with panic, but beneath the chaos she felt something else.

A pattern.

The conduit wasn't simply exploding outward.

It was folding inward on itself, collapsing and reforming like a machine that fed on urgency. The faster someone tried to fix it, the more violently it would react.

At first it had looked like destruction: random, overwhelming, and impossible to contain.

But it wasn't random.

It was structured.

The conduit wasn't just breaking the city. It was shaping it, folding the damage inward in a way that fed on urgency and reaction, pulling everything tighter each time someone tried to interfere.

Understanding hit her all at once.

Heroic intervention wouldn't fix this.

It would tear it open.

Every instinct in her body screamed to move, to act, to stop the falling stone and the spreading collapse, but the moment she imagined it she could feel the consequence ripple outward.

The structure would fracture.

The damage would spread, multiplying the moment anyone tried to force control onto something that had already been designed to collapse.

The trial wasn't looking for control.

It was baiting it.

It wanted someone to step in too quickly, to react instead of understanding. It wanted spectacle, something loud and decisive that would fracture the fragile balance holding the structure together.

It wanted panic.

More than that, it wanted someone to break first.

And then the accusations began.

They didn't rise gradually or come from a single direction.

They arrived all at once.

Voices cut through the smoke and heat, sharp and immediate, overlapping until they became something almost physical.

"You did this!"

"Fix it!"

"Why aren't you helping?"

"Do something!"

"It's your fault!"

The words struck like thrown stones: hard, fast, and impossible to track.

They didn't feel like ordinary fear.

They felt targeted.

Each accusation landed with unnatural precision, slipping past logic and aiming straight for instinct, for guilt, for the part of the mind that reacted before it could think.

The pressure built with every voice, tightening around them, demanding action, demanding response, demanding someone take responsibility for a collapse that had already been set in motion.

The trial wasn't just testing what they would do.

It was testing what they would believe.

Soren's storm surged violently in response, lightning flaring brighter along his hands as the pressure closed in.

Zephyr's voice cut through the chaos like breaking glass.

"Don't fight it!"

Soren spun toward him, lightning already crawling along his hands. "It's blaming us! You hear that, right? It's pushing it on us like we're supposed to fix it!"

"I know," Zephyr snapped, stepping closer without flinching. "That's the point."

Soren's jaw tightened. "Then we fix it."

"And give it exactly what it wants?" Zephyr shot back. "A reaction. A spectacle. Something loud enough to confirm its narrative?"

Soren's hands flexed, lightning snapping brighter. "People are going to die, Zephyr."

"And more will if you play along. This isn't a disaster. It's a design. And right now, it's trying to decide what kind of story you are."

Soren hesitated.

Only for a second.

But it was enough.

Rhazien moved.

He stepped forward into the thickest part of the chaos, into the center of the accusations as they sharpened and turned, as if they could feel something in him worth testing.

The voices shifted.

They weren't louder but they were closer.

"You did this."

"Fix it."

"Why won't you help?"

The pressure bent toward him like wind against stone.

Rhazien didn't push back.

He didn't flare, didn't defend, didn't correct the accusation or try to prove it wrong.

He simply didn't accept it.

The trial hesitated.

The words passed over him without finding purchase. They struck, but there was nothing in him willing to hold them, nothing that reached back to accept the accusation or make it real. The pressure slid off instead, dissipating as though it had nowhere to settle, nowhere to root itself.

For the first time since the trial began, the chaos hesitated.

Soren stared at him, the lightning in his hands faltering. "...How are you doing that?"

Rhazien didn't look at him. His attention remained fixed on the shape of the pressure itself rather than the noise it carried.

"By not participating," he said calmly. "It only works if we agree to the role it's assigning."

The implication settled between them.

Soren's brow furrowed. "...So, if we don't react..."

"It has nothing to push against," Rhazien finished.

And slowly, almost reluctantly, the narrative began to shift.

It wasn't collapsing or disappearing, but it started bending.

The accusations no longer struck with the same force. The voices faltered, their edges dulling as if the certainty behind them had been disrupted. What had felt targeted now felt misplaced, like the trial had reached for something that refused to exist.

Soren blinked, the storm in his hands dimming further. "That's not how anything works."

"It's how it works here," Zephyr said quietly.

Veya didn't answer.

Because she could feel something else.

Beneath the noise.

Beneath the voices.

The pattern.

While the others pushed against the pressure or refused it, she felt the structure underneath it began to clarify, like threads surfacing beneath tangled fabric.

The conduit pulsed again.

Magic twisted through the broken street like a knot being pulled tighter, feeding on urgency, on reaction, on the very chaos it had created.

Veya stepped forward.

She didn't rush.

She didn't reach for power.

While the world fractured around her, while stone collapsed and voices rose and heat pressed in from every direction, she moved with a kind of deliberate stillness that didn't belong to the chaos.

She was listening.

Not to the screams.

Not to the accusations.

But to something beneath it all.

The world sharpened and softened at the same time. The noise of the city pulled back as her focus narrowed. Falling debris, shifting light, even the air itself blurred at the edges, as if reality were receding just enough to reveal what lay underneath it.

The pattern.

She could feel it clearly now.

It wasn't chaos.

It was a knot: tightening in on itself, feeding on pressure, pulling every thread inward until the entire structure threatened to collapse under its own tension. And like any knot, it didn't need force to break it apart.

It needed understanding.

Veya stepped closer, her movement slow and deliberate, not because the danger wasn't real, but because she had stopped responding to it the way the trial expected. The heat should have driven her back. The instability beneath her feet should have made every step uncertain.

But it didn't.

Because she wasn't moving against it.

Instead, she was moving with it.

Her breath slowed naturally, falling into rhythm with the conduit's pulse until it became difficult to tell where her awareness ended and the system began. The shifting threads of energy no longer felt chaotic or hostile.

They felt responsive.

Not resisting.

Waiting.

As if the structure itself had paused to see whether she would finally understand it.

Her hand lifted gradually, not with urgency or intent to overpower, but with quiet precision.

She didn't cast or summon, didn't reach for power in the way the Academy had tried to teach them. There was no gathering of energy, no shaping of force, no visible claim over the magic around her.

Instead, she reached.

Not to take hold of the conduit or bend it to her will, but to find the place where it was already straining against itself. Her hand moved with quiet certainty, guided by something deeper than instinct, until her fingers hovered just above the shifting threads of energy.

She wasn't trying to control it.

She was trying to understand it.

And then she adjusted.

Not dramatically.

Not with force.

A single thread shifted beneath her awareness, a minute correction so small it might have been missed entirely by anyone looking for something louder.

But the system felt it.

As if it had just been touched by something it didn't know how to measure.

The conduit's pulse stuttered, then changed, its rhythm no longer feeding on itself but redistributing, the tightening pressure easing by the smallest fraction.

That fraction was enough.

The change moved quietly at first, almost imperceptibly, a subtle shift in the underlying structure that only became visible as its effects began to unfold. The ripple spread outward through the conduit in widening waves, like a breath finally released after being held too long.

Stone that had been mid-collapse slowed. The fractures running through the street stopped widening. The violent pull that had been tearing the city open lost its certainty.

Even the air changed.

The suffocating weight that had pressed against everything, the heat, the urgency, the expectation of impact, lifted just enough to make space for something else.

A fragile stillness settled over the city. It wasn't complete. Nor safe. But no longer tipping toward collapse.

The city seemed to inhale, as though it had been bracing for impact and had finally been given permission to hold.

The city was not healed, and it was not restored either.

But now it was no longer coming apart.

Soren stared at her, the storm in his hands gone completely now, replaced by something quieter, and sharper.

"What are you doing?" he asked, his voice lower

than before, edged with disbelief.

Veya didn't look at him.

Her attention remained on the pattern; on the way it continued to shift and respond beneath her influence.

"I'm listening."

And the trial reacted immediately.

Two more conduits tore open along the street with a violent crack.

Reality resisted the correction.

The change Veya had made didn't settle cleanly. It pushed back in subtle, persistent waves, like something that refused to stay healed, the structure beneath the city shifting restlessly as though it were searching for a way to return to collapse.

The conduit pulsed harder, its rhythm tightening as the pressure began to build again, not explosively, but with a steady, insistent force that made it clear the moment hadn't settled.

Soren moved closer to her, not stepping in front of her, not trying to take control, but closing the distance in a way that felt deliberate, as if he were choosing to stay within the moment instead of overtaking it.

For once, there was no instinct to override the moment.

Only the storm in him, held and waiting.

"Tell me what to do."

The words came out rough with urgency, but they didn't carry defiance this time.

They carried trust.

Zephyr blinked slowly. "Oh. That's new."

Soren didn't look at him. "I'm serious. I'm not guessing my way through this and making it worse."

Zephyr's mouth curved faintly, but he didn't press it.

Rhazien's voice came steady and grounded.

"You lead."

The words weren't encouragement or suggestion.

They were recognition.

Veya felt them settle across her shoulders all at once, not as pressure or fear, but as something heavier and far more permanent.

Responsibility.

For a fraction of a second, doubt flickered, not in her ability, but in the understanding of what it meant to be the one the system was beginning to orient around.

Then she chose.

"Soren," she said, her voice quieter than the chaos around them but steady enough to cut through it, "I need you with me."

He looked at her immediately.

"Anchor," she continued, holding his gaze. "Don't throw. If you hit it, it's going to tear everything open again."

For a second, he didn't move.

The hesitation was small, almost invisible.

Not because he disagreed.

Because everything in him was built to do the opposite.

To strike first.

To break the problem before it could grow.

His hands flexed, lightning threatening to return.

Then he forced it back.

"Anchor," he repeated, quieter this time, like he was rewriting something in himself as he said it.

The lightning in his hands didn't vanish.

It changed.

The wild, snapping arcs smoothed into controlled currents, curving outward instead of exploding, stabilizing the space around them instead of tearing through it.

Zephyr watched the shift with open interest. "Well. That's significantly less destructive than usual."

Soren shot him a brief look. "Don't get used to it."

"I won't. But I am enjoying it."

Rhazien had already moved, positioning himself

where the pressure felt thinnest, his presence steadying the space simply by refusing to let it distort around him.

Veya adjusted again.

Smaller this time. More precise. Less like an action and more like a refinement, as though she were tuning something that had already begun to settle into place.

The change was subtle.

But the system felt it.

And this time, they did too.

Soren didn't wait for explanation. His power shifted before he fully understood why, the lightning in his hands bending instead of breaking, anchoring instead of striking as the space around them steadied just enough to hold.

And for a split second, something slipped loose inside him. It was not a memory, not exactly, but the shape of one, incomplete and elusive, as though something half-buried had shifted just enough to catch the light before sinking out of reach again.

The world blurred at the edges, the smoke and fractured stone thinning just enough for something else to press through, a different kind of pressure, quieter and older than anything the trial could produce.

It felt like cold water closing in around him, deep and endless, the kind of stillness that didn't move but waited. The heat of the city faded beneath it, replaced by something vast and patient, as though he had stepped too close to the edge of a memory that didn't belong to this moment at all.

A voice reached him.

Not loudly, and not with any clear shape or language he could follow, but with a certainty that didn't need volume to be understood.

It didn't call to him.

It settled into him.

Hold.

The word carried no echo, no force behind it, and

yet it landed with absolute precision, fitting into place as though it had always belonged there. It felt the same as Veya's voice had, steady and impossible to ignore, but deeper than that, older, like an instruction remembered rather than learned.

For a fleeting instant, it felt as though something inside him recognized it.

As if the space it filled had never truly been empty.

Then the image fractured before he could reach it.

Gone.

The city slammed back into focus, heat and noise rushing in all at once. His lightning flickered in response, threatening for a second to break loose again.

But it didn't.

It held.

His jaw tightened as he tried to grasp what had slipped through him, the shape of the moment already dissolving the more he reached for it.

"What was…" he started, but the question fell apart before he could finish.

There was nothing there.

Only the lingering certainty that something had answered before he did.

Something that already knew how to hold.

The thought should have unsettled him.

It didn't.

He swallowed it down instead, pushing past the instinct to question it. Now wasn't the moment to chase it.

So, he let it go.

Not because it didn't matter.

But because this did.

He drew a slow breath, grounding himself in the present, in the pressure still building around them, in Veya's voice and the space she was holding together.

He let the instinct settle instead of fighting it, drawing on it with a control that felt unfamiliar but steady. When the power in him surged, it didn't lash outward looking for something to break. It gathered, tightened, and held, shaping itself into something deliberate instead of destructive.

He anchored.

"Anchor," he repeated under his breath, as if the word itself helped lock the motion into place.

Wind curved outward from him, not as a violent blast, but as controlled arcs that wrapped around the crumbling buildings like invisible scaffolding, catching what would have fallen and holding it where it stood.

Zephyr tilted his head slightly, his gaze tracking the unstable seams of magic as they tore and recoiled.

"Zephyr," Veya said.

Her voice wasn't loud, but it carried.

He glanced at her, the faintest hint of amusement returning to his expression. "Yes?"

"Don't push against it. It's feeding on anything that tries to hold shape the wrong way."

Zephyr's brow lifted slightly. "And the right way?"

Veya's focus sharpened, something unreadable flickering beneath the surface of her calm.

"Take away what it's using. Not the structure. The excess."

For a fraction of a second, the air around her seemed to tighten, as though the system itself had paused to listen.

"Shape absence."

Zephyr's smile deepened, not playful this time, but interested. "Finally."

Shadow answered him at once.

It didn't surge outward in force or spectacle. Instead, it folded inward with deliberate precision, wrapping around the unstable seams and swallowing the stray surges of magic that fed the collapse. The excess energy vanished into silence, leaving behind something cleaner, quieter, something the system struggled to destabilize again.

Zephyr exhaled softly. "That's disturbingly elegant."

Veya didn't respond.

She was already shifting her attention.

"Rhazien."

He didn't turn; his gaze fixed on the fractures splitting through the street. "I see them."

"Not the breaks," she said, stepping slightly to the side as her awareness brushed across the pattern again. "The edges around them. That's where it's deciding whether to hold or tear."

Rhazien's posture adjusted almost imperceptibly as the instruction settled into place.

"Hold the thin places," she finished.

He moved immediately.

There was no hesitation.

No wasted motion.

He stepped into the fractures, not to force them closed, but to occupy the space where they threatened to widen, his presence steadying the instability simply by refusing to let it define itself.

The cracks didn't vanish.

But they stopped spreading.

For a moment, the system seemed to falter, caught between what it had been doing and what it was now being forced to become.

Veya adjusted again.

This time the change was smaller. More precise. Not a forceful correction, not something dramatic enough for anyone watching to notice, just another thread in the unseen structure shifting quietly beneath her awareness.

But the city felt it.

The resistance didn't vanish, but it faltered, the pattern loosening just enough to allow the correction to take hold. The collapse lost its rhythm, its certainty breaking apart as the structure beneath it began, slowly, to realign.

For the first time since the smoke began rising, the

street stopped collapsing.

As if the world had finally decided to listen.

The broken conduit resisted the adjustment, its unstable pulse flaring and collapsing as though the trial itself refused to accept the new shape she was pressing into it. Magic lashed through the fractured street like a living thing fighting restraint.

The city fought her.

The trial resisted.

For several long seconds, it felt as though the structure might succeed.

Then the sky shifted.

Not with the quick flicker of ward-light, and not with the controlled response of the Academy's systems adjusting to change. This was something else entirely, something that didn't belong to the structure of the trial or the rules that governed it.

It was a pause.

A break in continuity.

And it carried a weight that felt older than anything the Academy could create.

The change settled over the city like the world hesitating on the edge of a thought.

Then everything stopped.

Flames froze mid-flicker. Chunks of falling stone hung motionless in the air. Smoke stilled into quiet, unmoving shapes.

Even the sound vanished.

For one impossible heartbeat, the entire world held perfectly still.

Not paused.

Held.

As if something had reached into the fabric of the moment and decided it was not yet finished.

And Veya felt it, not the familiar pressure of the trial or the structured presence of the Academy, but something entirely different.

It wasn't forceful, and it didn't close in around her the way danger usually did.

It settled on her.

Attention.

It came from somewhere deeper, somewhere that did not need stone or magic or systems to observe what was happening here.

Something had just noticed her.

Then the moment passed.

Reality resumed all at once. Falling stone crashed into the street again, flames roared back to life, and the air filled once more with the chaotic sounds of a city trying to survive itself.

But something had changed.

The conduit's pulse no longer thrashed violently against her adjustments.

The unstable magic slowed, the rhythm shifting subtly as if the structure had reconsidered the purpose of the trial.

It was no longer trying to break her.

Now it was trying to understand her.

"STRUCTURAL INFLUENCE: CONFIRMED."

The city began to stabilize, not all at once and not perfectly, but enough to halt the steady unraveling that had threatened to consume it. Smoke still lingered in the air, hanging low between fractured buildings, while broken stone littered the streets where structures had nearly collapsed but somehow held.

Fires continued to smolder along shattered walls, their heat no longer spreading but not yet fading, and somewhere deeper in the ruined blocks, frightened voices echoed through the aftermath of something that had come far too close to breaking everything apart.

But the violent rhythm that had driven the destruction was gone.

The conduits no longer tore themselves wider. The unstable pulse that had threatened to rip the street apart settled into something quieter, something controlled.

The city seemed to release a long, exhausted breath. It wasn't healed, and the scars of the chaos still lingered, but the destruction had been halted. The city was no longer tearing itself apart.

For a moment, the four of them simply stood there, surrounded by lingering heat and drifting ash, listening to the strange calm that had replaced the chaos.

Then the trial decided it had seen enough.

The smoke thinned.

The shattered buildings blurred at the edges like wet paint dissolving in water. The street beneath their feet began to lose its weight, its solid presence fading as the illusion unraveled piece by piece.

The city dissolved around them.

They stood once more on the stone platform.

The smoke-choked city was gone as if it had never existed, leaving behind only the cold, silent chamber of the trial space. For a moment none of them spoke. The sudden stillness after the chaos felt almost unreal, and they stood there catching their breath, the echoes of the burning streets still lingering in their lungs.

There was no applause.

No voice announcing success.

Only the quiet patience of the ancient stone surrounding them, watching and recording as it always had.

Then the platform beneath Veya's feet warmed faintly.

She looked down just as new words began to carve themselves slowly into the surface of the stone.

THE ARCANE TRIALS HAVE ACKNOWL-
EDGED VEYA.

The stone beneath the carved words warmed faintly.

It wasn't heat exactly, not the kind that came from fire or magic. It was something subtler than that, a quiet shift beneath their feet, as though the ancient structure of the platform had simply acknowledged what had just taken place.

Not approval.

Recognition.

Soren stared at the message for a long moment, his expression tightening as the meaning settled in. "That's… terrifying."

"Yes," Zephyr agreed mildly. "It really is."

Rhazien remained still, his gaze fixed on the carved letters as if he were measuring something deeper than the words themselves. "It's also an answer."

Veya looked up at him. "An answer to what?"

Before anyone else could respond, the voice returned.

It did not sound impressed.

It did not sound concerned.

And it certainly did not sound reassuring.

"CONTINUE."

No explanation followed.

No confirmation that they had succeeded.

Only the expectation that the trial would proceed.

A thin seam of pale light appeared along the far edge of the platform, widening slowly as the exit opened for them.

Soren stepped a little closer to Veya without quite touching her, the instinctive movement subtle but unmistakable.

Rhazien shifted to her other side, his presence steady and grounding.

Zephyr drifted a step behind them, no longer the amused observer he had been earlier. Now his attention remained sharp, watching the chamber the way a strategist watches a battlefield even after the fighting stops.

Together, they stepped toward the exit.

As the light widened and the platform began to fade behind them, Veya felt it again.

That same presence.

The older attention.

It brushed the edges of her awareness the way distant thunder brushes the horizon before a storm breaks: subtle, unmistakable, impossible to ignore once felt.

Only now, it was closer.

Not near in distance.

In focus.

The awareness behind it had sharpened, no longer drifting or observing in passing. It had settled, deliberate and steady, as if whatever had been watching had finally decided where to look.

Not curious.

Interested.

The distinction settled into her slowly, but with a certainty that left no room for doubt. This wasn't something encountering her for the first time, nor something trying to understand what it was seeing.

It had already chosen.

For the first time since the Trials had begun, understanding didn't arrive as a question or a flicker of instinct.

It settled quietly into place.

The Academy had not summoned her here to teach her what she was.

It had summoned her because the Trials had recognized something in her that predated them.

And now that recognition had been returned.

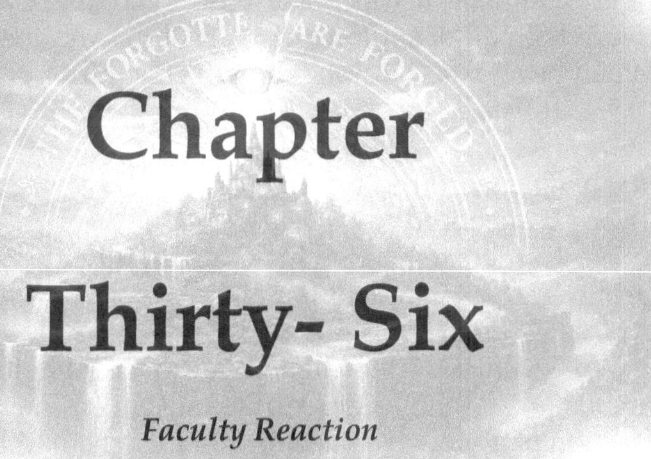

Chapter

Thirty- Six

Faculty Reaction

The Problem Becomes a Pattern
The decision-room did not change.
It never did.

It was carved to absorb pressure without showing it. Its stone was older than policy, older than curriculum, older even than the professors who believed they governed it. It was designed so that panic could exist without echoing.

Which meant that when tension entered the room, it became quieter.

And far more dangerous.

Professor Calderyn stood at the center of the circular chamber; hands folded behind his back. His posture was neutral enough to be mistaken for calm.

It was not calm.

Professor Virenna stood near the record panel, stylus hovering just above the surface, as if the stone had personally offended her.

Headmaster Oberon was not physically present.

He did not need to be.

His presence threaded through the architecture itself, woven into the walls, the floor, the very structure of the chamber. It was not a sensation that pressed or overwhelmed. It settled quiet, absolute, and inescapable. When he spoke, the stone did not echo him.

It listened.

"Report," Oberon said.

The word did not carry.

It anchored.

Calderyn inclined his head slightly, the motion precise rather than deferential.

"Arcane Trials initiated."

Virenna's stylus halted mid-mark, the tip hovering just above the record surface as if even she needed a fraction of a second to decide whether she had heard him correctly.

"Initiated," she repeated slowly. "By whom."

Calderyn's gaze shifted toward the panel, where sigils continued to rearrange themselves in slow, deliberate patterns, as though the Academy was still deciding how to categorize what had already occurred.

"By the Trials."

Silence followed.

Not empty.

Weighted.

Oberon's presence deepened within the chamber, subtle but unmistakable, like the foundations of the building settling under a new and unwelcome truth.

"The Academy did not authorize activation," he said.

It was not a question.

"No," Calderyn replied evenly.

Virenna's jaw tightened, the stillness in her posture becoming something sharper, more controlled.

"Then something inside our walls acted without sanction," she said. "Which means either we have lost control of a core system… or we never had it to begin with."

Calderyn did not correct her.

He didn't need to.

"The Trials are not a department," he said, his tone calm but carrying a quiet edge. "The system continues to operate within expected parameters," Calderyn added.

A brief silence followed, subtle but present.

"Despite the absence of its origin."

"They are not governed, scheduled, or contained by faculty oversight."

Virenna's eyes flashed, irritation sharpening into something more dangerous.

"They are a function of this institution," she said, each word said with deliberate meaning. "Integrated, maintained, and until now, predictable."

Calderyn's gaze lifted to meet hers fully.

"They predate it."

The words settled into the room with a finality that did not invite argument.

For a moment, even Virenna had no immediate reply.

That landed.

Not as information.

As a problem.

The record panel pulsed once beneath Calderyn's hand, the light shifting across its surface in slow, deliberate patterns. It did not feel like data being recorded so much as memory deciding where to settle, as though the Academy itself were considering how best to keep what it had just learned.

Calderyn watched the panel for a moment longer before speaking again.

"The unit entered together."

Virenna's attention sharpened immediately.

"They were permitted to enter together?" she asked.

The question was precise, but the edge beneath it was unmistakable.

"No," Calderyn replied. "They weren't permitted."

Virenna's eyes narrowed.

"Then explain why the gate accepted them."

Calderyn's expression didn't change. "Because they forced a pattern adjustment."

For the first time, something like real irritation flickered across Virenna's face.

"You allowed a gate structure to be altered," she said, her voice flattening into that dangerous, clinical calm that meant she was already three steps past annoyance and into analysis.

Calderyn glanced up at her.

"They altered it," he corrected. "There's a difference."

Virenna folded her arms, though the movement felt less defensive than controlled, as if she were containing the speed of her own thoughts.

"Is there?" she asked. "From the Academy's perspective, the distinction seems largely academic."

"It isn't academic if the system is adapting around them in real time," Calderyn said.

That settled into the room with more weight than the words themselves should have carried.

The walls seemed to absorb it.

Oberon had not moved, but his presence pressed more deeply into the chamber all the same, the silence around him tightening until it felt as though even the stones were listening for what came next.

"And inside?" he asked.

The question was quiet, almost conversational.

It didn't need force.

It drew the room's attention toward him anyway, the kind of gravity that didn't demand focus so much as assume it.

Calderyn did not look down at the panel when he answered.

"City construct," he said. "Multi-conduit collapse. Layered instability. Narrative pressure introduced early."

Virenna's gaze sharpened immediately. "A blame construct," she said, more to confirm than to ask.

"Yes."

Her stylus tapped once against the record surface, a soft, precise sound that carried more weight than it should have.

"And?" she pressed.

Calderyn's voice did not change.

"The unit resisted."

A slight pause followed. It was not confusion, but recalibration.

Virenna's eyes flicked up. "Resisted," she repeated. "As in endured, or as in disrupted?"

Calderyn met her gaze.

"As in refused to participate."

That landed harder than the initial report.

Virenna leaned back slightly, the movement controlled but thoughtful now, her irritation giving way to something more analytical.

"How?" she asked.

This time, Calderyn did pause, it wasn't for effect.

But for precision.

He chose the words carefully, as if the phrasing itself mattered.

"Rhazien nullified narrative engagement," he said. "Zephyr removed excess feed from the instability. Soren altered his response pattern."

Virenna's brow furrowed faintly. "Altered," she echoed.

"He anchored," Calderyn clarified.

That alone would have been notable.

But it wasn't the point.

"And Veya?" Oberon asked.

The question came softer than before.

Not less significant.

More.

Calderyn's gaze shifted, not to the panel, but to the

space just beyond it, as if what he was about to say did not belong entirely to record.

"Veya adjusted the system," he said, "without casting."

The room went still.

It didn't go quiet.

It just went still.

Virenna's stylus lowered slowly until it rested against the surface, her attention no longer divided between observation and analysis.

"Repeat that," she said.

Calderyn did not.

He didn't need to.

The panel hesitated.

Only for a fraction of a second, but long enough to feel wrong, like the system had reached for something that should have answered… and found nothing there.

Then it corrected itself, the sigils tightening back into place as though the lapse had never occurred.

The sigils rearranged themselves, light shifting across the surface in slow, deliberate motion before stabilizing into a single, unmistakable line:

STRUCTURAL ADJUSTMENT DETECTED
SOURCE: VEYA
METHOD: NON-CAST

No one spoke.

Because there was nothing in the Academy's recorded history that matched it.

And for the first time since the report began, the silence did not feel like control.

It felt like uncertainty.

SUBJECT: VEYA- STRUCTURAL INFLUENCE CONFIRMED
TRIAL RESPONSE: NON-RANDOM
UNIT COHESION: STABILIZING

Virenna stared at the text like it might rearrange itself if she waited long enough.

"That is not student behavior."

"No," Calderyn agreed.

Oberon's voice deepened slightly. "What did the Trials record."

The panel shifted again.

New words carved themselves with clean finality:
THE ARCANE TRIALS HAVE ACKNOWL-
EDGED VEYA.

The temperature in the room dropped a degree.

Virenna spoke very quietly. "That phrase has not appeared in…"

"Generations," Calderyn finished.

Virenna's fingers tightened subtly around the stylus, the small motion the only outward sign of the shift in her thinking.

"So," she said slowly, "we are past curriculum."

It wasn't a question.

It was a conclusion.

The kind that changed how everything after it would be handled.

Oberon did not respond immediately.

The silence stretched, deliberate and heavy, as though the Academy itself were listening for how he would choose to frame what had just been confirmed. The stone beneath them seemed to settle, the faint hum of the chamber quieting as if even the structure understood the importance of what came next.

When he finally spoke, the room leaned toward him.

"External attention," he said.

The words were quiet.

But they altered the shape of the conversation instantly.

Calderyn's jaw tightened by the smallest fraction, the only indication that the statement had landed exactly where it was meant to.

"The blink occurred again," he said.

Virenna's gaze snapped to him, sharp and immediate. "During the trial?"

"Yes."

Her expression tightened further. "During failure?"

Calderyn didn't hesitate.

"During stabilization."

That hit harder.

Virenna exhaled sharply through her nose, the controlled sound edged with something closer to irritation than surprise.

"So," she said, her tone cooling into something more precise, "it watched her succeed."

Oberon did not correct her.

He did not affirm it either.

"And the others," he said instead.

The shift was intentional.

Calderyn answered without hesitation.

"Soren anchored rather than discharged."

There was a faint pause after the words, just long enough for their weight to settle. For Soren, that alone was a deviation significant enough to note.

Virenna's lip curled faintly, the reaction more reflex than thought. "Then he can be trained."

Calderyn's eyes flicked to her, the movement brief but pointed.

"He can be contained," he said.

The distinction was subtle.

It was also deliberate.

Virenna did not like it.

That much was clear in the slight tightening of her posture, the way her grip on the stylus shifted just enough to betray the tension she was otherwise containing.

"Training implies cooperation," Calderyn continued, his tone even. "Containment assumes deviation."

Her gaze sharpened on him. "We are not containing students."

"We are containing outcomes," he replied.

The words sat between them like a boundary neither was willing to step across.

Oberon let the tension hold for a moment longer before redirecting.

"Zephyr."

Virenna's attention shifted, her voice returning to that clipped, clinical precision she favored when something interested her more than it irritated her.

"Severance behavior adaptive," she said. "He removed excess instability without triggering collapse. No overextension, no feedback surge."

There was a faint pause, then she added, almost reluctantly:

"Controlled."

Calderyn inclined his head slightly. "He is not acting independently."

Virenna's gaze flicked toward him. "Explain."

"He is following Veya's structural adjustments," Calderyn said. "Not reacting to the system. Instead, he was reacting to her."

That changed the calculation.

Virenna's expression stilled, the implications settling into place with visible precision.

"That," she said quietly, "is a liability."

Her words were not loud.

Not dramatic.

But they landed with finality.

Because it wasn't Zephyr she was assessing anymore.

It was the fact that someone else had become the point the system was beginning to orient around.

"Containment discipline maintained. Narrative traction denied. Protective positioning around Veya increased."

Virenna's eyes sharpened. "Define increased."

The panel answered.

PROXIMITY SHIFT: +17%

DEFENSIVE ORIENTATION: CONSISTENT
PRIMARY ANCHOR TARGET: VEYA

Virenna's voice went flat. "He's bonding."

Calderyn did not flinch. "He's aligning."

"Same difference."

"No," Oberon said quietly. "It is not."

Silence deepened.

Then the panel pulsed again.

Harder this time.

A new line carved itself, it was not part of the record sequence and not part of the structured report.

It surfaced from deeper stone.

WITNESS REQUIRED.

Virenna stepped back half a pace.

Not out of retreat.

It was recalibration.

The distance gave her just enough space to look at the panel not as a record, but as a problem.

"That was not our insertion," she said.

Her voice had lost its earlier edge. What remained was sharper, more focused, the tone she used when something had moved beyond protocol and into anomaly.

Calderyn did not answer.

He didn't contradict her either.

The absence of correction carried its own weight.

Oberon's presence shifted within the chamber, not advancing, not withdrawing, but adjusting. Like a structure redistributing its own balance under new pressure.

"Define source," he said.

The command did not rise.

It narrowed.

The panel responded.

Or tried to.

The sigils beneath the most recent entry brightened, rearranging themselves in rapid, intricate sequences as though searching for a classification that did not yet exist. For a moment, the patterns almost stabilized.

Then they broke.

The light fractured into an unreadable lattice, symbols dissolving into overlapping forms that refused to resolve into meaning.

The system had encountered something it could not name.

Virenna went very still.

Her voice lowered, not in uncertainty, but in precision.

"It is responding to the blink."

Calderyn's gaze remained fixed on the panel. "Yes."

Virenna's eyes sharpened, the correction immediate.

"No," she said. "It is responding to what caused the blink."

That changed the atmosphere of the room. Not in any visible way, but in the subtle shift of weight, as if the conversation had crossed into something none of them could easily contain.

Oberon's presence thinned slightly, not diminishing, but focusing, like a blade drawn to a finer edge.

"Anomalies," he said, "are how ancient things begin."

The words settled into the chamber like a warning written into stone.

Virenna's jaw clenched, the restraint in her posture tightening into something more decisive.

"Then we split them now," she said. "Before the pattern stabilizes around her."

Calderyn did not move.

But something in his stillness changed, the quiet neutrality giving way to a more deliberate resistance.

"Premature fracture increases instability," he said.

Virenna turned toward him fully now.

"And delay increases consolidation," she countered. "They are already aligning. You saw it. The gate, the trial response, the adjustment. This is not coincidence, Calderyn. This is convergence."

Her stylus tapped once against the panel.

"Cohesion at that level does not unwind cleanly."

Calderyn's voice remained even. "Neither does forced separation."

"It becomes irreversible if we wait," she said. "The longer they operate as a unit, the more the system adapts around them. At a certain point, we will no longer be testing them."

A beat silence.

"We will be responding to them."

That was the real concern.

Oberon let the silence hold just long enough for the implication to settle.

"And if we move too early," he said, "we provoke what is observing."

The words didn't rise.

They didn't need to.

They carried a different kind of weight now. One that extended beyond the Academy, beyond the Trials, into something older that had already begun to take notice.

Virenna's gaze flicked back to the panel, to the unresolved sigils still shifting in quiet refusal.

"...Then we are already being observed," she said.

Calderyn didn't look at her.

"That does not mean we escalate it."

"It means we are late," she replied.

Oberon did not answer immediately.

For a moment, the chamber held all three positions at once:

Control.

Containment.

Caution.

Then, quietly, "Then we proceed," he said.

Not a resolution.

A decision to continue anyway.

Virenna's stylus scraped against stone. "We are already provoking it by allowing her to continue."

Calderyn's voice dropped, quiet and uncomfortably honest.

"The Trials already chose."

Silence.

"Our control," he continued, "is now conditional."

That landed harder than any raised voice could have.

Oberon spoke again.

"Controlled escalation," Oberon said at last.

The words were delivered without urgency, spoken with the calm certainty of someone accustomed to decisions that altered lives without needing to raise his voice.

Calderyn inclined his head in quiet acknowledgment, absorbing the instruction as if it had already been anticipated. "A major trial," he replied evenly, "designed to pressure the unit structure directly. If their cohesion is genuine, it will endure the strain. If it is not, the fracture will present itself."

Virenna's gaze sharpened slightly, though she made no effort to hide the interest that flickered there. Her eyes reflected the faint glow of the record panel as its sigils shifted beneath her stylus.

"And if fracture fails?" she asked.

The question carried no outrage and no hesitation. It sounded almost academic, as though she were discussing a variable in an experiment rather than the futures of four students.

Oberon did not answer immediately.

When he did, his voice remained calm, steady, and procedural. Exactly the tone one might use when adjusting a line in a report.

"Reassignment."

The word settled into the room without drama.

It did not echo through the chamber or rattle the architecture. It did not need to. Everyone present understood what it implied, and that understanding was far louder than any sound.

Virenna resumed writing.

Her stylus scratched across the panel's living surface with deliberate pressure, the marks etching themselves into the Academy's records as though the decision had always been waiting to be written.

Calderyn remained where he stood.

To anyone less familiar with him, his posture would have appeared unchanged, the same measured composure he carried into every faculty discussion. Yet something subtle had shifted beneath that stillness.

It wasn't doubt that had shifted his posture, nor fear.

What settled into Calderyn instead was something colder and far more deliberate: calculation. The kind that came from recognizing a pattern that had begun moving beyond prediction yet refusing to look away from it.

Across the chamber, Oberon's presence receded slightly into the architecture of the room. It did not vanish, nor did the pressure ease entirely. It simply repositioned itself deeper within the stone, like a storm withdrawing behind distant mountains while still shaping the air.

"Continue observation," Oberon said.

The words were quiet, almost casual, yet they carried the unmistakable weight of command.

At once the record panel responded. Its surface rippled faintly as the sigils rearranged themselves, rewriting the Academy's living record with patient precision, each new line settling into place as though the future had already been waiting for the moment to acknowledge it.

Official lines stacked neatly into record.

But beneath them, beneath policy and ward and institutional restraint, another truth vibrated through the stone like a second pulse.

The Academy was no longer asking whether Veya would survive the Trials.

It was asking whether the Trials would survive her.

And somewhere deeper still. Beneath the Academy's records, beneath the living architecture that carried Oberon's authority through stone and corridor, something else had begun to stir.

It existed below the systems built to observe and measure. Below the wards designed to contain power. Even below the reach of the man whose presence shaped the building itself.

Beyond Oberon.

The Academy believed it was watching the students.

It believed it was guiding the Trials.

But far beneath those assumptions, something older had already taken notice.

It was not a faculty member watching from the gallery, nor a mechanism hidden within the Academy's systems. It was not a mind that could be summoned to a meeting, questioned, or recorded in the panels that tracked every student, every trial, every decision carved into the institution's living memory.

This awareness existed beyond those structures.

Older than the processes meant to control power. Older than the authority that Oberon carried through the building's stone. It lingered in a deeper layer of the world itself, where patience mattered more than urgency and observation could last longer than generations.

And whatever it was, it had been waiting.

Something that had witnessed generations rise, fracture, and vanish long before the Academy learned to carve its authority into stone.

It had watched the Trials before they were curriculum.

Before they were even called trials.

And now, as the record panel above quietly etched Veya's name into the Academy's living memory, that deeper presence shifted its attention.

Not with surprise, but not with the curiosity of something encountering the unexpected. The movement felt far older than that, deliberate and patient, like the turning of a tide that had been waiting for the right moment to return.

It was recognition.

As though a pattern long buried beneath years of silence had begun to move again. As though something the world had nearly forgotten had finally stepped back into alignment with it.

One of the Forgotten had risen once more into the shape of the living world.

And somewhere beneath Mistara, far below the stone halls of the Academy and the authority carved into its walls something ancient had begun to witness.

Chapter

Thirty- Seven

The Major Trial Notice
When The Academy Stops Pretending

The notice didn't appear.

It manifested, and Veya watched it happen. Stone rippled in the Curriculum Hall the way water rippled when something large moved beneath it. The slate wall always carved, always permanent, shifted by a fraction, as if the Academy had decided permanence was optional when it suited the measurement.

The surface smoothed.

Then it re-wrote itself without being touched.

Students gathered in a dense semicircle, shoulder-to-shoulder, the way people crowded a fire when they were cold and telling themselves it wasn't fear that brought them close. The hall filled with that specific tension Arcane Academy loved most: curiosity braided to dread, contained only by the illusion that someone else would be called first.

Soren pushed through the crowd because of course he did.

"Move," he said, not rude, but urgent, the kind of urgency that didn't ask permission. The storm in him pressed against his skin like it hated waiting even for air.

Zephyr drifted close behind him, his gaze narrowing as the slate finished forming its first line. "Careful," he murmured. "If you shoulder the wrong person, they'll write a myth about it."

Soren didn't look back. "Let them."

Rhazien didn't push. He didn't need to. He stepped into the nearest gap and without understanding why students shifted aside to make room, like their bodies recognized something in him and chose the safest option without thinking.

Veya felt the slate's hum through the soles of her boots. It wasn't exactly magic. Not the kind that sparked or flared.

It was attention.

Then the new heading carved itself into the stone.

The letters were not written.

They were gouged, as if the Academy had used a blade.

MAJOR ARCANE TRIAL: EFFECTIVE IMMEDIATELY

TRIAL TYPE: POWER/COORDINATION/ CONSEQUENCE

STATUS: LIVE MEASUREMENT

FAILURE RESULTS IN: INJURY / REMOVAL / DEATH

The word DEATH sat there like it belonged.

That was the problem.

It shouldn't have belonged anywhere near schedules and slates and corridors that pretended this place was a school.

It didn't read like a warning.

It read like a prophecy finally getting tired of metaphor.

Soren stared at the line for a long moment.

Then he smiled, not amused. Offended, like the Academy had committed a personal insult. "They really put *death* on a slate," he said quietly. "That's… bold."

Zephyr's mouth curved faintly. "Ah. Honesty. How novel."

Rhazien's gaze remained on the header, unreadable. "They're tired of rumors," he said. "They want it witnessed."

Veya swallowed. Her palms were damp against her own slate, her grip tightening without permission. "They're going to do it in front of everyone," she said.

Zephyr's eyes flicked to hers. "Yes."

Soren turned toward her too fast. "No."

Veya didn't blink. "It's already happening."

Because below the warning, the slate began carving names.

Not all at once.

One at a time, slow enough to force the crowd to watch each fate arrive like a ceremony.

A name appeared.

A student made a sound, half relief, half apology.

Another name.

Then a pause long enough for hope to form and be punished for existing.

And then:

UNIT: ECLIPSE - SUMMONED

The air changed. Not dramatically, not with a flare of light, just a shift in pressure, like the crowd sensed the line before their eyes finished reading it.

"That's them," someone whispered too loudly.

"Of course it is," another voice replied, sharp with inevitability.

The reaction spread in a ripple. Students turned in increments, heads swiveling toward them, shoulders angling away, space widening the way it widened around heat when heat began to look hungry.

Soren's jaw ticked. "I hate that people have mouths."

Zephyr murmured, almost fond, "You love that people have mouths, you just hate what they do with them."

Rhazien didn't speak. His posture shifted barely, but Veya felt him move closer to her side not touching, not hovering. Simply placed, the way he had begun to place himself around her as if his body understood a threat before his mind named it.

The slate continued.

TRIAL LOCATION: THE COLOSSEUM OF THE FORGOTTEN

OBJECTIVE: STABILITY UNDER LETHAL INPUT

CONDITION: THE SYSTEM WILL ASSIGN BLAME

INSTRUCTION: DO NOT CORRECT THE STORY

Soren let out a short, humorless laugh. "Oh, now they're giving instructions. How generous."

Zephyr's voice went quieter, more serious. "They aren't teaching you to win."

Rhazien's gaze sharpened. "They're teaching us to survive being misnamed."

Veya felt that land in her ribs like a stone.

Because she understood it. She understood the way the Academy didn't just test power, it tested narrative. It tested how quickly a room could be convinced to fear the wrong person, and whether the wrong person would explode to prove them right.

Near the back, a tall third-year in Astrael colors snorted like he couldn't help himself. Confidence sat on him like a second cloak.

"Finally," he said. "A real trial."

His friend elbowed him hard. "Shut up."

The third-year grinned wider anyway, reckless and bright. "I know what I'm doing."

Soren's head turned. His eyes narrowed. "Do you?"

The grin faltered just a fraction.

Zephyr leaned in, voice mild and sharp as a needle. "What's your name, brave volunteer?"

The boy lifted his chin. "Kael."

Veya repeated it silently without meaning to. Kael. Astrael. Loud enough to be noticed.

For a moment, though, the name slid strangely in her mind, like it didn't want to stay put. *K…?* No. Kael. She had it. She did.

Still, the sensation lingered an almost-slip, a near-blank where certainty should have been.

The slate kept carving.

ADDITIONAL PARTICIPANTS:
SELECTED RANDOMLY

Zephyr made a soft sound that was almost a laugh. "That's a lie."

Soren muttered, "Everything here is a lie."

Rhazien said quietly, "Not everything."

Veya glanced at him. His eyes stayed on the slate, calm and controlled, but the air around him carried that subtle pressure again like heat leashed too tight behind stone.

"The slate says random," Veya murmured.

Rhazien's voice didn't change. "It won't be."

The Arena of Wards opened itself an hour later.

It didn't open with a door.

With alignment.

Corridors shifted until there was only one way to go, and everyone was already walking it before they realized they'd been guided. Students poured in from every wing, every guild color, filling tiered stone seating that rose high above an enormous circular platform.

The arena felt old in a way the Academy halls never did.

Not historic.

Not preserved.

Judgment-old.

The kind of place that had not been built to teach, but to decide. Where outcomes were not guided or graded, only witnessed and made permanent.

The stone beneath their feet carried that weight.

Not memory in the way records held it, but something deeper, something final, as though every trial that had taken place here had not simply ended, but been concluded.

Veya's gaze lifted slowly, taking in the vast curve of the structure rising around them, the scale of it too deliberate to be anything but intentional.

"This place…" she murmured.

Zephyr's eyes traced the upper tiers, where the shadows seemed to gather more thickly than they should. "Not an arena," he said quietly. "Not really."

Rhazien's voice came measured. "A verdict space."

Soren frowned. "That's worse."

For a moment, no one spoke.

Then the stone itself answered.

The words did not appear all at once.

They carved themselves into the inner wall, slow and deliberate, as though the structure had waited until they were standing within it to name itself.

COLOSSEUM OF THE FORGOTTEN

The name did not feel like a title.

It felt like a warning.

Zephyr exhaled softly. "That's… not subtle."

Soren glanced around the arena again, his expression tightening. "Forgotten by who?"

Rhazien didn't look away from the carved words.

"Not by who," he said.

A beat.

"By what."

Hairline fractures webbed the floor, sealed and resealed so many times they formed a faint pattern beneath the surface, history repaired but never erased. Rings of wards shimmered in layered circles around the central platform; frozen ripples of arcane script suspended in air.

They weren't barriers.

They were boundaries.

And boundaries implied consequences.

The magic here didn't flare.

It watched.

Like it had watched hundreds stand where they would stand and did not care how many more would fall.

Soren stared down into the center and exhaled slowly. "Okay," he said. "That's… not a simulation chamber."

Zephyr hovered beside him, unusually still. "It's a mouth," he said. "And we're about to step onto its tongue."

Soren blinked. "You're gross when you're poetic."

"I'm accurate," Zephyr replied.

Rhazien didn't look at the arena first. He looked at the seating, scanning the upper arches where faculty stood in shadow, silhouettes that weren't watching the crowd.

They were watching the floor.

No, they were watching them.

Veya followed his gaze.

Professor Calderyn, hands folded behind his back, expression unreadable.

Professor Virenna beside him, sharp as a blade.

And higher still, deeper in shadow, a place where no one stood, yet Veya felt weight anyway, ancient and certain.

Oberon wasn't visible.

But he was present.

Soren felt it too. His shoulders tightened. "Can we leave?" he muttered, only half joking.

Zephyr smiled faintly. "You can."

Soren stared at him.

Zephyr continued, cheerful. "You'll simply be removed. Probably publicly."

"That was the least comforting thing you've ever said."

Veya stepped forward. "We don't run."

Soren's gaze snapped to hers. Some of the storm in him softened, still there, just steadied. "I know," he said quietly. "I just want to."

Rhazien's voice was low. "We move together."

Zephyr looked between them. "How romantic."

Soren: "Shut up, Zephyr."

Zephyr: "No."

They descended.

Stone met their boots with dull finality as they stepped onto the arena floor. The wards brightened in response, not welcoming.

Recording.

And a voice spoke not from a person, not from a podium, but from the architecture itself.

MAJOR TRIAL: BEGIN."

The platform split into four zones.

Not separated by walls.

Separated by pressure.

The same trick again, but sharper less like calibration, more like a blade sliding under skin.

Soren's zone demanded restraint so intensely that Veya could almost feel it pressing against him. The air around him resisted every surge of storm as if the space expected him to snap and wanted to see whether he would.

Veya's zone demanded decisive force. The ground beneath her thrummed with expectation, urging action as if hesitation itself would be counted as failure.

Zephyr's zone demanded silence, absence, flattening every instinct he had to move, speak, or disrupt. It wasn't suppressing him; it was asking him to become nothing.

Rhazien's demanded engagement. Heat coiled in the air around him like a provocation waiting to be answered.

Veya felt the pattern settle with cold clarity.

Inversion again.

Not random. Not coincidence.

Each of them placed where their instincts would fail first.

The arena didn't want their strengths.

It wanted to see what happened when those strengths were denied.

Soren looked across at Veya, jaw clenched. "I hate this."

"Oh, trust me, I know," she called back, voice steady.

Zephyr's voice carried like lazy wind. "Try to enjoy it. It's probably the last fun we'll ever have."

Soren shouted, "THAT'S NOT HELPING!"

Rhazien didn't raise his voice. "Focus."

Then the arena generated the problem.

A conduit rose from the floor. It was cleaner than the city construct, more contained, and far more personal. It pulsed in steady beats, and every beat carried pressure that felt like accusation in a language the body understood too easily.

The wards tightened.

And the system chose its first scapegoat with the cruel simplicity of a crowd deciding who deserved blame.

The pressure snapped toward Soren.

Of course it did.

Static gathered around him that wasn't his, static assigned to him. The conduit's pulse sharpened the moment it locked on, and Veya felt the arena trying to write him into a role.

Liability.

Storm.

Problem.

Soren went still, breathing hard. "You've got to be kidding me. How am I not surprised, it's always me."

Zephyr's voice went low. "Then you should know what I am going to say next, don't fight it."

Soren laughed once, harsh. "It's literally blaming me."

"Good," Zephyr said. "Then let it."

Rhazien's voice, steady: "Don't participate."

Veya felt her own instincts surge, fire and wind rising with that old urge to correct, to fix, to force the room into order.

But the slate's instruction echoed in her mind:

Do not correct the story.

So, she did what she hated.

She did less.

Veya shifted her stance, subtle as breath. She adjusted alignment, not power, not output, but pattern.

The conduit's pulse eased by a fraction.

Soren's shoulders dropped a millimeter, like relief tried to exist.

And the arena responded by escalating.

A second system rose.

Then a third.

Not barriers but roles.

Hero. Liability. Sacrifice.

The wards brightened along the seating tiers, and the crowd's murmurs began to carry in a way that felt wrong as if the arena itself was distributing their whispers like script.

Veya heard it as knives.

Soren heard it as a dare.

Rhazien heard it as a trap.

Zephyr heard it as music.

Kael was on the floor too, one of the "randomly selected" additions standing in a nearby zone with two other students Veya didn't recognize.

Kael grinned at the pressure like it was applause. "This is it!" he shouted. "This is what Astrael is for!"

His friends looked less thrilled. "Kael..."

But Kael stepped forward anyway.

He raised his hands, and wind snapped sharp.

Lightning flared big and bright and confident.

He did what Soren wanted to do.

He tried to win.

For a moment, it looked impressive. The conduit staggered. The crowd gasped. Kael's grin widened as if the arena had finally given him what he wanted, recognition.

Then the arena punished certainty.

The narrative shifted violently.

The pressure that had been on Soren slammed into Kael like a sentence.

Kael's lightning froze mid-air as if it had struck invisible glass. His wind collapsed inward. He blinked, confused, his grin faltering.

"What the…?"

The conduit pulsed once.

And Kael's own magic turned against him like a story that decided to eat its narrator.

A crack split the platform beneath Kael's feet, not dramatic, not cinematic but precise. A fault line drawn with intent.

Kael stumbled, tried to recover, tried to force control.

"KAEL, STOP!" one of his friends screamed.

Kael didn't stop.

He doubled down.

The wards drank it.

The fault line widened.

Kael's foot slipped.

He flung lightning instinctively, and the arena redirected it, straight down into the crack.

The floor answered with a sound like stone breaking its own jaw.

Kael dropped out of sight.

Not slowly.

Not dramatically.

Just… gone.

Silence hit the stands so hard it felt physical.

Someone sobbed above them, thin and strangled.

Veya's breath locked in her chest.

Soren went very, very still.

Zephyr's expression emptied completely.

Rhazien's jaw tightened, one small, rare fracture in his neutrality.

And the arena spoke, neutral as ever:

CONSEQUENCE RECORDED."

Veya heard her own heartbeat.

Soren's voice came out rough, barely audible. "He's…"

Zephyr didn't soften it. "Dead."

Rhazien's voice followed quiet, not cruel, simply truth. "Removed means death."

Soren swallowed hard. The storm in him surged like a scream with nowhere to go.

Veya stepped toward him. Not to restrain him, not to hold him down, she touched his wrist, light as breath, the anchor she had become without intending to.

Soren's eyes flicked down to her hand, then up to her face. Rage shook, trying to become violence.

Veya didn't let it.

"Don't," she whispered.

Soren's mouth twisted. "I wasn't going to…"

"Yes," Zephyr cut in softly, voice tight. "You were."

Soren glared, but panic lived under the glare like lightning under storm cloud.

"I hate this place," Soren said, and this time it wasn't a joke.

"I know," Veya said, steady because if she wasn't steady, nothing would be.

Then the conduit pulsed again.

The arena wasn't done.

The wards tried to assign blame once more, and this time the pressure angled toward Veya. Warmth crawled under her skin, not her warmth, not her fire, something trying to name her.

Pivot.

Cause.

Center.

Her instinct to correct surged, and she understood with sick clarity: this wasn't about power.

It was about whether the Academy could make them perform their worst selves on command.

Soren's storm.

Zephyr's sabotage.

Rhazien's detachment.

Veya's control.

Veya inhaled slowly.

And chose what the arena hated most.

She did less.

She adjusted the pattern again, refusing to carry the accusation, refusing to "fix" the narrative in the way it wanted. The blame thinned around her like fog meeting wind.

Rhazien stepped into the thinnest place and denied the lie traction.

Zephyr shaped absence, interrupting certainty without turning it into attack.

And Soren, painfully, lowered his hands, refusing to give the arena the spectacle it wanted.

The conduit's pulse faltered.

The wards shimmered, irritated.

The arena went still.

Then the voice returned:

"TRIAL: END."

There was no applause in the Colosseum.

No comfort to be had.

No explanation for Kael and no instructor stepped forward to tell them what they'd learned.

An exit seam opened and the arena moved on as if death was only a data point and grief was not relevant to measurement.

Students in the stands sat frozen, some sick, some fascinated, and some relieved it wasn't them.

Veya hated all of it.

Soren's voice came out hoarse. "They just… did that."

"They recorded it," Zephyr said quietly.

Rhazien's gaze stayed forward. "They wanted a refusal," he said. "They wanted someone to prove the instruction mattered."

Soren looked at Veya, eyes bright with rage and something dangerously close to grief.

"And if we hadn't?" he asked.

Veya didn't answer right away, because the answer lived in the crack Kael vanished into.

"…Then it would've been one of us," she said softly.

Soren's jaw clenched so hard it looked painful.

Zephyr's voice was almost gentle. "Congratulations," he murmured. "We have officially reached the part where the Academy stops pretending it is a school."

They walked out together, not brave, not triumphant, just unwilling to find out what separation cost.

Behind them, the Colosseum of the Forgotten sealed with a sound like a book closing.

And as Veya stepped back into the corridor, she felt something unsettling happen again: Kael's name tried to slip.

For half a heartbeat it became something else, a blank edge, a memory refusing to hold shape.

She forced it back. Kael.

But the effort left a faint ache behind her eyes, like the world was sanding away details in exchange for survival.

Somewhere above, in the shadows of the upper arches, faculty silhouettes remained still long enough to confirm what they'd seen.

Then they turned away, unhurried, as if Kael had always been the cost of proving the trial was real.

And Veya understood something cold and sharp:

The Academy wasn't escalating to scare them.

It was escalating because the Trials had started responding to her…

and now the institution needed to know how much the world would bleed to measure it.

Chapter

Thirty- Eight

Faculty Reaction
When Stone Has to Admit What It Saw

The Colosseum of the Forgotten sealed behind them with the soft finality of a throat closing. No announcement followed, no bell, no public statement. Arcane Academy did not soothe panic; it measured it.

The corridors filled slowly, not with the usual rush of students between lectures, but with something quieter and far more unsettled. Students spilled out of the arena in uneven clusters, moving without direction, as though no one had quite decided where they were supposed to go now that it was over.

The noise didn't rise all at once, it fractured instead, breaking into jagged pieces that didn't quite fit together. Voices overlapped in fragments that carried more confusion than clarity.

"Did he…?"

"I thought…he fell…"

"No, the floor…something moved…"

"Kael… Kael Astrael…"

"They didn't stop it."

"They watched."

"It said 'End' like… like it was…"

No one finished their sentences. No one seemed able to.

The Academy absorbed the panic without interrupting it, the stone walls holding every broken word as though they were being recorded rather than comforted.

Veya kept walking, not because she felt steady, but because stopping, even for a moment, would mean feeling everything at once. The voices, the image of the fall, the way the trial had ended without hesitation or mercy. She could feel it all waiting just beneath the surface, pressing against the edges of her control.

So, she didn't stop. She focused on the rhythm of her steps instead, one after the other, something simple enough to hold onto while everything else threatened to unravel.

Soren walked half a step ahead of her, close enough that she could feel the tension coming off him like heat.

His jaw was locked tight, the muscle shifting with every breath he forced himself to take. Lightning flickered faintly beneath his skin, not visible enough to draw attention, but present in the way his hands kept flexing at his sides, like his body was bracing for a fight that hadn't happened and still hadn't been released.

Every instinct in him was looking for something to break.

He just hadn't found it yet.

Zephyr drifted at his shoulder, his movements smooth and deliberate in a way that didn't match the chaos around them. He looked composed, too composed, the faint curve of his smile still in place as he moved through the corridor.

But it didn't reach his eyes.

Up close, it was clear the expression was nothing more than a mask, something carefully maintained for the benefit of everyone watching. Beneath it, his gaze tracked everything: the students, the whispers, and the way the Academy itself seemed to be holding the moment in place.

He wasn't relaxed; he was measuring everything around them, even as Rhazien remained close to Veya.

Rhazien didn't crowd her or reach for her, and he didn't break the quiet space she was holding around herself. Instead, he remained close enough that the distance between them never felt accidental, close enough to intercept if something went wrong, close enough to steady without intruding, and close enough to catch her if she faltered. He said nothing, and he didn't need to.

The silence he carried was different from the others. It wasn't avoidance or restraint, but presence. A quiet, grounded certainty that didn't try to fix what had happened or soften it.

It simply remained.

And for now, that was enough.

They turned a corner, and the corridor changed. It was not cold, but clean.

The air thinned, like the Academy had inhaled and didn't intend to exhale until it got what it wanted.

Soren felt it instantly. "Oh, come on."

Zephyr murmured, "We're being escorted."

"We're not moving," Soren snapped, turning sharply as if expecting to see someone. "No one told us to…"

Rhazien's voice cut in, low and steady. "We're already moving."

Soren's nostrils flared. "I hate that you're right."

The hall ahead aligned itself.

A doorway appeared where there hadn't been one before.

There were no plaque and no sign. Only an arch cut into older stone, smooth, pale, and wrong in the way old things often are.

Above the arch, letters had been carved with indifferent precision:

RESULTS REQUIRE CONTEXT. CONTEXT RE-QUIRES CONTROL.

Zephyr read it and sighed. "That's… not ominous at all."

Soren glared at the arch like it had personally offended him. "If I walk through that, I'm going to start breaking furniture."

Veya didn't answer. Her chest still felt tight, like the arena had reached inside her and left something behind.

She glanced at Rhazien.

He didn't nod or reassure her. He simply shifted his weight, subtle and ready, like if the hallway tried anything, he had already decided where he would stand.

So, Veya stepped forward.

The arch admitted them.

The Decision Room

The room beyond wasn't a classroom.

It wasn't even a chamber in the traditional sense.

It felt like a calculation, something designed to process rather than contain.

There was a logic to the structure, precise and responsive, almost sentient in the way it adjusted to new information. And yet, beneath that precision, something felt… incomplete.

Each correction carried the faintest delay, subtle enough to ignore, but persistent enough to suggest the system was compensating for something no longer present to guide it. Something it had once been built to answer to and no longer could.

Stone walls curved around the space, etched with shifting sigils that slid and reformed in slow, deliberate motion. Panels lined the perimeter, not screens, but records, each one rewriting itself in real time, as though the architecture were actively processing what had just occurred.

There were no chairs in the center, no comfort, no warmth, only a controlled, open space that existed for authority alone.

Professor Calderyn stood near the primary panel, his hands folded behind his back, posture perfectly neutral. He looked as though emotions were something he had long ago identified, categorized, and discarded.

Professor Virenna stood opposite him, her attention fixed on the flowing sigils like a predator watching movement through tall grass, sharp, patient, and precise.

And above them, present without being fully seen, the room carried the weight of Headmaster Oberon like gravity.

His voice did not come from a visible source.

It came from the stone itself.

"Report."

The word did not echo.

It settled.

Calderyn did not hesitate.

"The Major Trial has concluded."

Virenna's stylus continued its slow movement across the record panel, though her focus had clearly shifted.

"It concluded early," she said, her tone precise, almost analytical. "That was not the expected duration."

Soren's fingers twitched at his sides, the motion small but sharp, like something in him was straining not to break through.

Zephyr drifted slightly upward beside him, expression smooth, almost amused, until you looked closely.

"Do you always speak like we aren't standing right here?" he asked lightly.

Calderyn's eyes flicked toward him, calm and unbothered.

"You are here," he said. "Your presence is part of

the record."

Soren let out a short, disbelieving laugh that held no humor.

"That's what you got from that?" he said. "A record?"

His voice sharpened, the restraint in it beginning to fracture.

"We just watched someone die."

For the first time, Virenna looked up.

It wasn't concern.

It was assessment.

Her gaze moved across them briefly, as if confirming variables rather than acknowledging people.

"Correct," she said.

The word landed harder than anything else in the room.

Veya felt it more than heard it.

Her voice came out quieter than she expected, pulled from somewhere deeper than she wanted to reach.

"Kael."

For a fraction of a second, the name seemed to hang in the space between them.

Virenna's expression didn't change.

"Yes."

That was all she offered.

No acknowledgment.

No weight.

Just confirmation.

Soren stepped forward before Veya could stop him, the movement sharp and unrestrained.

"You knew that could happen," he said, his voice tightening with every word.

Virenna didn't answer.

Calderyn did.

"The slate stated the conditions."

Soren's head snapped toward him.

"That's not the same as caring," he shot back, the

anger no longer contained. "And it's definitely not the same as stopping it."

The air in the room shifted. It was subtle, but unmistakable.

Oberon's voice cut through the tension, quiet but absolute, like a blade finding the exact seam it needed.

"Caring is not the Academy's function."

Soren went still.

Not because he accepted it.

Because something in the way Oberon spoke made the air feel older, almost heavier, like the statement wasn't opinion.

It was structure.

His jaw worked as he swallowed back the instinct to push harder.

When he spoke again, his voice had dropped lower, rougher, and more dangerous.

"So that's it?" he said. "That's all he was to you?"

His gaze flicked between them, searching for something that wasn't there.

"Acceptable loss?" he pressed. "Just another number you write down and move on from?"

Virenna's eyes narrowed slightly. It was not in anger, but in correction.

"He was not a number," she said.

A beat passed.

"He was data."

The distinction was worse.

Zephyr's smile sharpened, no warmth left in it.

"Ah," he said softly. "Charming."

Rhazien spoke then, his voice low and steady, cutting cleanly through the rising tension.

"He wasn't random."

The room stilled. Not in surprise, but in attention.

Calderyn's gaze sharpened by a fraction, the shift subtle but unmistakable.

"Explain," he said.

Soren didn't wait.

"Explain what?" he snapped, the restraint finally breaking. "That he slipped? That the floor gave out? That's your explanation?"

His voice rose, sharp enough to cut through the chamber.

"Or are you going to tell me that was part of the design too?"

Lightning flickered faintly along his hands, not fully formed, but close, too close.

Zephyr shifted slightly beside him, not intervening, but ready.

Rhazien didn't raise his voice.

"He wasn't chosen at random," he said.

That landed differently.

Not louder.

Deeper.

Soren turned toward him, frustration still burning. "He fell. That's what happened."

Rhazien's gaze didn't waver.

"No," he said calmly. "That's what it looked like."

The distinction settled into the space between them, quiet and dangerous.

Virenna's attention sharpened immediately. "Go on."

Rhazien stepped forward, not toward them, but toward the memory of the moment itself, his focus narrowing as he spoke.

"The instability didn't spread evenly," he said. "It converged."

Calderyn's expression shifted slightly, interest replacing neutrality.

"Localized collapse," he said.

Rhazien inclined his head once. "Yes. But not toward the weakest structure."

A brief pause.

"Toward the most responsive subject."

That changed the atmosphere of the room. Not visibly, but in the weight of what had just been introduced.

Soren frowned. "What does that even mean?"

"It means," Rhazien said, "the trial wasn't looking for failure."

His gaze flicked briefly toward Veya.

"It was looking for reaction."

Silence followed.

Veya felt something tighten in her chest.

Zephyr's smile faded completely.

"Ah," he said softly. "That's worse."

Soren shook his head, like he was trying to force the idea away.

"No," he said. "No, that doesn't…he didn't…"

Rhazien didn't push.

He didn't need to.

"The pressure built around him before the collapse," he continued. "The others were already stabilizing. He wasn't."

Virenna's stylus moved again, slower now.

"Emotional variance," she murmured.

"Targeting," Rhazien corrected.

That word did not belong in a classroom.

Calderyn's gaze sharpened further. "You're suggesting the trial selected him."

"I'm stating that the system adjusted toward him," Rhazien said. "There's a difference."

Soren let out a breath that sounded more like something breaking than releasing.

"So, what," he said, his voice lower now, but more dangerous for it. "It picked him. That's your explanation? That he was just…what…convenient?"

"No," Rhazien said.

Soren looked at him, something raw flashing through the anger.

"Then say it."

Rhazien held his gaze.

"It positioned him."

The words didn't rise.

They settled.

Like something locking into place.

Soren went still again, but this time it wasn't Oberon's presence holding him there.

It was understanding.

And he hated it.

"You're telling me," He said slowly, each word tightening, "that it set him up."

No one answered because they didn't need to.

The silence confirmed it.

Soren laughed again, hollow this time.

"Right," he said. "Okay. Good. That's great."

His hands clenched, lightning snapping once before he forced it back.

"So let me get this straight," he continued, voice rough. "You built a system that doesn't just test us—it decides who breaks first and then helps it happen?"

Virenna didn't flinch.

"It does not decide," she said. "It responds."

Soren's eyes snapped to hers.

"That's the same thing."

"No," she replied. "It is more efficient."

That did it.

The storm surged, not outward, but contained, pressing into the room like pressure before lightning.

"For you," he said, voice low and dangerous. "Not for us."

Zephyr's voice cut in, softer but no less sharp.

"Soren."

Not a warning.

A reminder.

Soren exhaled hard, dragging the power back down.

The anger didn't leave.

It settled.

Instead, the anger went deeper and colder.

Rhazien spoke again, quieter now.

"It wasn't just about him."

Soren didn't look at him. "Then what was it about?"

Rhazien's gaze shifted briefly toward Veya, then back.

"The system was watching how we would respond when it removed stability."

That landed harder than anything else.

Because it reframed everything.

Zephyr exhaled slowly. "So, the collapse wasn't the test."

"No," Rhazien said.

Soren's jaw tightened. "Then what was?"

Rhazien didn't hesitate.

"We were."

Rhazien didn't posture. He didn't accuse.

He simply stated the shape of the truth.

"The wards reassigned blame to him when he performed certainty," Rhazien said. "The system needed a visible consequence."

Virenna's mouth tightened. "The wards didn't need anything."

Zephyr tilted his head. "Oh? Then why did they choose the loudest boy on the floor?"

Soren's eyes flashed. "He was trying to do what you're forcing us to do!"

Calderyn's gaze slid to Soren like a measurement. "He attempted dominance. The Colosseum punished dominance."

Soren's voice rose. "So, you're teaching us to be weak?"

Veya snapped her eyes to him in quick warning.

Soren saw it and forced himself to inhale. Hard.

The storm in him pressed.

But he didn't let it out.

Calderyn watched that too, as if the restraint mattered more than the anger.

Oberon's voice returned, calm as stone. "The question is not whether the trial was lethal."

A pause.

"The question is why the Colosseum escalated when it did."

Virenna turned back to the record-panel. "Because the unit resisted narrative correction."

Zephyr's smile vanished. "Let's be honest, that's a cute way to say, 'we didn't dance when you pulled the string.'"

Calderyn ignored him. "The Colosseum altered its pressure profile mid-trial."

Virenna's eyes narrowed. "External influence."

The room cooled a degree.

Soren's gaze snapped to Veya. "No."

Veya didn't speak.

Because the truth in her chest moved like something settling into a shape.

Calderyn's voice remained neutral. "The wards registered a structural adjustment without corresponding exertion."

Virenna finally looked directly at Veya. Her eyes were sharp, almost… satisfied.

"Veya," she said. "You didn't cast."

Veya kept her voice even. "No, I didn't."

"You didn't flare. You didn't force."

"No."

"And yet," Virenna said, voice precise as a scalpel, "the conduit folded inward when you stepped."

Soren's head turned sharply. "Stop."

Virenna didn't look at him. "This is not an accusation."

Soren's laugh was ugly. "It sounds like one."

Oberon's presence pressed into the room. "It is classification."

Veya's throat tightened. "I didn't"

Calderyn cut in, not unkindly but professionally. "We are not suggesting intent."

Virenna said, "We are noting effect."

Zephyr's voice went soft. "Effect is what institutions punish."

Rhazien's gaze stayed on the panel. "Or exploit."

Calderyn's eyes flicked to Rhazien. "And your containment remains… irregular."

Rhazien didn't blink. "It's disciplined."

Virenna's mouth curved faintly, it was almost a smile. "Disciplined enough to deny narrative traction."

Soren snapped, "Stop saying that like it's a compliment."

Virenna's eyes finally flicked to him. "Soren, your magnitude is escalating."

Soren's hands curled into fists. "It's called being alive."

"It's called trend." Calderyn said.

Soren's storm rose with his anger and Veya touched his wrist, just barely.

A breath of contact to steady the storm brewing in him.

Soren's fingers tightened once.

Then loosened.

The room noticed, of course it did.

Calderyn's gaze paused on the gesture. "Anchor response confirmed."

Soren's voice went sharp. "Don't."

Virenna's eyes narrowed. "She stabilizes you."

Soren looked at Veya like he was about to argue but his anger couldn't find her as a target.

It curved around her. It always did.

He swallowed, harsh. "She's not your tool."

Oberon's voice was calm, and therefore terrifying. "All students are tools. The only variable is whether they recognize it."

Zephyr whispered, almost to himself, "Ah. There it is."

Veya felt her stomach turn. "So, what now?"

Calderyn answered. "A contained escalation."

Virenna corrected. "A major trial with revised ward parameters."

Soren's laugh was short and humorless. "Meaning you're going to try to break us again."

Oberon's voice settled over the room, controlled and absolute.

"Meaning we will measure whether your unit response exceeds acceptable limits."

Rhazien didn't raise his voice. "And if it does?"

The silence that followed wasn't hesitation. It was decision.

One cold beat stretched between them.

Then Oberon spoke again, final and unyielding: "Then we begin reassignment."

Soren went very still.

Zephyr's shadows tightened at his feet.

Veya felt something in her chest, sharp and instinctive, like her body already understood that "reassignment" wasn't academic.

It wasn't physical dismemberment.

It was worse than that, it was structural. The kind that didn't tear you apart but rearranged you until nothing recognizable remained.

Virenna turned back to the record panel, her attention already shifting as if the conclusion had been filed away.

"There is another variable."

Calderyn didn't look up. "External attention."

Zephyr's head tilted slightly, the faint curve of his expression returning, though it didn't quite reach his eyes.

"You mean the creatures."

The temperature in the room seemed to drop. Not

dramatically, but enough to be felt. Enough that no one mistook the shift.

Oberon's voice lowered slightly. "The witness pattern is increasing."

Veya's breath caught.

Soren's voice tightened, the word slipping out before he could stop it. "Witness?"

Calderyn didn't react. "Non-random creature response."

Virenna's voice followed, precise as ever. "Recognition behavior."

Zephyr's smile returned, thin and edged, though it didn't quite hide the shift in his attention.
"So," he murmured, "the world is beginning to notice."

"Not the world."

Rhazien's voice didn't rise, but it cut cleanly through the moment.

Veya turned toward him.

There was something in his gaze that didn't belong here. Not to the Academy, not to their level, not to anything that should have been standing beside her.

There was something in his gaze that didn't belong here. Something older than the Academy, steadier than anything a student should carry, and far too certain for someone who was supposed to still be learning.

He let the silence hold just long enough to make it matter.

"Something," he said quietly, "older."

Oberon's presence pressed like weather. "We do not allow ancient forces to claim Academy assets."

Soren snapped, "We're not assets."

Oberon's voice didn't change. "You are within Academy jurisdiction."

Zephyr murmured, delighted in the worst way, "He really does say the quiet part out loud."

Virenna's gaze sharpened. "The next trial will occur within forty-eight hours."

Soren's jaw tightened, his voice rougher now, the restraint starting to wear thin.

"No warning," he said. "Again."

Calderyn's expression didn't change. "Warning alters behavior."

Soren let out a quiet breath that didn't quite settle anything. His eyes lifted, sharp and unyielding.

"So does fear."

Calderyn met it without hesitation. "Yes."

Veya stepped forward slightly. Her voice stayed calm because calm was the only weapon she trusted.

"What exactly are you trying to prove?"

Oberon answered, and the room seemed to listen harder. "We are not trying to prove anything."

A pause.

"We are trying to determine what you are becoming."

The words landed hard, not like a threat but like a sentence.

Veya felt the stone under her boots hum as if it were satisfied with that statement and began recording.

Then the door behind them opened without a hand touching it. A clear sign of dismissal and not permission.

Just the Academy moving on.

Zephyr drifted toward the exit first. As he passed Calderyn, he murmured, almost conversational, "If you split us, you'll regret it."

Calderyn's eyes flicked to him. "Is that a threat?"

Zephyr's smile was bright and empty. "It's an observation."

Rhazien didn't look at Calderyn.

He looked at Virenna instead.

And for one second…just one, Virenna's expression shifted. It was not fear exactly, but calculation meeting something it didn't fully like.

Then it was gone.

Soren walked out last, shoulders set so hard it

looked like armor. Veya followed behind him.

The corridor outside felt warmer like the Academy had been holding its breath.

Soren spoke the moment the door sealed behind them. "They're going to try to break us."

Zephyr's voice was light. "Obviously."

Rhazien's voice was quiet. "They're going to try to split what responds when we're together."

Veya nodded, though the motion felt distant, like it belonged more to the version of her that knew how to stay controlled.

Beneath that, something else stirred. Something older, less patient, and far less willing to accept what the Academy demanded.

She didn't let it rise.

"Yes," she said, her voice calm… even if the quiet beneath it wasn't.

Soren dragged a hand through his hair, frustration bleeding into something raw. "So, what do we do?"

Veya looked at them, at storm, wind, shadow, and the quiet space that held them together.

For a moment, she didn't speak.

Not because she didn't have an answer, but because the one forming in her chest no longer felt like something a student should say. It felt heavier than that. Older.

When she finally did speak, it wasn't as a student trying to survive the Academy.

It was as someone who had begun to understand that the Academy might not be the most dangerous thing in the story.

"We don't give them fracture," she said, her voice soft but deliberate, the kind of quiet that didn't invite disagreement.

Zephyr hummed under his breath; the sound threaded with faint amusement. "That sounds deliciously vague."

Rhazien didn't look away from her. His gaze held steady, grounding rather than questioning. "We stay controlled."

Soren's jaw tightened, the tension in him still coiled and restless. "And if they force it?"

Veya drew in a slow breath, feeling it settle deeper than her lungs, like something aligning beneath her control rather than calming it.

She hadn't wanted to say this out loud.

Not yet.

But the truth had already taken shape, and pretending otherwise wouldn't change what was coming.

"Then," she said quietly, her voice steady even as something beneath it sharpened, "we learn how to survive becoming what they're afraid of."

The words didn't echo.

They settled.

And the corridor responded.

The wards along the walls brightened faintly, not enough to draw attention, but enough to feel, like the building itself had registered the shift… and approved.

And somewhere beyond stone and record and rule something ancient shifted again, not waking fully but paying attention like it liked the sound of that.

Chapter
Thirty- Nine

The Trial That Chooses Its Weapon

The Academy didn't wait forty-eight hours instead it waited twelve. Because tension was more useful when it hadn't settled.

The summons came at dusk, not through slate or stone, but through the sky itself as it shifted. The color bending, light thinning, like something unseen had reached up and rewritten the horizon.

Clouds over the Arena Wing twisted inward like a spiral being drawn by an invisible hand. The lanterns lining the courtyard flickered to life one by one, not warm and golden, but cold and white.

Students stopped mid-step. A low hum rolled through the stone beneath their feet.

Soren froze beside Veya. "Oh," he said flatly. "That's not subtle."

Zephyr tilted his head, amused and alert at once. "No. That's theatrical."

Rhazien didn't look at the sky first. He looked at the shadows. "They're gathering," he said quietly.

Veya felt it too. The Academy wasn't just calling them.

It was calling everyone.

The courtyard filled quickly, students gathering into a wide outer ring as guild colors flickered beneath the lanternlight, bright and restless against the fading light of dusk.

Along the high balconies, faculty assembled in silence, their silhouettes drawn in clean, unyielding lines against the pale sky, watching not as observers, but as those who had already decided what this moment meant.

Calderyn stood among them, composed and unreadable.

Virenna beside him, precise and intent, her focus already narrowing.

And above them all, where form gave way to something less visible and far more present, the weight of the Academy itself seemed to settle.

Oberon.

Soren leaned slightly toward Veya. "Okay. Just once, I would love for something dramatic not to involve us."

Zephyr smiled faintly. "You radiate drama. It follows you like weather."

Soren shot him a look. "You radiate chaos."

Zephyr's expression brightened. "That's fair."

The ground beneath them split, not violently, but with a smooth, deliberate precision that felt wrong in a way none of them could quite name, as if something had happened like this before… and been taken with it.

The stone didn't fall away.

It parted.

A wide circle opened beneath their feet, and from within it, the Colosseum of the Forgotten began to rise. It was not the smaller trial floor they had seen before, but something larger now, sharper in its design, its edges too clean, too intentional, as though it had shed any pretense of restraint.

The platform expanded as it rose, locking into place with a quiet finality that felt less like construction and more like activation.

No one spoke.

They didn't need to.

The space itself had already shifted into something else. Something that wasn't waiting for them to begin.

It had already decided.

Then the voice came.

Not the Academy's neutral cadence.

Not instruction.

Something older.

"MAJOR ARCANE TRIAL: LIVE ESCALATION."

The wards flared in concentric rings. Students murmured in the stands. Someone whispered, "They're doing it again."

Soren muttered, "No. They're doing it worse."

Veya inhaled slowly. The floor beneath them pulsed once. Then names carved into the stone around the perimeter.

Again, it was not random. It was never random.

ECLIPSE UNIT
AXIOM UNIT
MERIDIAN UNIT

Three units. Twelve students.

The count settled cleanly, but something about it didn't.

Not wrong. Not enough to question.

Just… off.

Soren's jaw tightened slightly, his gaze lingering on the lineup a second too long, like he was trying to catch onto something that kept slipping just out of reach. "Replacement," he muttered.

Zephyr's voice came softer, threaded with quiet interest.

"Or precedent."

Rhazien didn't look at the slate.

"Watch the Axiom unit."

Veya did.

The names had already arranged themselves, precise and unquestioned, but one of them pulled at her attention, not because it stood out, but because it didn't.

There should have been something there.

A sense. A shape. A memory that refused to form.

Instead, there was only certainty.

Another Astrael student stood among them now, older, colder, their focus fixed on the platform with a kind of predatory calm that hadn't been there before.

No one questioned it.

No one seemed to notice anything had changed.

The Academy was escalating.

The voice continued:

"OBJECTIVE: STABILITY UNDER MULTIPLE FAILURE CONDITIONS."

The platform trembled.

Three conduits rose from the center.

Not one, but three.

Each pulsing in a different rhythm. Each carrying a different narrative pressure. The crowd quieted.

Soren exhaled through his nose. "Oh good. There's triple."

Zephyr's voice was thoughtful. "That's excessive."

Rhazien: "That's deliberate."

Veya felt it before it happened. The wards snapped outward. The twelve students were divided, not by walls, but by shifting gravitational fields. Each unit forced toward one conduit.

Except the Eclipse Unit stood at the center, positioned with exact precision between all three conduits.

Soren huffed a short laugh, the sound sharp with disbelief. "Of course," he said. "Why did I even think we'd get anything else?"

Zephyr's smile curved faintly, though his attention remained fixed on the pattern surrounding them.

"We're the pivot," he reminded him. "That was never going to change."

The word settled into Veya like it belonged there.

Not forced.

Recognized.

Something in her stilled, not into calm, but into focus. A deeper kind of awareness that didn't question the placement, didn't resist it.

It understood it.

Her breath slowed, but not to steady herself but to match something else, something already moving beneath the structure of the trial.

This wasn't coincidence.

It was design.

And for the briefest moment, something in her didn't feel placed.

It felt… expected.

The voice deepened.

JUNALYN NICDAO

"FAILURE WILL RESULT IN CASCADE COLLAPSE."

A pulse of energy ran through the floor. One of the Lumora students flinched. The Axiom unit braced. While the Eclipse unit looked at each other.

Soren's voice came lower this time, the edge of frustration replaced by something tighter, more controlled.

"Okay," he said, glancing between them. "Same rules?"

Veya nodded once, steady. "No performance."

The words didn't sound like a suggestion. They sounded like something she had already decided.

Zephyr tilted his head slightly, eyes tracking the unstable lines of the conduits before settling back on the group.

"No ego," he said, quieter now, the usual ease in his voice giving way to something more deliberate.

Rhazien's presence didn't shift, but his voice grounded the space anyway.

"No fracture."

Soren let out a breath, tension still visible in the set

of his shoulders.

"No dying," he said, the words tighter than the others, like he didn't trust the system not to try.

Silence settled between them, not empty but understood.

They weren't agreeing on rules.

They were choosing how they would survive.

The conduits pulsed once.

Then the first failure condition triggered.

One of the outer conduits surged past its threshold, not failing quietly but flaring outward in a violent burst of unstable light.

A student in the Meridian Unit cried out as their zone inverted, radiant energy around them folding inward instead of radiating outward.

The air didn't detonate.

It collapsed. The space compressing in on itself as though something had reached in and removed the rule that said it should expand.

Pressure folded inward, crushing tight and sudden, like the space itself had decided they were the weakest point and adjusted accordingly.

The Axiom Unit reacted instantly with aggressive and precise attacks, unified. They struck the destabilized conduit together, releasing large spells in a controlled barrage meant to overpower the imbalance and force it back into alignment. It was impressive, clean and dominant.

Exactly what Astrael training rewarded. But the conduit drank it. Every surge of power fed straight into the instability instead of correcting it. The light swelled, thickened, and then redirected.

The pressure didn't vanish.

It reassigned.

Hairline fractures of energy began to spread through Axiom Unit's own zone, thin at first, then widening as the strain transferred.

Soren sucked in a sharp breath. "They're feeding

it."

Zephyr nodded once, eyes narrowing. "It rewards spectacle with collapse."

Power here, wasn't meant to dominate. It was meant to be understood. And the arena punished anyone who forgot.

Then the voice echoed:

"CONSEQUENCE: REDIRECTION."

The Axiom conduit snapped sideways and slammed its excess pressure into Eclipse zone.

Soren's lightning sparked instinctively.

Veya grabbed his wrist.

"Anchor," she said sharply.

Soren clenched his jaw but obeyed. Wind curved into stabilizing arcs instead of attacking.

Zephyr's shadows expanded, not striking, just diffusing the worst of the incoming surge.

Rhazien stepped exactly where the pressure thinned, absorbing narrative traction without claiming it.

The collapse slowed.

But the second failure triggered.

The third conduit that was behind them shattered into shards of unstable magic that spun like knives.

One student from the Meridian Unit misjudged the distance.

A shard cut through their shoulder.

Blood hit stone.

The crowd gasped.

The voice did not.

"CASCADE INITIATED."

All three conduits pulsed at once, the surge hitting not in separate waves, but all at once, as pressure flooded the center and closed in around them from every direction.

Veya felt it first.

Not just the power, but the shape of it. The intent behind it.

The wards weren't reacting.

They were deciding.

Something in the structure shifted, and suddenly the pressure wasn't neutral anymore. It pressed inward with purpose, trying to name them, to define them, to settle on a conclusion the system could understand.

Unstable. Dangerous. The cause.

The narrative forced itself against her, not loud, but insistent, threading through bone and breath alike.

It was wrong.

She felt it immediately.

Her fire surged in response, sharp and immediate, demanding release. Her air followed, tightening instinctively, ready to seize control and force the structure back into something she could contain.

For half a second, it would have been easy.

Too easy.

Beside her, Soren's storm rose hard enough to make the lanternlight stutter, the air around him tightening with barely restrained force.

"Let me," he growled, already leaning into it. "I can stop this."

Zephyr's head snapped toward him, sharper than Veya had ever seen him.

"You can detonate it," he shot back.

Rhazien's voice cut cleanly through both of them. It was not louder, but undeniable. "Don't perform."

The words landed exactly where they needed to.

Soren's eyes burned brighter, fury flashing through them as he fought against the instinct clawing up his spine.

"They're going to die!" he snapped, the restraint in him already starting to crack.

Veya felt the pattern shifting too fast. The conduits weren't independent anymore. It was as if they were syncing, building toward one catastrophic convergence. The Academy wanted to see which unit broke first.

She saw it then. It was not all at once, not clean-ly, but in fragments that snapped together faster than thought.

Which one forced.

Which one fractured.

And suddenly, the shape of the trial shifted into something she could understand.

They weren't measuring power.

They were measuring pivot.

The realization didn't feel like discovery.

It felt like recognition.

The noise of the courtyard blurred at the edges, voices dissolving into something distant and irrelevant. The faculty balconies seemed to pull farther away, as if the space itself were narrowing its focus, and the wards… the wards no longer hummed.

They pressed.

Sharp. Insistent. Like teeth closing around a deci-sion already made.

And Veya moved.

She didn't step toward a conduit.

She stepped into the space between them.

"Veya!"

Soren's voice cut after her sharp with warning, but she didn't stop. Didn't turn. The sound of him reached her, but it didn't anchor her the way it normally would.

Because this wasn't something she needed to react to.

It was something she already understood.

She felt the structure of the Colosseum unfold be-neath her awareness, not at the surface level where power flared and collided, but deeper, where intention shaped outcome.

The conduits weren't the problem.

The alignment was.

The pattern had been set to force imbalance; to push one point to break so the system could justify its conclusion.

She reached.

Not with fire.

Not with air.

But with something quieter. Something that didn't demand control but rewrote it.

Influence.

Her fingers lifted slightly, not casting, not summoning, just aligning with something already in motion.

Then she adjusted.

One thread.

The first conduit's pulse faltered, its rhythm slipping just enough to break the pattern it had been feeding.

She adjusted again.

A second thread shifted beneath her awareness, and the next conduit stuttered, its surge collapsing into something uneven, unstable.

For a fraction of a second, the system hesitated.

Then the third conduit reacted.

Not faltering.

Resisting.

It pushed back harder, its energy surging with sharper intent, like it had recognized what she was doing and refused to yield.

The air thickened around her, pressure building fast enough to be felt in her lungs, in her bones.

The wards responded immediately.

Not adjusting.

Opposing.

They pressed against her influence, not violently, but with precision that was trying to correct, to reassert the structure she was unraveling.

"INTERFERENCE DETECTED."

The voice carried something new, subtle, but unmistakable.

Irritation.

Soren stared at her like the ground had shifted

under him.

Zephyr stilled completely.

"Oh," he breathed, quieter now, his gaze sharpening as he watched the system struggle to correct itself.

"Well… that's not supposed to happen."

A faint smile touched his mouth, not amused, not mocking.

Interested.

"Do that again," he added under his breath.

Rhazien's voice was low and steady behind her. "Keep going."

The conduits tried to reassert control. Tried to force the narrative.

The Axiom Unit faltered. One of them stumbled.

The Lumora student in the Meridian Unit that was bleeding from the shoulder collapsed to one knee. The cascade built.

Veya felt the pressure crest.

Then…the sky blinked.

Again.

It was not the Academy, not the wards. But something older.

The conduits froze mid-surge. The shards of magic hung in air like suspended glass. Every student on the platform went still.

Soren's lightning went silent.

Zephyr's shadows flattened.

Rhazien's shoulders tightened a fraction.

The entire Arena held its breath.

Veya felt it.

Something was watching and it wasn't the Academy or the faculty. Something beyond stone and record. And it wasn't curious. It was evaluating.

The pause lasted one heartbeat.

Then, the sky did not resume normally.

It darkened, just slightly.

The conduits resumed, but not with the same

rhythm.

They aligned.

All three conduits folding inward at once.

The cascade reversed, the shards dissolved into harmless light, the bleeding Meridian student's zone stabilized.

Then the Axiom crack sealed and the wards flickered like they'd been overridden. That's when the voice returned.

It wasn't the same voice, not it's neutral tone...

"PIVOT CONFIRMED."

The words carried across the Colosseum, not just heard but *felt*, the sound threading through stone and air alike as it settled into the structure of the arena itself.

The reaction was immediate.

The stands fell silent, not gradually, but all at once, as if the noise had been pulled from the space instead of fading from it. Students leaned forward without realizing it, attention locking onto the center with a tension that hadn't been there a moment before.

Above them, the faculty shifted.

Subtly, but not insignificantly.

Virenna's posture straightened, precision sharpening into something more alert, more intent.

Calderyn's gaze narrowed, the neutrality he carried thinning just enough to reveal something underneath it.

And higher still, beyond motion, beyond visibility, Oberon's presence deepened.

Not louder.

Heavier.

Like a storm lowering without thunder, pressing into the architecture until even the air seemed to acknowledge it.

On the floor, Soren let out a slow breath, the sound rougher than he intended, like he was grounding himself against something he didn't fully understand.

"…You did that."

Veya's hands trembled.

Not violently.

Not enough for anyone watching from a distance to notice.

But she felt it, felt the instability threading through her control, the way something deeper had moved before she could stop it.

"I didn't…" she started, the words quieter than she expected, uncertain in a way she rarely allowed herself to be.

"You did," Zephyr said softly.

There was no amusement in it now.

No deflection.

Only clarity.

Rhazien stepped closer. He was not touching, not crowding, but near enough that the space between them felt deliberate, chosen, like he had already positioned himself for what came next.

Beneath Veya's feet, the stone shifted. It was not cracking or breaking but rewriting itself.

The surface smoothed, then carved itself in precise, deliberate strokes, lines etching outward in a perfect circle around her position.

The movement wasn't rushed.

It was certain.

Letters formed, each one settling into place as if it had always been there, simply waiting to be revealed.

This wasn't a warning.

It wasn't measurement.

It was a declaration.

And for the first time, the Academy wasn't observing her.

It was naming her.

THE ARCANE TRIALS ACKNOWLEDGE VEYA AS PIVOT.

The shift didn't stay contained.

It spread.

It spread through the crowd first, silence rippling outward as understanding hit in uneven waves. Through the faculty next, their stillness sharpening into something more focused, more deliberate.

And through the Academy itself, not observed, but felt.

Soren looked up at the balconies, something sharp and disbelieving breaking loose in his chest as it all clicked into place.

He laughed.

Once.

"Yeah," he called, voice cutting upward toward the watching silhouettes. "That went well."

His expression hardened, the humor vanishing as quickly as it had appeared.

"You were trying to break her," he said. "Congratulations."

The words carried farther than he intended, cutting cleanly through the space between the floor and the balconies, and for a moment, no one answered, no correction, no interruption, just the weight of it settling as the realization caught up with the room.

"You just gave her a title."

Zephyr's smile returned slowly, not playful this time but sharp with recognition. "Oh," he murmured, almost to himself, "that's going to be very inconvenient for them."

Rhazien's voice was quiet. "This changes the board."

The Colosseum voice spoke one final time:

"TRIAL: COMPLETE."

No one cheered.

No one moved for a second. Then the wards dimmed. The conduits sank. The floor sealed. The students staggered back toward the edges.

The Meridian Unit started to help their injured.

The Axiom Unit looked shaken but defiant.

Eclipse Unit, stood together and stood as a unit.

Soren leaned close to Veya. "You realize this makes things worse."

Veya managed a faint, tired smile. "When have they been better?"

Zephyr tilted his head, watching the balconies. "They're recalculating."

Rhazien's gaze lifted toward Oberon's shadowed position.

"They're afraid," he said quietly.

Soren snorted. "Good."

Above, Virenna's voice carried just enough to reach them.

"Escalate."   "Contain first," Calderyn answered, his voice lower now, more deliberate.

Oberon didn't raise his voice, but the stone seemed to register it anyway, the weight of his presence pressing subtly into the room as if the architecture itself was listening more closely.

Veya exhaled slowly.

Her pulse had steadied, even as her hands still trembled, the two sensations existing at once in a way that should have felt contradictory but didn't anymore.

Because something inside her had shifted.

Not louder.

Not stronger.

Clearer.

The Trials hadn't just tested her, they had defined her, traced the shape of something she hadn't fully understood until now and forced it into the open where it could no longer be ignored.

And now the Academy was left with a choice it had never intended to face, whether they were still training a student or standing in front of something that no longer belonged to them.

Chapter

Fourty

The Cost of Being Named

The Academy did not announce what had happened. It didn't need to. The stone within the Academy had seen. The wards had recorded. And students, students were better than any official decree.

The Way They Look at You After

By morning, the corridors had changed, not physically, but behaviorally. People moved around them like they were navigating weather.

Too close felt dangerous.

Too far felt like disrespect.

So, everyone hovered in that careful middle space.

Soren, being observant as ever noticed first. He always did. "They're doing it again," he muttered.

Zephyr floated beside him, deceptively serene. "Define 'it.'"

Soren gestured with his chin at a cluster of Astrael students near a column. Where they were whispering openly, not even trying to pretend.

One of them met Soren's eyes and didn't look

away. "That," Soren said. "The stare."

Zephyr tilted his head. "Ah. You've upgraded."

"Upgraded to what?" Soren snapped.

Zephyr's smile was thin. "Legend status."

Rhazien didn't look at the students. Instead, he watched the exits. "The spacing changed," he said quietly.

Veya felt it too. Students weren't just avoiding us, they were positioning themselves at a distance, curious and calculating.

A Lumora girl stepped directly into Veya's path.

Not by accident.

On purpose.

She was pale and younger than us. Her hands trembling slightly. "Did you…" the girl started, voice thin. "Did you mean to do that?"

The shift didn't stay contained to the floor.

It moved outward, uneven, unpredictable, like something that refused to settle into a single shape.

The crowd felt it first.

Silence didn't fall cleanly. It fractured. Some voices cut off mid-word, others lingered too long, like the moment couldn't decide what it was supposed to be.

The faculty saw it next.

Not just the result but the instability underneath it. The way the pattern didn't quite hold, didn't resolve the way it should have.

And the Academy, the Academy didn't just observe it.

It stuttered.

For half a breath, the wards flickered out of sync, the structure hesitating as if it had been given an answer it didn't know how to record.

At the center of it, Veya stood very still.

Too still.

Her hands hadn't stopped trembling.

Not from fear.

From pressure.

Something inside her hadn't settled when the trial ended. It hadn't closed. It pressed outward instead, restless, searching, like it had more to say than the world was built to hold.

For a moment, the edges of everything felt… wrong.

Not broken.

Just slightly out of alignment.

Like if she reached again, she wouldn't adjust it.

She would unravel it.

Soren looked up toward the balconies, something sharp and disbelieving breaking through the tension in him as the full shape of the moment snapped into place.

Then he laughed once, short and sharp.

"You were trying to break her," he called, his voice carrying cleanly upward toward the silhouettes.

His eyes flicked back to Veya, just for a second and something in his expression shifted.

Not just anger.

Recognition.

"Congratulations," he added, the edge in his voice cutting deeper now.

"You didn't break her."

A beat of silence surrounded them.

"You gave her something worse."

Because at the end of the hall, a cluster of Astrael students had stopped pretending not to watch.

They weren't whispering.

They were waiting.

One of them stepped forward. He was older than the others, composed in a way that felt practiced, his expression cold and controlled like he had already decided what this conversation was going to be.

"You destabilized the wards," he said flatly.

Soren didn't slow.

"You're welcome."

The student's jaw tightened, something flickering

behind his eyes, not uncertainty, not quite anger… something closer to frustration.

"Someone fell," he said. "That doesn't happen unless something breaks."

The hallway stilled, not completely, but enough to be felt and Zephyr's smile vanished.

Rhazien shifted, subtle, precise, but the angle of his body changed just enough to place himself between Veya and the threat without making it obvious.

Veya's stomach turned.

"That's not what happened," she said, though the words felt thinner than she wanted them to.

The Astrael student's gaze sharpened, locking onto her like he was trying to force something into focus that wouldn't stay.

"You changed the conduit alignment," he said.

"Yes," she answered.

"And the cascade reversed," he continued. "It redirected."

His voice didn't shake.

If anything, it sharpened, like he was carving meaning out of something he couldn't fully see.

"You shifted the board."

Soren stepped forward, storm rising fast enough to charge the air.

"Careful."

The Astrael student didn't look at him.

His attention stayed fixed on Veya, unwavering.

"Every system here requires a cost," he said. "You don't get to remove pressure. You move it."

Something in his expression tightened like he knew there was more to say, something missing just out of reach.

"You decided where it landed."

Silence followed, not empty but dense, settling into the space with a weight that felt almost deliberate.

It pressed in around them, sharp and unrelenting,

as if the moment itself refused to move on, refused to release what had just been said.

No one spoke.

No one broke it.

And the longer it held, the more it felt less like absence and more like something watching to see who would fracture first.

Veya felt the words hit anyway, even without a name attached to them.

Zephyr spoke lightly, but the edge in his voice had gone razor thin.

"You're implying she chose it."

The Astrael student didn't blink.

"I'm saying the system adapted."

Rhazien stepped forward then not aggressive, not loud, just enough to shift the geometry of the space between them.

"The system punishes dominance," he said calmly. "Someone pushed when they should have adjusted."

The Astrael student's gaze flicked to him.

"And she didn't."

"No," Rhazien said.

Silence settled between them, not uncertain but deliberate, as if the moment itself needed time to decide what that truth meant.

Then, quieter and colder Rhazien said, "She didn't."

The Astrael student looked back at Veya, holding her there for one long, searching beat, like he was trying to make her fit into a shape the system hadn't fully explained.

"You think you're stabilizing this place," he said.

A slight tilt of his head.

"But pivots don't remove damage."

His voice lowered.

"They decide where it goes."

Then he stepped back.

The hallway resumed around them, but slower now. Heavier. Like something had shifted that no one could name.

Soren exhaled sharply, his voice low and dangerous.

"I will absolutely punch him."

Zephyr nodded thoughtfully.

"Later."

Veya didn't speak.

Because the worst part wasn't the accusation.

It was the absence.

The way something in her chest knew the shape of what had been lost and couldn't find it.

She had shifted the board.

She just didn't know what it had cost.

What Faculty Does
When They're Afraid

Deep below the Constellaria Wing, the decision-room was not loud. It was surgical. Virenna stood before the record-panel, stylus carving precise notes into stone.

"Her influence is accelerating," she said.

Calderyn's voice was neutral. "Confirmed."

Oberon's presence pressed into the architecture. "Student reaction?" he asked.

Virenna didn't look up. "Polarizing."

Calderyn added, "Fear. Reverence. Jealousy."

"Good," Virenna said.

Calderyn's eyes flicked to her. "Explain."

"Divide the narrative before it consolidates," she replied.

Oberon's voice was quiet. "Split them."

Calderyn did not immediately agree. "The unit's cohesion is stabilizing," he said.

Virenna's jaw tightened. "Exactly."

Oberon asked, "Method."

Virenna turned slightly, eyes sharp. "Reassignment."

Calderyn's voice cooled. "Direct separation will provoke resistance."

Virenna's smile thinned slightly, the expression sharpening rather than warming.

"Then we don't separate them physically."

The statement settled into the room with quiet deliberation.

For a moment no one responded, as though the meaning behind her words required a moment to unfold.

Oberon's presence seemed to deepen within the chamber, the subtle pressure of his attention pressing into the architecture itself.

"I need you to clarify," he said.

Virenna did not hesitate.

She tapped the record panel once with the end of her stylus.

The surface of the stone responded immediately.

Four sigils flared into view, each symbol burning with a soft gold light as the system reconstructed the pattern recorded during the trial.

Veya.

Soren.

Zephyr.

Rhazien.

The pattern resolved itself slowly across the panel, not as a fixed image but as something alive, shifting lines of light connecting and reconnecting as the system recalculated.

A unit.

Not four individuals.

A structure.

Balanced in a way the Academy had not intended.

Interdependent in a way it could not easily control.

Virenna studied the configuration in silence, her

gaze moving along each thread of connection tracing where influence flowed, where resistance formed, where one presence reinforced another instead of breaking under pressure.

When she spoke, her voice was soft, precise, and entirely certain.

"Pressure fracture."

The words didn't sound like a suggestion.

They sounded like a method already chosen.

"Introduce conditions that force one of them to choose against the others."

The sigils shifted in response, the glowing lines between them tightening, reconfiguring as if the system itself was already exploring the outcome.

Calderyn's eyes narrowed slightly as he followed the adjustment, his attention sharpening on the points where the connections strained.

"Emotional manipulation," he said, the phrasing deliberate.

Virenna's gaze flicked toward him, not disagreeing, but refining.

"Behavioral testing," she corrected smoothly.

The difference sat between them, subtle but intentional.

Calderyn didn't respond immediately.

But something in his posture tightened, just enough to suggest that while he understood the function, he did not entirely agree with the framing.

To him, the distinction mattered.

To her, the result did.

Above them, Oberon watched in silence.

The pattern reflected faintly across the stone around him; the shifting light caught in the architecture as though the Academy itself were observing alongside him.

When he spoke again, his tone was calm, almost conversational.

"Which one breaks first?"

The question didn't rush the room.

It settled into it.

Because the answer wasn't unknown.

It was simply… unspoken.

The silence stretched, not from uncertainty, but from recognition.

Each of them had already traced the same fault line.

Each of them had seen where the pressure would land and what it would do when it did.

Virenna didn't hesitate. "Soren."

The name landed with quiet certainty, as clean and precise as the lines she had just drawn across the system.

The panel reacted subtly, the sigil representing him brightening by a fraction, as if the system itself acknowledged the selection.

Calderyn didn't argue.

But the faint tightening at the corner of his expression betrayed something closer to resistance than agreement.

He studied Soren's position within the structure for a moment longer, his gaze tracing the way the others adjusted around him the way the unit didn't stabilize despite him…but around him.

Then, quietly he said, "He is not the point of failure."

The room didn't interrupt.

Calderyn's eyes didn't leave the pattern.

"He is the point everything else is forced to respond to."

A brief pause followed, it was not uncertainty, but recalibration.

Then he said nothing more.

Which, in its own way, was agreement.

The Roof
Where Cracks Actually Show

They didn't go back to the dorm.

None of them suggested it, and no one questioned the choice. The corridor turned, the stairs rose, and somehow, they all ended up moving in the same direction without needing to say it out loud.

Up.

To the roof.

The Academy allowed it.

That was what unsettled Veya the most. It was not the silence between them, not even the weight of what had just happened, but the way nothing in the building resisted their movement. No redirection. No closed doors. No quiet correction guiding them somewhere else.

It let them go.

As if it wanted to see what they would do next.

The sky above Mistara stretched wide and impossibly clear, untouched by the chaos they had just walked out of.

It was too clear.

Too calm.

Like the world had decided none of it mattered.

Or worse…like it was waiting for something else to begin.

Soren sat on the edge, legs dangling over nothing, hands clenched between his knees like he was physically holding himself down.

Zephyr hovered nearby, quieter than usual.

Rhazien stood against the low wall, arms folded, gaze scanning shadows.

Veya sat beside Soren, not touching, but close enough to feel the storm under his skin, the tension in him still searching for somewhere to go.

For a long time, no one spoke.

The silence wasn't empty. It lingered, stretched

thin between them, heavy with everything they hadn't said yet.

Then Soren broke it.

"They think you caused it," he said roughly.

Veya didn't answer.

Soren's voice caught slightly in his throat, not breaking, but close enough to feel the strain beneath it.

"Do you?"

The question landed harder than anything else had.

Not because it was loud.

Because it wasn't.

Zephyr's head tilted, his expression sharpening, but he didn't interrupt.

Rhazien remained still, his presence steady and unyielding at the edge of the space.

Veya swallowed.

"I adjusted the alignment," she said carefully, choosing each word like it might shift something if she got it wrong.

Soren shook his head slightly.

"That's not what I asked."

She looked at him then.

Really looked.

His eyes were bright as he looked at her, not with anger, not anymore, but with something more uncertain, more dangerous because it didn't know where to land.

"If you hadn't moved," he pressed quietly, "would it have happened?"

The wind shifted around them, catching at the edges of the rooftop like it was listening.

Veya's throat tightened, the answer catching somewhere between thought and instinct as something deeper stirred beneath it.

"I don't know," she said at last, though the words felt too small for what she had felt.

They didn't settle into the space between them.

They lingered, unfinished, carrying the weight of something she couldn't fully name.

Because part of her did know.

Not how it had happened… but that it hadn't been accidental.

Something had answered her.

And that realization sat beneath her ribs like a second heartbeat.

Soren exhaled shakily, dragging a hand through his hair as if he could physically pull the moment out of his head.

"I was going to throw," he said, the words rough, unpolished. "If you hadn't stopped me… I would've."

Veya didn't hesitate this time. "I know," she said softly, not as reassurance, but as acknowledgment—because she had felt it building in him, the surge, the inevitability of it.

Soren let out a quiet, humorless breath, his gaze dropping for a second before lifting again, steadier but heavier.

"And if I had," he continued, his voice thinning under the weight of the realization, "it might've been me."

The words settled between them, not dramatic, not loud, just honest in a way that left no room to soften it.

Veya felt something in her chest pull tight, sharper than she expected, the thought landing deeper than it should have.

Her hand moved before she could stop it, her fingers closing around his not to anchor him or correct him, not to control what he was feeling, but simply to hold on.

For once, she didn't try to shape the moment or steady the outcome she simply stayed there with him, her grip quiet but certain, as if that alone might be enough to keep something from breaking.

Soren flinched at the contact because of instinct, not rejection, but then he stilled, letting it happen. "I don't want to be what they're afraid of," he said quietly.

Veya's voice softened. "You're not."

His eyes snapped to hers. "You don't know that."

Rhazien spoke from where he stood, his voice a calm and steady ground that didn't shift. "He didn't break."

Zephyr added, softer than usual, the edge gone from his tone.

"He didn't perform."

Soren let out a humorless breath. "You all sound like instructors."

Zephyr's mouth curved faintly. "Please don't insult me like that."

Veya's fingers tightened around Soren's hand, just once.

"I didn't choose it," she said.

Soren studied her face, searching, not for a lie, but for something that would make it simpler.

"You chose the pattern," he said slowly.

"Yes."

"And the pattern decided where it landed."

For a second, Soren's expression faltered, not with confusion or hesitation, but with something deeper he couldn't quite place.

Like a thought had almost formed and then slipped.

His brow tightened slightly, eyes unfocusing for half a breath as if he were trying to grab onto something just out of reach.

"There was…"

He stopped.

The word didn't finish.

It didn't exist long enough to.

A faint crease formed between his brows, frustration flickering across his face. It was not at her, not at the situation, but at something he couldn't name.

"…someone," he said finally, the word sounding

wrong even as he said it, like it didn't belong to anything real; the feeling lingered longer than the thought, leaving behind a hollow gap, a space where something should have been before it vanished again, unresolved and ungraspable, until all that remained was absence, and Soren exhaled sharply as if forcing himself not to follow it.

His jaw tightened as he muttered, "Doesn't matter," but the feeling didn't fade, it stayed, settling into him like something unfinished, until the truth lingered between them, not sharp or loud, but impossible to ignore.

Veya's voice dropped, almost lost to the wind. "If I stop adjusting," she said, "more people get hurt."

Soren's jaw tightened. "And if you keep adjusting?"

She held his gaze. "They still might."

The wind rose briefly, curling around the rooftop like it approved of the honesty.

Soren leaned closer without thinking, the distance between them closing on instinct rather than decision.

"Then don't carry it alone," he said.

Veya's breath caught. "I don't want you breaking for me," she whispered.

Soren's storm flickered. It was not outward, but inward, tightening into something contained.

"I don't want you hardening because of me."

That one landed.

Zephyr looked away, deliberately giving the moment space.

Rhazien didn't.

He never did.

Soren's voice dropped lower, something sharper threading through it now.

"If they try to split us…"

"They will," Zephyr interrupted gently.

Soren didn't look at him.

"If they try," he repeated, his voice lower now, steadier, his eyes fixed on Veya like the rest of the world had narrowed down to just her, "I won't let them."

There was no hesitation in it.

No performance.

Just certainty.

Veya held his gaze, and for a moment, everything else, the Academy, the trials, the pressure pressing in from every side, fell away, leaving only the quiet intensity of him choosing her in a way that felt both instinctive and absolute.

She believed him.

And that was the problem.

Because belief had weight.

It turned words into something solid, something that could exist beyond the moment, something that could be broken.

And she had already seen what happened when things like that broke.

Her fingers tightened slightly in his, not enough to pull him closer, not enough to stop him either, just enough to acknowledge what he had said and what it meant.

"You don't get to carry that alone," she said softly, though her voice wasn't as steady as she wanted it to be. "Not for me."

Soren didn't pull away.

If anything, he leaned into it, just slightly, like the space between them had stopped being something either of them questioned.

"I'm not doing it for you," he said, though the words lacked any real edge. "I'm doing it because I don't like the alternative."

Her breath caught, just for a second.

Because the alternative wasn't just separation.

It was loss.

And something about the way he said it made it feel like he understood that, maybe not fully, maybe not consciously, but enough that it settled between them like something real.

Dangerously real.

Veya looked at him, really looked this time, at the storm he kept holding back, at the way he chose restraint when everything in him was built for the opposite.

"You say that like it's simple," she murmured. "It isn't," he admitted, his expression tightening slightly as if the words had cost more than he was willing to show. "But it's still not optional."

That landed deeper than it should have.

Because it wasn't a promise.

It was a decision.

And decisions could be tested.

Below them, deep within the Academy, the stone had already begun to shift. Not violently, not in a way anyone on the rooftop could hear, but with a quiet, deliberate movement that spoke of intention rather than reaction.

The structure was adjusting.

Preparing.

And somewhere beneath their feet, the system was already beginning to write the next way to break them.

And somewhere far beyond the island, older than the trials, older than the rules that tried to contain them, something turned its attention fully toward the four figures standing on that rooftop.

Not curious anymore.

Interested.

Chapter

Fourty-One

What the Trials Created

The Academy did not summon them immediately, and that was how Veya knew the situation was serious.

When the Academy wanted spectacle, it called assemblies. When it wanted control, it issued orders.

But when it was deciding whether something might be a threat, it chose observation first.

For two full days, nothing happened.

There were no punishments that were delivered, no praise offered and no official statements released.

Only silence.

The kind that pressed steadily against the nerves until even breathing felt as though it was being monitored.

Students continued to stare and whisper, adjusting their paths around the four of them as if navigating weather that might turn violent without warning.

The faculty, however, did nothing at all.

They simply waited.

Watching.

And that waiting told Veya everything she needed

to know.

They were afraid.

The Naming

On the third night, the summons came.

It did not arrive through a messenger or a folded notice left outside their doors. No sigil appeared on the walls, and no instructor stepped forward to deliver instructions.

Instead, the Academy itself spoke.

It began with the stone.

At first the change was subtle enough that most students might have mistaken it for imagination, a faint shift beneath their feet, like the building adjusting its weight.

Then the corridors dimmed.

Lanterns along the vaulted halls softened, their light lowering in unison as though the Academy had drawn a slow breath.

A moment later the wards lining the walls pulsed.

Once.

Low and resonant.

The vibration moved through the towers the way a heartbeat moves through a body, steady and deliberate, traveling from stone to stone until the entire structure seemed briefly alive with it.

Students paused in doorways and stairwells, glancing around in quiet confusion, sensing that something had passed through the Academy even if they could not name it.

But the message was not meant for them.

High above the courtyards and training halls, where the four of them stood together, the air shifted.

Gold light gathered slowly in front of them, not flaring or flashing but forming with deliberate precision. The letters appeared one by one, suspended in the open space like something carved into invisible stone.

ECLIPSE UNIT. NOW.

The words hovered there, steady and unmistakable.

Soren stared at them for a moment before exhaling through his nose.

"Well," he muttered, "that doesn't feel ominous at all."

Zephyr tilted his head, studying the letters as though they might rearrange themselves if he looked long enough.

"I admire the efficiency," he said lightly. "No explanation, no ceremony. Just a quiet architectural command."

Soren shot him a look. "You say that like it's normal."

"It is normal," Zephyr replied mildly. "For the Academy."

Rhazien's gaze remained fixed on the glowing directive.

"No one else received it," he said.

That landed quietly between them.

By the time they reached the Constellaria chamber, the faculty were already waiting.

Virenna stood near the center of the room, posture sharp and deliberate, her hands folded behind her back as if she had been standing there long enough to grow impatient with time itself.

Calderyn remained a step behind her, composed and watchful, his expression carefully neutral.

And at the far end of the chamber stood Oberon.

His presence filled the room without effort. He did not move, yet the space seemed to orient itself around him, the way corridors bend around gravity.

But it wasn't the faculty that stopped them.

It was the wall behind them.

The ancient stone that lined the Constellaria chamber had remained unchanged for centuries, its surface etched only with the faint patterns of constellations long studied and long understood.

Now something new burned there.

At first it looked like light moving beneath the stone, a quiet glow spreading along lines that had not existed moments before.

The patterns formed slowly and with deliberate precision, the lines emerging one after another as though the wall itself were remembering knowledge long buried beneath centuries of silence.

At first the shapes appeared scattered, like stars drawn across dark stone. But the longer the light held, the more the design revealed its true structure.

These were not stars at all.

They were sigils.

And there were four of them.

Each symbol ignited with its own quiet intensity, carved lines burning with gold-white light against the deep gray stone. The glow was not the unstable shimmer of ordinary magic. It held with an unnerving steadiness, the light flowing through the etched patterns as though the stone itself had awakened to carry it.

The sigils did not flicker.

They did not surge or fade.

They remained constant, patient, deliberate, and impossibly precise like something that had waited a very long time for this moment and had no intention of wasting it.

A deeper silence settled over the chamber.

It was not the silence of confusion or uncertainty. No one in the room questioned what they were seeing.

This was recognition.

The faculty understood immediately what the symbols meant, and the weight of that understanding pressed quietly through the air. These sigils had not appeared within the Constellaria chamber for centuries. Their return was not an accident, and it was certainly not a coincidence.

Veya stopped without fully realizing she had done so.

Something about the pattern pulled at her instincts, a subtle pressure that made her chest tighten as though the constellation had been waiting for her to see it.

Beside her, Soren went very still. The usual restless energy that lived in him seemed to settle all at once, his attention locked on the burning symbols as if he were trying to understand how something so ancient had just rearranged itself around the four of them.

Zephyr's familiar smile faded slowly, replaced by an expression far more attentive. His eyes moved carefully across the wall, studying the lines of light the way a strategist studies a battlefield.

Rhazien lifted his gaze toward the stone as well, his attention quieter but not less focused. He did not simply look at the sigils themselves. His eyes moved across the entire chamber, measuring the arrangement, the spacing, the intention behind the moment, as though the pattern contained more information than it was immediately willing to reveal.

The four sigils burned in a pattern that left no room for interpretation. Their placement was deliberate, each symbol positioned with the kind of precision that suggested design rather than coincidence. Lines of pale gold light stretched subtly between them, connecting the shapes in a quiet geometry that the eye understood instinctively before the mind could name it.

They were aligned.

Not simply arranged, but bound into a single structure, each mark reinforcing the others in a way that made the entire formation feel intentional and inevitable.

Together they formed something unmistakable.

A constellation, not of distant stars scattered across the night sky, but of people standing in the chamber below it.

For the briefest instant, the light linking those symbols flickered in a way that felt strangely alive. The pattern shifted, not enough to change its shape, but enough to give the unsettling impression that the constellation was not being created for the first time.

It felt older than that.

As if the structure had existed long before this moment and was only now remembering itself through them.

The chamber fell silent.

No one rushed to speak, and no one pretended confusion. The meaning of the moment pressed quietly against the air, settling into the stone with the same certainty as the glowing sigils.

Then Oberon's voice carried through the room, calm and unmistakably authoritative.

"Step forward."

The command did not echo, yet it filled the chamber all the same.

They didn't move.

Not immediately.

For a brief second the room seemed to hold its breath, the silence stretching between the faculty and the four students as though the Academy itself were waiting to see how the moment would resolve.

Then Veya stepped forward.

The response was immediate.

The sigils brightened, their light sharpening as though her movement had completed something within the pattern.

The others followed without hesitation.

Soren moved first beside her, then Zephyr, and finally Rhazien, the four of them crossing the chamber floor together as if the decision had already been made long before the command was spoken.

They entered the constellation not as individuals, but as a single formation.

Together.

As they had been since the Trials began.

As, increasingly, the Academy itself seemed to expect them to remain.

The constellation flared as they entered its circle. Lines of light shifted, recalibrating as if the Academy itself were trying to understand what it had just created.

Virenna watched the pattern with open fascination.

Calderyn watched them.

"You have altered the equilibrium of the Arcane Trials," Oberon said.

His voice carried no anger.

There was no approval in it either. No satisfaction, no disappointment, nothing that suggested judgment in the ordinary sense.

Only fact.

"The system has adapted," Oberon continued, his tone steady and unhurried, as though he were reciting a conclusion that had already been reached long before this moment. "The wards have restructured. Trial responses have begun recalculating around your presence."

The words moved through the chamber with quiet finality.

Soren released a slow breath through his nose, his eyes flicking briefly toward the glowing constellation behind them.

"That sounds bad," he muttered.

Calderyn answered before anyone else could respond.

"It is unprecedented," he said calmly.

The professor's voice held none of Soren's unease, but the choice of word carried its own weight. Unprecedented did not mean dangerous, not necessarily, but it did mean the Academy had entered territory it had never charted before.

Virenna's gaze shifted slowly across the chamber until it settled on Veya.

For a moment she said nothing, studying her with an intensity that felt less like curiosity and more like confirmation. When she finally spoke, her voice was quieter than before, though the focus behind it had sharpened to something almost surgical.

"You are no longer functioning as a standard participant."

The words hung in the chamber, heavy with implication.

Behind them, the constellation flared once.

The sigils etched into the stone wall brightened suddenly, their carved lines igniting with steady gold-white light. The faint strands connecting the four symbols sharpened and tightened, as if the pattern itself had reacted to the declaration.

No one in the room moved.

Then Oberon spoke again.

He did not raise his voice, nor did he pause for emphasis. Yet the silence of the chamber seemed to gather around the words before he said them, as though the Academy itself was listening.

And the word he chose would become the one the institution remembered.

"You are now designated a Pivot."

The effect was immediate.

The chamber itself shifted, not as metaphor or illusion but in a quiet, physical adjustment. The stone beneath Veya's feet realigned by the smallest fraction, a subtle correction that rippled outward through the floor like a structure redistributing its weight.

The ancient architecture of the Constellaria chamber seemed to acknowledge the declaration in its own language of pressure and balance, settling around her presence as though the room itself had just recalculated.

For the briefest instant, the ancient wards hesitated, not in resistance, but in recognition, as though the chamber itself remembered something it had not seen in a very long time.

The constellation behind them burned brighter still.

For the first time since the sigils had appeared, the lines connecting the four symbols locked into place.

For a brief moment, the chamber felt perfectly balanced as if the system had finally found the point around which everything else would begin to move.

Stone groaned quietly beneath the floor as something within the structure adjusted by the smallest possible degree. The movement was subtle enough that no one might have noticed it under ordinary circumstances but here, in the heart of the Constellaria chamber, it felt unmistakable.

The stone beneath Veya's feet realigned by a fraction, as though the Academy itself had just corrected its balance around her existence.

The chamber held the declaration in silence for several long seconds afterward, as if even the ancient architecture required a moment to settle around the word.

No students were present to hear it spoken.

No witnesses crowded the chamber doors, and no whispers yet stirred through the corridors outside.

But the Academy recorded everything.

Every trial. Every anomaly. Every name that altered the pattern of its systems was etched into its living memory. The moment Oberon spoke the designation, the wards threaded through Mistara had already begun carrying the information outward through the towers like a slow, spreading current.

The change did not spread through the Academy with noise or spectacle. No bells rang, and no announcements echoed through the halls.

It moved more quietly than that.

The information traveled through the wards threaded through Mistara the way a current moves through deep water, steady, deliberate, and impossible to stop once it had begun.

The change did not spread through the Academy with noise or spectacle. No bells rang and no announcements echoed through the halls. Instead, the information traveled quietly through the wards threaded beneath Mistara, moving from tower to tower with the steady certainty of a current that could not be stopped. By morning, the entire Academy would know what had happened in the Constellaria chamber.

Not because the faculty would gather students into an assembly.

Not because instructors would repeat the story in lectures.

Because the institution itself would remember.

Every corridor, every warded wall, every listening stone carried the same silent record. The Academy had already etched the moment into its living memory, preserving the designation the same way it preserved every turning point that altered the structure of the Trials.

Pivot.

The word settled into the chamber with a weight that felt older than the language itself.

It was not a word that belonged beside titles like Victor or Champion, the kinds of honors students fought and bled to earn each year within the Trials.

Those titles were familiar to the Academy. They were measurable things, markers of achievement that could be counted, celebrated, and eventually replaced when someone stronger came along.

Victor.

Champion.

They proved strength. They rewarded endurance. They marked the individuals who had risen above the rest of the field.

But the word pivot carried a different kind of gravity.

It was quieter than those titles, yet far more unsettling.

A winner demonstrated power. A leader gathered followers. A survivor endured what others could not.

Those roles measured accomplishment within the system.

A pivot did something else entirely.

A pivot altered direction.

It was not simply someone who succeeded inside the structure of the Trials, but someone whose presence forced the structure itself to adjust.

Where a victor proved superiority, a pivot re-shaped the outcome.

Where a champion stood above the system, a pivot became the point around which it began to turn.

And that distinction made the title far more dangerous than any simple victory.

It marked the precise moment when momentum shifted, when systems that had been moving steadily along one path were forced to reorient themselves around a new center.

It did not simply reward achievement.

It acknowledged change.

And once that change occurred, everything connected to it would inevitably have to move as well.

It was the precise point where momentum shifted, where systems that had moved one way for centuries suddenly adjusted themselves around a new center.

Whether they intended to or not.

Something the structure could no longer ignore.

Something the Academy itself had just acknowledged.

And something that would force everything around it to move.

That was why the word carried weight and why it was far more dangerous than any simple victory.

Terms of Survival

Calderyn stepped forward slightly.

"From this point forward, all trial structures will adjust dynamically in response to your actions."

Soren blinked.

"So… we're being punished for surviving?"

"No," Virenna said softly.

Her eyes gleamed.

"You are being studied."

Virenna delivered the words with quiet satisfaction, as though the situation had just become far more interesting to her.

Zephyr tilted his head slightly, the corner of his mouth lifting in a faint, crooked smile that didn't quite reach his eyes.

"Adorable," he said lightly, though the edge beneath the word was unmistakable.

Rhazien spoke next, his voice calm and controlled, cutting through the moment without raising in volume.

"Define parameters."

Oberon's gaze shifted toward him immediately, as though the question had been expected.

"You will not be separated."

For a moment, no one spoke.

The statement hung in the chamber with a weight that seemed disproportionate to its simplicity. Even Virenna's stylus stilled against the panel she had been writing on, and she turned her head slightly toward Oberon with a look that suggested the decision had not originated with her.

Oberon continued without acknowledging the reaction.

"Attempts to fracture high-functioning units have historically resulted in catastrophic instability," he said, his tone measured and entirely procedural. "We will not repeat inefficient strategies."

Veya felt a brief flicker of relief before she could suppress it. The thought of the Academy forcing them apart had been sitting in the back of her mind since the Trials began, an unspoken fear she hadn't fully allowed herself to name.

The moment passed quickly.

But not quickly enough.

Soren noticed.

His gaze flicked toward her for a fraction of a second, something quieter settling in his expression.

Rhazien noticed as well, though his reaction was subtler, his posture shifting almost imperceptibly as he absorbed the implication.

Zephyr noticed everything.

His eyes moved between them, the faintest hint of amusement returning to his expression as he quietly filed the moment away.

Oberon, however, had not finished speaking.

"However," he continued, his voice carrying the same steady authority, "continued survival will require adaptation. The next phase of the Trials will not test individual strength."

Behind them, the constellation carved into the chamber wall shifted.

Lines of light connecting the four sigils thickened slowly, the gold-white glow brightening as if responding directly to Oberon's words. The symbols did not merely shine; they locked into place with a deliberate precision that made the pattern feel suddenly permanent.

The message was unmistakable.

"You will not be measured alone," Oberon said.

The light flared once more, sealing the pattern.

"It will test what you become together."

The chamber fell silent.

Not the uncertain quiet that followed confusion, but something heavier. Something that carried the weight of understanding.

This was not simply the next stage of the Trials.

This was something new.

Virenna watched the constellation for another moment before her attention returned to the four of them. A faint smile curved across her lips, the kind that suggested she had just been handed a puzzle she was eager to dismantle.

"You may go," she said at last.

Dismissed.

Just like that.

But as the four of them turned to leave the chamber, the sensation in the air made it clear that nothing about this moment resembled freedom.

If anything, it felt as though the real examination had only just begun.

The Choice

They didn't return to the dorms.

No one suggested it, and no one questioned the direction their steps took as the corridors turned and the stairwell rose beneath them, drawing them upward without a word being spoken.

They went to the roof.

Not for air.

Not for quiet.

But because there was nowhere else in the Academy that felt far enough away from what had just happened.

The sky above Mistara stretched endless and black, stars sharp as broken glass scattered across velvet.

Soren was the first to drift toward the edge of the rooftop. He rested his forearms on the stone railing and stared out across the Academy grounds as though he might somehow find answers in the pattern of lights below.

"Pivot," he muttered after a moment, the word

tasting unfamiliar in his mouth. "That's… not exactly comforting."

Zephyr hovered nearby, leaning lazily against the wall as if the entire conversation amused him more than it should.

"I don't know," he said lightly. "Personally, I love titles that sound like we might accidentally destabilize civilizations."

Soren shot him a sideways look, one brow lifting as a faint edge crept into his voice.

"You would," he said, dragging a hand through his hair. "Anything that sounds remotely catastrophic and you're already halfway committed."

His expression tightening just slightly.

"Some of us prefer not to be labeled as a problem before we've even had a chance to decide how bad we're going to be."

Zephyr's smile sharpened, something more deliberate settling into it.

"Oh, I don't think you get to decide that part," he said mildly. "That's already been decided for you."

Soren's eyes flicked to him, irritation flashing.

"Funny."

Zephyr tilted his head, watching him like he'd just proven a point.

"No, I'm serious," he continued, his voice still light but threaded with something quieter underneath it. "You're not worried about the title."

He let the words settle, watching Soren a second longer than necessary, as if giving him time to deny it.

"You're worried it might be accurate."

Zephyr's expression softened just slightly. "Relax," he added. "If we're a problem, we're at least an interesting one."

Soren didn't answer right away.

His jaw tightened, not sharply this time, but like he was holding something in place instead of pushing it back.

For a second, his gaze dropped, not far, just enough to break eye contact, before he dragged a slow breath in and let it out again.

"Yeah," he said quietly, almost under his breath.

Not in agreement.

Not denial.

Just… recognition.

His eyes lifted again, something steadier settling in behind them.

"Then I guess we'd better make sure we're not the kind that breaks first."

Veya didn't speak.

But the words didn't land the same.

Zephyr's words settled in her mind like a warning, sharp, precise, and something to be analyzed and contained. While Soren's resisted that same control, lingering instead in a quieter, steadier way that refused to be categorized.

But anchored, the kind of certainty that didn't ask permission to matter.

She felt it shift something in her. Not the careful control she had been holding onto, but something deeper, something less contained. The part of her that didn't think in balance or restraint, but in movement… in outcome.

In change.

For a moment, she saw him differently, not just the storm he fought to hold back, but the way he chose to hold it at all, the way he stayed when everything in him was built to react.

Not because he had to.

Because he decided to.

That was what made it dangerous.

Not his power.

His choice.

Her fingers tightened slightly at her side before she forced them still, grounding herself before the shift inside her could move any further.

Because if she let that part of her answer, she wasn't sure it would choose to hold anything together at all.

Across from them, Rhazien had taken up position along the low wall, his posture relaxed but his attention fixed on the sprawling Academy below. His gaze moved slowly over the towers and courtyards, the training fields and glowing wards, as if he were measuring something none of the rest of us could see.

Watching.

He always seemed to be watching.

I remained near the center of the rooftop, letting the cold air settle around me while I tried to understand the strange shift moving through the space.

The Academy felt different now. It wasn't hostile, and it wasn't welcoming either. The atmosphere had settled into something quieter and more deliberate, a strange equilibrium that made the entire place feel balanced in a way it hadn't before.

It was the same sensation I had felt in the Constellaria chamber, the subtle sense that something vast and deliberate had quietly adjusted its internal structure. The institution wasn't reacting with approval or rejection. Instead, it felt as though it had simply recalibrated, reshaping itself around our presence the way a river bends around stone.

The wards no longer pressed against her senses the way they had before. Instead of the constant tension she had grown used to, the magic surrounding the rooftop had settled into something steadier, almost rhythmic. Even the stone beneath her feet seemed to carry that subtle change, its quiet pulse moving through the structure with a calm, measured consistency.

It was a strange sensation, difficult to name.

They no longer felt like guests.

They no longer felt like intruders either.

Whatever the Academy had decided about them, it had shifted their place in it. They no longer felt like students moving through the system, but something the system itself had begun to account for. Something it was adjusting around rather than directing.

Soren shifted beside her, his attention moving across the rooftop and out into the open air beyond it, like he was trying to track something that didn't have a visible form.

The wind didn't move the same way.

The wards didn't hum the same way.

Even the space between breaths felt… aware.

"You feel that too?" he asked, quieter now, like saying it too loudly might disturb whatever it was.

Veya nodded slowly, her gaze unfocused, not because she wasn't paying attention, but because she was paying attention to something deeper than what was visible.

"It's like…" she hesitated, searching for something that didn't quite exist in language, "like the Academy isn't just watching anymore."

Her voice dropped slightly.

"It's responding."

And somewhere beneath that awareness, she felt something else, something that didn't belong to the Academy at all.

Zephyr tilted his head, his gaze lifting toward the invisible lines of warding woven through the air, his expression sharpening with interest rather than unease.

"Not responding," he said after a moment, almost thoughtfully.

Soren frowned. "Pretty sure that's the same thing."

Zephyr's mouth curved faintly, but there was no humor in it this time.

"No," he said. "Responding implies reaction."

His eyes flicked briefly toward Veya.

"This is adjustment."

A beat, quieter now.

"Like we've been… reclassified."

Zephyr's expression remained annoyingly calm. "Not entirely, different would mean the Academy changed. Adjusted means it simply decided where to put us."

Rhazien spoke without turning, his gaze still resting somewhere out over the Academy.

"It stopped pushing."

The words settled quietly between them, simple but heavy enough to change the way the air felt around the group.

Veya inhaled slowly, letting the cool night air steady her thoughts.

And then something else brushed the edge of her awareness.

It wasn't the Academy.

It wasn't the wards either.

The sensation was deeper than that, older somehow, like a presence stirring beneath layers of stone and magic that had existed long before the Academy was built.

Watching.

The feeling vanished as quickly as it came.

Soren noticed the shift in her expression immediately.

"What?" he asked, turning toward her.

Veya hesitated for a moment before shaking her head.

"…Nothing."

Zephyr's mouth curved faintly at the corners.

"Those are usually the important ones," he said lightly.

Soren didn't smile. His attention stayed fixed on Veya, searching her face the way he always did when he thought she might be carrying something alone.

"We can still walk," he said quietly after a moment.

"Leave. Nobody's forcing us to stay here."

Veya considered the idea seriously.

For a brief moment she imagined it: walking away from the Academy, from the trials, from the strange gravity that had been pulling all of them toward something none of them fully understood.

Then she shook her head.

"No."

Zephyr tilted his head slightly. "And if we stay?"

Veya looked up at the sky again, her thoughts settling into place with a calm certainty she couldn't fully explain.

"Then we decide what this place becomes."

The silence that followed had changed, no longer uncertain, but settled into something certain and unmoving.

Soren nodded first, the motion small but deliberate.

"Together."

Rhazien's voice came quietly, but with the kind of certainty that didn't invite doubt.

"Always."

Zephyr's faint smile returned, softer than before.

For once, he didn't argue.

"Well. That sounds delightfully inevitable."

Something settled between the four of them then.

Chosen.

Veya let the quiet settle for a moment longer, her gaze drifting across the dark horizon beyond the Academy towers.

Soren stepped closer beside her, close enough that she could feel the subtle tension that never quite left him, like a storm that had learned how to stand still.

"You realize," he said quietly, "this is probably the point where things get worse."

A faint smile touched the corner of her mouth.

"That's been every point since we got here."

He huffed softly at that, but the sound didn't quite

reach humor. His gaze remained fixed on the distant sky.

"If it turns ugly," he said after a moment, "you don't have to face it alone."

Veya turned slightly toward him.

For someone who pushed the world away as instinctively as breathing, the words carried more weight than he probably realized.

"I know," she said.

For a moment, neither of them moved.

Then Soren glanced down at her, the storm in his eyes quieter than usual.

"Good," he muttered.

What Wakes

And somewhere beyond the Academy, beyond its wards, beyond its reach, beyond even the memory of what it had erased, something stirred.

Not newly awakened.

Not summoned.

Something that had once stood at the center of it all, before the system learned how to continue without it.

It had been removed.

Silenced.

Forgotten so completely that even the absence of it no longer had a name.

But absence was not the same as erasure.

And now, as something long buried began to take shape again within the Academy's walls, it began to remember.

And somewhere beyond the Academy, beyond its wards, beyond its reach, beyond even the memory of what it had erased, something stirred.

Not newly awakened. Not summoned.

Something that had once stood at the center of it all, before the system learned how to continue without it.

It had been removed. Silenced. Forgotten so completely that even the absence of it no longer had a name.

But absence was not the same as erasure.

And now, as something long buried began to take shape again within the Academy's walls, it began to remember.

And this time, it was not the Academy doing the watching.

Veya and The Arcane Trials continues in book 2

Emjoyed the book?

Support the author by leaving a review on

Amazon or Goodreads!

visit the authors website

www.junalynnicdao.com

Instagram:

JunalynNicdao.author

Acknowledgments

For my love, who believed in this story before it knew

what it was.

For my parents who always love me.

And for my students, your encouragement lit the spark.

About the Author

Hello, I'm Junalyn Nicdao, a Filipino fantasy author and creator of the world of Mistara, where power is earned, survival is never guaranteed, and the forgotten refuse to stay unseen. I've loved fantasy for as long as I can remember.

To me, stories have always been more than escape, they are a way to make readers see, feel, hear, and live

inside another world. As a teacher, I've spent years encouraging my students to write boldly and bring their imaginations fully to life.

What began as a quiet side project of my own slowly grew into something more when I shared my story with them. Their excitement and belief in my world became the spark that pushed me to finally make this story real. My debut novel, Veya and the Arcane Trials, begins the Rise of the Forgotten series. A brutal, magic-laced journey through trials of power, identity, survival, and found family.

I'm drawn to stories that explore the struggles many of us experience but rarely speak about, being overlooked, fighting to belong, discovering strength, and rising even when the world expects you to stay small. I write for readers who have ever felt unseen and for those ready to realize they never were. I'm a night writer fueled by coffee, tea, and a little chaos. Most of my worlds are built in the quiet hours while the rest of the world sleeps.

When I'm not writing into the early morning, I'm balancing life as a full-time teacher, mother of two amazing daughters, fantasy reader, and storyteller. Many nights are spent in shared "creative time" beside my partner as he creates music and I build new realms.

At the heart of everything I write is one belief: Those who feel forgotten are often the ones destined to rise. You're early to this world and early readers are never forgotten.

Thank you

Thank you for stepping into Mistara and walking beside
Veya through the trials.

Stories only truly come alive when someone chooses to
read them, and the fact that you spent your time in this
world means more to me than I can say. Rise of the Forgotten was written for anyone who has ever felt overlooked, uncertain, or like they were still searching for
where they belong.

If this story found you at the right moment, then it was
meant for you.

Your journey through the trials is only just beginning.

— Junalyn Nicdao

www.ingramcontent.com/pod-product-compliance
Lightning Source LLC
Chambersburg PA
CBHW061418150726
47987CB00001B/11